FOOL'S JOUST

CRYSTAL WOOD

TATTERSALL
PUBLISHING
Denton, Texas

(9)
PL

Tattersall Publishing
P.O. Box 308194
Denton, Texas 76203-8194
www.tattersallpub.com

First Edition

Copyright © 1998 by Crystal Wood

Printed in the United States of America

01 00 99 98   010   1 2 3 4 5

This book is a work of fiction. Names, characters,
places and incidents are either products of the author's
imagination or are used fictitiously. Any resemblance
to actual events or locales, or persons, living or dead,
is entirely coincidental.

Cover Illustration by James Hobdy

Library of Congress Catalog Card Number: 98-90179

ISBN 0-9640513-7-0

ACKNOWLEDGMENTS

For their assistance in the creation of this book, the author wishes to express sincere appreciation to the following: Pati Haworth, Jim Hobdy, Jonathan Reynolds, Cheryl Wolfe, George A. Wood, and George W. Wood.

To *my* knight in shining armor,
George "Frosty" Wood

FOOL'S JOUST

Yet some men say in many parts of England that King Arthur is not dead, but had by the will of Our Lord Jesu into another place; and men say that he shall come again, and he shall win the holy cross. Yet I will not say that it shall be so, but rather I will say, here in this world he changed his life.

Sir Thomas Malory, ca. 1469

Looking to us, and desiring to be a part of my Father's Kingdom, can offer to those . . . that chance to connect with the Level Above Human, and begin that transition. Your separation from the world and reliance upon the Kingdom of Heaven through its Representatives can open to you the opportunity to become a new creature, one of the Next Evolutionary Level . . .

"Do," Heaven's Gate, 1997

You can't believe in what you don't understand.

David Koresh, 1993

PROLOGUE

THE TALL HORSE PRANCED IN PLACE IN THE SOFT SANDY DIRT AT THE west end of the list, its rider holding tight the rein with his gloved left hand and balancing with his right a long, gaily painted lance. He sat up tall in the saddle and called out toward the east end, "Say thou, sir, art thou prepared to meet thy fate this day?"

"Prepare thyself, knave!" came the reply from the other rider, whose horse was equally impatient to charge.

"Then come, sir!" cried the first, and with the touch of a spur, the horse leaped forward and was almost immediately at full gallop. Likewise, the rider at the opposite end of the list spurred his horse and leveled his own lance at his swiftly closing rival.

The two horses passed each other at breakneck speed, close enough to draw the same breath of air . . . and the lances passed also, piercing only the dust clouds kicked up by the flying hooves. Once at opposite ends of the list, the two riders turned and calmed their quivering steeds. The first rider lowered his lance and cried, "Close, sir! Far *too* close for my nose! I can smell thy fulsome feet e'en now!"

"Not my feet, sir. Surely 'twas thyself breaking wind in fear of my approach!"

"Prithee, sir, I fear thee not, for thou art my own master's fool— as am I."

"And no master ever had two finer fools than we! Come, sir, and let us tell our master that his good horses are practiced and will serve him well in tonight's tournament. Perhaps he will reward us with flagons of stout!"

The spectators who had witnessed the fool's joust cheered and applauded the two liveried horsemen as they dismounted, took their bows, and led the animals into the stables to await the full-contact armored joust later that day. The crowd dispersed from the rails that enclosed the jousting list and moved along to experience other sights and sounds and scents of the faire. Those who were dressed in plain cottons and leathers mingled freely with those attired in satin finery, for all men, women and children were equal on this glorious spring afternoon. From the spires atop the stone and wooden bailey that ringed the fairegrounds, colorful pennants fluttered in the breeze beneath a cloudless blue sky and drew all together in camaraderie and merriment.

Not far from the jousting list, a trio of performers gathered another group of spectators around a small platform and amazed them with knife-throwing, juggling, and balancing tricks. One *jongleur,* dressed in gaudy breeches, an outrageous waistcoat, and a ridiculous cap with bells upon it, peppered the act with salty jokes while the other two made the audience gasp at the precision of their entertaining craft.

Just beyond the stage, a gypsy loitered upon the front steps of her brightly painted wagon, inviting passers-by to come inside and have their fortunes told. Blacksmiths and glassblowers went about their work, scarcely noticing the onlookers admiring their skills. A falconer displayed his prize birds, each one hooded, belled, and jessed so that it would not fly until commanded. Exotic dancers writhed sinuously, trailing silken veils across their faces as coins jingled upon their undulating hips and bodices.

Vendors hawked hot meat pies and roasted turkey legs, along with ale and wine and soft beverages. Craftsmen sold pottery, jewelry, leather goods, and many other items not commonly available in town. This merry medieval faire offered something for everyone with a few shillings to spare. But they didn't take American Express.

On this lusty June afternoon in the latter part of the twentieth century, half an hour's drive west of Fort Worth, Texas, the annual Merrie Olde Tymes Faire continued its six-week run. For a twelve-dollar admission fee, visitors could experience a day in the life of the imaginary medieval English village of Merryborough, which was peopled by actors who portrayed everyone from thieves and wenches to wizards and witches to knights and ladies. Even the artisans and crafters, who came from all across the country, were trained to conduct business in character before being granted licenses to sell their wares in Merryborough.

The faire was the largest historical festival of its kind in the Southwest, and it attracted thousands of visitors from all across the state. Many came to the faire in costume and participated to the fullest in its anachronistic spectacle. Many more who came in with a Texas drawl left with a British brogue, and, to some extent, each and every person who came to the faire became one with the abandoned yet innocent atmosphere of a time long past.

As another crowd began to gather at the jousting list for the next show, an old man, his hands lightly clasping the rail, stood gazing out over the list, imagining the scent of horseflesh, leather, soil and sweat. It was a good smell, a manly smell, a reminder of real warfare. And he remembered it now as clearly as when he first had become a Traveler, more than half a millenium ago.

He could not explain how he had arrived in this bewildering century, but he knew why. There was another Traveler who had forsaken the sacred vows, who desired what never had been rightfully his, and who had found in this world the means to obtain it. Already this evil one gathered believers about him, filling their heads with falsehoods and spurious promises in return for their loyalty, gaining strength from their devotion, swallowing their souls. He had to be stopped.

But the old man could not do it alone. He sought a knight to aid him, one with a strong arm and a stronger heart, who would submit his will to the greater good. Where in this perplexing age could such a man be found?

To this faire, so familiar and yet so strange, he returned now and anon, though his quest lay elsewhere. Surely in this place he would find among these latter-day wayfarers a true knight to wield the sword of righteousness against the evil one.

A sturdy young man of eighteen or twenty summers strode up to the rail next to the Traveler, laughing with his companions. Tall and solidly built, with prickly-short sandy hair, he was clad in a livery of murrey with the emblem of a snarling soldier and the puzzling motto *Gig 'em Aggies* upon it in white. This young man seemed a likely candidate for his champion.

"Good day to you, young sir," said the Traveler, allowing himself to be seen.

"Yo, pops," replied the young man, cordially but cautiously.

The Traveler closed his eyes, and a moment later opened them in the halls of the young man's thoughts. He discerned a disturbing lack of character: There were no moral absolutes in evidence, and whatever convictions the young man might have seemed to be geared more toward satisfying his own pleasures than serving others. This boy would be no match for his opponent—he was too much like him. Disappointed, the Traveler moved on.

The young man flinched, swayed slightly, and clutched at the rail to steady himself. It was as if a veil had been drawn from before his eyes. He shook his head, as if to clear it of cobwebs, and rubbed the back of his neck. One of his friends noticed his sudden discomfort and asked, "Dude, you okay?"

"Yeah, I'm fine," he replied, confused. "Where's the old man I was talking to just now?"

"*What* old man?"

"He was right here—!" Suddenly he could not remember where the old man had stood. But he had seen him. Hadn't he?

CHAPTER ONE

TRICK McGUIRE TUGGED AT HIS STIFF COLLAR FOR THE UMPTEENTH time and wished he were back on the ranch, wearing his boots and jeans and a layer of honest dirt. The rented tuxedo was styled Western, which made it vaguely bearable from an aesthetic standpoint, but it was as confining and uncomfortable as any other monkeysuit he had been compelled to wear in his life. The Adolphus Hotel ballroom was undeniably elegant, the drinks and hors d'oeuvres were plentiful and delicious, the music was outstanding, but the reason for his presence at this upscale affair escaped him.

Then she returned to the room and slipped her hand into the crook of his arm, and he smiled and remembered and agreed that there was no other place in the world he'd rather be.

"Is my face on straight?" whispered Tay Silvestri, his very significant other, with her customary spin on a phrase.

"If you mean, did you color inside the lines with your makeup, yes," he replied. "But if you mean, do you look like you're about to crack up laughing the next time somebody asks how you like your new boss, that'd be a big no."

"The thought of my new boss makes me want to crack up, but not laughing. Furniture and costly *objets d'art* come to mind. God, I'm gonna miss Shack!"

Nothing Trick could say would change the circumstances or

assuage her disdain for the situation, so he merely patted the hand tucked inside his elbow and shrugged. In spite of her attitude, she looked fabulous in the long black sheath that followed every curve of the body that could bench-press two hundred pounds, but remained soft to his touch. Her long dark hair was pulled up in an elegant twist, and her brief trip to the ladies' room had enhanced cosmetic accents to her jade-green eyes and rose-red lips. He could not help but wonder where on her person she was concealing her service weapon and pager, for although they were guests at this formal reception, she was on duty as a Special Agent of the FBI.

"Here comes the guest of honor and the missus," remarked Trick, and released her hand so that Tay could go and speak to them. Tay's slender form was briefly enveloped in the ponderous embrace of O. D. Shackleford, former Deputy Director of Operations for the FBI's Dallas field office, whose retirement was being celebrated this evening. She then greeted Nancy Shackleford with a more reserved hug and beckoned to Trick to join them.

Trick watched his hand disappear into the big man's giant but surprisingly gentle mitt as he said, "Good to see you again, Trick. How are things back in Alpine?"

"Mighty dry and the cows are skinny," replied Trick. "In other words, just about normal. So what's next for you, big guy? I hope *I* get to retire at fifty-eight."

Shackleford shrugged, and his shoulders in the outsize tuxedo jacket heaved like a mountain under considerable seismic stress. "Well, I thought I might do a little carpentry for fun and profit, and maybe once in a while some private investigations for a lawyer friend of mine."

"Orrin built the addition to our house all by himself," beamed Nancy, "and I hope he does more of that kind of thing than he does stakeouts on cheating husbands."

"I think I'll build a boat," mused Shackleford, and gazed off into the distance as he took a drink of champagne.

"Shack, why did Padgett have to get your job?" blurted Tay

undiplomatically, as if she could no longer contain the question.

Shack grinned. "What's the matter, Silvestri, don't you like your new boss?"

Trick glanced around quickly to make sure there were no costly *objets d'art* or small furniture pieces within her reach as she answered, "You know as well as I do what a ... yutz! ... he is! Benavides was next in seniority, and he's twice the investigator and ten times the man."

"I agree on all counts, Tay. I recommended Benavides, but I didn't get to make the decision. All I can tell you is to do your best, hang in there, and check your piece at the door before you go into Padgett's office."

"I'm gonna miss you, Shack," she said sadly, shaking her head. Suddenly the strident tones of a pager cut through the convivial clamor all around. "Damn," she said, and reached into the tiny handbag she clutched in her left hand to silence the device. "Guess I gotta go to work now. Let's stay in touch, okay?" She hugged Shack and Nancy once more, and headed for the nearest telephone.

"Let me know when you finish that boat and you're ready to go fishin'," said Trick as he shook hands with both Shacklefords before following Tay out of the ballroom.

Out of earshot, Trick whispered to Tay, "I didn't know his name was Orrin."

"Yeah, Orrin Doyle. But he likes that about as much as I like to be called Phyllis Jean and you like to be called Pat." She took the pager from her handbag and read the display. "Hmm, I wonder what *she* wants," she said, and her forehead furrowed slightly.

"What who wants?" asked Trick, as Tay dropped a quarter into the pay phone and quickly punched in a number without referring to the display.

"My sister, Gina. I just talked to her yesterday. I hope nothing's wrong with Mom or Dad, or ... Bob? Hi, it's Tay. Did you beep me? ... uh, yeah, I guess so. We're downtown, so give us half an hour to get there. ... Trick's with me. ... Okay. ... Just stay calm, and try to get Gina to lie down till we get there. Then you can both tell me all about it. 'Bye." She hung up the phone.

"What's wrong?" asked Trick.

"I don't know. He was really upset, and he said Gina was nearly hysterical. Trick, do you want me to drop you off at my place first? This might take awhile."

Trick shook his head. "If I can help, I will."

"I hoped you'd say that. Come on."

They walked quickly to the valet parking area and presented their claim check, and in a moment, Tay's white minivan came hurtling out of the hotel's underground parking garage. The valet jumped out and held the door open for Tay, who got in and peeled out of the driveway before Trick even had the passenger door completely shut. Fortunately, he was accustomed to Tay's daredevil driving, which he now regarded as the accepted, if not legal, way to maneuver Dallas freeways.

The stars over Texas on this cloudless summer night were so bright that the biggest of them were even visible even through the glare of the city lights. As they raced up North Central Expressway, Trick thought about how bright were the stars over his hometown of Alpine, 'way out west, the gateway to the rugged Big Bend of Texas. On a clear night, as most there were, these same stars that twinkled timidly over Dallas would shine like beacons through the shimmering curtain of the Milky Way. Though he missed being home on the ranch, which he managed for his father, Trick was content to be wherever Tay might be. He thanked God for the bizarre circumstances that had brought them together on an FBI investigation—he as a civilian deputy, she as his partner—and for the subsequent success of their mismatched, long-distance relationship.

He was forty-six, she was thirty-five; he was a cattleman who had seldom strayed from his own acreage, and she was a seasoned field agent of the FBI who traveled all over the country, often in undercover roles. He lived on the ranch near Alpine with his aging parents, and she lived in a condo in Las Colinas with three cats. Yet they somehow found time to be together, and the time they spent with one another—whether attending a black-tie reception or vegging out in front of the television—was always quality time, and always too brief.

He hoped that this diversion to comfort a sister would not take up too much of the rest of Trick's stay in Dallas, which had already been short on private time. He had only one more day and night before he needed to return to Alpine and the unending chores of cattle ranching. The reception for Shackleford had been their one undodgeable social obligation. He certainly did not mind visiting Tay's family, but he would much rather spend the remainder of evening with only feline chaperonage.

The home of Bob and Regina Brannan was situated in a subdivision of late-model zero-lot-line homes in the suburban city of Plano. The houses were all large, brick, of many colors and designs, with high-pitched roofs and tiny, well-landscaped front yards. All the homes on this side of the street shared a common driveway to garages in the back, so Tay parked the minivan at the curb, next to a mailbox set in a monolith of brick that matched the house. Except for some exterior accent lighting, the house was dark—no lights showed in any of the windows, nor was the porch light on.

"Are you sure they're home?" asked Trick as he climbed out of the vehicle.

"Yeah, pretty sure," answered Tay, with apprehension in her voice. "Maybe they're in the kitchen or in their bedroom, in the back. Just in case—" She reached into her handbag and extracted the small, semi-automatic, FBI-issue handgun which she usually packed in a shoulder holster beneath a jacket. Trick heard a round click into the chamber as they approached the front door, and he felt marginally safer, though not sure from what.

Trick rang the doorbell and stood in front of the door; Tay flattened her back against the wall beside it with her weapon poised.

After a long, silent moment, the porch light blinked on, the door opened, and Trick jumped out of the way as Tay spun around to face the door with the gun aimed and ready.

"Go ahead and shoot me, Tay," sighed the tired voice of Bob Brannan. "I couldn't hurt any worse."

"Jeez, Bob!" gasped Tay, lowering the weapon. "The house was dark, so I thought you'd been robbed or something! You didn't exactly tell me why you needed me in such a hurry, so I didn't know what to expect. Where's Gina? Is she okay?"

"In the kitchen. She's better. Come on in."

Trick and Tay followed Bob through the dark house toward the glow of a single lighted room in the back. They emerged from the gloom into a breakfast area adjacent to the kitchen, where a stylish fixture over a contemporary dinette illuminated the form of a woman slumped in a chair, staring at a coffee mug on the table. Her face was drawn tight, as if to restrain a tempest. Her eyes were red and her cheeks flushed, but she was composed.

Immediately Tay was at her sister's side, and embraced her warmly. Gina responded with a weak smile. "You look so pretty tonight, Kit-Tay," she whispered, employing the full version of the childhood pet name that had stuck to Tay all her life. "I'm sorry we dragged you away from your date."

"We were just leaving the party anyway," Trick offered. He had met Bob and Gina before, and was sure they knew that he was more to Tay than a "date." He chalked it up to whatever it was that had drawn them to the single light in the dark house like a couple of sluggish moths.

"Y'all have a seat," said Bob. "I'll pour us some coffee." This he did, but without much style or energy. He sank into the chair beside his wife, and for a moment, Trick thought they both looked very old—although he knew Gina was only two years older than Tay, and Bob wasn't much older than that.

"So how's the cattle business these days, Trick?" asked Bob without enthusiasm.

"It's steady. Yourself?" Trick couldn't remember exactly what Bob did, but it had something to do with computers.

"Promising. I think our company is really onto something with our new computer security software. It'll run on your home PC as easily as on your mainframe, and it's absolutely hackproof. All you have to do is—"

"Bob," said Tay, with an impatient edge on her voice, "do you want to talk shop or tell me why you called us to hurry over here, and I almost blew you to kingdom come?"

Bob took a deep breath and heaved a long sigh, and then said softly, "It's Brian."

The mere mention of their son's name cracked Gina's composure. Her lip began to quiver and she squeezed her eyes tightly shut.

"What about Brian?"

"He's gone."

"Gone? You mean dead?"

"He may as well be. He's gone off to join some kind of cult."

With this pronouncement, Gina could no longer bear the strain of containment. She broke down and sobbed loudly, hiding her face in her hands. Trick fidgeted helplessly in his chair while Tay and Bob attempted to comfort the hysterical woman. After what seemed a long time of patting, murmuring, and cajoling, Bob persuaded Gina to swallow a capsule with the last of the cold coffee in her mug, and a few seconds later, her tears began to abate. He encouraged her to stand, and she shuffled unsteadily along beside him as he led her into the darkness toward their bedroom.

Once they were out of earshot, Tay said, "I'm sorry about all this, Trick. If you want to take the van to my house, go ahead. I'll get Bob to drive me home in the morning."

Trick thought the offer tempting, but he shook his head. "I'll stay. How are *you*, darlin'? This can't be easy, seeing your sister all tore up like this."

"Well, no, but maybe she's overreacting a little. I mean, all kids go through phases when they're seventeen."

"Yeah, but a *cult*."

She shrugged. "Bob and Gina aren't big into organized religion. For all I know, they probably think *Methodists* are a cult. But Methodists or Moonies, there's nothing I—or the Bureau—can do, unless there's evidence of some criminal activity or intent exhibited by this so-called cult. It's not illegal to practice your religion in this country, last time I checked the Constitution."

Bob returned in a moment, an apologetic little grin masking his own sadness. "She's resting now," he said, returning to his place at the table. He raised his mug and swirled the lukewarm coffee around in it before taking a sip. "I'm sorry about all this. I guess it's even sort of our fault Brian's gone, the way we handled it. I just—"

"Bob, now's not the time to cut to the chase," said Tay. "Start at the top."

Bob dabbed at his eyes, sighed convulsively, then said, "Well, up until about three months ago, Brian was a sane, level-headed, normal kid, doing well in school and looking forward to graduation. He was going to the University of Texas next fall to study computer science, and we were really proud of him. Then he started coming home and telling us all these stories about King Arthur and the Knights of the Round Table."

"Like in English Literature class?"

"That's what I thought at first, but he kept on and on about it. Then he told me he'd met some people who claimed to *be* King Arthur and the Knights of the Round Table."

Trick and Tay glanced at each other, but returned their attention to Bob, who went on. "He said they were called The Knights of the Once and Forever King. It sounded to me like one of those 'Dungeons and Dragons'-style role-playing games that can go on for weeks at a time. He'd played them before, but he always got bored with them, so I didn't worry much at first. A couple of weeks later, he came home real excited and said he'd earned his first degree of knighthood. I asked him what that meant, and he said it gave him the right to bear arms and something about administering justice in the kingdom to come. I thought he meant he was progressing well in the game he was playing with his friends. Then he asked me if I believed we were living in the last days as described in Revelations, and I said I didn't know—I don't understand that apocalyptic stuff. He said that King Arthur will be the leader of the final battle, and the battle is coming soon. He said that when King Arthur claims his eternal throne, the age of chivalry will return to the whole world.

"Well, his mother and I tried to discourage his interest in this stuff, but no matter what we said to debunk it, he had an answer for it, straight from 'King Arthur' himself. That's when we started having the fights and when he started staying out late every night. We took his car away, but he'd ride with a friend or take the city bus. We cut his allowance down to lunch money only, but he'd buy a week's worth of peanut butter and day-old bread and pocket the rest. Whatever we did to separate him from this group, he found a way to get past us. Somehow, in just a few weeks, he'd changed from the boy we knew and loved into a proselytizing fanatic we could hardly bear to be around.

"Yesterday, his school counselor called Gina and asked to meet with us. I wanted to be there, but I had a meeting with a client that I thought I couldn't afford to miss, so she went by herself. The counselor told Gina that Brian had been cutting classes regularly for about a month and was in danger of losing credit for the whole semester, and not being able to graduate. She asked Gina if there was any trouble at home that would account for Brian's sudden strange behavior, and Gina told her about the Knights of the Once and Forever King game he was playing. The counselor said she hadn't heard of it, but that it probably wasn't a game, that it might be some kind of New Age or militia group, and to get him away from those people by any means possible.

"Gina called me, and I came home from work and we talked.

We knew there was nothing else we could do by ourselves, so today we made arrangements to check him in to a psychiatric facility for an evaluation. We were going to take him there in the morning. But when he came home tonight and announced that he was going to spend the weekend with 'a friend,' we told him no, we had some-place else to go. It was like he sensed what we were planning. He stiffened up and got this horrible expression on his face. He pointed at us and reamed us out in some weird kind of language, then he did this—" Bob raised both arms, elbows bent and fists clenched, then snapped his right arm across his left, forming a crooked cross, as if in some kind of malediction.

"He yelled at us that we weren't his family anymore—his fel-low knights were his family and King Arthur was his father. He said he'd be at his father's right hand to bring in the kingdom of heaven on earth, and we would look upon him with terror and beg for mercy when 'the dragon would rise and the lion would fall,' or something like that. There was something awful in his eyes, and for a minute, I was really afraid he might try to hurt us. But he just kept staring at us with that evil look on his face, and it was like we were paralyzed or something, as he backed out the door and just . . . vanished.

"It was probably five minutes before we could even move. Then Gina came unglued, and that's when I called you, Tay."

"Did you call the police?" asked Tay.

Bob shook his head, and smiled weakly. "Why should I, when I can have the FBI?" His expression crumbled as he went on. "Tay, I've never asked a favor of you . . . I wouldn't take advantage of your connections . . . but Brian's our only child. Help us. Please." He covered his face with his hands to hide the tears he could no longer hold back.

Tay gently patted his arm. "I'll see what I can do," she assured him. "Is it okay if I take a look at Brian's room?" Bob shrugged acquiescence, and Tay cast Trick an apologetic look as she faded into the darkness of the hallway. He returned an understanding one, but he couldn't help but feel cheated. Tomorrow, instead of whatever pleasurable diversions they might have pursued, he would be sitting in the visitors' area at the FBI field office while she searched through tons of files for information leading to the whereabouts of this alleged recent incarnation of King Arthur. He was slightly relieved when she did not volunteer to spend the night with her sister—at least they had until morning together.

Tay returned in about ten minutes. Bob thanked them, then shuffled off to the bedroom to check on Gina's drug-assisted slumber as they left the dark house. The thirty-minute drive to Tay's condo was silent except for the radio, which played country tunes at the level of a whisper. Trick glanced at Tay as she drove, and in the dim vehicle, the glare of streetlights seemed to illuminate a deepening worry on her face. By the time they arrived at the door of the two-story duplex on the upscale side of Irving, her brows were drawn tight, her lips were set, and she looked almost exactly like her sister before the breakdown earlier that evening.

When they went inside, Tay was warmly greeted by two of the three resident felines, Scully and Mulder, who were named for FBI agents on a popular TV show. She scooped up one of them and hugged it as she climbed the stairs to the bedroom, and the other impeded Trick's ascent by slaloming between his ankles. Gratefully, Trick pulled off his black bow tie and unbuttoned the stiff tuxedo shirt, and carefully hung everything up, out of reach of the copiously shedding cats. He offered assistance when Tay struggled with the zipper of her dress, and as he slid it open, he admired the firm curve of her back. He expressed his appreciation by planting a kiss on the back of her neck, which usually made her shiver with delight. Tonight, however, she only sighed and gave him a wan smile as she disappeared into the bathroom.

Trick also sighed as he climbed into bed, listening to the water filling the bathtub for what might be a two-hour soak. He would be asleep by the time she emerged, pruney but with her investigative strategy all mapped out. Maybe her soapy ruminations tonight would save some time tomorrow, and the weekend wouldn't be a total waste.

He punched his pillow into a more comfortable shape, switched off the light on his side of the bed and settled in. He felt only a twinge of guilt about his selfish demand of her time until doing some contemplation of his own. What if it were his own sister's or brother's child who had transformed into a wicked caricature of his former self? He thought of his own nieces and nephews who were, for the most part, sensible, well-reared teenagers and young adults. Certainly if something like this had happened to one of them, he would be appropriately commiserative with his sibling and would offer whatever assistance in his scope of experience.

And then he could not help but wonder: what if this were his *own* child? Laura, his daughter by a previous marriage, lived in Dallas with her mother and stepfather. She also was seventeen, but one grade in school behind Brian. For most of her childhood, Trick had not been an active part of her life, due partly to the geographical distance that had separated them and partly to the emotional distance he had placed between himself and Laura's mother. Now that Trick came to Dallas at regular intervals and spent some time during each visit with Laura, their friendship had grown quite close. She could confide in Trick in ways she could not with any other adult. Usually these confidences involved the everyday crises of attending high school in a big city, or conflicts with her mother and stepfather—both college professors, whom she regarded as unbearably dull and rigid—or a boy named Scooter who sported an earring and, recently, a tattoo.

Trick knew pretty well what bubbled near the surface of Laura's mind; yet he had no idea what occupied her thoughts when they turned to subjects of a spiritual nature, if they ever did. If so, how easily could she be captivated by a fanciful and possibly dangerous vision of a perfect world, as Brian seemed to have been? And if she had been, at what point would Trick have intervened beyond yanking her car keys and allowance? *Bob and Gina should've pushed their private Fibbie button a long time ago,* Trick thought.

He glanced at the bathroom door, behind which he was certain a plan was formulating amidst a mountain of Estee Lauder-scented bubbles, and abandoned his resentment. He was glad Tay could provide some significant assistance, and he would help her in whatever way he could.

In spite of a brief but noisy feline disagreement over rights to the foot of the bed, Trick was able to relax and drift off to sleep. Still he held on to the faint hope that all of this would be resolved in time for him to have a few hours of Tay's undivided attention between now and his Sunday morning departure.

CHAPTER TWO

Floating on the wakeful side of a pleasant dream, Trick turned over in bed and got a face full of Agatha. Spluttering, cursing, he recoiled and almost tumbled onto the floor. When he recovered, he was irritably awake, and he glared menacingly at the feline dowager that had commandeered the pillow where Tay's head should have been. The overweight silver Persian glared back with an expression of bored superiority on her broad, squashed face, then resumed her catnap. As he picked strands of cat hair out of his mouth, Trick had a feeling that this day would not improve.

The scent of coffee gave him a bit of hope, and he pulled on a pair of plaid flannel boxer shorts and followed the fragrance downstairs into the kitchen. There he found Tay, wearing only an oversize T-shirt, seated at the breakfast table with her notebook computer open and a pencil clutched in her teeth as she typed, paused, and typed some more.

"Surfing in cyberspace?" asked Trick, as he poured himself a cup of coffee. His own computer knowledge was limited to programming a VCR occasionally, but he had seen the Web browser screen over Tay's shoulder before.

"Uh-huh," she responded, without removing the pencil from her mouth. "I didn't really find much when I gave Brian's room about half a good toss, but I did notice some stuff missing. I remember he had a computer and printer, and a TV and VCR, and they were gone. I figured if he took his computer with him somehow, he might have left a trail on that proverbial information superhighway. I finally found something."

After a moment, she punched a few keys decisively, and the notebook's portable desktop printer began to whir. She removed the pencil long enough to greet Trick with a kiss and then gathered up the pages as they rolled out.

"The FBI database didn't have squat about the Knights of the Once and Forever King, but I gave the Gopher and Yahoo a bunch of keyword combinations and found their homepage."

" 'Gopher and Yahoo'—didn't they used to be on 'Hee Haw'?" remarked Trick with a grin. "What did you find?"

"It's sort of a classified ad. Here, read it." Tay handed the pages to Trick.

At the top of the first sheet, an elaborate coat-of-arms was printed as a fuzzy, low-resolution graphic, but Trick could tell that the principal emblem on it was a dragon. Below the graphic was the headline, "What Are You Searching For?", and beneath that he read:

> If you are searching for:
> - high adventure
> - companionship
> - a purpose in life
> - a chance to live FOREVER
>
> . . . you will find them all if you will accept the bold challenge that awaits each seeker who finds and surrenders to THE KNIGHTS OF THE ONCE AND FOREVER KING!
>
> Every day, TV and newspapers shout about bitter conflicts between nations and ideologies. You are shocked and sickened when you see starvation, crime, disaster, immorality and hatred. These are

symptoms of a disease called EVIL . . . and there IS a cure!

You may have heard that someday there will be a final battle between good and evil for supremacy over the earth. The battle is at hand! And leading the forces of good is the King whose power and influence ruled the entirety of Western Civilization in the obscure and turbulent years known as the Dark Ages. He has gone beyond life, but lives again among the faithful. He is Arthur, the Once and Forever King, and His mighty army is gathering behind Him to lead his people to final victory over Evil.

It is a perilous journey to Avalon (heaven), but those strong enough of heart to take up His sword and follow shall stand at His side as the Returned King claims His eternal throne when Evil is vanquished. If you are searching for true meaning in your life . . . if you seek fellowship and love with others who are bold . . . if you seek the eternal peace and prosperity that is Avalon . . . then pray that God will lead you to the Once and Forever King!

(In the Dallas-Fort Worth area, hear our Sovereign speak each Sunday at 1:00 a.m. on the KVXP-FM program, "Voices from Beyond," or visit Joyous Gard, a waystation for apprentice Knights and loyal friends, at 4633 West Redwing Drive in Fort Worth, Texas.)

"Pretty weird," remarked Trick. He noticed some more Internet gobbledygook at the bottom of the page as he handed the paper back to Tay.

"Want to hear something weirder? I've got a meeting with Padgett about this at ten, and I'm actually looking forward to it!"

"Is it gonna take very long?" Trick asked. He smiled, but his voice betrayed his frustration. "I mean, will you have some time for me today? Remember, I gotta go home tomorrow."

"Of course I will!" she exclaimed, and slid her arms around his waist. "I've got the game plan all mapped out. All I have to do now is submit my request to begin an official investigation on these Knights, and get a warrant to pick up Brian. That probably won't come through till Monday. Tell you what—come downtown with me, and after I'm through, I'll buy you lunch in the West End."

"Take me to Hooters and you've got yourself a deal!"

Shortly before ten o'clock, Trick and Tay arrived at the Cabell Federal Building in downtown Dallas. On Saturday morning, the building was practically deserted, but Tay was dressed for a typical day at the FBI field office in a summer suit of light gray wool with a violet scarf bow tie, her leather portfolio tucked under her arm. Trick's black denim jeans were crisply pressed, and he clipped his visitor's pass to the pocket flap of his subdued-Southwestern-patterned band-collar shirt as they rode the elevator to the FBI's administrative offices on an upper floor. On the way up, he took his pocket comb and smoothed his reddish-blond hair back from his face so that its unruly waves hung over his collar only in the back.

In the public area of the FBI offices, it was a regular business day, with phones ringing, office machines humming, dozens of clerical employees busy at their desks. To the casual visitor, it looked no different from the offices of a bank or a newspaper or any other large private-sector corporation. But Trick knew that just out of public view operated a model of efficient law enforcement, utilizing the most advanced techniques of investigation and analysis in the world. The men and women who worked here were among the most highly trained officers of the American criminal justice system . . . and it frequently amazed him that the woman he loved was one of them.

Tay checked in with the receptionist, noting her ten o'clock meeting with the new Deputy Director of Operations (DDO), her immediate superior. "Mr. Padgett hasn't arrived yet," said the receptionist. "I'm sure he's just running a little late. You can wait in his office if you like, Agent Silvestri."

"I'll just wait here with my guest," Tay replied. She gave Trick a smug look and whispered to him, *"Mister* Padgett isn't totally with the program. Shack was here every Saturday morning at eight o'clock sharp, whether he had anything urgent on the desk or not."

"New boss never has a chance when he has to follow a good one," remarked Trick, who had met Gordon Padgett only briefly at the reception.

"He does if he's a good one, too. If it had been Benavides . . . and speak of the devil, there he is now." She waved and called out, "Hi, Jim!"

Special Agent Diego "Jim" Benavides smiled as he crossed the clerical area from one of the offices that opened onto it. He was about Trick's age, with neatly styled light brown hair and dark twinkling eyes behind stylish eyeglasses. He was handsome in spite of deep scars inflicted on his face by adolescent acne, especially when he flashed a big, sincere smile full of even white teeth. His suit was a modest off-the-rack model but fit him well, enhancing broad shoulders and a trim waist. "A very good morning to you, Tay," he said, clasping her hand in his. "And you must be Patrick. Tay's told me all about you, most of it very flattering."

"She's said the same of you, Mr. Benavides," said Trick, shaking hands. "And call me Trick—only my mom calls me Patrick, and then only when I've ticked her off."

"Nice to meet you, and I'm Jim to everyone but *my* mom, who still calls me Diego. What brings you to the office on Saturday morning, Tay? I thought you pulled the evening on-call shift last night."

"I did," she answered. "Something's come up, and I've got to see Padgett."

Benavides grinned and said softly, "Well, I always heard that if you ate a live frog first thing in the morning, whatever happened the rest of the day would seem fabulous by comparison." He shared the laugh with them, then excused himself and returned to his office.

In a moment, the elevator door opened and in strode the DDO. Gordon Padgett was forty, but his encroaching baldness and expanding middle made him look years older. He was dressed in a knit polo shirt, light poplin pants and penny loafers, and in the same hand with his briefcase he carried by the laces a pair of golf shoes. If there was any doubt that his appointment at the office this morning had coincided with something of a higher priority, he confirmed it when he said without greeting, "I can give you fifteen minutes, Agent Silvestri. What is so damned important that it can't wait till Monday?" Without waiting for an answer, he stormed into his office, leaving the door open for Tay to follow him in.

Tay glanced apprehensively at Trick, who grinned and said, "A little sugar'll help that ol' frog slide right down." He discreetly touched a finger to his lips to symbolize a kiss. She was smiling as she turned and disappeared into Padgett's office. The door closed.

Trick took a seat in the visitors' waiting area and picked up the sports section from the morning newspaper. He figured he could finish it in fifteen minutes. But he was through with the sports, the funnies, and the classified automobile ads before Tay reappeared. About half an hour had gone by, but she looked like she had already put in a hard day. Her face was as drawn as it had been on the way home from her sister's house last night. She didn't say a word; she simply jerked her head in the direction of the elevator, and Trick rose and followed her. He had a feeling that all of the plans she had hatched in the bathtub last night had just gone down the drain.

Alone together in the elevator, she released a stream of invective that described Gordon Padgett as everything but a jolly good fellow. When the elevator door opened at the ground floor, she bottled it up and remained silent until they got to her minivan.

She was so upset that she fumbled her car keys, and she began to curse again as they went sliding under the vehicle. Trick recovered them and insisted that he drive, lest in her agitated state she become an even greater hazard on the road than she usually was. She had yet to state the reason for her distress, but Trick knew she would eventually get around to it when she simmered down, so he drove aimlessly through downtown Dallas to give her time to do so. When he discovered a parking space by a small city park, he skillfully maneuvered the van into it and cut the engine.

"Come on," he said gently, and urged her out of the van. They walked across the little green island to a bench beneath a shady live oak. Her anger vented, she sank slowly onto the bench and sat quietly for a moment, staring at a squirrel browsing in the grass nearby. Trick sat silently also, waiting until she was ready to talk before he said a word.

Finally she said, "You might have already guessed that things did not go well."

"I sort of picked up on that," he answered.

"The short version goes something like this. The good and wise Mr. Padgett stated that the fact that the Bureau database has nothing on the Knights suggests there is no evidence of criminal activity. If no such evidence exists, no warrants will be issued, no investigation will be authorized. He offered a reminder of what happened down around Waco a few years ago between the FBI and another 'character' with delusions of divinity. Until the Knights actually *do* something, they are free to operate their sect as they choose."

"But what about Brian?"

"The fact that Brian has associated himself with the Knights is not the issue, since he apparently chose to do so of his own free will. But because he's just seventeen, he's technically a runaway, and so we have been advised to seek the assistance of our local police. I have also been advised to stay the hell out of it, with warnings about interjurisdictional interference, conflicts of interest and professional ethics violations. End of transmission."

She sighed, and slumped down on the bench. "What am I going to tell my sister? 'Sorry, Gina, my boss says I can't do anything
to help you. Just call the cops and wait in line for the next available
officer, who already has more to do than he can say grace over.' I've
got half a mind to go back there right now and give my notice. I
can't work for that . . . that . . . bureaucrat!"

Trick reached over and patted her shoulder. "Now, honey, sim-
mer down," he soothed. "You don't really want to quit. Maybe
there's something else we can do."

"I'm open to suggestion."

"Well . . . we have an address in Fort Worth where Brian might
be, from that thing you got off the computer. Why don't we just
happen to be in the neighborhood and have a look? At least you
could tell Gina and Bob you'd accomplished that much."

Tay's dark expression brightened a little. "It's worth a shot. We
could at least drive by."

"Yeah, and then you could buy me lunch in the Stockyards."

"I do believe I have a Fort Worth map in the van. Let's do it!"

They drove west on Interstate 30, with Tay at the wheel and
Trick navigating from the map he found in the glove compartment. The address turned out to be almost an hour's drive from
downtown Dallas, on the far southwest side of Fort Worth in an
ordinary middle-class subdivision. It was an unremarkable brick
house on a corner lot with a mowed but weedy front lawn. Cars of
all descriptions were parked in the driveway and along the curbs of
the intersecting streets. The mailbox bore no name, only the street
number, and it had its red flag up to signal that outgoing mail
awaited the postal carrier's attention. Blinds covered the windows,
and behind the front door screen, some kind of colorful plaque
decorated the main door.

"This must be Joyous Gard," remarked Trick as they passed
slowly by. "Want to go knock on the door?"

"No, I better not—if Brian's there, he's going to recognize me.

He'll either bolt and run, or he'll announce the arrival of the FBI, and there's no telling what might happen next . . . and suddenly I recall that little Branch Davidian incident."

"Well, *I* could do it. Brian doesn't know me, but I'd recognize him from the pictures I saw in Bob and Gina's house."

"Would you do that?"

"You know I would. Why don't you drop me off, make the block, and pick me up in about five minutes?"

Tay slowed the van at the next intersection, but sped on through it. "Hey, where are you going?" asked Trick, looking backward at the neighborhood as they turned onto the main road and headed out of the subdivision.

She shook her head sadly as they continued back toward the downtown area. "No, we can't do that, either. You'd be doing it at my behest, and that makes it infiltration, which is still a violation of FBI ethics. There's nothing in the least bit suspicious about that house back there. Padgett was right: there's not a damned thing we can really do to help Brian. I might as well hang up my badge." She pounded her fist on the steering wheel once, hard, then said, with strained cheerfulness, "Now I'm going to feed you lunch at the Stockyards like I promised."

Neither said much during the half-hour's drive to the north side of Fort Worth, to the historic Stockyards—now primarily a tourist attraction full of shops, restaurants, and nightclubs. Billy Bob's Texas, still reigning as the world's largest honky-tonk, was located at one end of the Stockyards, and was one of their favorite evening destinations on Trick's visits to the Dallas-Fort Worth Metroplex.

Nearby was Rowdy's Rib Ranch, which served up all sorts of barbecue, but specialized in big, meaty ribs, dripping with sweet, piquant sauce, which waiters and waitresses brought to the table in galvanized pails until diners begged them to stop. Their timing was excellent; the lunch crush had peaked, and they were seated immediately and set up with iced tea and hot rolls to await their bucket of beef.

They sat in silence in the noisy restaurant. Trick watched Tay poking absently with her tea spoon at the lemon wedge in the bottom of her glass, and the disappointment on her face could not have been more pronounced if she had been a child who had just learned the truth about Santa Claus. Soon the bucket of ribs arrived at the table, along with plates heaped with coleslaw and potato salad. It was as glorious a feast for the eyes as for the tastebuds, and Trick eagerly took a rib and began eating with gusto. She pushed the side dishes around on her plate with a fork, but did not take a bite. Her utter lack of interest in the meal dulled his own appetite, and when they left a few minutes later, they abandoned enough food to nourish a Bengal tiger for two days.

They returned to Dallas, to Tay's condominium, where the remainder of the afternoon was spent in silence, as Tay's mood swung from angry frustration to helpless depression. Trick went to take a dip in the complex's pool, while Tay curled up for a nap on the couch. The nap seemed to refresh her a bit, but she declined an evening on the town. Instead they spent the evening cuddling in front of the television, watching old movies on cable TV and eating ice cream out of the carton. Neither of them said a word about Brian or Joyous Gard or the strict policies followed by the FBI.

Everything seemed back to normal, until they finally climbed into bed and turned out the lights. The cats jumped up on the bed and began staking out the territory between Trick and Tay. Usually, Tay would gently shoo them away, and they would return after things settled down, but this time, she made no effort to close the distance they placed between herself and Trick.

"I'm sorry, honey," she said, "I know it's our last night together for awhile, but I'm just not up to it right now. Maybe in the morning."

"It's okay, darlin'," he answered. "I understand."

They kissed like old married people, and settled down for sleep. But Trick—eye to eye with Agatha on the pillow, Mulder curled up in the small of his back, and Scully tucked into the crook of his knees—began to wish he'd never heard of the Knights of the Once and Future King, Joyous Gard, or the ungrateful brat of a kid who had robbed him of his beloved's full and pleasurable attention.

The next morning, Trick rose early and quietly gathered his things. He showered, but neglected to shave—it usually took two or three days for his blond stubble to show. He got dressed, brewed a pot of coffee, then sat at the kitchen table and glanced through the Sunday paper. After he sorted out the sections he wanted to read more thoroughly, he poured himself a cup and began with the sports. By the time he'd finished the golf standings, he could hear water running in the bathroom, so he knew Tay would be joining him soon. He looked forward to greeting her this morning, but not without some apprehension. Goodbyes would have to be said soon.

After he'd read the funnies, the opinion page, and the Sunday magazine, Tay appeared in her pink terry bathrobe with a towel wrapped like a turban around her wet hair. He liked the look, and loved the fragrance of soap and shampoo that followed her into the kitchen as she poured herself a cup of coffee. He smiled as she sat at the table across from him. " 'Mornin'," he said warmly.

"I'm sorry about last night," she said.

"Nothing to be sorry for. We'll make it up next time. When do you think you can come out west?"

"Gosh, I don't know. It may be around the first of September before I can take any vacation time."

"So you've decided not to quit?"

Tay shrugged. "For the time being. I may go ahead and send out some résumés."

"I guess that's all right. Just don't do anything you'll regret. Maybe I can come back to Dallas again before September."

Then she became very quiet again. Trick could hear the clock over the stove ticking. Finally he could no longer stand it, and he rose from the table. "I better get going," he said softly. "It's nine solid hours to Alpine."

"When will you ever learn to buy airplane tickets?" she asked as she put her arms around his waist and leaned her warm, damp head against his chest.

"Honey, I got a lot more time than I do money, and my truck's already paid for." He pressed her close, and drank in the steamy, clean scent of her. Already his chest ached, as if he were seeing her for the last time. "I'll miss you, Tay."

"I'll miss you, too, cowboy. You keep that truck between the fences, okay?"

"I will. Make sure you only shoot bad guys—your boss doesn't count," he teased, and they shared a kiss that lasted a long time, but not nearly long enough. Although she was smiling as she waved at him from the front porch, he couldn't help but think she was still preoccupied with thoughts of leaving the Bureau because of her inability to help Gina and Bob.

As he drove away, he decided he would go ahead and do what she could not ask him to do. It would make her happy to be able to report something . . . anything . . . to her distressed sister. And it wasn't really infiltration—after all, it would only take a few minutes—but he did need a little plan, which he concocted as he drove.

Sunday morning traffic on the freeways was light, and he was in Fort Worth before he even realized he'd left Dallas. He kept a rein on his speed as he navigated the loop around the city, waiting to drop the hammer when he got onto the rural stretches of Interstate 20 just west of Weatherford. But as he got to the cutoff, instead of turning west, he continued on south a few miles to the exit that led to Joyous Gard.

He stopped his red Chevy half-ton at a Whataburger restaurant and went in and ordered breakfast. While he waited for his name to be called, he went into the restroom and exchanged his good jeans and shirt for the clothes he'd brought to do yard work in, if Tay had needed it done—threadbare jeans and a blue workshirt with holes in both elbows, clean but stained with grass, sweat, paint and motor oil. He tugged off his good snakeskin boots and pulled on the ancient, cracked and stained cowhide Ropers he had worn in the years he had worked as a roughneck on oil leases in different parts of the world, which made good mowing boots now. Finally he ran both hands through his hair, disheveling the careful work he'd done earlier with comb and hair dryer. He inspected his work in the mirror, and was pleased that the man looking back at him could have been any random derelict.

He carefully folded his clothes and stowed them in his truck, and returned to the dining room just in time to hear the name "Patrick" called by the friendly Whataburger employee who had taken his order. When he claimed his platter of scrambled eggs, bacon and biscuits, she looked askance at him, as if he were a freeloader grabbing someone else's order. He sat by the window as he ate and reviewed his plan to approach Joyous Gard, the way Tay would do, formulating options for any contingency. Unfortunately, his mind did not operate in the same analytical, methodical ways that hers did, and he could only plan as far as walking through the front door. He would just have to get that far and let whatever might happen, happen.

He finished his breakfast and headed for the parking lot. Before he got in the truck, he hesitated by the pay phone; in the event his little mini-investigation involved more than a few minutes, he decided he should alert his parents that his estimated time of arrival home might be later than expected. He dropped in a quarter and punched in his credit card number, and after a few rings, the phone at his home in Alpine was answered by a recorded message. His mother's voice chirped an apology for their not being able to answer the phone, but invited the caller to leave a message. Trick glanced at his watch and remembered that it was Sunday and his mother and dad would be at church. At the beep, he said, "Hi, it's me. Uh, Tay has some stuff she needs me to do today, so I might be late getting in. Don't wait up for me. See you later." He hung up the phone and got in his truck.

Before he started the engine, he stripped off his watch and

strapped it around his billfold, and tucked them deep under the seat for safekeeping during his reconnaisance mission. He drove to a large grocery store that was about a half mile from the Joyous Gard neighborhood. He parked close to the building, then got out, tossed the keys under the seat, and checked to make sure his spare key was safe in its magnetic box under the front bumper before locking the door. He set off walking down the street that led to the subdivision with nothing but some change in his jeans and a folded-up piece of paper in his shirt pocket—the filched hardcopy of the information Tay had gleaned from the Internet about the Knights of the Once and Forever King.

Ten minutes later, Trick stood on the front porch of the corner house. The colorful plaque on the front door was a coat-of-arms cut out of wood with a scrollsaw. Painted upon it with a good degree of skill was the same dragon emblem featured on the piece of paper in his pocket. He took a deep breath and rang the bell.

In a moment, a woman opened the door and said, "Can I help you?"

"Is this, uh, Joyous Gard?" asked Trick, comparing the number on the door to the one on the paper which he had extracted from his pocket. He made sure he had a lost expression on his face which would serve him whether he was in the right place or not.

"It is. Would you like to come in?" The woman held the door open and Trick went in. If he had expected a Turkish opium den, he would have been disappointed—it was an ordinary living room with a sofa, chairs, a coffee table, a television with VCR, and inexpensive framed pictures of castles on the paneled walls. It seemed that he and his hostess were the only people at home; only two cars were parked along the corner curbs this morning.

"Have a seat," offered the woman. "Would you like some coffee?"

"Yes, thanks. This is a nice place."

"Thank you. We like it. Make yourself comfortable, and I'll be right back."

Trick took a seat in a worn wing-back chair near the door, and looked all around for evidence that this was actually the headquarters of some kind of dangerous cult. Obviously he would have to dig a little deeper if there were any bodies to find.

His hostess returned in a moment, stirring a steaming mug which he handed to Trick. He took a sip. Instant, but acceptable. "My name is Diane," said the younger woman, who seated herself on the sofa across from Trick. She looked about thirty-five, with short brown hair frosted blonde and pulled into a stubby ponytail. Her somewhat matronly figure was disguised by a long red T-shirt decorated with blue and white ribbons over matching leggings, and red sneakers added a youthful touch. "What's yours?"

"Pat—" Trick caught himself about to give his real name, and quickly pulled one out of the blue. "—terson. Jack Patterson."

"Welcome to Joyous Gard, Jack. What brings you here this morning?"

Trick took another deep breath, and it came out in a ragged sigh as an image of the reason for his presence here filled his mind— Tay Silvestri, looking very unhappy, and waving goodbye. Something about her expression, the way she had looked when they parted, gave him a chilling little feeling that it might be the last time they would be together. Quite unexpectedly, tears clouded his eyes. "I—I dunno," he said softly. "I guess I'm—looking for something." He shrugged, and let his mouth run. "I found this paper in a dumpster. I need somethin' to live for, like it says. I been living on the street awhile, and I know there's gotta be a better way."

"There is, Jack, and you've come to the right place," said Diane earnestly, reaching out her hand to him.

Trick smiled, and let a tear escape to meander the creases on his weatherbeaten face. If he was going to play a part, he would play it to the hilt. Tay, the FBI's reigning master of undercover disguise, would be thoroughly proud of him.

Fibs, don't fail me now, he thought, as he took Diane's hand.

CHAPTER THREE

S O TELL ME A LITTLE ABOUT YOURSELF, JACK," said DIANE, ONCE the cup of coffee had restored her guest's composure.

"There's not much to tell, really," said Trick. "I don't call any-place home, especially. I travel around. Usually I work someplace for awhile, finish the job, and move on."

"What kind of work do you do?"

"Oh, lots of things. Construction. Truck drivin'. Oil field. Cowboyin'." *Undercover investigations,* he added to himself.

"Are you working now?"

"No, I haven't worked for a couple of weeks. Kinda hard for a guy my age to get anything these days."

"What about your family, Jack?"

"Not much to tell there, either. I got no folks, no brothers or sisters. Used to have a wife, but she took the kid and split a long time ago. Guess you could say I'm pretty much alone in this old world."

"Well, you don't have to be alone anymore, Jack," said Diane warmly, patting his arm. "Let me see that piece of paper you brought with you."

Trick fished the paper out of his ragged shirt pocket and care-fully unfolded it. He turned it so Diane could see it, but did not let it go, as if he feared he would lose something valuable. She smiled as she glanced at it, then asked, "Do you understand what it says, Jack?"

"Kinda," he replied. He pointed to the first paragraph. "I sure believe all this about evil in the world. I've seen enough of it to last me two lifetimes. And I sure would like to get some of the peace and prosperity like it says here. What do I have to do?"

"Well, the first thing you need to do is come to our study tonight here at Joyous Gard, when the others get back. There'll be singing, and we'll talk about different things, and Sir Jeffrey will bring a message from King Arthur, and you'll know you made the right decision."

"I dunno, Diane. I don't really think I can hang around that long. Can't *you* just tell me more about it?"

"Oh, I couldn't do it justice. You really just have to experience it."

"What does it mean about King Arthur and joining his army and all?"

"Like I said, Jack, you really have to hear it from Sir Jeffrey and listen to what the others say. I think you'll understand it better from them. I'm kind of new here myself, and I don't know everything there is to know, but I could tell when you came in that you're the type of person King Arthur needs in his army, Jack. You seem like someone who only needs a little guidance to reach a superior potential. You can get that here, Jack. I promise you. I'll help you, and so will the others."

Trick could see he was getting nowhere—Diane wasn't going to tell him anything. As much as he wanted to get a tidbit of information for Tay, he certainly could not wait around for it all day. He needed to get home in time to get a good night's sleep so he could get up early for his day's work on the ranch. He shook his head and stood up slowly. "I better get going, Diane," he said. "Thanks for your time, and the coffee."

"Jack, don't leave. You'll regret it the rest of your life if you don't stay." She rose also, and gently clasped his hand. "Besides, if you stay," she added, and her voice dropped into a husky whisper,

"I'll *personally* make it worth your while."

Trick recoiled as if her hand had suddenly transformed into a hot poker. He blushed, and stammered, "Oh, no, ma'am, that's not necessary—not at all! I *definitely* got to go now!" He backed up to the door, and fumbled behind him for the knob.

Diane giggled, and smiled, and said in her normal voice, "Wait, Jack! I didn't mean it! It was a test—a test of character. One of the qualities a Knight must have is virtue, and you proved you're a virtuous man. Don't you see, Jack? Not everybody is cut out to be a Knight—only a few will be chosen to stand with the King at the final battle. You can be one, I know you can! Please stay. I won't test you again, I promise."

Trick's heart slowed down a little, and he chuckled nervously. He would have to omit this incident in his report to Tay. "I guess I don't get that offer often enough to know how to behave when I do," he said.

"You behaved chivalrously—which is what being a Knight is all about."

Now his interest in the workings of this group was genuinely piqued, but he was still hesitant to invest the time it was obviously going to take to find out more about them. "Well, what time does this deal start tonight?" he asked.

"The others will start getting back later this afternoon. We'll have a meal together about six, and then after that we'll have a study. Will you stay? I'll tell you a secret if you say you will."

Trick sighed; he'd started this charade, and now it looked like he'd have to finish it. If he stayed until the "others" returned, maybe he would see Brian among them, and he could make excuses and leave before he would be obliged to sit for a meal and the study. He could then phone his parents to let them know it would be daylight before he would be home, and report to Tay that Brian was all right. He said, "Okay, I'll hang around. What's your big secret?"

"You have to promise you won't tell Sir Jeffrey or anyone that I told you," she whispered, as if they might already be listening.

"I promise."

"Once you're admitted to the fellowship, you start working toward becoming a Knight. One of the ways you can get your first degree of Knighthood is by bringing a worthy candidate into the fellowship. If you stay, I could be qualified for Knighthood!"

"Why's that such a secret?"

"It's not really a *secret* secret—but silence is part of our discipline. I just thought you'd be happy for me that you've helped me to earn my Knighthood."

Trick nodded as if in agreement, but he was actually processing the first bit of useful information he had gleaned: Tay's brother-in-law had said Brian had come home one evening with the news that he'd received his first degree of Knighthood. What had he done to earn that honor? "What else can you do to be a Knight?" he asked innocently.

"Well, you can—uh, maybe I better not say anything else right now. More coffee?"

He declined, and slowly finished the last lukewarm sips from his mug. *Silence is part of the discipline,* he thought. Maybe the Knights *did* have something to hide. But the only way he would be able to find out would be to gain the trust of Diane and all the other inhabitants of Joyous Gard—and the quicker, the better. "Do you have any little odd jobs around here that I can do today?" he asked. "Might as well be busy while I wait."

"Oh, this place needs *tons* of work," she answered gratefully. "Would you like to work on the weeds in the front yard? I'll get you something to dig with." She added conspiratorially, "I can't guarantee anything, but it might get you a head start on your Knighthood—if you want it."

Trick had hoped for something a little more intellectually demanding for his first task at Joyous Gard, but within minutes he was armed with a rusty paring knife and kneeling in the crabgrass by the curb. A grease-stained gimme cap produced from one of the bedrooms in the house helped to shade his eyes from the sun, which crept toward its zenith on this cloudless June morning and promised a scorcher of an afternoon.

At noon, Diane brought him a tuna salad sandwich and a tall insulated plastic jug full of sweetened iced tea, and complimented his work. She then invited him to continue his efforts in the back yard, and was pleased at how he eagerly accepted his assignment. What she did not know was that when she went back into the air-conditioned house, the eager newcomer cursed the weather, the weeds, and his decision to detour to Joyous Gard.

Trick was certainly no stranger to heat and the sun, having worked outdoors all of his life, but he was accustomed to the thin, dry air of mountainous west Texas; here in Fort Worth, the humidity felt like being submerged in a tropical fish tank. Shucking the shirt helped, but before long, his bare shoulders were broiled medium rare. Sweat streamed from every crevice on his face and collected around the stubble of his beard, and soaked his jeans. The moisture in his clothes invited an invasion of chiggers—they burrowed in around his waist, behind his knees, and a few especially sadistic ones targeted the tender area in between. Pausing occasionally to scratch and curse, Trick forged on until the middle of the afternoon.

When the Joyous Gard grounds, front and back, were pitted with hundreds of tiny divots where the crabgrass, dandelions, and milkweed had been, Trick rapped on the back door to report completion of his assignment. Diane admitted him to the utility room after glancing out into the yard to check his work. "You did really well, Jack," she praised. "The yard's never looked better. Would you like to take a shower and change clothes?"

"Well, uh, I don't have any other clothes," Trick said.

"Don't worry. I'll find something you can put on, and I'll wash your things. Go ahead and take a shower. There are towels in the closet outside the bathroom."

"Thanks, Diane. You're mighty nice."

She smiled. "This is just how we do things at Joyous Gard."

On the way to the bathroom, Trick had a quick look around the back part of the house. There were three bedrooms, each furnished with multiple sets of bunk beds. One room with four beds had a feminine appearance, and was a little neater than the other two. One of the other bedrooms had an unfinished plywood partition which offered privacy to the occupant who lived behind it— Trick guessed Sir Jeffrey, the absent leader of the Joyous Gard gang. He wondered which was Brian's bunk; it would be impossible to determine from the few personal belongings that were visible in the two men's bedrooms. The only thing remarkable about the bathroom was the number of used towels hanging on racks—almost a dozen of them, all different, neatly folded and draped to dry.

As he stood beneath the shower spigot, wishing that calamine lotion would pour from it to soothe the burn on his back and the itch of the rest of him, he decided he had seen enough. For all he could tell, the inhabitants of this house were just a latter-day Waltons family with an unusually strong interest in medieval chivalry. If he left by five, he could be home by two or three in the morning, grab a couple of hours of shut-eye, and maybe accomplish a good day's work on the ranch. Then he could call Tay and tell her not to worry about Brian—he would get over this silly infatuation eventually.

He wrapped a towel around himself and opened the bathroom door a crack to see if Diane had found him something to wear. She had—on the floor beside the door lay a folded red T-shirt with the Coca-Cola logo on it, a pair of gray sweatpants with a drawstring waist, and a pair of worn white tube socks. He hung his towel neatly over the shower curtain bar, bringing the number to an even dozen. He tugged the shirt over his head and winced as it gently abraded the tender, sunburned skin of his shoulders, then stepped into the sweatpants, which felt odd without underwear. Finally, he stuffed his feet into the socks and padded out into the hallway, combing through his wet hair with his fingers. He stopped when he heard Diane's voice, then another voice, speaking.

"His name is Jack Patterson," she said, and Trick perked up his ears. "Says he doesn't have a home or a job, but he's real interested in the Knights."

"He may just be after a free meal," said a male voice. "What did you tell him?"

"Nothing. I told him that he'd find out more tonight at the study."

"Good work. Is he going to stay?"

"He said he would. I think he's okay, Josh. He passed the test of virtue. And I think Sir Jeffrey will pass him on diligence and sacrifice for the yard work."

"Well, if he shows two more chivalrous traits, he'll be acceptable as an apprentice. His not having a job is a bit of a problem, but he does seem willing enough to work. He can work for us if he doesn't have any other way to contribute to our budget. Speaking of working, New Cadbury is beginning to look like Camelot at last."

"Will it be ready in time for the Convergence?"

"It's *got* to be. As soon as Merryborough shuts down, we'll have more help from our Knights. The Faire is the best recruiting tool we have, but most of those novices won't become residents. Do you think your new guy will stay on here?"

"I'm not sure. He seems a little anxious to leave."

"Well, I'll work on him a little. If he's really worthy, once he hears King Arthur for himself, he'll want to stay."

Trick stood in the hallway a moment, trying to puzzle out what he had just heard. The name "Camelot" was familiar, but "New Cadbury" and "Merryborough" meant nothing to him. And though he had no idea what was meant by "worked on," he knew he wanted no part of it. Still, he was curious about "King Arthur's plan" . . . and at least for the moment, he wasn't dressed for egress.

Bravely, he ventured into the living room, where Diane introduced "Sir Joshua," a stocky, pleasant-looking fellow about thirty years old, with curly brown hair and twinkling blue eyes. He was dressed casually, in jeans and a golf shirt, and looked like a young businessman at his leisure on a Sunday—except for the red armband tied around his left bicep. Embroidered upon the band was a gold dragon, similar to the one on the coat-of-arms on the front door, and beneath the image was sewn an embroidered double chevron.

"Diane says you came to Joyous Gard looking for a purpose," said the amiable Knight. "Forgive me if I presume too much, but you seem to be a nice enough kind of guy who's sort of fallen through the cracks of society."

"I reckon that's true, Sir Joshua," answered Trick, with convincing humility. Standing there barely dressed, it wasn't difficult to feel submissive.

"I'll bet you've worked hard all your life, and you have nothing to show for it."

Trick nodded. The young Knight leaned forward and asked, "Do you believe in God, Jack?"

"Yes, sir, I do," Trick said, truthfully. "I grew up in a Christian home, and was baptized and everything."

"Who do you trust more: God or the government?"

"That's easy," Trick chuckled. " 'In God We Trust'—all others, cash up front."

Sir Joshua was only slightly amused. "Seriously, Jack. If I told you that you could become prosperous beyond your wildest dreams, simply by putting all your trust in God and none in the government, could you do it?"

"Well, I . . . I dunno. There's nothing illegal involved, is there?"

"Jack, when we're talking about the law, which is the higher authority—God's law or man's?"

"God's law, of course."

"Then would you agree that God's law supersedes laws made by mortal men?"

"I guess if you put it that way, yes."

"What I want you to understand, Jack, is that you have come of your own free will into the keeping of the Knights of the Once and Forever King, and before you decide to stay, you need to know a little bit about us. We are a small group, but our numbers and our power are growing under the influence of one whom God has chosen to lead us. Our mission is to rid the world of evil, poverty and hopelessness by restoring it to chivalry. Chivalry is based on godly principles, but it is often necessary to defend those principles. And when I say *defend*, I may be implying a certain degree of physical and spiritual danger. Does that frighten you?"

"No, Sir Joshua, it sounds exciting! Tell me more!"

The Knight smiled and leaned back in his chair. "Sir Jeffrey will tell you the rest tonight after supper, when we gather to hear the latest revelations from our leader."

"I'll have your clothes ready before then," Diane chimed in.

"So, Jack, are you still interested? We're tough and demanding and not for the faint-hearted or feeble-minded. We need good people to be good Knights, and I believe you may have what it takes. But if you hear King Arthur's message tonight and you decide it's not for you, for whatever reason, then you can go on your way. But remember as you go that one day soon, you'll be ruled rather than ruling."

"I'll stick around," Trick said, and this time, he meant it. The Knight had thrown him just enough bait to hook him. Without actually saying so, Sir Joshua had revealed that what the Knights of the Once and Forever King did might not be totally within man's laws—which was what Tay Silvestri had sworn as an FBI Special Agent to defend. If he could gather just enough information to make a case, he could offer it as a "tip" to help her open a real investigation. In the meantime, if he could just get a glimpse of Brian, that would fulfill his initial mission.

For the next couple of hours, Trick relaxed at the insistence of his host and hostess. He watched TV and dozed in his chair, made sleepy by the fever of his sunburn. During that time, others began to arrive, and he was introduced to each of them as they trailed in, one or two at a time. The men ranged from sixteen-year-old Sir Dylan, a skinny, serious, taciturn kid with an earring and limp blond

hair that hung over his eyes like a ragged window curtain, to Sir
Barry, a fiftyish, diminutive, professorial type with thick eyeglasses
and a goatee. In between there was Sir Cody, a shy, good-natured,
rather handsome hulk in his mid-twenties with enormous hands,
who looked strong enough to juggle haybales; and Russell, a small,
rotund man in his late twenties, whose belly strained the buttons
of his shirt the same way his nasal, asthmatic giggle strained Trick's
ears. There were three female Knights, whose honorary title was
"Dame": Anne, Tonya, and Jennifer. All three were in their early-
to- mid-twenties and attractive enough in their own way, Anne
and Jennifer on the stout side and Tonya just a little too thin, and
all were very pleasant and seemed glad to welcome "Jack" to Joyous
Gard. They all came in wearing armbands like Sir Joshua's, most
with only one chevron—Dame Jennifer's had two, but Russell's
had none. Conspicuous by his absence was the object of his investigation, Brian Brannan.

Last to arrive, minutes before dinner was served, was Sir Jeffrey.
He was young, perhaps twenty-five, with black wavy hair carefully
styled back from his face and sleek as a helmet. His dark eyes peered
out from under a bow of black eyebrows that extended all the way
across his forehead. Although he wore gray dress slacks and a white
Oxford cloth shirt, with a red and black striped tie loose at his
neck, he had the bearing of a soldier. His armband insignia showed
three chevrons, and it was clear from the moment he walked through
the door that he was in charge: each person stopped what he or she
was doing to greet him respectfully. He was the first person to sit at
the dining table, and took the head chair.

All the others came to the table when Diane and Dame Anne
announced that supper was ready. Trick, dressed once more in his
tattered but clean clothes, stood beside Sir Joshua as he said, "My
liege, allow me to present Jack Patterson, who came of his own will
this morning to Joyous Gard. Jack, this is Sir Jeffrey Lancelot, lord
of the Knights of Joyous Gard."

Sir Jeffrey nodded toward him, and said in a deep, authoritative voice, "Please be welcome as a guest at this table. Everyone may now be seated. Jack, you may take the seat beside Sir Joshua." With that, all the Knights moved as one into their crowded places around the long dining room table and bowed their heads. Sir Jeffrey spoke a brief blessing, and then plates were passed for servings of a flavorless hamburger casserole, green beans and salad. Everyone ate diligently for a time, speaking only to ask that additional food be passed. There was no chatter, none of the warmth shown him by the Knights as they arrived at Joyous Gard. Trick watched each person at the table, wondering if it was his presence or Sir Jeffrey's that was stifling the conversation.

Finally, after cookies and fruit for dessert, Sir Jeffrey rose from his chair. "It is time to hear the word of King Arthur," he announced ominously. "Will our guest attend?"

Trick felt a slight jab in his ribs from Sir Joshua's elbow, and he quickly replied, "Yes, Sir Jeffrey, I'd be honored."

Sir Jeffrey nodded, and everyone at the table rose. With the mysterious Knight in the lead, they trooped from the dining room through the kitchen into the garage, which had been converted into a kind of chapel. There, a dozen or more mismatched folding chairs were set in rows in front of a small table draped with a white cloth. Upon it were a Bible lying open, a flat wooden box with brass fittings, and a carefully-trimmed candle in a brass candlestick on each side. Adding an anachronous touch to the formal furnishings on the table was a portable stereo with a formidable array of speakers. Its aerial was fully telescoped and pointed out to one side. Above the table, on the wall, were a pair of gleaming swords crossed below an ornate coat of arms. Like the one on the front door, it featured a gold dragon on a red shield, but was rendered in greater detail.

On the other walls were displayed maps of the United States and Europe, and more pictures of castles. Off in one corner was a steel cabinet the size of a wardrobe, chained tightly shut and locked with a large combination padlock. A small window air conditioner labored to cool the uninsulated room, which seemed to have gathered all the day's heat. The twelve people jamming the room did not enhance the appliance's performance, and Trick began to itch and perspire again. He hoped this ceremony would be brief.

"Knights, apprentices, honored guest," said Sir Jeffrey as he stood before the group. "Let us stand and begin this time of meditation with our anthem. Dame Jennifer, will you lead us?" Dame Jennifer stood, and with a clear, sweet voice she began a chorus which the others followed. Trick knew the tune—it was the familiar Doxology, "Old One Hundredth"—but just as he began to join in, the words changed.

> *Praise God, from whom all blessings flow;*
> *Soon all who dwell on earth shall know*
> *The day of Arthur now hath dawned,*
> *The King of Earth and Avalon.*

"Thank you, Dame Jennifer," said Sir Jeffrey. "Now let us pray." Trick's impulse was to bow his head and possibly fold his hands, but instead, the Knights all stared straight ahead at the crossed swords over the open Bible, then clenched their right hands into fists and struck them on the left sides of their chests, as if preparing to speak the Pledge of Allegiance with a vengeance. They spoke no words aloud, but stared at the cross of steel and the emblem above it, as though they were offering prayers in the privacy of their thoughts. After about a half minute, Sir Jeffrey said, "You may be seated."

The leader of the Knights of Joyous Gard opened the wooden box on the table and removed a small, worn book with a red cover. He opened it to the pages in the back and said, "Hear now the covenant from the Malory Revelation: 'Yet some men say that King Arthur is not dead, but had by the will of our Lord Jesu into another place; and men say that he shall come again, and he shall win the holy cross. And many men say that there is written upon his tomb this verse: *Hic iacet Arthurus, Rex quondam, Rexque futurus.* ' "

"Amen," agreed several members of the small assembly.

Sir Jeffrey then thumbed to a place marked with a red ribbon and said, "Our study tonight from the Malory Revelation is from the book of Excalibur."

All the Knights leaned forward with anticipation, but the name "Excalibur" meant nothing to Trick except a very expensive sports car. Even so, he feigned interest as Sir Jeffrey, with a deep, resonant voice, read from the little book the story of how the Lady of the Lake led King Arthur to find the great sword Excalibur and its magic scabbard, which, when worn by the King, would protect him from shedding blood, no matter how badly wounded. He then closed the book and embellished the story with the legend of how this same sword had been the one that Arthur had pulled from the stone in the churchyard and thereby proved himself to be the rightful King of all Britain.

"And now our Lord King Arthur has fulfilled the promise that he will return, and with him has come Excalibur, the mighty sword that will one day smite the forces of Evil in this world. It is this sword that we all must take up. The time is almost at hand, good Knights. We must take up his sword and follow our Lord King Arthur into battle against the heretic, the blasphemer, the unbeliever, and win the heavenly kingdom of Avalon for all the earth." He paused for effect, then said dramatically, "It is now time for revelation from Lord Arthur himself."

The Knights all squirmed forward in their seats, as if moving that much closer could help them hear better. Sir Jeffrey pressed a button on the tape player, and after a few seconds of silence, another voice began speaking. This one was also deep, musical, full of kindness and authority, and graced with a British accent.

"Pentecost has passed, and we are preparing for our Convergence, when the Round Table shall gather at Camelot. Behold, I give you good news: the Convergence shall be on Midsummer's Eve in this third year of our Resurrection, by the grace of God. I, the King, have spoken it. If you would know more, if you would stand with your King victorious at the final battle for the throne of Earth, if you would dare to live forever in legend and in fact, then seek my Knights. For it is written that no one may come to the Father but through me, and none to me but through my Knights, who stand for the fulfillment of my new covenant. Come then, and be exalted with your King when the Lion and the Eagle shall fall, the Dragon shall arise, and the new Kingdom is come on earth. As I, Arthur, son of Uther Pendragon, speak, so mote it be!"

The room was now hot with excitement. Trick was hot also, with sunburn and chigger bites and not enough air-conditioning. He felt a bit light-headed, and especially so when Sir Jeffrey called out, "Stand, Jack Patterson!" He rose carefully, feeling as if he had left his stomach on the folding chair.

"Jack Patterson, it has been reported to me that you have displayed the following chivalrous traits: virtue, diligence, sacrifice, courage, humility, and honesty. I have been told that you came to Joyous Gard of your own free will, seeking 'something.' It is my belief that you will find that 'something' here in service to the resurrected King Arthur. You have been apprised of our mission by Sir Joshua. We may reveal no more until you commit yourself to apprenticeship as a Knight of the Once and Forever King. I call upon you now to choose: will you stand with us, or will you fall without us? Stay and become a Knight and one day a King? Or leave, knowing that one day you will be enslaved? If you stay, you will learn things that may at first sound fantastic to you, but as you study and work, you will find in them the truth that will make of you a man beyond your dearest dreams."

"Stay, Jack," whispered Diane beside him. "You won't regret it."

"Yes, Jack, please stay," said Dame Tonya. The others also spoke, softly encouraging him to stay. Their whispers grew into a chorus of approval around him, which, coupled with his light-headedness, seemed to surround him with a feeling of acceptance, purposefulness, and strength.

A strange euphoria bubbled up from inside him, and it was hard to remember that he had his own agenda here. He knew he should not stay . . . yet he could not abandon what he had begun. He had seen only the tip of the iceberg, and now he needed to know the secrets of the Knights of the Once and Forever King as much as he needed to find Brian for Tay. He had to stay a little while longer at Joyous Gard to do either; somehow he would get a message to Tay to let her know he was okay, and she could notify his parents so his dad could hire some help on the ranch for a few days.

"What is your choice, Jack Patterson?" demanded Sir Jeffrey.

"I want to stay," Trick said evenly and easily.

"Then kneel before me."

Slowly, Trick moved to the front of the room and carefully got down on one knee in front of Sir Jeffrey. He could feel all the eyes in the room upon him as he looked up at the Knight's stern face. "Are you, Jack Patterson, willing to accept the responsibilities of the fellowship into which you are about to enter, to uphold all that it believes without question or hesitation, to live your earthly life in preparation for eternal life in Avalon as a loyal Knight of the Once and Forever King, the Returned King Arthur?"

"Yes," agreed Trick, as the heat swirled around him like the silken veils of a dancer.

"Will you, Jack Patterson, abide in love and fraternity with your fellow Knights, obey your liege at all times, serve with dignity and willingness, keep secret all that you learn, and strive to bring forth Camelot as a fortress on earth for the soldiers of Chivalry at the final battle for Avalon?"

"I will," said Trick. His heart was pounding with genuine excitement.

"Then repeat after me. 'I, Jack Patterson . . .' "

"I, Jack Patterson . . ."

". . . do solemnly swear my faith and allegiance to the Knights of the Once and Forever King, the Returned King Arthur; that I will dedicate my heart, hands, and mind to service and loyalty to him, so help me God." Trick repeated the words.

"Then rise and be one with this fellowship as an apprentice and novice Knight. Congratulations, Jack. You've made the right decision."

As he rose, he swayed a little, but kept his balance. There was applause, but Sir Jeffrey silenced it by raising his hand. "Let us have a benediction," he said, " and then we may rejoice with our newest member." He spoke a brief prayer, and then the other members of the Joyous Gard household crowded around "Jack" to welcome him with hugs and handshakes. Even serious Sir Jeffrey permitted himself a little smile.

After awhile, Sir Cody led Trick to one of the men's bedrooms—the one without the privacy partition—and showed him an upper bunk which he could call his own while at Joyous Gard. Trick was fading fast after his long, hard day, and crawled gratefully between the cool sheets. All the excitement had given him a pounding headache to compound his sunburn and chigger bites. He hoped most of the discomfort would be gone by morning. Even though he had just taken an oath to be a loyal Knight-apprentice, he hadn't ruled out completely the possibility of sneaking out just before daylight and heading home to Alpine, where there might still be a little sanity left.

As he drifted off to sleep, an image of the magic sword Excalibur formed in his mind . . .

CHAPTER FOUR

W HEN A NEW ERUPTION OF ITCHING BROKE OUT DOWN HIS BACK, waking him to semi-darkness, Trick squirmed miserably against the sheet and found that he was not at Joyous Gard, but in his cot in a tent in a jungle outpost south of Khe Sanh, near the Demilitarized Zone. The heat was sweltering even in the hours of dawn, and the smell boiling in from the jungle was foul, as of decay. He itched all over—what with the mosquitoes, the body lice, the fleas and the fungus, there was little reason *not* to itch.

Trick was immediately aware that he was dreaming; some variation of this dream had intruded upon his sleep at irregular intervals for years. It was a movie without a soundtrack, a pantomime in monochrome accompanied only by a heightened awareness of the sound of his own heartbeat and breathing. But there was nothing he could do to stop it—he just had to let it play out.

Like all the others in his outfit, Corporal Patrick A. McGuire was conditioned to awaken at duty time without the aid of Reveille. His duty time was an hour ahead of everyone else's, anyway; by the time the rest of the men were awake, Trick would be turning the Spam on the grill, shuffling biscuit pans in and out of the oven, and enduring the inefficient supervision of chief cook Smitty, who started swigging his homemade whiskey the instant he got up in the morning, and was drunk by sunrise.

Trick sat up slowly, his plastic-edged dogtags sliding off his shoulder to thump gently upon his chest. He pulled on his pants and boots after checking both for vermin, and tugged the least dirty of his olive-drab T-shirts over his head. He smoothed his closely mown G.I. haircut with his fingers and parked his cap atop it, then shuffled sleepily through the humid darkness of the hootch, trying to make as little noise as possible to disturb the sleep of the other men. The ever-present mud sucked at his feet as he made a stop by the latrine on the way to the mess tent. The stink in that place was only slightly more pungent than the usual outside air, but it made a guy appreciate the fresher outdoors. Sometimes the mess tent didn't smell much better.

Sergeant Vernal Smith looked like a huge mound of the biscuit dough he was stirring—his face was lumpy and colorless, except for his misshapen nose, which was streaked with varicose veins in a maplike array of reds and blues. His hair was buzzed to the scalp for comfort, giving his head, with the folds of flab down the back of his neck, the appearance of a melted tennis ball. He had stoked the wood-burning oven and grill for the morning meal by the time Trick arrived, so Trick washed his hands, tied on a grease-stained apron, and got to work without greetings or chatter. He decided to stir up a little gravy with the Spam drippings to make the biscuits a little more palatable, and possibly conceal the fine ash of Smitty's cigarette, which floated into the mix as he grunted and stirred.

As he flung slices of canned meat product onto the sizzling grill, Trick wondered why the other grunts in the unit considered the job of assistant camp cook a soft one. Sure, every day they faced graver danger than he. Their daily routine included various futile search-and-report missions, where they had to fight the jungle, the mud, the filth, and the occasional Viet Cong. So far, the greatest danger Trick had faced was when Smitty had accidentally set the mess tent on fire. But the daily routine in Operations Support was no picnic, either. When he wasn't prepping, cooking or serving, he was cleaning up and getting ready to do it all over again. Day in and day out, there were only dirty pots and pans, and canned meat, and sickly produce, and dozens of men who were still hungry after all he could do to feed them. Whether a soldier fought on the front lines or in the mess tent, it was all in a day's work in Vietnam in 1971.

The day began as the men began filing into the mess tent. A few of them he knew well enough to greet by name, and they knew him well enough to call him "Trick" as they moved down the serving line with their compartmented aluminum trays: Garcia, Van Eyck, Hayes, Whiteman, Kaplan, Connally, Hill, Montelione. There were dozens of others whose faces he could not remember from day to day, much less their names; he only recognized their thumbs gripping the top side of their trays, and he tried to avoid these as he spooned up steaming clumps of odorless reconstituted scrambled eggs next to the browned meat slice, and ladled gravy over crumbled biscuits.

Finally, there was Reggie, always the last in line. Reggie had just turned eighteen; in order to escape the poverty of rural Mississippi, he had lied about his age and enlisted. His olive complexion was practically beardless, and dotted with darker freckles that made him look even younger. He was assigned to Operations Support in the motor pool, and there he kept the unit's jeeps and transports purring with a skill that surpassed his years. But in many ways he was still a child, and getting out of bed on time was a chore beyond his maturity, so he always got leftovers for breakfast. Everybody liked Reggie and tried to look after him, and Trick always saved a slice of meat for him, since it was the item they usually had the least of. When Trick slipped it onto his plate next to the last cold scrapings of eggs, Reggie grinned broadly, with teeth so widely spaced that they looked like piano keys. Trick couldn't help but smile back; the poor kid had once confessed that his family's diet included squirrel and opossum, so to him, a piece of Spam was like a T-bone steak. Trick wished all of his mess hall guests were as grateful as Reggie— it made the job a little more bearable.

Once everybody was served, Trick ate his own breakfast alone, out back of the mess tent where it was slightly cooler. Then he returned to scrape the grill and wash the pans in a tub of water heated on the stove. It was a hot, tedious job, and Smitty was no help at all—while Trick scrubbed and sweated, the chief cook sat and smoked and drank and mumbled to himself.

Trick finished the cleanup with about half an hour to spare before lunch preparations had to begin, so he walked out into the compound to have a smoke and a quiet moment to think. In the mid-morning, the camp was all but deserted. The troops were out performing their usual duties, and hardly anyone else stirred among the camouflaged tents that formed a crude circle around the quonset hut that was the area base of operations. Trick had no desire to go outside the circle—not more than ten feet away in any direction was the stinking jungle. He had to take this walk around the camp about once a day to remind himself that though the job of assistant cook was just as hot and nasty as being in the infantry, he was on an island of relative safety. And it was nowhere near as scary as having to deal directly with that fetid ocean of jungle beyond the camp. It was also comforting to remind himself that the period of his active service in-country was growing ever shorter, and soon, when he spoke of his forthcoming rotation back to the States, he could reckon it in "weeks" rather than "months." And when it became thirty *days*, he would get to serve the rest of his hitch in a much friendlier location, like the famed China Beach, or maybe as far away from Vietnam as Okinawa, or Subic Bay in the Philippines.

A thin wisp of smoke drifted up from under his boot as he crushed his cigarette into the mud. He didn't much like to smoke, but it was a social ritual he practiced here to fit in with the other guys. He made a stop by the latrine on the way back to the mess tent, not so much from need as from habit. It gave him a reason to wash his hands.

Back at the mess tent, Smitty had spared himself enough brain cells to begin opening packages of dried beef, which Trick began converting into creamed chipped beef to be served on toasted bread—that military mess hall staple known as "S.O.S." The lack of a variety of menu items made it a frequent lunch feature, and Trick knew the men would groan when they saw it plop onto their plates again—all of them except Reggie, of course. As he stirred the mixture and the peppery aroma drifted upward enticingly, Trick grinned at the memory of the day Reggie found out that "S.O.S." did not stand for "Same Old Stuff" or "Smitty's Obnoxious Substance." At first the kid had stared incredulously at his plate, as if it actually contained roofing materials, et cetera . . . and then he had burst out laughing, as if it were the funniest thing he had ever heard, and had devoured it with renewed enthusiasm. It was good to have Reggie around—not only was he amusing in his simple, naive way, he reminded everyone what they had been like before coming to Vietnam and learning its bitter lessons.

The soundtrack of his dream—heartbeat and respiration—gained speed and intensity in anticipation of the next scenes, which Trick remembered so well, yet which always seemed to be happening for the first time. Trick saw himself meticulously arranging square slices of white sandwich bread onto a baking sheet, hoping the oven would toast away some of their staleness. The bread was never fresh—it came in from Guam—but it was one of the few American luxuries afforded this unit. He opened the oven door, and the dry heat that rushed out over his hands as he slid in the pan was like a cool breeze in the ambient humidity. He shut the door, but before he straightened up, he got a sinking sensation in his stomach, a premonition of imminent disaster.

In the dream he could not hear anything except his accelerating heartbeat and breathing, but he remembered what he had heard that day as he slowly raised up from behind the wood-burning cookstove. It was always quiet in the middle of the day, but now it was absolutely silent—no chirp of insect, no swish of vegetation in the breeze, no distant gunfire. He glanced over at Smitty, who, though deep in his cups, had noticed it, too. Trick moved slowly toward the main opening of the mess tent and carefully peeked out. The camp was as deserted as it ever was around noon, before the morning patrol shift rotated off duty and came in for lunch. But the silence that had descended on the camp was as tangible as the humidity that bore down upon it.

Operations Support personnel also were expected to be soldiers at need, but Trick was separated from his weapons, which were safely locked in the weapons depot on the other side of camp. He had to retrieve them somehow and stand ready to face whatever was hovering in the silent shroud over the camp. Other members of the resident staff were already doing the same, scrambling for weapons and/or cover. Still clad in his floury, greasy apron, he dashed from the mess tent, just as a burst of gunfire from outside the camp ripped it a new side door. Reflexively, he dove for the ground, and slid on his bare elbows through the mud. The side of the tent bulged out as the bulk of Sergeant Smith fell against it, and one flabby arm, now spattered with blood, flopped limply through the bullet-torn opening.

Terror such as he had never known gripped Trick's heart, as if a hand had reached up from a grave beneath the mud where he lay and clutched his chest with icy fingers. Staccato bursts of automatic weapons fire and occasional single shots continued to echo around him. It was still a hundred yards to the ordnance tent through a path of certain death. The cold hand still clutched him close to the mud, and his mind whirled in what might be his last dilemma: Should he go for it and die quickly, or stay where he was and wait for death?

Suddenly a truck parked near the quonset hut headquarters was engulfed in a fireball as a rocket roared through its windshield. Tiny bits of hot debris rained on Trick when its fuel tank exploded, and he scuttled beneath a piece of corrugated metal that was lying, sagging and rusting, in a pile of trash on the edge of the camp as thick black smoke billowed upward and outward.

From his meager shelter, Trick saw a figure moving swiftly

through the smoke, returning fire with a rifle. There was another spatter of automatic fire, and the soldier dropped to his knees, then to the ground. As he fell beneath the cloaking smoke, within mere yards of Trick, Trick recognized the brave defender—it was Reggie! His smooth brown adolescent face was briefly twisted in agony, but as his olive T-shirt quickly darkened to a wet black, his face and body sagged into a slack stillness.

Now there was fire in Trick's chest where the ice had been. He launched himself from his shelter in the trash heap and grabbed the rifle from Reggie's lifeless hand. His body shook from anger, terror, and the recoil of the weapon as he emptied the clip into the jungle. Grim satisfaction flooded him, even though his fire showed no apparent results except the shredded bits of leaves that drifted like tiny green snowflakes onto the soggy ground.

It took a moment for him to realize that his clip was spent, and in that moment's confusion, the enemy was upon him. Four Viet Cong soldiers—apparently renegades, with no insignia upon their drab, tattered uniforms—stepped purposefully out of the jungle and surrounded Trick with rifles aimed. He dropped the useless weapon, and placed his hands on top of his head in a show of surrender. They barked at him in their own language, of which Trick understood nothing, but it was clear that they wanted him to march.

With their four rifles pointed at him, Trick shuffled toward the center of camp, where other Operations Support people were kneeling in a line like penitents in a mosque, except with guns trained on them. Trick took his place on his knees at the end of the line; he was the last of eight. The apparent leader of the VC renegades made a brief speech to the prisoners as if he thought they all understood Vietnamese. Then, with the flick of his hand, the first of the Americans—a kid named Rodriguez from California—died with one shot to the back of his head. His body was knocked forward by the impact of the shot, so that the remaining seven knew what was in store for them. For an instant, Trick was glad that Reggie had died on his feet and was spared this. One after the other, the soldiers fell face down into the mud. One tried to make a break and was dropped before he'd gotten to his feet.

There were three left. The mud beneath Trick's knees was soggy because he'd already voided his bladder. He tried to pray, but his brain had voided, too, and he could not form coherent thoughts. So he simply squeezed his eyes shut and waited his turn. There was another gunshot, and his world exploded in a burst of brilliant light.

It was at this point in the dream that Trick would always wake up in a tangle of sweat-soaked sheets; it had been a long time since he had actually screamed. But this time, he did not wake up.

Suddenly, the pounding, panting soundtrack of his dream attenuated. Into the silence thundered a voice: *Behold Excalibur!*

He opened his eyes. Before him was a sword . . . a long broadsword with a shining steel blade and an enormous hilt worked in gold filigree, studded with glittering jewels. Its blade was thrust into the mud, inches in front of him.

Slowly he raised his hands toward it, but they never got there. The sword dissolved into a swirling shower of sparks and vanished.

Trick gasped, and suddenly it was dark again, and he lay on his back, his entire body in such rigid contraction that he quivered like a spring wound too tight. Cold sweat poured from every crevice, soaking his hair and the twisted sheets beneath him. His heart was pounding like a rabbit pursued, and he was panting like the dog pursuant.

"Jack!" repeated the voice—it was Sir Cody, whose bunk was beneath his. "C'mon, Jack, wake up!"

His hands were still clenched around the hilt of Excalibur; but he blinked, and stared in the dark at his empty fists. He groaned, and they fell to his sides. He still trembled all over, but his heartbeat began to return to normal. Now he was wide awake.

"What's going on in here?" came the stern voice of Sir Jeffrey.

"Jack's havin' a bad dream," answered Sir Cody.

"I'm okay," panted Trick.

"I want a full report in the morning," declared Sir Jeffrey, and he stalked back to his room.

Sir Cody said, "Are you sure you're okay, Jack? You wanna go get a drink of water or somethin'?"

Trick rubbed his face and shook his head. "I'm okay," he repeated.

"Okay. You let me know if you need anything," said the young Knight as he crawled back into his lower bunk.

Little by little, Trick unwound, but he could not return to sleep. He lay quietly upon his bunk for another three hours, alert but strangely relaxed. Never had the dream, which had once been a living nightmare, progressed beyond his last clear memory before waking him—and never had any new element been introduced. Already he felt the power of the Knights at work; a subtle psychological seed planted during their rituals had swiftly bloomed in the darkest part of his soul. Someone unaware of this secret suggestion might regard it as some kind of epiphany, which would banish any doubt from his or her mind about turning away from the Knights. Even with his awareness of their ability to persuade, it was still disturbing—the Knights could get into your dreams.

Now more than ever, he needed to stay awhile longer, to find out what else these Knights were capable of doing—and what they had done with Brian Brannan.

And somehow, he had to get a message to Tay. He needed somebody whose sanity was not suspect to know where he was . . . while he himself still knew.

CHAPTER FIVE

W HEN THE SUN FINALLY CAME UP AND THERE WERE STIRRINGS OF activity in the house, Trick slid silently out of his bunk, put on his ragged jeans and shirt, and tiptoed to the kitchen where Diane, dressed in another set of decorated T-shirt and leggings with matching sneakers—this time, lavender—sleepily gathered cereal bowls and juice glasses for the breakfast at Joyous Gard.

"Need some help?" he asked cordially. "I'm a pretty good little breakfast chef."

"Oh, really?" she asked, without much enthusiasm. "There's eggs and stuff in the fridge. Help yourself."

With the memory of his days as an Army cook fresh in his mind, Trick rummaged the refrigerator and assembled the ingredients for *huevos rancheros*, one of his favorite civilian breakfasts. He quickly sauteed some bell peppers and onions, and mixed a spicy sauce with some canned tomato paste and a small jar of salsa. The tasty aroma wafting through the house drew sleepy but curious Knights into the kitchen, where he began scrambling eggs to order, and frying bacon in a cast iron skillet.

Those who made the effort to rise a little earlier than usual on this Monday morning were rewarded with plates of fluffy scrambled eggs, topped with the piquant tomato sauce and grated cheddar cheese, with some crisp bacon on the side. Sir Jeffrey was one of these, and he practically licked his chops as Trick served him a plateful.

"I'm sorry about last night, Sir Jeffrey," Trick said when the leader of the Joyous Gard Knights returned for a second helping. "I was in Vietnam a long time ago, and sometimes I still get nightmares about it."

"Oh, you were a soldier?" asked Sir Jeffrey, with interest.

"Yes, sir, but my main assignment was as a cook."

"A soldier *and* a cook, eh? We need both at New Cadbury . . . but we probably need a cook a little more desperately. I'll get back to you on that."

Sir Jeffrey and most of the rest of the members of the household thanked Trick and complimented his work on their way out of the house to their various jobs. When only he and Diane remained, together they washed and put away the dishes. She was more cheerful when she was fully awake, and Trick asked her, "So are you gonna get knighted now, or what?"

"Sir Jeffrey didn't say, but since you took the vow of apprenticeship, it's a done deal," she answered. "And how about *you*, Mr. Jack-can-cook Patterson? You'll be going to New Cadbury in no time, too! How will you like being the chief cook at Camelot?"

"Sounds like a great title for a book," he laughed. "Maybe I'll write my memoirs one day, and that's what I'll call it."

"Oh, you'll be much more than a cook in the coming Kingdom, when the Lion and the Eagle fall and the Dragon arises!"

"I heard that expression last night. What does it mean?"

"That's the prophecy. You'll learn more about it in the next few days, and about a lot of other things. Welcome to the Knights of the Once and Forever King, Jack!"

"It's mighty good to be here, Diane," he said with an earnest smile, which was genuine. Even after his traumatic first night at Joyous Gard, Trick felt at ease. He had won their approval and possibly their trust, had learned an interesting though cryptic bit of "prophecy," and had established a toehold on the bigger secret of New Cadbury. It looked like he was in for the whole game, and it might go into overtime. There was just one thing he needed to do right now—and it would risk all he had accomplished so far.

When Diane excused herself for a bathroom break, Trick searched quickly and found the one telephone in the house, which was located, as he supposed, in Sir Jeffrey's private quarters. While listening for Diane to emerge from the bathroom, he dialed a 1-800 number and entered a PIN code. At the prompt, he entered another code, then the number 46337777—the street address of Joyous Gard, plus four sevens which meant "everything's okay" in Trick's and Tay's private code—then hung up the phone. He returned to the kitchen to finish scrubbing the pots and pans, and when Diane reappeared, she smiled her approval.

MOMENTS LATER, SPECIAL AGENT TAY SILVESTRI'S PAGER BUZZED. WHEN she saw the display, she murmured an expletive which was frequently thought but not usually said aloud in Monday morning staff meetings at the FBI field office.

"Agent Silvestri, do you have something you wish to add at this point?" asked Deputy Director of Operations Gordon Padgett icily, and all eyes in the briefing room turned upon her inquisitively.

"No, sir," she responded with cool politeness. "My pager. It's not urgent."

Padgett grunted with annoyance, and moved on to the next item on the agenda. He droned on for another hour, but Tay did not hear another word until the meeting was dismissed. *What the hell is Trick doing at Joyous Gard?* she wondered, for she had immediately recognized the street address in the coded message. Since late last night, she had looked for a code of 21627777, which meant Trick had arrived safely home at Rural Route 2, Box 16B, in Alpine—but it had not come. For that reason, she had been more concerned that he was unhappy with her for the way their last few hours together had turned out, than for his physical safety, for she knew Trick was a good driver. Now, she was relieved to know he was all right, and evidently thinking of her interests above his own by going to Joyous Gard for a closer look for Brian. Yet mixed with the relief were both anger, for putting himself in a situation where she herself could not go, and fear, that the situation could develop into something he could not handle. Although there was little she could do to support him, she had to do something, and she needed some help.

When the meeting broke up, and all the agents filed out of the briefing room to their various assignments, Tay hurried to catch up with senior agent Diego Benavides. "Jim, you got a minute?" she asked, just before he turned into his office door.

"Sure, Tay, come on in," he answered cordially, and beckoned her into his office.

"Let's go get some coffee," she responded. "But not here. Can you meet me down the street at Denny's in ten minutes?"

"I could use some fresh air after Padgett's briefing. Sure. See you there."

Tay smiled her thanks as she ducked into her cubicle, where she rifled her briefcase looking for the hard copy of the information she'd gotten from the Internet. It was gone. She knew Trick must have taken it, and gave the wastebasket under her desk a swift kick in his stead for getting into her briefcase without permission. But then, she had to smile a little; he had the right instincts to be a good investigator.

Quickly she opened her notebook computer and plugged the cord from her desk telephone into its modem port. She dialed up her Internet provider, and called up the "bookmark" she'd placed to the World Wide Web homepage about the Knights of the Once and Forever King. This time, she downloaded the information and saved it to a diskette, which she plugged into her desktop computer. She opened the file, then sent it to the laser printer in the workroom. She knew it would be a moment before it printed out, since that printer was used by half the users on the office network, so she restored the cord to the phone and dialed up Trick's parents in Alpine.

"Maureen, hi, it's Tay," she said, when Trick's mother answered. "Just wanted to let you know everything's okay, but something's come up, and Trick might be here a couple more days . . . He's fine, he's just doing a little work for me—you know, like he did before. . . . No, nothing dangerous, but it's sort of secret, so I can't tell you. I know he'd want me to ask you to have Hugh get Pablo and his boys to help out while he's gone . . . Sure, I'll let you know as soon as I can when he'll be coming home. I gotta run now. Take care. 'Bye!"

She made a dash by the workroom and grabbed her hardcopy just as it rolled out of the printer, and hurried out of the Federal Building to the Denny's restaurant two blocks away, where Jim Benavides waited for her at a corner booth. He had a carafe of coffee on the table, and poured her a cup as she slid into the booth.

"Twenty minutes," he said with a smile, glancing at his watch. "Not bad for you, Tay."

"Very funny, Benavides. *You* try running in heels sometime."

"Hey, I used to be in Covert Ops. How do you know I haven't?"

Tay chuckled. If Trick had not bungled into her life, she might have considered Jim attractive. But she had learned the hard way not to become involved with a fellow agent—her husband of less than one year, Special Agent Dan Bailey, had died in a drug raid gone sour almost five years ago. She was entirely content with Jim's friendship, and hoped she could count on his help on that level now.

She took a sip of her coffee, then said, "Jim, I got a problem, and his name is Trick McGuire."

"Whoa right there, Silvestri. I'm not getting mixed up in your love life. That is, unless you're including me in it—which I somehow doubt."

"No, my problem with Trick is he thinks he's a junior G-man, playing undercover agent, but I think he might be onto something." Tay showed Benavides the new print-out of the Knights of the Once and Forever King information, and summarized the story of her nephew's disappearance. She told of the drive she and Trick had taken by the place called Joyous Gard on the day DDO Padgett had refused to authorize an investigation, and of the message she had received from Trick this morning, which indicated that he was at Joyous Gard.

"I think he went there with the intention of having a quick look around, to see if Brian was there and if he was all right, just as a favor to me," she said. "He wouldn't stay overnight there, and not show up for work when he was expected—unless he's found something, and he's staying with it. If I know Trick, he won't leave a job half done. Is there anything we can do to help him?"

"Not much, I'm afraid, if Padgett won't approve it," said Benavides. "We could go straight to the DO, but I think we'd get the same answer, and then we'd catch hell from Padgett for going over his head."

"You know, we shouldn't bother either of them about this. Forget I even brought it up. You know I would *never* disobey my supervisor."

Benavides rolled his eyes skyward. "Uh-huh. And I suppose you won't be checking with the county tax office to see who owns the house?"

"Absolutely not."

"And you wouldn't run the tag numbers of the Joyous Gard vehicles through the DPS computer?"

"Wouldn't dream of it."

"And you won't be checking with the private-sector carriers for records of package deliveries to Joyous Gard?"

"Goodness, I don't think so!"

"Well, that's good. Because if you did, you might discover something. Then I'd have to exercise my negligible authority to approve some kind of surveillance, which might lead to warrants and arrests. I'm glad we understand each other on this matter."

Tay summoned all her skill to restrain a smile. "Yes, I'm happy we didn't have this little talk," she said.

"Just remember while you're not doing these things that you have other cases," he added pointedly as he slid out of the booth, "and we'd better get back to them. Thanks for the coffee, Agent Silvestri."

It was a small check, and one she didn't mind picking up. Tay was energized by Benavides' support—however cautious—and by noon she had the unauthorized investigation underway. She quickly learned that the Joyous Gard house was owned by a property management company and leased to one Jeffrey Dale Matthews. A routine background check on the lessee turned up no criminal record, except for a minor traffic violation which had been dismissed after a defensive driving course.

That evening, just before dark, a white minivan cruised slowly down West Redwing Drive in Fort Worth. Tay scribbled down the license numbers of the six vehicles that surrounded the house on the corner. Conspicuous by its absence was Trick's red pickup; she hoped he had bailed out of Joyous Gard and was on his way home to Alpine. She then returned to her office to check the tags against the Texas Department of Public Safety database. Each of the registrations came up as current and clean, and she checked criminal records on each of the listed owners. Again, there was nothing suspect in any of them.

She had already called the FBI liaison officers with Federal Express, United Parcel Service, and other major package delivery services, but it would take a few days for them to gather information about package deliveries to the Joyous Gard address. Tay mused as she drove home late that night that unless one of them came up with something useful, all this hard work she wasn't doing would be wasted.

As THE MINIVAN DROVE SLOWLY PAST, THE INHABITANTS OF JOYOUS GARD were feasting on the Word of God and King Arthur in the garage, having already feasted on spaghetti and meat sauce prepared by the newest member of the fellowship. Satisfied expressions adorned each face, and even Sir Jeffrey seemed content as he taught the day's lesson.

"Let's review the Code of Chivalry," he said, delicately stifling a belch. "We all need to keep it fresh in our minds, and our new apprentice needs the instruction. Pay close attention, Jack, this is basic preparation for Knighthood. Diane, give us the first three tenets of the Code."

Diane stood up, as if in a schoolroom, and carefully recited, "One: Championship of the right and the good, in every place and at all times, against the forces of evil. Two: Generosity in giving and in service. Three: Loyalty to truth and the pledged word."

"Very good, Diane. You may be seated. Russell, give us the next three."

Russell giggled as he stood, and wheezed as he took a breath before beginning. "Four: Purity in thought, word and deed. Five: Diligent study and practice of Knightly conduct. Six . . . uh . . ." He giggled, scratched his chin, then shrugged. "Sorry, Sir Jeffrey, I forgot."

"Somebody help him, then—Sir Dylan, what's the sixth te-net?"

The young Knight stood and declared, "Six: Strict obedience to the liege lord of the castle." He turned to Russell and said impa-tiently, "Why's this so hard, Russell?"

Sir Jeffrey glowered. "Sir Dylan, what are the seventh and eighth tenets?"

"Seven: Humility and a spirit of servitude, even in victory. Eight: Respect for fellow Knights at all times, even in their folly." His smug expression melted once he realized he had violated the com-mandments he seemed to know so well.

Sir Jeffrey said sternly, "Perhaps we should review this more often. Sir Dylan, you'll assist Jack with the dishes tonight. Russell, you'll recite all ten tenets before breakfast or you'll do without. Both of you may be seated. Now, Dame Anne, the final tenets of the Code of Chivalry."

The eldest of the female Knights stood and said slowly, in a soft, confident voice, "Nine: Unswerving belief in the coming Kingdom ordained by God. Ten: Willing submission to the King, even unto death."

Trick had been following along with a photocopy of the Code of Chivalry, which had originally been rendered by hand in ornate calligraphy. Up until Nine and Ten, Trick found no quarrel with the basic beliefs of the Knights of the Once and Forever King; they were all admirable qualities. But the last two were a little scary, and what he found scarier still was the fact that when Dame Anne quoted the part about submission and self-sacrifice, nobody in the room blinked. What, he wondered, was worth that price? He hoped to find out before someone had to pay up.

After Sir Jeffrey read a bit more from the "Malory Revelation" about the relationship between the young King and the wizard, Merlin, the evening meeting was adjourned. Trick returned to the kitchen, where the supper dishes and cooking utensils awaited his attention. Young Sir Dylan shuffled along after him to do his penance, and unenthusiastically took up a dish towel when Trick suggested that he do the drying.

He was about the same age as Tay's nephew and his own daughter. Theirs was an incomprehensible generation, by and large, but Trick had gained some skill in communicating with Laura and her circle of friends. The kid looked more sad than surly tonight, so Trick tried to cheer him with chatter as they worked. "So, where do you come from, Sir Dylan?"

"Dallas," he answered curtly.

"Are you in school, or do you have a job?"

"I work."

"Oh, yeah? What do you do?"

"Shelve videos and stuff at the video store up on Chapin Road."

"How long have you been a Knight?"

The boy shrugged. "About two months."

"Why'd you decide to join?"

"Why do you want to know?" asked the teenager suspiciously.

"I don't mean to be nosy, Sir Dylan. I'd just like to get to know everybody here at Joyous Gard."

He shrugged again. "Beats livin' with my parents."

"Kind of rough on you, huh? Like Sir Jeffrey tonight."

A wry smile twisted Sir Dylan's pale lips. "Sir Jeffrey is cool. I wish *he* was my dad. *My* dad acts like he's scared of me—like if he makes a mistake, I won't love him or something. Sir Jeffrey don't take crap from nobody."

Trick did not press him further as they finished the dishes. Now he had a clue about the Knights' appeal—in Dylan's case, they met his need for an authority figure. He wondered if Brian felt the same way about his parents. Although it was evident that Bob and Regina accommodated his physical needs more than adequately, and that they loved him unconditionally, there had to be something lacking that the Knights were providing. Perhaps they had failed to establish their authority as parents, and Brian had come to the Knights seeking more stern guidance and discipline than he received at home.

It was an acceptable explanation for Dylan and Brian, but what about the many adults who populated Joyous Gard? What had brought them here? He recalled the reason "Jack Patterson" said he had come: He was homeless, seeking a reason to stop drifting. Diane seemed eager for acceptance. She had told him more about herself during his first full day at Joyous Gard as a Knight-apprentice, including the fact that she came from the nearby town of Bedford, had never married, had flunked out of nursing school, and had made a meager living by maintaining a booth at a crafter's mall, selling the decorated daytime pajamas and sneakers that she liked to wear. She had learned about the Knights when she visited the

Merrie Olde Tymes Faire out west of Weatherford, looking for ideas for her craft items.

At Merryborough, she told him, she felt as if time had stopped in a simpler century, where people treated one another with courtesy, and a person's worth wasn't dependent upon physical appearance. She had come to Joyous Gard at Sir Joshua's invitation and immediately decided to stay when she found the atmosphere at the "waystation for novice Knights and loyal friends" just as courteous and accepting as the fictional Merryborough. "When King Arthur is restored to his throne," she had said with earnest excitement, "the whole world will be like this, only better."

When the last of the pots and pans had been put away, his young assistant hurried to claim some time on the Nintendo system in one of the men's bedrooms, and Trick joined the rest of the amiable Joyous Gard gang in the living room around the TV. It was, at first glance, simply a large, diverse family: Dames Jennifer and Tonya were reading paperback novels, and Sir Barry was reading the newspaper; Dame Anne and Sir Joshua were playing cards at the dining table; Sir Cody was in the bedroom playing Nintendo with Sir Dylan; Sir Jeffrey was in his private quarters on the phone; Russell's attention was riveted on the noisy comedy playing on the television, and he giggled annoyingly every fifteen seconds. Trick hoped to learn more about these people who were ready to die at King Arthur's command in order to establish a more chivalrous society on earth.

Trick sat on a sofa next to Diane, who was embroidering a red armband stretched tight across a plastic hoop. He watched as she swiftly but meticulously placed long stitches of gold thread side by side until they formed the silhouette of a golden dragon. When she finished, she held it up for him to admire.

"It's nice," he said. "Did you make everybody's armband?"

"No, but I've made a bunch of them," she answered. She added proudly, "Sir Jeffrey says mine are the best. He and the rest of the Round Table Knights all wear them."

"Whose is this one gonna be?"

She smiled. "Yours, Jack."

Trick felt his stomach sink; he was one of them now.

CHAPTER SIX

AGAINST HIS BETTER JUDGMENT, TRICK REMAINED AT JOYOUS GARD for five more nights, but Tay's nephew, Brian Brannan, neither appeared nor was mentioned. Compounding his frustration was resentment that he'd wasted so much time and had not uncovered a single particle of evidence that the Knights of the Once and Forever King were anything but a group of otherwise ordinary people who enjoyed the trappings and ceremony of the Middle Ages. There was very little "cultish" behavior exhibited, as far as Trick knew how to define it. However, when he had volunteered to go grocery shopping with Sir Joshua, he was politely refused.

"You mustn't return to the outside world yet, Jack," explained Sir Joshua. "You might be tempted to go back to the way you were. Do you really want that, after all you've learned at Joyous Gard? We must be *above* the world if we are to rule it."

"Well, we still gotta eat," Trick had protested. "I don't see how I'm gonna be tempted at the Piggly Wiggly, except maybe in the cookie aisle."

"Isolation is part of the discipline. We are few among the many, yet we few will rule the many. You must trust no one but your fellow Knights, Jack, and we'll take good care of you until you're strong enough. You're making very good progress, and you'll be a full-fledged Knight in no time."

Trick mentally pencilled *isolation* beneath *silence* in his list of the Knightly disciplines he must learn; what it really meant that he was a prisoner at Joyous Gard. It was at that moment that he decided that if nothing of substance that the FBI would find worthy of investigation came to light by Friday night, Joyous Gard would wake up Saturday morning minus one cook.

In the meantime, "Jack" learned his lessons in basic Knighthood while preparing the evening meals at Joyous Gard, and performing small maintenance tasks around the house. He first learned the organizational structure of the Knights of the Once and Forever King. One was admitted to the fellowship as an apprentice only after proving worthy by displaying traits of chivalry, as "Jack" had apparently done. There were three degrees of Knighthood: the first conferred certain basic rights and privileges, such as the privilege of living at New Cadbury, where Camelot, the King's royal city, would someday rise; the second granted more rights and access to classified information. The third degree was reserved for those Knights whose exemplary service and dedication earned them a seat at the Round Table as the King's elite guard and advisors. One honor bestowed upon Third Degree Knights was a legendary Round Table Knight's name. Trick had learned that Sir Jeffrey had been given the name of Lancelot because he was the leader of the Knights at the "waystation for Knights and loyal friends," and that *La Joyeuse Garde* was the name of the historical Sir Lancelot's castle in France, which had served as a waystation for the King of the Britons.

There had been some basic instruction in the art of heraldry, as it applied to the coat of arms displayed upon the door of Joyous Gard and the wall of its chapel. The golden dragon, which was the central figure on a red shield, was shown springing forward while looking backward. While studying with fellow apprentices Diane and Russell, Trick remarked that the dragon looked like "Emmitt Smith runnin' and lookin' for Troy Aikman's pass." They were amused, but he knew the serious Sir Jeffrey wouldn't be, so he committed to memory the term *rampant regardant*, the proper heraldic description of the pose.

He had learned the tenets of the Code of Chivalry, and could recite them all—even Number Ten—without flinching. Trick had asked Diane as they dried the dishes together one night how she felt about that ultimate requirement for Knighthood. "Doesn't it scare you to think that you might have to put your life on the line for the King someday?" he had asked.

Diane had shrugged, and answered, "Well, we all have to die sometime. Better to go out in a blaze of glory than just snuff out all alone in the dark." Her calm reply gave Trick a creepy little shiver: Had David Koresh drummed the same self-fulfilling prophecy into his doomed followers' heads?

Just who *was* this King to demand such sacrifice, Trick wanted to know. If he had heard of this latter-day incarnation in any other way than through the involvement of Tay's nephew, he would have dismissed it as hogwash without another thought. But there apparently *was* someone who claimed to be King Arthur, and it was his voice on tape that issued from the boombox on the altar in the Joyous Gard chapel about every other night. It was a nice voice, one that not only commanded respect, but radiated a peculiar warmth. It was deep and mellow, and graced with an English accent that had a Welsh lilt to it, and a musical quality that was like nothing Trick had heard before. It was almost as if it really *had* come from another century, when spoken English was a young language that relied upon inflection as well as vocabulary.

Each evening, Sir Jeffrey read from *Le Mort d'Arthur*, the fifteenth-century work by Sir Thomas Malory accepted by the Knights as the true account of King Arthur's "first life." After each reading, Sir Jeffrey would give his interpretation of the passage as it applied to the Returned King's new purpose. Sometimes Trick understood it; other times, he pretended that he did. Whether he did or not, it was often difficult to swallow some of it. Tales of sorcery, ghosts and bloody warfare were liberally sprinkled among lessons of chivalry in this "Revelation."

And then there was the prophecy that was repeated every time the Knights assembled in the chapel: *The Lion and the Eagle shall fall and the Dragon arise.* Evidently the King considered himself the Dragon, since according to the Malory Revelation, his father was the duke Uther Pendragon—and *Gules, a dragon Or* was the chief emblem of the coat of arms. On either side of the shield stood a lion and an eagle, but the lessons in heraldry taught the apprentices only that they were "supporters," a part of the total heraldic design or "achievement." Whatever the prophecy actually meant, it was not yet time for him to know, but Trick was certain it wasn't going to be good news for somebody.

That Friday evening, which Trick was sincerely hoping was his last, Joyous Gard received a distinguished visitor: Sir Kevin Kay, the seneschal, or chief of staff, at New Cadbury. He had taken his Round Table name from the adopted brother of King Arthur, who was the seneschal of Camelot. He was about the same age as Sir Jeffrey—late twenties, early thirties—but with a much more laid-back aspect in both appearance and manner. He wore jeans and a cotton knit polo shirt with a trendy designer name stitched on the pocket, and round, wire-framed eyeglasses. His hair was light brown and lightly salted with premature gray, as was the short, neatly-trimmed Vandyke beard that made him look somewhat older than he was. He was a much less intense young man than Sir Jeffrey, smiling easily and putting the residents of Joyous Gard at ease.

In honor of Sir Kevin's visit, Trick prepared lasagna, a main course that was easier to make in large quantities, a tossed green salad and a congealed fruit salad, and homemade garlic cheese rolls. He enjoyed the opportunity to practice his culinary skills—his mother did most of the cooking at home, and when he was with Tay, who did not like to cook, they usually dined out. The meal was a success, as all of the evening meals had been during his week at Joyous Gard, and afterward, Sir Jeffrey summoned him into the chapel for a private conference before the evening devotional.

Trick entered the garage apprehensively, expecting to be quizzed on his Knightly knowledge. He was prepared, though, for he and the other candidates for Knighthood had studied together every night. He was not prepared for Sir Kevin to be there also, and for the question asked by the young Knight.

"Jack, can you be ready to leave with me in the morning for New Cadbury?" asked Sir Kevin.

For an instant, Trick's heart sank: this would put a crimp in his plans to escape in the wee hours. But then his heart rose in anticipation of an opportunity to dig deeper into the Knights' affairs—at New Cadbury, where the Lord King himself lived. "Well, yes, sir, I reckon I can," he answered. "But don't I have to be a Knight before I can go there?"

Sir Kevin chuckled. "You've learned your stuff well, Jack. Yes, that's the rule, but because New Cadbury needs a good cook with the Convergence coming up, Lord Arthur has relaxed that restriction for you. I'd be willing to bet that you'll be granted your Knighthood soon after you get there, if it all works out."

"It sounds great, Sir Kevin. What time do we leave?"

Sir Jeffrey asked wistfully, "Can we keep him for one more breakfast?" The senior Knight of Joyous Gard had been seen wearing his belt a notch looser since the arrival of Jack Patterson.

Sir Kevin laughed. "Hooked on good eats, are you, Jeff? Don't worry—I won't take him away before breakfast and leave you hungry. Besides, you'll be coming to New Cadbury for the Convergence next week, and afterward, depending on . . . well, you know . . . " The young Knight cleared his throat, as if to dislodge some words that had suddenly smashed into one another there. He quickly changed the subject. "Well, let's not hold up the lessons any longer. I've got the tape from New Cadbury for tonight."

Trick returned to the kitchen briefly while Sir Jeffrey rounded up the Joyous Gard Knights for the evening lessons. There he found Diane, who had already started scraping the supper dishes and stacking them in soapy water. She looked up with deep concern on her face when she heard Trick coming.

"Jack, is everything okay?" she asked softly, wiping her hands on a dishtowel.

"Sure, Diane," he answered. "Why wouldn't it be?"

She pointed to the garage entrance through the utility room, indicating she knew Trick had met privately with the senior Knights. "Oh, that," he said. "Well, they need a cook at New Cadbury. Knighted or not, I'm off in the morning with Sir Kevin."

The concern on her face deepened, and she swallowed hard. "You're leaving?"

"It looks that way. Hey, what's the matter?"

"Nothing," she said, casting down her eyes. The dishtowel slipped from her fingers to the floor, and Trick gallantly bent to pick it up for her. When he placed it in her hand, her fingers curled around his briefly, then shrank away.

"Whoa, are you mad at me because I'm going to New Cadbury before you?" he asked. "I didn't mean for that to happen. I'm just doing what I'm told."

"I know. I just kinda hoped . . . we'd go there together."

Trick hoped Diane couldn't hear the alarm that suddenly went off in his head. *Oh my God, she's in love with me!* he thought. All week long, he had worked with Diane and studied with her and sat with her at meals and at the studies, but he had never given her the slightest hint that he might be attracted to her. He'd treated her kindly, to be sure, but he had never said or done anything to give her the idea that what he felt for her was anything but friendship. How could he respond without damaging his cover—or her feelings?

What would Tay do? he wondered, but the warm perpetual presence of Tay Silvestri in his heart and mind only compounded his panic. As one of the FBI's most successful undercover operatives, she had portrayed everything from hookers to princesses in the line of duty. In the process of winning the trust of a suspect, she must have had to deal occasionally with that suspect's affections. How far would she go to keep the fish on the line long enough for her FBI partners to net him? He privately feared that there had been times when the job unavoidably demanded her all, and in his mind, that was more dangerous than being shot at. In this fear he found an answer: Tay would probably do whatever was necessary *at the moment* to maintain the subject's trust and to avoid confrontation. He needed to keep Diane happy, if for no other reason than he didn't need to leave behind any bad feelings about him at Joyous Gard.

"Hey," he said softly, and reached for Diane's pudgy fingers clutched around the threadbare towel. He gathered them into his firm grip and smiled shyly as he said, "I kinda hoped that, too. But one of us has to be here to fatten up Sir Jeffrey, and you're the only one here who can cook as good as me. Anyway, you'll be coming to New Cadbury next week for the Convergence . . . and I'll be waitin' for you."

Diane sniffled, but smiled. "Thank you, Jack, I just—well, I'll miss you."

"Not for long. Hey, we better not be late for school. Come on!"

All during the evening study time, Trick sat in his usual place and Diane sat in hers, but he felt like she was wedged right between his shoulderblades. He hoped no one could see him kicking himself for being anything but truthful with someone who trusted him. The customary sweltering heat in the chapel that evening served to remind him of the place prepared especially for liars.

The next morning, Trick arose long before anyone else, but he did not tiptoe out the front door as he had originally hoped to do. Instead, he began preparing his special McGuire Family Reunion/ Christmas Morning Breakfast, which included just about every-thing in the pantry. As he peeled and chopped and shredded and mixed, he admitted to himself that he was just showing off—but it fit well with eager "Jack's" character. While he worked, he hoped that somehow he'd be able to let Tay know that he was about to leave Joyous Gard. He missed her desperately—it had been almost a week since they had spoken. He wondered if she would ever speak to him again.

His longing for Tay only increased when sleepy Diane padded into the kitchen to help him with breakfast preparations. Since he had taken over kitchen ops, as he privately called his principal duty at Joyous Gard, she had assisted him at every meal. Now he knew why. He hoped his impending absence from Joyous Gard would cool her infatuation.

Still, he remarked, "That's a pretty outfit. I haven't seen that one before."

"Thank you. It's one of my favorites," she answered. This morning's T-shirt and leggings ensemble was sunny yellow with an appliquéd daisy design.

"Well, don't get anything on it. Here, put this on." Trick tugged a worn apron out of a drawer and tied it around her thick waist, and she smiled as if he were crowning her Miss America. He put her to work cleaning and slicing fresh cantaloupe while he rolled out biscuit dough on the counter. Soon the fragrance of biscuits baking, sausage frying, coffee brewing, and potatoes hash-browning drew even the most determined Saturday morning sleepers from their cozy racks . . . with Sir Jeffrey in the lead.

When all the residents and guests of Joyous Gard had been served, Trick and Diane filled their plates and joined them at the table in the dining room. Before Trick had gotten much more than a bite, Sir Jeffrey stood with coffee mug in hand and announced, "I have some bad news and some good news. The bad news is that our trusty chef, Jack Patterson, will be leaving us this morning."

There were moans and protests, but Sir Jeffrey continued, with something like a grin on his face. "The good news is that by special request of our Lord King Arthur, Jack is going to New Cadbury with Sir Kevin to serve as chef there. In other words, it won't be long until the Convergence, when we'll all be together again. In the meantime, let's hear three cheers for stout Jack."

"Hip, hip, hurray!" chorused the Knights of Joyous Gard with enthusiasm, and Trick felt his face glowing warm with the praise. If nothing else, he considered, being in the Knights certainly conveyed a strong sense of belonging—which was as powerful a way of keeping recruits as bars on the windows, and much more pleasant.

After the breakfast was a happy memory and the dishes were cleared away, Trick gathered his meager belongings. He'd been given some worn but serviceable hand-me-down clothing: a couple of Sir Joshua's old shirts, a pair of Sir Cody's jeans, and some assorted, if not matching, socks and underwear. These he folded neatly into a bundle and tucked into it his photocopied Knighthood study materials. Those who had not already wished him well before leaving for Saturday morning jobs followed him to Sir Kevin's late-model Honda Civic to see him off. Dames Anne, Jennifer, and Tonya gave him hugs and Sirs Barry and Cody shook his hand warmly. Even Sir Jeffrey seemed a bit reluctant to see him off.

It was Diane who brought him a gift. "You'll be needing this, Jack," she said, and displayed a neatly-folded embroidered red armband—the one she'd been making—which she carefully tucked into his shirt pocket.

"Thank you, honey," he said, genuinely touched by the gesture. "I'll see you soon." Impulsively, he leaned down and gave her a little peck on the cheek. She said nothing, but her bright yellow ensemble was dimmed by her smile.

"Let's roll, Jack," said Sir Kevin from behind the wheel, and Trick climbed into the small car's passenger seat, tossing his bundle of clothes into the back seat. As they pulled away from the curb, Trick wished there had been some way to alert Tay to his departure from Joyous Gard. Maybe there would be some way to communicate from New Cadbury.

TRICK DID NOT NOTICE THE CABLE TV TRUCK PARKED AT A HOUSE TWO doors down and across the street. The technician who sat behind the wheel, having completed his assignment, put the truck in gear and drove off just as the small black Honda departed the house on the corner. Diego Benavides, in a nondescript blue uniform and hard hat, drove casually but carefully, following the Honda at a discreet distance. Thank goodness something was finally happening! He and Tay had taken turns at the stakeout all week long, as their schedules permitted, covered as everything from carpet cleaners to salespeople. It had not been a barrel of laughs. Now he remembered why he'd allowed himself to be promoted out of the field—most of the time, investigative work was criminally boring.

While he followed the Honda out of the subdivision and onto the freeway, he wondered whether he should tell Tay that he'd seen Trick kiss one of the female suspects. He wasn't sure how she'd react, but it couldn't hurt his private hope that she would someday soon get over that unsophisticated cowpoke and look his way.

The Honda failed to signal before exiting to westbound Interstate 30, and Benavides almost missed the turn. As soon as it merged onto the straight, wide highway that shortly blended seamlessly into Interstate 20, it accelerated above the speed limit, and rapidly outdistanced the cable TV truck. Quickly, Benavides pulled his cellular phone from his briefcase and dialed it with his thumb while keeping his other hand on the wheel and his eyes on the Honda.

"Baxter, this is Jim Benavides," he said when the call was answered. Lonnie Baxter was a rookie agent who lived on the west side of Fort Worth. "You want to earn some brownie points? Good. Get in your car right now—no, don't change clothes, you'll be fine—and get out on westbound I-20. Watch for a newish black Honda Civic, Texas tag BQF86J, going pretty fast, with two white males inside. Follow them wherever they're going and call my pager when they get there. You got my number? Good! Oh, and don't say anything about this to Padgett or anyone else. Thanks, Baxter. I'll get you another day off later this week."

Benavides stayed on the road until he could no longer see the Honda, then turned around and headed back to Fort Worth to return the borrowed truck. Less than half an hour later, his pager vibrated urgently, and he flipped open his cell phone and dialed the unfamiliar number that appeared in the pager's display.

"Baxter," said the voice that answered the phone.

"It's Jim. Where'd you end up?"

"Weeeelll, it's kind of hard to describe."

"If you're going to be a Special Agent of the FBI, Baxter, you'd better learn fast to observe everything and report in detail."

"Okay, then, here goes. It's like Six Flags meets *Monty Python and the Holy Grail*," reported the junior agent. He took a deep breath and began describing what he saw. "It's a great big outdoor festival, about two miles south of I-20 on Farm-to-Market Road 4450. There's a sign out by the road that says 'Merrie Olde Tymes Faire,' but there's another sign over a gate in a tall wooden fence that says 'Welcome to Merryborough.' There are big stone-castle-looking towers at each of the two corners of fence that I can see, with flags all along the fence. There are people everywhere. A lot of them are dressed like they came out of fairy tales or something. I'd estimate . . . maybe three or four hundred cars parked in the field out in front of the gate. This place is *big*."

"Did you see the two men get out of the Honda?"

"They haven't yet. They're still looking for a place to park. I flashed my badge to an attendant and parked right up front. I'm standing at a pay phone by the front gate. I can't really see inside the place—you have to pay to get in. Wait a minute, they've parked, and they're getting out. Driver's about medium height, thirtyish, brown hair, glasses, little fag beard—"

"Sensitivity, please, Mr. Baxter."

"Other guy's taller, mid-forties, kind of long reddish-blond hair. These guys seriously heinous or what?"

"Proceed with extreme caution, Bax. Just stay with them awhile and see what they do. Call me again if anything goes down."

Benavides grinned; Baxter would be a good agent someday, but he had to learn that it wasn't all danger and glamour in the field. Before he returned his cellular phone to its case, he decided boldly to see if Tay would be interested in hearing his report over dinner, and punched in her number.

THERE HAD NOT BEEN MUCH CONVERSATION ON THE DRIVE FROM Joyous Gard to Merryborough. When they talked at all, it was of insignificant things: baseball, music, the weather. In the long silences, Trick worried about his truck and its contents; when they drove by the grocery store, he saw that it was not in the parking lot where he'd left it. He hoped it had only been tagged as abandoned and towed to a storage facility, not stolen and stripped. If the latter were the case, then someone was having a grand time with his credit cards by now. Worst of all, someone else was wearing his snakeskin boots.

Sir Kevin had told him that they were detouring by Merryborough, but had not really prepared him for the spectacle. As they trudged across the flattened grass of the parking area toward the gate, Trick was amazed at the number of cars arranged in orderly rows, and at the number of people streaming into the gates just before noon. They had to stand in line at the gate, and Trick noticed that another queue had formed at a ticket window: the posted price of admission was twelve dollars for adults, eight for children.

"Sir Kevin, I don't have any money to get in this place," he whispered.

"Don't worry, Jack, I have season passes for us," said Sir Kevin with a smile. "Here, take a couple of bucks. You might want to get yourself a cold drink." Trick accepted the folded dollar bills with thanks.

A few minutes later, Trick and Sir Kevin were greeted at the gate by a young woman dressed in a plain long jumper-style dress made of muslin, unevenly dyed light blue, over an off-white chemise with long blousy sleeves. The dress laced tightly up the front, and the chemise was rolled and tucked at the top, revealing a significant amount of tanned, freckled cleavage. She wore no makeup, and her face matched her bodice, freckle for freckle. Her blond hair was modestly covered by a crocheted *snood*, which formed it into a soft roll at the nape of her neck. She glanced at the passes in Sir Kevin's hand and said with a light Cockney accent, "Thank thee, good sirs. Welcome to Merryborough!"

And as they pushed past the turnstile, Trick found himself in another world.

CHAPTER SEVEN

BEYOND THE GATE LAY MERRYBOROUGH, A COLORFUL VILLAGE
sprawled out over a hundred acres or more of verdant north
Texas countryside. Around the perimeter were dozens of quaint
little shops in permanent buildings, all designed and painted to
resemble the rustic architecture of an English village in the fifteenth
century: some with rough wooden siding, some half-timbered and
stuccoed, many with thatched roofs and others with shingles. All
were festively bedecked with flags, banners, and ribbons that streamed
in the breeze, as if the little English town of Merryborough were
perpetually celebrating the arrival of spring.

In the shops and along the pathways, the costumed inhabitants of Merryborough conducted their business and their pleasure
as if nothing out of the ordinary were happening, only their little
country faire. There were lords and ladies in satin finery admiring
one another and the wares in the shops, common working folk
selling those wares, and beggars in tatters and rags picking up scraps
of litter. Most of the men sported beards and long hair, and tight
trousers with high boots; upperclass men wore elaborate doublets
with puffed sleeves, while the middle-class men wore loose, laced-
up shirts and vests. All of the women wore long dresses, most with
tight bodices that caused the tops of their breasts to bulge over the
low necklines; most were plain, like the greeter at the gate, but

some were intricately decorated with jewels, ribbons, flowers, and other ornaments. When they spoke, their voices were melodiously British, from the careful, graceful speech of the uppercrust to the varied and amusing brogues of the commoners.

Across the wide open center of the village, music drifted from every corner: flutes and drums from one side, bagpipes from another, a chorus of voices from yet another. Somehow, they all blended into a harmonious underscore for the laughter and excited buzz of the visitors who continued to stream into the park, who seemed more out of time and place in their shorts and T-shirts and sneakers than any of the Merryborough villagers. Twentieth-century types found plentiful food, entertaining shows, simple rides, and many wondrous things to separate them from their money: cash, "Master Card" and "Lady VISA" cheerfully accepted in Merryborough.

"This is sure somethin' else," remarked Trick with honest amazement as they made their way through the crowds.

"It is pretty awesome, isn't it?" answered Sir Kevin. "I never get tired of coming here. But this is the last weekend of the festival for the year. It's starting to get too hot."

"I'll say," agreed Trick, who'd already broken a sweat. He wondered how the Merryborough performers, in their heavy costumes, kept from dropping like flies from heat exhaustion.

"Let's put on our armbands now, Jack. We need some visibility while we're here."

Trick tugged the folded armband out of his pocket and wrapped it around his right arm. It fastened easily with a strip of Velcro underneath. He remembered overhearing Diane and Sir Joshua talking about how the "faire" was a good recruiting tool for the Knights, and now he could see why: some people with a strong enough interest in things medieval might be interested in making it a way of life.

"How many of the people who work here are . . . are Knights?" asked Trick.

"Only two. You'll meet one of them in a moment. We're not sanctioned by the Merryborough people—that's why we waited to get inside before putting on our identification. If anyone in regular clothes asks about your armband, speak up proudly and tell them about the Returned King. Try not to get into a conversation with one of the Merryborough performers, though—they can have us kicked out if they think we're here to recruit."

"Aren't we?"

"Well, today our primary mission isn't recruitment. Since this is the last weekend, we expect sales to be pretty good at our booth. I'm going to check the inventory and see what needs to be brought in from New Cadbury, and pick up the cash."

"We have a booth here? But I thought you said we weren't sanctioned."

"No one's against honest trade, Jack—not in this world or the next, and in this one, we have bills to pay." Sir Kevin said no more until they came to a row of shops at the far end of the fairgrounds, near a large fenced enclosure that looked—and smelled—like a corral. Behind it was a wooden structure that looked like a castle wall with tall gates. Pennants featuring all sorts of colorful heraldic devices fluttered from flagpoles set atop each of the turrets.

"Funny place for a rodeo arena," said Trick, pointing to the enclosure, where a team of costumed lackeys was smoothing out hoofprints in the sandy soil with long-handled rakes. "They need to get 'em a tractor with a good rotary harrow."

Sir Kevin laughed. "They probably wish they could, in this heat, but that wouldn't be in character for Merryborough. No, it's not for rodeo . . . well, maybe the medieval version of it. It's a jousting list."

"Jousting? You mean, like knights in armor knockin' each other off their horses?"

"That's an accurate, if inelegant, description. It's really quite thrilling."

"Man, I might like to see some of that."

Sir Kevin glanced at his watch. "It's a little early for jousting, but we might get to see some questing before we have to leave. Over there's our booth—and it looks like we're busy!"

Before Trick could ask what "questing" might be, his gaze followed Sir Kevin's pointed finger to one of the shops in the colorful structure near the jousting list. Beneath a brightly-painted awning that stirred lazily in the warm breeze, Trick and Sir Kevin joined eager shoppers clustered around display cases filled with a wide assortment of swords, daggers, knives, even maces and axes. Behind the cases stood a trim middle-aged man with black hair and beard, dressed in the mode of Merryborough and patiently answering questions about the workmanship and prices of the handsome weapons therein.

"These are replicas, m'lady," he said to a customer, with a country British accent, pointing to the open display cases in front of him and the weapons lying upon a bed of deep green velvet. "They're made of resin, each one painted by hand to resemble steel, but they're only for show. You'll find they are modestly priced." Then he turned to an upright display case behind him, which had a glass front and an antique padlock. In it, nestled among dark purple velvet, were four swords whose blades gleamed like mirrors—obviously of greater quality and value. He stroked his hand lovingly down the side of the case. "But if my lady wishes an extraordinary gift for her lord, these are true steel blades, keen of edge, and if it please you, laid upon with the blessing of the King himself."

"How much is the one on the right?" asked the customer. The merchant leaned close to the cabinet and opened the lock with a tiny key that dangled on a chain around his neck. He opened the glass door and used a piece of black velvet to lift the sword out of its cradle. Holding it closer to the customer, but still out of her reach, he stroked the velvet along the blade, and it sparkled like sunlight on still water. The ornate hilt had a grip wrapped with golden cord, and its cross-guard was studded with glittering faceted gems. Runic writing was engraved upon the blade where it joined the hilt.

"This one is . . . ah . . . pardon me, my lady, but it is five hundred pounds." He started to restore it to its case, but the woman said, "No, wait—I'll take it. It's perfect. You do take plastic, don't you?"

"Aye, my lady, but not, I fear, ye American Express."

"Discover?"

"Gladly."

In a matter of moments, the electronic processing device hidden beneath the front display case returned an approval of the customer's credit card. The merchant sheathed the long blade in a leather scabbard, and wrapped the hilt in a piece of authentic medieval plastic bubble-wrap before handing it across the counter to the delighted woman. She seemed a bit dismayed by its weight as she took it, but she balanced it on her shoulder like a parade rifle and went away happy.

Other customers purchased the replicas, which were priced between fifty and one hundred dollars, or "pounds" in the Merryborough lexicon. While Trick and Sir Kevin stood and watched, almost a thousand dollars was exchanged by the sword merchant. Finally, there was a lull in business, and when the last customer took his purchase away, Sir Kevin said to him, "Looks like brisk early sales today, Greg!"

"Oh, fair to middlin'," replied the merchant, whose British accent vanished to reveal his twentieth-century Texas heritage.

"Sir Gregory, I'd like you to meet Jack Patterson from Joyous Gard. He's going to be the chef at New Cadbury, and you're in for a treat when you get there. Jack, this is Sir Gregory, who operates our booth—and quite profitably, I should add."

Trick shook hands with Sir Gregory and said, "These are neat weapons, Sir Gregory. Do you make them?"

"No, I just sell them, but thank you—they *are* nice. The replicas are made at New Cadbury; they have the molds, and they pour 'em and paint 'em, and do a really good job. They're worth the price, if you just want 'em for decoration, or stage props. The real ones are made by Sir Robert Tristram, who's got an art studio in Fort Worth. You can actually fence with them if you want—although you have to be pretty doggone strong just to lift 'em! Here, check it out."

Sir Gregory selected another sword from the locking cabinet, and lifted it out with the piece of black velvet wrapped around the blade. This one was the nicest of the bunch, with gold and silver cord wrapped around the grip, a jeweled cross-guard, and a large, round, clear jewel in a setting that looked like a talon as its pommel.

Trick wiped his right hand on his jeans before accepting the sword. It *was* heavy; he had to hold the blade in his left hand in its protective velvet cloth until he determined the sword's balance. Only when he was comfortable with its weight did he raise the blade upward to admire its sheen. The gleaming blade caught the sunlight in brilliant little sparks as he raised it, and Trick felt inexplicably energized by it—it was as if it channelled its strength into his arm.

A voice at his side said, "It looks well on thee, lad."

Trick turned his head to the right and glimpsed an elderly man standing beside him, wearing the costume of a Merryborough commoner. He had white hair and a neatly trimmed white beard, but that was all Trick noticed of him.

"It's a beauty, all right," he agreed, and began to lower the blade once more into its velvet touch-cloth. But something stopped him. Instead, Trick raised the blade once again, and gazed intently at it. It suddenly seemed farther away than arm's length, as if he were looking at it over someone else's shoulder. Impulsively, almost against his will, he ran his bare fingers gently up the flat side of the blade to its point, then gingerly down the edge. A rough spot on the edge nicked his left middle finger, and a small drop of blood oozed up.

"Your pardon, sir," said the old man beside him.

"Careful, man, Sir Robert puts a real edge on these things," cautioned Sir Gregory, taking the sword out of Trick's hands and polishing the blade before placing it back in its velvet-covered holder. "You could slice a tomato thin as *baklava* with that one."

Trick reflexively put his finger in his mouth, and his saliva made the small cut sting a bit. He turned to reply to the old man's apparent concern, but he was gone; he wasn't in the shop, nor anywhere around it. Trick blinked; surely the old man hadn't just vanished into thin air. "Did you see which way that old man went?" he asked.

"What old man?" asked Sir Kevin.

"The one who was standing right beside me just now."

Sir Kevin inclined his head quizzically. "Are you okay, Jack? There hasn't been anyone beside you."

"But . . ." Trick began to protest, but let it drop. He didn't think Sir Kevin would be pulling his leg. Still, he *had* seen—and heard—someone. Hadn't he?

"Maybe I'd better get me that cold drink now, Sir Kevin. I think the heat's gettin' to me."

"You go ahead, Jack. Cruise around the faire a little while, if you want to. I'll meet you back here."

Trick strolled to a nearby concessions stand and purchased a large Dr Pepper for "one pound and seventy-five pence." With his quarter in change and a few moments of liberty from the watchful eye of his Knightly companion, Trick determined to take the opportunity to call Tay and let her know he was okay, and still on the case. He wandered from shop to shop, looking with genuine interest at the unusual and attractive items in each one, but in fact searching for a telephone. He found not a one, not even at the central food service area—although he saw a couple of visitors sitting at rough-hewn picnic tables munching turkey legs, with small cellular phones pressed to their ears. At last he bravely asked a buxom lass who served sherbet frozen inside scooped-out oranges where he might find a phone.

"Alas, good sir, you'll not be finding one of those inside

Merryborough," she answered, with an Irish lilt to her speech. "You must go outside the village, where time has not stopped as it has for us here inside."

Trick thanked her, and made his way to the main gate. He peered past the costumed gatekeeper, and saw a rack of pay telephones just outside. In order to leave the fairegrounds, even for a moment, he saw that he would have to have his hand stamped with the kind of ink that did not wash off easily. That would be difficult to explain to Sir Kevin: He couldn't tell the truth about having to make a phone call, since "Jack" was supposed to be estranged from his family and friends, and would have no need to make a call. He sighed, frustrated, turned around and headed back toward the shop where Sir Gregory sold swords to help support the Knights. His chest tightened a little at the thought that the longer he was out of touch with Tay, the more likely it was that the days of their relationship were numbered.

When he reached the jousting list, a crowd was forming at the rails around it, and up on top of the castle-like structure behind, performers dressed as heralds and musicians were getting into place. Curious, Trick made his way toward the front, where he could see that down one side of the arena had been set a row of five upright wooden pillars, each one about five feet tall and a foot wide. On the other side, four tall wooden L-shaped structures resembling a hangman's gallows were spaced down the length of the list; suspended on a chain from each one swung a metal ring about six inches in diameter, about six feet from the ground. In the center of the arena were four brightly-painted wooden barrels set in a square formation.

A trumpet fanfare rang out from atop the structure overlooking the jousting list, and a voice cried out, "Hear ye, ladies and gentlemen, boys and girls!" A barrel-chested man in an "uppercrust" costume, whose voice required no artificial amplification, boomed, "I am Jacob Spittle, Master of the Revels of Merryborough, and I welcome you to this demonstration of the knightly art of questing!

Questing is a sport requiring speed, accuracy, and perfect horse-manship. It is my pleasure to introduce to you one of Merry-borough's mightiest, most fearless, most courageous, strongest, bravest, stoutest . . . did I say fearless? . . . largest and most worthy knights, Sir Bruno of Buckingham, and his mighty stallion, Black Lightning!"

The crowd applauded as the gate beneath the announcer swung slowly open, then burst into laughter as the knight who appeared was not the promised behemoth on a fiery steed, but a petite woman on a light-limbed brown and white paint horse. Above a long forest green skirt, she wore a silver breastplate that was molded more to show off her lithe figure than to protect it from jousting lances, and a long violet cape draped attractively from her shoulders and over the horse's rump. Her long red hair was pulled into a tight braid that hung down her back, and around her forehead was a silver band with a green jewel in the center. She rode out proudly, with a long, brightly-painted jousting lance held upright like a flag-pole in her right hand, and a long sword in a scabbard hanging at her left side.

"What trickery is this?" demanded the Master of the Revels. "You are not Sir Bruno! Where is the mighty Sir Bruno?"

"Alas, my lord, the mighty Sir Bruno is unable to quest today," cried the woman. "He was defeated last night . . . by a barrel of ale. I am Valerie, the Lady Bruno, and I will quest in his place today."

"Sir Bruno sends his *wife* to quest? Oh, this is madness! This is devilry! Who among these good people would wish to see a—a *woman* ride the questing gauntlet?" The crowd whooped and cheered enthusiastically, and Jacob Spittle shrugged broadly and called out, "Then let it be so. God have mercy upon such a world!"

The trumpeters blew another fanfare, and Valerie spurred her horse into a canter around the ring. Her cape fluttered above the animal's hooves, while flutes and drums provided a lively under-score. She returned to the top end of the list, below the gate struc-ture, removed her cape and handed it to a young squire, along with her lance. Jacob called out, "The questing knight must train his horse to respond to the slightest touch of the rein and spur. At the signal, Lady Bruno will guide her mount close around each of the four casks in the center of the list. If any of them topples, my lady, you will forfeit the event. Art thou ready, Lady Bruno?"

"Aye, my lord, I am." Valerie wriggled down in the saddle, and at the drop of a flag by a squire at the far end of the list, she spurred the horse toward the formation of four barrels. The horse approached the first barrel at top speed, and his rider skillfully reined him in a tight circle around it before proceeding to the next. The third barrel teetered a bit as they circled it, but it remained upright, and they completed the course in less than twenty seconds.

As Valerie galloped her horse back to the starting point, Trick cheered and applauded with the rest of the spectators. He'd seen some good old-fashioned barrel-racing in his time, but this woman was one of the best he'd ever seen. He could only speculate about her equestrian training, but he was willing to bet she had a couple of rodeo award belt buckles in her trophy case.

"Forsooth, my lady," called the Master of the Revels. "Perhaps I was a bit hasty. But let us see your work with the lance. A questing knight must have the eye of an eagle. As Lady Bruno rides, she will attempt to pluck the rings hanging from these gallows with the tip of her lance. You may ride when ready, Lady Bruno!"

The squire returned the lance to Valerie, who raised it in a salute to the crowd as she trotted her horse to the far end of the list. She leveled the lance, which was an elongated cone about six feet in length, then touched her heels to the horse's sides. The horse sprang forward and held a straight course down the side of the list, where, one by one, the lance pierced the rings dead center, leaving only the chains swinging and jingling in the clouds of dust kicked up by the galloping horse. Triumphantly, Valerie circled the list, holding the lance high to show that all four rings were neatly stacked midway down its shaft.

"Methinks the lady doth make a good shish kebab!" called Jacob approvingly. "But there is one final test: a questing knight must also be a warrior. Behold, here are five godless heathens on the battlefield." He pointed to the other side of the list, where squires had set a large head of cabbage upon the top of each wooden pillar. "It is good for a knight to die for his king, but it is much better to make the enemy die for his! Have you the stomach for this, Lady Bruno?"

"My lord, it is I who launders Sir Bruno's codpiece. I can stomach much."

"Then ride, my lady, and slay the heathen!"

With a cry, Valerie drew her sword and spurred the horse around the list once to pick up speed. The steel blade flashed in the sunlight, and she hacked each head of cabbage in half as they charged by the pillars at a full gallop. When the cheering abated, Valerie stopped in the center of the arena and stood up in the stirrups. She raised the sword, which still had shreds of cabbage hanging from it, and called out, "My lord, wouldst thou care to repeat that bit about the madness of a woman riding the questing gauntlet?"

"Good my lady, I meant only that I was *enchanted* by the idea. As are we all! Ladies and gentlemen, three cheers for Valerie, Lady Bruno, and her gallant steed! Hip, hip, huzzah!" Valerie bowed from the saddle with the applause, which rang out anew when her horse also took a "bow" at her cue. The gates opened, and horse and rider disappeared behind them as flutes, drums, and trumpets played an exit chorus while the crowd dispersed from the jousting arena.

Trick had enjoyed the show so much that he had almost forgotten his frustration at being unable to contact Tay. Sir Kevin met him in the crowd and said, "I see you got to watch the questing show. So what do you think of Dame Valerie?"

"*Dame* Valerie?" asked Trick in amazement. "She's one of—of *us?*"

"Otherwise known as Dame Valerie Percival. You'll be seeing her around New Cadbury after the faire closes tomorrow. Speaking of which, we're running late getting there. We'd better hit the road."

Trick waved goodbye to Sir Gregory, then he and Sir Kevin

crossed the fairegrounds toward the main gate without stopping to look at any other shops or attractions. In spite of himself, he'd enjoyed the visit to Merryborough, and had begun to understand why some people would relish the thought of living in a simpler time such as this one—the color, the spectacle, the simple courtesies extended by each one to everyone. He even considered bringing Tay here to next year's festival—that is, if there *was* a next year for them. His mood dipped again, after having been much improved by the prospect of meeting the talented Dame Valerie later at New Cadbury.

Just as they approached the gates, Trick spotted a familiar face in the crowd: the old man who'd spoken to him back at Sir Gregory's shop. Trick was relieved—so he hadn't imagined him, after all! He raised his arm and waved; the old man smiled and returned the gesture gracefully.

"Who are you waving at, Jack?" asked Sir Kevin.

"The old guy from the sword shop. He's over there by the exit."

"Where? I don't see him."

"He's right by—" Trick stopped in mid-sentence and mid-step. The old man was there . . . and then he wasn't. Trick hurried ahead of Sir Kevin to the exit gate, but there wasn't a trace of him anywhere to be seen, on either side of the passage from Merryborough to the real world.

"Jack, are you sure you're okay?"

"I did see that guy, I'm sure of it! He waved at me."

"Come on, Jack old boy, let's get you into the air-conditioned car," said Sir Kevin with deep concern. "You can lean the seat back and relax the rest of the way to New Cadbury."

Trick took one more look back across the green fields of Merryborough before following Sir Kevin out into the parking lot, but saw no one who resembled the mysterious old man. As they walked to the car, Trick felt like he was being watched . . . very *closely* watched . . . by a figment of his imagination.

CHAPTER EIGHT

AFTER LEAVING MERRYBOROUGH, TRICK AND SIR KEVIN RETURNED to the main highway and traveled farther west a short distance, into the rolling ranch land west of Weatherford. Having driven the same road more than a dozen times during the past couple of years, Trick was familiar with most of the landmarks along the way and was confident of his geographical bearings when they took the exit for Millsap, a tiny community north of the Interstate. However, instead of heading toward the town, they crossed over the highway and backtracked about a mile down the eastbound access road. Then they turned south down a rough, poorly maintained road marked only by a reflector post that had been bent over and straightened up many times. The pavement gradually ran out and became packed dirt, so Sir Kevin slowed the Honda's pace slightly to lessen the jolt of the rocks and ruts on the vehicle and its occupants.

On either side of the narrow road ran slack barbed-wire fences strung between gnarled wooden posts. Like most ranchmen, Trick had a profound disdain for people who didn't keep their fences maintained, but he could see little beyond these that required strong containment. Mesquite, live oak, and cottonwood trees, large chunks of limestone, and an occasional prickly-pear cactus were all that lay behind the sagging fence lines. The land rolled in gentle waves from one horizon to the next, around bushy hillocks and into shallow draws, and in the distance, silhouettes of flat-topped *mesas* were visible. Trick was pleased to note the slight similarity of this undeveloped land just west of Fort Worth to his home out near Alpine. There, the land alternated between ruggedly mountainous and dance-floor flat, but it shared some of the same wild vegetation and sedimentary evidence of having been carved out and smoothed by the primordial ocean. "A land of mighty contrasts is your Texas," someone had once told him; yet on a fundamental level that was deeper than geology, every distinct pebble of Texas was Texas, just the same.

"New Cadbury coming up around this turn," announced Sir Kevin. Trick shook off the homesickness he felt at being this much closer to home to sit up and pay attention. The road took a bend to the left at the foot of a wooded hillock, and the rustic barbed-wire fence on the hillock side abruptly stopped. In its place, a tall steel fencepost embedded in concrete supported the corner of a section of sturdy chain-link. About a hundred yards of it faced the road, with another steel corner-post at the opposite end. A cross-fence, also made of chain-link, ran back from the road and up the back side of the hill. Along the top of it all was a triple row of barbed wire, which angled back about thirty degrees. Trick could tell by the look of the fence that it wasn't new; it sagged in places, and appeared to have been patched in others, but it still looked strong enough to keep out casual intruders.

Sir Kevin drove up to a gate in the center of the fence facing the road. He stopped and put the Honda in neutral, and dust swirled around the car as he got out and approached the gate. Trick could see a rusty chain and double padlocks securing the gate, and a weathered wooden sign attached to it. Pale letters stenciled in faded black upon the flaking white background read "U.S. Government Property. No Trespassing."

"Sir Kevin, are you sure this is where we want to be?" asked Trick as the Knight fumbled in his pockets, finally extracting a set of keys on a split ring.

"This is where everybody will *wish* they could be when the King regains his throne," replied Sir Kevin. He unlocked the padlocks, unwound the chain from the center of the gate, and swung the portal open wide. He got back in the car and drove it through, past a small wooden structure that resembled a tollbooth that was grown over with weeds, with creeping vines twining in and out of its shattered, empty windows. Then he got out and secured the gate once again before returning to the driver's seat. The tires made a quiet crushing sound in the softer dirt of the road inside the fence as Sir Kevin slowly drove over a rise that secluded New Cadbury from view from the rest of the world.

Just below the rise was a row of weather-beaten cinder-block structures with sagging flat asphalt roofs. All the windows were broken out, and weeds grew high around them. They had been painted white at one time, but years of wind and rain, summer heat and winter cold had rubbed them all to a speckled pentimento effect, revealing the cold gray brick underneath. Trick recognized the buildings for what they had been—military barracks, not unlike some he had lived in during his brief Army career. He felt his diaphragm contracting uncomfortably, as if in anticipation of the ghost of a Military Police officer stepping out to guard this phantom fortress.

His fear subsided when they drove around the back of the old barracks, and Trick saw that the entire back wall had been removed, so that what once had been staff rooms and sleeping quarters were now carports. A dozen assorted vehicles, including a couple of motorcycles, were parked inside the gutted barracks. Sir Kevin drove the Honda into an empty space that had been a shower area— ceramic tiles still covered the walls and floors, with a drain in the center of the room, and rusty shower spigots protruded uselessly from one wall.

"Car wash?" asked Trick.

Sir Kevin laughed. "No, just a garage. Last spring we had golfball-size hail out here. Besides, the less that can be seen from the road or the air right now, the better." Without elaborating, he switched off the engine and pulled a handle to pop open the trunk. Trick loaded his arms with a soft-sided suitcase, a duffel, and his small bundle of "Jack's" belongings, and followed Sir Kevin from the "carport" back to the road, and farther down the hill a short distance to where another set of barracks stood behind another chain-link fence. The gate in this fence was secured only with a small chain and padlock, both of recent make, and Sir Kevin opened it with another key on his ring. He instructed Trick to lock it back once they were inside, and Trick did so. Across a yard that had once been solid with caliche, their feet alternately crunched in powdery gravel and swished in ankle-high grass and weeds as they went up to the end door of the row of cinderblock barracks. These were in slightly better condition than the first ones Trick had seen—at least most of the windows looked intact.

Sir Kevin opened the door and switched on a light, and they entered a small reception room. Trick looked around the room, and he experienced the same lack of awe as he had upon entering Joyous Gard for the first time—once again disappointed at the un-cult-likeness of the place. It was stark, as could be expected of a military barracks, but its dreariness was warmed by a recent coat of pinkish paint on the walls and ceiling, and a worn but neatly swept carpet that covered most of the concrete floor. It was simply furnished with a threadbare sofa and a small occasional table by the door. Another door in the center of the wall opposite the entrance opened onto a long, dim hallway.

"Let's find you a bunk, Jack, and then I'd better report to the Round Table," said Sir Kevin. "First, you can just put the stuff in my room, right down the hall here." Trick followed him down the narrow hallway, onto which opened a dozen small rooms, and at the end of which was a shower room. All of these rooms were taken, explained the young Knight, by senior Knights and some of the members of the Round Table, such as himself. Sir Kevin's room was across from the showers, a tiny cubicle hardly large enough to hold a single bed and a makeshift desk and still have room to turn around in. Here Trick put down the suitcase and duffel and joined Sir Kevin out in the hallway once more.

Just beyond the showers was a door to the outside underneath a shattered "Exit" sign. They went outside, and behind the building where they had been were two more cinderblock buildings; on the left, another row of barracks, but on the right, a concrete building that seemed at first glance a building-and-a-half high. Trick saw, as he studied it, that it was definitely two-storied, with the lower floor recessed into the ground so that they had to descend a set of concrete steps to enter it. It made sense to him that whatever this remote military base had been used for, it had been designed to maintain a low profile—literally and figuratively—and this larger barracks had been designed to be no more conspicuous than the buildings around it.

It was a dormitory, or in military jargon, a Bachelor Officers' Quarters. Although Trick had never been more than a corporal in his entire brief military career, he recognized it as such. The large open room that they entered on the lower level was obviously the B.O.Q. mess hall, which now contained several contemporary folding banquet tables and chairs. They walked briefly through the dingy kitchen, which had been recently used but not thoroughly cleaned. Trick winced at the smell of stale grease—some of which, he feared privately, had been there since this base was new. "How many people eat here?" asked Trick, trying to estimate from the number of folding chairs.

"Not very many right now, maybe thirty per meal," answered Sir Kevin, "but once your reputation gets around, you could probably cook for about fifty or so."

"Is that everybody here at New Cadbury?"

"Nearly everybody. The Innermost Circle dines at the Round Table, of course."

"Where's that?"

Sir Kevin smiled enigmatically. "Maybe one day you'll sit there, too, Jack."

Trick knew it was time to button his lip; he only hoped that the Innermost Circle's kitchen, wherever it was, had been policed a little better than this one. He followed Sir Kevin up a flight of concrete stairs and into the first of several large rooms on the upper floor. In this room were a dozen bunk beds, with a garage-sale assortment of chests of drawers, wardrobes and lockers. Each bed was neatly made, with extra shoes lined up underneath each lower bunk. Personal effects were arranged carefully on dresser-tops, and clothes that hung exposed in open lockers were orderly and tidy. Although the floor was cracked and two of the four windows were broken out, the room was cool, even in the middle of the hot day, as the breezes blew through.

"I'm going on to the Round Table now, Jack," said Sir Kevin. "I'll have Sir Floyd come up and show you where you'll sleep and where to put your things. Any questions for me before I go?"

"No, sir. Thank you, Sir Kevin."

"All right, then. I'll see you later. Glad to have you at New Cadbury, Jack."

Sir Kevin's footsteps dopplered away down the stairs, but in only a moment, another pair started up. "Must be Sir Floyd," Trick thought, and he mused on the incongruity of a knight named *Floyd*. It wasn't exactly a name that inspired awe, like Bruno or Lancelot or even Kevin—it was an old man's name.

An old man . . . could it be? Trick thought of the old man he'd seen at the faire, but quickly dismissed the thought. Even if he wasn't just a figment of his imagination, there was no way the old man could have gotten to New Cadbury ahead of him. Besides, the footsteps on the stairs were solid and swift, and the voice in the stairwell that called out, "Jack Patterson?" was clear and strong.

"In here," answered Trick, and he took a step toward the stairwell to meet Sir Floyd.

"Hi, Jack, I'm—" began the voice of the man who turned the

corner into the dorm room.

Trick's eyes widened, and as if equipped with zoom lenses brought into focus the figure of a man a little younger than himself, about his height, with close-cropped black hair and a look of astonishment on his dark face that mirrored the one on Trick's.

The two men faced each other across the room, and as Trick stared, the dust blew away from memories more than half his life old. Trick found his tongue at last and asked, "Aren't you supposed to be dead?"

"They said *you* were," answered the man, and in the next second, they rushed together into an embrace.

"Reggie! My God, Reggie! What are *you* doin' here?"

"Trick McGuire! Trick McGuire! I cannot believe this!" Their voices overlapped, and they laughed and hugged and pounded one another upon the back like the old friends and fellow soldiers that they had been. Over a quarter of a century had passed, but the memories of the days they had spent together in Operations Support on the ragged edge of the Vietnam war were still clear in their minds.

"Jesus, Trick, it's good to see you," said Reggie, once the shock and joy of their meeting had settled. "You haven't changed a bit."

"Neither have you, Reggie," replied Trick sincerely. Time had not diminished the memory of the face of the soldier chronically last in line in the mess tent, but it had etched some lines upon it. The light hazel eyes still seemed almost golden in the smooth olive complexion that was as dotted with darker freckles as ever, even upon the full lips that revealed a mouthful of widely spaced teeth when he smiled. It finally occurred to Trick that *Floyd* was Reggie's last name—a picture from the depths of his memory showed the name stencilled on the fatigue shirt that always seemed too big for Reggie's youthful frame.

They chuckled uncertainly, once the initial excitement had given way to awkwardness about what to say or do next. They sat down together on some other Knight's lower bunk, and Trick ventured, "So tell me, Reggie, how did you get out of 'Nam alive? I saw you shot."

"Shot, but not killed," answered Reggie calmly, as if it had happened to someone else. "All I know is what they told me when I came to in the hospital in Saigon, that you and a bunch of other guys had been executed—"

"Let's not talk about it, okay? What did you do after 'Nam? How'd you get here?"

Reggie shrugged, grinned. "Well, I had enough holes in me to qualify for full disability, so I got on out of the Army. I went back to Mississippi, lived at home for awhile, and worked as a mechanic while I got my G.E.D. Then I went to college, and got a degree in business, and went to work for the state of Mississippi. I got married, and we had three kids, all grown up now. My wife—well, she died last year with cancer. I guess that's part of why I'm here now. How 'bout you, Trick? What happened after your tour? How'd you end up at New Cadbury?"

"After I got discharged, I went back home to Texas. I went to college awhile, but I dropped out and went to work on the ranch. I got married . . . and got discharged again. I have a daughter, lives with her mama." Trick felt that was a much truth as he could afford to share, even with an old friend—especially since this old friend now wore a red armband with two chevrons on it, signifying the second degree of Knighthood. He let "Jack" do the rest of the talking. "I been drifting awhile, and I just got tired of it, so that's how I ended up here. But I got in a little trouble a while back over my support payments, and my 'ex' swore out a warrant on me. I've been going under the name of Jack Patterson for about a year. You won't blow my cover, will you, Reggie?"

Reggie laughed. "You know I won't. Names are no big deal here. Me, for instance. After the Army, for some reason, everybody just started calling me by my last name—I don't know why, but I've gone by 'Floyd' ever since. Since we don't use last names here, bein' as we're all sons and daughters of the King, it's as good as any. You can still call me Reggie when we're by ourselves, but be sure to call me Sir Floyd if anyone's listening. Speaking of which, Sir Kevin wanted me to show you where to bunk and put your stuff. How about here?" Reggie indicated an unmade upper bunk, upon which extra pillows and bedding were piled.

"Good enough," replied Trick, and tossed his small bundle of belongings onto it.

"Did Sir Kevin show you around at all?"

"No, we came straight on up here. Didn't look like there was much to see."

"Well, then, you'll be surprised. Hey, we got a little time before you need to start cooking. Come with me, and I'll give you the nickel tour and show you what I've been working on."

Trick followed Reggie back downstairs to the dining hall, where they found signs of life: A young woman was rummaging in the kitchen for snacks for three fussy toddlers. She and Reggie greeted one another briefly, but she kept her attention on doling out graham crackers spread with low-fat peanut butter to the trio of two-year-olds clamoring around her.

"Many kids here?" asked Trick as they climbed the steps out of the B.O.Q. into the hot afternoon sun and moved out into the middle of the compound.

"Oh, a few. The mothers take turns looking out for each other's young 'uns, especially those who work off campus. We have a pretty good little cottage industry here, though. Did you see the replica weaponry at Merryborough? It's made in the building next to this one. We've also got a little print shop, and a vegetable garden. There's something for everybody to do here. Sure will be good to have a real, live cook on the premises—everybody's tired of sandwiches and tuna casserole."

"I'll do my best, Reggie. But I haven't improved much beyond S.O.S."

Reggie laughed out loud and slapped Trick on the back jovially. "Who could ask for anything more? I'm glad you're here, Trick, and not just for your cookin'. We're gonna have a good time while we're workin' on immortality."

For awhile, they followed a ruined sidewalk from which the heat was reflecting in rippling-water mirages. Then, they came to the rear of the compound, where the back fence stood against a tall earthen embankment that followed a vague roadway grown over with weeds. A narrow gate that sagged on its hinges was secured with a late-model chain and padlock, and Reggie jingled a ring of keys out of his pocket and quickly opened it. He secured the gate behind them once they had passed through. There were an awful lot of fences and gates, Trick thought. What had this place been? It was obviously designed for maximum security, though it was fairly easily reached from the highway. Yet it had no airstrip, nor even a helicopter landing pad. Even the roads looked like they had been minimal, even when the place was new. Trick pointed out the lack of road to Reggie as they continued on around the embankment.

"We don't usually take any vehicles out here in the daylight," Reggie explained. "They're too easy to spot from the air. When we haul supplies out here, we do it after dark."

"Aren't we taking a risk by being out here now?"

"A little. But we can hide ourselves a lot easier than we can hide a truck, if we need to."

Around the end of the embankment, a small empty guardhouse came into view, next to a tall gate that stood in the inner row of a double fence of chain-link, topped not with ordinary barbed wire but with coils of perilous anti-personnel wire. The inner fence was set back from the outer fence about six feet, and Trick guessed that this was the area in which vicious Dobermans and German Shepherds had patrolled the perimeter of the relatively small enclosure that lay before them. Inside the enclosure, which was about a hundred yards long and fifty yards wide, was nothing but an absolutely flat surface of gravel and concrete, littered with what appeared to be rusty air-conditioning parts and scrap iron.

Reggie unlocked the gate and opened it just wide enough for the two of them to squeeze through. "Here's the best-kept secret of

New Cadbury," he said, gesturing grandly at the blighted expanse before them, then beckoning to Trick to follow.

There, flush upon the surface of the eroded concrete were three immense metal double doors, which had at one time been painted with yellow and black diagonal stripes. Now they were mostly rusted, with only hints of the paint still visible as vague chevrons upon the pocked metal surfaces. Reggie led Trick to the center door, and they stood at one end while Reggie fumbled for more keys. The door was about forty feet long, but only about twelve feet wide, with one half of the door overlapping the other slightly in the center. Beside it was a smaller metal door, mounted in the concrete slightly above the surface, like a storm cellar door. This one had at one time been sealed; the seam where the halves of the door met had been pried up, and rusted broken hasps were swung uselessly to one side, the old locks still intact. A new hasp had been welded on, and Reggie unlocked the padlock that secured it. He pulled open one side of the door, and let it stand open as he stepped in and invited Trick to join him with a grand, gallant gesture.

"Watch your step," he cautioned. "There might be water standing at the bottom. Maybe snakes, too."

Apprehensively, Trick stepped inside, and found himself on a concrete stair, painted dull gray, descending into darkness. The concrete of the stairwell was cold in contrast to the outside temperature. Trick trailed his hands along both sides of it as he followed Reggie underground ten, twenty, thirty short steps into increasing darkness. Sure enough, just as Reggie had warned, at the bottom stood about one inch of stale water, and the sound of his boots sloshing into it echoed into a greater darkness beyond.

"Wait here a minute," Reggie said, and Trick paused in the dim gray corridor listening to Reggie's feet splashing in the water, then clipping hollowly on dry concrete. The footfalls reverberated louder and louder, then stopped abruptly. Then: a sharp click, a dull hum, and light flowed into the corridor where Trick stood, his hands still pressed against its opposite walls as if to brace himself for what he was about to see. As his eyes blinked into focus in the underground chamber, he saw a room large enough to enclose two full-size basketball courts side by side, with a ceiling more than high enough to permit aerial slam-dunking. Dull green enamel clung tightly to the concrete walls, and upon them were stencilled legends; in black, reminding personnel to keep doors closed, and in red, where fire extinguishers once could be found. In the center of the ceiling, daylight drew a narrow outline around the immense metal door Trick had seen on the surface. On the floor directly underneath the door was a rusted steel platform, roughly its same size. Four upright steel beams cornered the platform from floor to ceiling. In the dim but adequate light given off by four electrical fixtures in safety cages mounted on the ceiling, Trick could see heavy machinery underneath the platform in the space around it where it was more or less flush with the floor. Other than this, the room was empty, except for some building materials and paint cans stacked nearby.

"What *is* this place, Reg?" he asked, and the reverberation of his voice in the cavernous room gave him a chill.

Reggie grinned and said, "Well, Trick, old buddy, you're standing in a missile silo."

Trick felt his stomach reach up and clutch his throat. *Missiles!* No wonder this military base had been built to be so secure! As if Reggie sensed his discomfort, he explained, "Oh, don't worry; Uncle Sam took out all the firecrackers thirty years ago. Once we slap on a little new paint, and bring in some chairs and stuff, this place will become New Glastonbury Abbey—the place for the Convergence of our King!"

If he had believed in ghosts, Trick would have been convinced that this place was full of them. He had been a young teenager during the Cuban missile crisis in the early 1960s; no doubt this base had been built during that very tense time in history. He now felt the same gnawing trepidation as he had felt back then—a sense of disaster hovering at the edge of his world.

He swallowed his uneasiness for the sake of his cover. "Is that an elevator?" he asked, pointing to the metal platform.

"Uh-huh," said Reggie. "And it still works, too. Well, after a fashion. I've been messin' with it, while I've been workin' on the electrical system. Watch."

He beckoned to Trick to follow him, and they went behind a steel mesh fence at one end of the elevator, where an electrical circuit panel stood open. A broken padlock, some melted fuses, bits of wire insulation, and other evidence of tampering littered the floor around it. Reggie flipped on a large circuit breaker, and the machinery rumbled to life, vibrating the room. Trick watched as the metal doors in the ceiling opened slowly downward into the room, their rusty hinges screaming from the strain of disuse, and sunlight streamed down into the dull green room. As Reggie manipulated the antiquated manual controls, the platform quivered and began to rise toward the open doorway. It groaned and creaked and shuddered, and stalled halfway there. He shut off the motors before they could burn out, and the room was silent again except for the hum of electrical consumption.

"Still needs some work," he said, " but by the Convergence, this baby ought to be back in Def-Con readiness."

Unable to continue merely wondering, Trick asked, "Reg, were there nuclear missiles at this place?"

"Oh, yes, you can bet on it. Judging by the size of this base and its location, I'm guessing that they were big SAMs, surface-to-air missiles, probably in the Nike class. They were deployed in the late fifties, early sixties. If I'm guessin' right, there's probably one of these bases at all four compass points around the Dallas-Fort Worth Metroplex, stuck off in the boonies, far enough out to be hidden but close enough to do some good."

"How were the missiles supposed to be launched? I thought they came straight up out of a silo."

"Well, I guess maybe technically, this is actually a *bunker*. I took a military history class in college, and we studied some of this stuff. The missiles would sit down here nice and harmless, one on the lift and one on each side, till we got to a volatile Defense Condition. Then the guys who worked this pop-stand would go and get the warheads and screw 'em on, the doors would open and up she'd go. The guys on the surface would push the missile onto a launcher and raise her into firing position, and then they'd come down here and wait. The order to fire would come from Washington through the command center, which is the part of the base where we live now. Fortunately, Mr. Castro did not choose to heave any firecrackers at us, so upright and ready was as far as these probably ever got. When LBJ was pretty sure Fidel had cooled off enough, most of these little surface missiles were decommissioned and their bases closed. But for awhile, they were supposed to be the last line of defense against air strikes in the Dallas-Fort Worth area. That was back in the days when people believed we could *win* a nuclear war."

Reggie shook his head sadly, then reached for the controls. The elevator grumbled and creaked back down into the room, bringing the platform flush with the floor once again. The metal doors slowly strained upward to close off the sunlight once more from the cold, mildewed concrete room.

All was dim and silent once again, and once Reggie had secured the bunker, they climbed the steps to the surface to continue Trick's tour of New Cadbury. Even though they emerged into direct sunlight, with waves of heat rippling across the flat concrete surface, Trick shivered. As they left behind the ghosts of the Cold War, Trick could not help but feel that some other evil was gathering about this unlikely cathedral for the coronation of a King.

CHAPTER NINE

THIRTY-ONE MEN, WOMEN, AND ASSORTED CHILDREN QUEUED UP AT the B.O.Q. mess hall that night for the first meal prepared by Jack Patterson. They stood in line expectantly, gripping their compartmented school-cafeteria trays in both hands, whispering among themselves about the delicious possibilities that awaited. Rumor had it that the new arrival had actually been some kind of chef, or at least a short-order cook, before coming to Joyous Gard; this was what had won him a pre-Knighthood transfer to New Cadbury. Whatever they believed, they were not disappointed, for when they presented their trays, the new cook served up spaghetti with as good a homestyle meat sauce as any they had ever tasted. A crisp salad with a light oil-and-vinegar dressing, and toasted triangles of garlic bread completed the simple feast.

"Jack" modestly acknowledged each compliment paid him as the diners filed by once again to scrape their plates and stack them, tossing their silverware into a basin of soapy water. But Trick McGuire was deeply disappointed, for in all those thirty-one pairs of thumbs gripping trays, none of them belonged to Brian Brannan. Trick began to worry that perhaps Brian had not flown to the bosom of the Knights after all; maybe the kid was still in Dallas, crashing at the home of a friend. On the other hand, Sir Kevin had mentioned an "Innermost Circle" which dined at "the Round Table"—

perhaps Brian was one of that elite group. Maybe Reggie would enlighten him about them if he couched his questions just right.

After supper, Trick was dismissed to the living quarters for one hour so the Knights could hold their evening studies in the mess hall. "I know you're disappointed, Jack," said Sir Kevin kindly, "but you can't study at this level until you're Knighted. Why don't you use the time to rest up a little, and to review your apprenticeship materials? When we're through, you can come back down and put away the dishes."

"Yes, sir," agreed Trick without much enthusiasm.

"While you're at it, I need to visit with you about the Convergence feast. It's only a week away now, and I want you to cook something extra special. Be thinking about that, too."

Reluctantly, Trick climbed the stairs to the room he would share with ten other men and made up his upper bunk with some of the extra bedding that was piled upon it. He found an empty locker with a couple of bent hangers inside and hung up his other hand-me-down shirt and pants. His moving-in process took all of eight minutes and left him bored and fretting, all alone in the dim upstairs of the B.O.Q.

He wandered over to the open window to catch the full benefit of the light breeze that cooled the room. It looked out over the front of the compound, toward the entrance on the lonely country road that led to the old missile base. All he could see, however, were the cars lined up in the old gutted barracks fifty yards away. The place seemed deserted once more—everybody was gathered in the mess hall with Sir Kevin, and all was silent except for some singing which he could hear faintly through the concrete floor. The sun was still high in the west, so he guessed it was about seven o'clock; but it had been a long, eventful day and he was feeling sleepy.

He sat on the windowsill, and as he gazed off into the west, he thought of home, five hundred miles toward the coming sunset. He hoped everything was all right on the ranch and with his folks, and that they hadn't given him up for dead and sold all his stuff. Thoughts of hearth and home inevitably brought bittersweet memories of Tay, who no doubt had already crossed his name off her Christmas card list as well. If he could not dig up one noteworthy bit of dirt on the Knights on their own hallowed land, then this whole exercise would be more than just a colossal waste of time— it would be the end of all the things that made his life most pleasant.

As Trick marked the slow sinking of the sun, a cloud of dust suddenly rose up on the horizon, heralding the arrival of a vehicle. In a moment, a small teal-green pickup appeared, tearing along New Cadbury's unpaved, unkempt main road at an inadvisable speed. It wheeled into the shed next to Sir Kevin's car, the brake lights glaring red in a whirlwind of pale dust. The driver leaped from the cab and made a beeline for the B.O.Q. Trick immediately recognized the red hair pulled into a long, tight braid, and smiled appreciatively as Dame Valerie Percival jogged toward the door downstairs. Instead of her elegant costume from the faire, she now wore jeans, a sleeveless denim vest open over a white T-shirt, and white leather athletic shoes with riding heels. Apparently she did not notice Trick at the upstairs window before she disappeared into the building, but Trick watched her closely and admired her firm pulchritude rippling alluringly with the impact of each step.

He glanced back toward the shed, where he saw another figure slowly moving through the settling dust. Trick was a bit disappointed in Dame Valerie, if she was in such a big hurry that she couldn't wait for her passenger. The man had not changed out of his faire costume, and still wore his plain brown tunic and leggings. When he stopped abruptly in the middle of the yard between the shed and the B.O.Q. and looked around, Trick recognized the old man he had seen at the faire! Almost reflexively, he called out, "Hey!" and waved from the window.

The old man looked up and his eyes met Trick's. There seemed to be a slight smile twisting the lips behind the grizzled beard, but he gave no other response. Suddenly Trick flinched, and the sunlight seemed to dim for a moment; he felt as if he'd fallen asleep sitting up, then awakened with a twitch. When he blinked his eyes into focus again, the old man had vanished.

"Oh, man, I am definitely losin' it," Trick groaned as he arose from the sill and shuffled wearily to his bunk, where he lay down and closed his eyes, but remained alert. Soon he heard voices and footsteps on the stairs, signalling that the Knights-only study session had come to an end.

"Hey, Jack, are you in there?" called Reggie's voice from the hall, and then he appeared in the doorway. He glanced around quickly, saw that Trick was alone, and said softly, "We're done now, Trick. Sir Kevin wants to see you in the kitchen."

Trick sat up and slid carefully from his upper bunk to his feet. "Hi, Reggie. Did I miss anything important?" he asked.

"Nothing that you won't hear many times after you're Knighted," said his friend. "I'll give you the non-classified highlights sometime soon. Right now, me and the boys have to get to work out at the site. Come on out later, if you want."

Trick tucked in his shirt tail as he hurried down the concrete stairs to the mess hall, where the assembly was breaking up. A couple of the women carried sleepy children up another set of stairs, and a few of the Knights remained in the mess hall, chatting in small groups around the cleared banquet tables, but most of the others drifted outside. Trick passed them all, acknowledging their brief greetings, and entered the kitchen. There he found Sir Kevin, talking amiably with Dame Valerie.

"Ah, here's Jack now," said Sir Kevin. "I bet he can find you something to eat. Jack, you remember Dame Valerie Percival from the questing demonstration at the faire. Valerie, this is our new chef, Jack."

"Nice to meet you, Jack," said Dame Valerie, offering her hand. Trick grasped it gently, and was not surprised at how strong her grip was. Neither was he surprised to hear that the British brogue affected for her role at the faire had vanished to reveal the twangy drawl particular to west central Texas. "I hope it's not too much trouble—I just got back from the faire, and I'm starvin'."

"It'd be no trouble at all, ma'am," Trick said with a smile. "I'll warm up some of tonight's spaghetti, but it'll take a minute, since we don't have a microwave."

"That'd be great, thanks," she answered.

Sir Kevin said, "Jack, I know this is much to ask of you since you've only just arrived, but next Friday, as you know, is the Convergence. There could be as many as two hundred people present, possibly more, for the feast prior to the ceremony. What would you recommend for a gathering that size? Can our kitchen even handle it?"

Trick answered as he stirred sauce in a small pan on the ancient gas stove and dropped a small handful of dry spaghetti into a pan of boiling water. "Well, everybody likes barbecue. If we can get hold of some kind of smoker, I can cook enough briskets in two days to feed two hundred, easy. If not, well, I can do it in the oven, but it's not as good without the smoke flavor. Brisket and potato salad and beans, maybe a big ol' peach cobbler for dessert. If I can have a couple of helpers, it'll be a snap."

"That shouldn't be difficult to arrange. Make up a shopping list for that and for what we'll need for next week's meals, and I'll see that it's bought. Ask Sir Floyd to find you a smoker—he's a pretty clever scrounger of supplies and equipment."

"Yes, sir, I will."

"Great! That's a load off my mind. Now I can concentrate on getting New Glastonbury Abbey ready on time." Sir Kevin glanced at his watch. "Valerie, will you be joining us at the Round Table tonight?"

"I'll be there as soon as I've had a bite," she replied.

"Then I'll leave you to it. See you soon." He turned and left Trick and Dame Valerie alone in the kitchen.

"I'm sorry we don't have any salad left, Dame Valerie," he said as he heaped the freshly-cooked pasta onto a plastic plate, and covered it with steaming meat sauce.

"No problem," she replied, and hungrily dug her fork into the plate of spaghetti Trick handed her.

"Don't you want to go sit in the dining room?"

" 'S fine," she answered with her mouth full, leaning against the prep counter by the stove. "Mmm, this is good."

"Thank you, ma'am. Here's you a glass of tea."

Dame Valerie stood and ate while Trick began washing the dishes that he had piled in the sink after supper. He could not help but glance occasionally at the young woman; he guessed her to be in her late twenties, discounting the crinkles around her light blue eyes as the price she paid for working outdoors. Her skin was tanned, with a spattering of freckles across her nose and cheeks, and the fine hair on her arms glowed golden against it. She appeared not to be wearing any makeup, but her reddish-blond lashes were long and her lips were a deep natural pink.

"Dame Valerie, can I ask you something?" he ventured bravely.

She took a drink of tea, and her fork hovered over her plate, waiting to dive again. "Sure, Jack, what do you want to know?"

"Well, today I watched you at the faire . . . and I was just wondering if you'd ever rodeoed, because you ride like you do."

She laughed gently. "The secret's out! Yeah, I was a pretty good barrel racer and pole bender in my younger days. When I was in high school in San Angelo, I was state-ranked, and I was All-Around Cowgirl my senior year. But that was a long time ago."

"I was a calf roper myself, an even longer time ago. You must keep in practice to do what you do at the faire."

"I have to. During the week, I ride in the shows at the Medieval Nights Dinner Theatre in Dallas. Mostly I just ride in the opening procession, and later I'm the Persian Ambassador in the *dressage* exhibition. My costume covers my face so you can't tell I'm a woman. Sometimes I get to do the questing show as myself, but I never get to joust—only the stunt guys do that."

"Well, I bet you could do it, and from what I've seen you do so far, you'd be mighty good at it."

"Why, thank you, Jack. It's nice of you to say so. And you're a pretty fine cook, if you don't mind my saying so. I can hardly wait for the Convergence, now that I know you'll be barbecuing." She wolfed the last bite of the spaghetti and handed the empty plate to Trick. "Gotta go now. I was late for lessons, so I better not be late to the Round Table. Thanks for the supper. Be seein' you!"

Trick watched her hurrying through the mess hall, and out the back door. He tried to see which direction she went after that, but now that the sun was setting, the shadows of the buildings were long and she vanished into them. He truly wanted to know where the Round Table might be located . . . but he also wanted one more glimpse of Dame Valerie. He guiltily admitted to himself that in spite of his deep feelings for Tay, he found Dame Valerie quite appealing. He also had to admit that he was twice her age—and that was depressing.

He completed the kitchen chores, but hesitated before heading out to the site where Reggie and the others were working on New Glastonbury Abbey, under cover of the approaching darkness. He was bushed, and yearned for a good night's sleep, but knew that he should at least make an appearance out at the renovation of the missile bunker. If the Knights worked mostly at night and rested during the day, it was unlikely he would get to know any of them well enough to ask questions, so his opportunities for encountering Brian Brannan would narrow once again.

He found a beat-up five-gallon insulated container, stained pink inside from some long-ago batch of fruit punch, and filled it with tea brewed on the propane stove. He dumped in the last of the day's ice from the freezer and clamped on the lid, grabbed a sleeve of plastic beverage cups, and hoisted the heavy jug up onto his shoulder before striking out alone for the underground installation. As Trick followed the pathways in the waning daylight, he found all the gates shut but unlocked, and he was careful to shut them behind him as he passed through.

When he got within sight of the missile bay doors, he could hear the buzz of electric saws and the pounding of manual and pneumatic hammers. He made his way down the concrete steps cautiously, still balancing the jug of tea on his shoulder. At the bottom, he found a beehive of activity: a team of a dozen men had already begun the transformation of the concrete box in the ground into the venue for the coming Convergence of their King. Some were up on ladders, sanding away flakes of paint that decades of seeping moisture had peeled from the ceiling. Others were sawing two-by-fours and assembling them into small rectangular trusses. Over to one side, Reggie was pulling wires through a pipe conduit toward a newly-installed circuit breaker box. He saw Trick and called out, "Hey, Jack! Glad you're here! Come on in and pick your project—we need help with everything."

"I brought a jug of iced tea for everybody," Trick announced. "Figured we'd be thirsty before long." The men voiced their thanks, and he set the jug on top of a paint can. Almost immediately he was recruited by the building crew, and learned they were constructing a chancel—a stage upon which the Convergence ceremony would be performed. The trusses would become supports for levels of two different heights, plus steps up to it.

Once he had gotten busy again, Trick forgot how tired he was and worked far into the night with the rest of the men. Conversation around him was cordial, but guarded, since he had not yet been officially admitted to the fellowship as a full-fledged Knight. Still, he felt welcome and appreciated for his efforts, and when the building crew finally did knock off, an hour or two before daylight, he felt as if he had won the trust of all his companions.

Sleep came quickly when he climbed into his bunk in the B.O.Q. in the room he shared with Reggie and the other unmarried Knights, but so did his wakeup time. Born a ranchman, his eyes opened automatically every morning at five-thirty, Central Standard or Daylight Savings Time, no matter what time he had closed them the night before. It was Sunday morning; he doubted that anyone here would arise early except for whatever worship services were customarily practiced, so there would be no need of early breakfast.

Still, once awake, he could not linger in bed, so he got up and took advantage of the deserted community shower room, adjacent to the sleeping area. When he was finished, he dried off with the small, threadbare towel he'd brought with him from Joyous Gard, and checked his reflection in the cracked and clouded mirror. What he saw startled him—had he not looked at himself all week? The man staring back at him could not be the same one who had left Tay's condominium only a week ago.

He realized he hadn't shaved since Shack's reception, but the blond stubble he'd neglected last weekend now bronzed the lower half of his face with something that looked like a real beard. It was even and well-defined, even in its early stage of growth, and its few strands of gray at the corners of his mouth gave him a rather digni-fied appearance. He stroked his hands down his cheeks, amazed at the transformation. With his damp hair slicked back from his face, drying into unkempt waves down the back of his neck, he looked like a character out of Merryborough. *All I need now is an earring,* he thought, grinning.

Quietly, he dressed in his one other set of clean clothes and tiptoed down the stairs to the dim kitchen, where he filled an old-fashioned percolator with water and coffee and set it on the stove, just in case someone got up before noon. While waiting for it to perk and wishing for a Sunday newspaper, he watched the sun come up from the eastern horizon and let his mind wander in pleasant thoughts of being out on the ranch at sunrise, miles from any-where, with a horse under him and cows all around him. He cursed his decision to be here instead of there; if all he did in a week on the ranch was to find and bring in one stray, he would have accom-plished more than he had since he had taken on the same task here.

He poured himself a cup when the coffee was ready, and drifted back to the narrow window that was at eye level to the ground outside. Something moving caught his eye, but he passed it off as another "figment" until he saw two sets of red brake lights and white backup lights blink on in the shed. He didn't hear engines until the two vehicles had backed out and started down the road toward the main gate. One was Dame Valerie's turquoise pickup, the other was an older, four-door Pontiac. Since he'd heard no stirring in the B.O.Q., he assumed that both Dame Valerie and the occupant(s) of the other car were dwellers in the private quarters he'd walked through briefly upon his arrival here. Trick guessed Dame Valerie was heading for her last performance of the season at Merryborough; he was disappointed that she had not come by for breakfast first, even though he was convinced that someone her age wouldn't be attracted to someone his age. Still, it didn't hurt to pretend.

Soon he did get a couple of breakfast customers: a young woman and a girl of about eight came into the kitchen, apparently ready to scrounge for some cold cereal, and were delighted by the Trick's offer of a hot breakfast on a Sunday morning. Although pickings were skimpy in the New Cadbury pantry, Trick was able to stir up some pancakes, which he served with some thin maple syrup and some fried bologna on the side. He delighted the little girl (and charmed her mother) by singing the Oscar Meyer jingle for her as he served the sizzling bologna from the grill.

Before long, others trailed down the stairs—men from one end of the building and women from the other—for a share of the simple breakfast feast. Each one praised "Jack" profusely, and Trick accepted their compliments with shy thanks. Last but not least, after most of the others had gone, Reggie appeared at the kitchen door, yawning. Trick laughed and said for his ears only, "It's good to know some things never change. I don't know what I'd do if you made it to breakfast on time."

Revealing the gappy grin that Trick remembered so well, Reggie said simply, "Old habits are hard to break."

"Well, it just so happens, I have one piece o' baloney left." Trick lifted the last slice of bologna from the grill with a spatula and placed it next to a short stack of pancakes. He neglected to tell Reggie that it really was the last slice, and he had planned to eat it himself.

Reggie accepted the plate and a cup of coffee with thanks, and started to take it into the dining room. He stopped, turned, and with a disturbingly serious expression on his dark face, said, "You always were good to me, Trick. I hope I can do something for you someday soon."

Before Trick could reply, Reggie turned away and went into the mess hall to eat.

At eleven, Trick was banished from the mess hall once more while Sir Kevin led a study hour for the Knights. He was getting a little tired of working so hard for the Knights and being excluded from their activities, but he was in no position to argue about it. Instead of going upstairs, Trick decided to walk around outside in the clear summer morning and enjoy some fresh air. The old building had a musty aroma of mildew, and in the kitchen, the smell was compounded by the odor of old grease.

The sun was sailing toward its meridian, promising another scorching afternoon. Trick clung to the shadows of the buildings, partially to keep cool and partially to conceal himself from any who might notice a trespasser on the old abandoned missile base. Between the B.O.Q. and the gate to the missile launch area, there was a small stucco-covered storage shed which he had not especially noticed before, but when he saw someone emerging from its front door, he paid attention. He pulled deeper into the shadow of the B.O.Q. and watched two men and a woman he had not seen before walk out into the sunshine. They paused while one of the men locked the door, but apparently did not see him lurking nearby. The woman was in her twenties, with short blond hair, and attractive legs revealed by medium-length shorts. The man locking the door was about the same age, with long dark hair slicked into a ponytail, and muscles that bulged through a tight T-shirt and jeans. The other man was much older, slightly stocky in khaki coveralls, with graying hair grown rather long. For a moment, Trick thought he was seeing his genial "ghost" again, but this man had no beard, and his feet crunched lightly in the gravel as did the others' as they moved quickly from the small shed to the gutted barracks where the vehicles were parked. They did not speak during their short walk, and they all got into a compact station wagon and drove away toward the main gate.

When he was certain the strangers were completely out of rear-view mirror range, he crossed over to the shed and peered through its solitary window, which was cracked and jammed open about three inches. Inside was a small, old-fashioned duplicator, with paper and printing supplies neatly stacked on shelves along the opposite side of the interior. Beneath the window was a rusty metal sink in a narrow, ink-spattered countertop. Opposite the front door, behind the duplicator, was another door that did not lead outside. Trick thought it odd that such a small storage shed would have an enclosed closet; and it was also odd that three adults would be comfortable for very long inside the tiny room that looked barely big enough for one person to move comfortably around the duplicator. Maybe, he thought hopefully, this simple shed, which housed the print shop, also concealed the way to the mysterious Round Table, and the people he had seen were some of its privileged inhabitants.

Trick returned to the sheltering shadows of the B.O.Q. just in time to look totally innocent as the Knights were dismissed from their lessons. He was much less resentful of his exclusion now, because, for the first time in a week, he felt like he had at least a slim lead on where the Knights hid whatever secrets they kept, and, possibly, the whereabouts of Brian Brannan. He now looked forward to the next opportunity to be excluded from Knightly duties so he could snoop a little more in that direction.

One way or another, I'll get the information Tay needs, he thought. *That is, if she's still interested in hearing it from me . . . and if I ever get out of here.*

ONE MILE AWAY, CROUCHING BEHIND THE CREST OF A HILL, TAY SILVESTRI peered through binoculars and watched the third vehicle she'd seen leaving the compound today emerge from the main gate and turn onto the gravel road toward the Interstate. "Baxter," she said into her handset. "Here comes another one. Looks like a Subaru wagon, dark gray."

"Roger that," replied Lonnie Baxter, as if speaking over a two-way radio instead of on a crystal-clear connection through the FBI's satellite phone system. After a moment, he said, "Got it. I'll run the tag while Jim tails 'em."

"Who's in the car?"

"Front seat, man and woman, early twenties, she's driving. Back seat, older guy with long hair."

"Is it Trick?"

"Not unless he's turned gray-headed since you've seen him. No, this guy's closer to sixty."

"Damn," grumbled Tay. "Okay, Bax, call me when you have something. I'm calling Jim now." Tay pushed the *end* button, then punched in Jim Benavides' car phone number.

"Benavides," came the immediate answer.

"Gray Subaru wagon, coming your way. Baxter's chasing tags and title now."

"I'm on 'em. How are you, Tay?"

"Hot. I wish I could see something besides the front gate and the top of a building."

"I should be able to get that satellite photo and thermal analysis later today. It'll be from night before last, but I can't get anything newer without a higher clearance."

"What about a night scope for tonight?"

"Impossible. And even if I could get one, we're not sitting out there tonight."

"Whattaya mean, we're not?"

"I mean *I'm* not, and *you're* not. We both have to work tomorrow, Tay. On real, official, authorized cases. I know this is important, too, but we don't even know for sure that Trick or your nephew are there. And until we can get a better view of the place, there's no point in a twenty-four-hour stakeout."

Tay sighed. "You're probably right. I appreciate what you're doing, Jim, I really do. You and Baxter are great to help me with this."

"You can thank us by not getting us caught."

"Where are you now?"

"Eastbound, about halfway through the Weatherford corridor. They're minding the speed limit, and so am I, about five cars back. They're in the center lane, so they won't be exiting right away. Traffic's easy, so I can stay with them. How long are you going to be there?"

"I don't know. Maybe till dark."

"Call me when you come in. I'll bring the satellite imagery and some Chinese to your place, and you bring whatever Bax digs up."

"Okay. Be careful, Benavides."

"You too, Silvestri."

Tay switched off her phone and laid it down in the dirt beside her. She hated to admit that Benavides was right, but apart from giving Baxter a heads-up—he was on the county road, a quarter of a mile from the front gate, disguised as a telephone lineman up on a cherry-picker—there was little she could do from her current vantage point. And unless Bax could turn up anything through the Department of Public Safety computer, there wasn't much hope of getting a warrant and approaching the compound. They couldn't even make a case for trespassing on Federal property, because the U.S. Government no longer owned the land—it now belonged to Tarleton State University in Stephenville, but no one she talked to at the college seemed to know anything about it.

It was the most frustrating thing she had ever banged her head on as a trained investigator: Without the use of the FBI's vast resources, except for what Jim could finagle for her, her effectiveness was practically zero. She found herself resenting Trick for butting in and getting her mixed up in it. Maybe Jim was right about other things as well . . . maybe she *did* need some space in that relationship, and she determined to discuss it with Trick the moment he emerged from his role as the dilettante detective.

In the meantime, she could only sit in the hot sunshine, gaze through her high-powered binoculars at all the inactivity at the old military base, and hope that he was all right.

CHAPTER TEN

As THE TIME OF THE PROMISED CONVERGENCE DREW NEARER, THE level of excitement at New Cadbury compounded daily; and though he was smack in the middle of it all, Trick was forced to remain outside of it. Isolated by his un-Knighted status and saddled with the growing responsibility of the New Cadbury food service, his only contact with the Knights at all was when he served their meals or when he joined the building crew down in the missile bunker. If it had not been for Reggie, who found some time each day to visit with him, friend to friend, Trick might have gone for days without speaking to anyone except in passing.

On the Monday night before the scheduled Convergence, Trick was working alongside the other Knights, stapling a black fabric "skirt" to the front of the now-completed chancel/stage, when a loud whistle echoed in the emptiness of the underground concrete cathedral. Everyone looked up when a voice called out, "Anybody up for a little recreation?" Standing at the bottom of the main stairs were Sir Kevin Kay and the young man Trick had seen leaving the printing shed Sunday morning.

"Who's the guy with Sir Kevin?" whispered Trick to the Knight he was assisting with the skirting.

"That's Sir Travis Gawaine," answered the Knight, making a gesture for silence.

Sir Kevin announced, "The Grand Arms has arrived, and I need everyone's help bringing it down and hanging it. Afterward, since you've all been working so hard, Sir Travis will take you on a night maneuver, just for fun!"

The response from the Knights was enthusiastic, and everyone followed the two Round Table Knights up the stairs and into the warm, dark cover of the Texas summer night. No one objected to his accompanying them, so Trick fell in and waited in silence for further instructions.

In a moment, a flatbed truck with its headlights dark approached from the gate in the double fence, and parked beside the missile bay door. In the soft starlight, what appeared to be a large roll of thick carpet was secured to the truck bed with ropes. Trick hefted his share of it when it was untied, and the coarse backing scraped his bearded cheek as it came off onto his shoulder. It smelled woolly but clean, like new carpet ought to smell. The Knights moved as one toward the missile bay door, and the ground beneath their feet vibrated with the dull rumble that sounded underground. The missile bay doors creaked and opened slowly downward, and light streamed out into the summer darkness.

Just as the doors reached maximum clearance, the light began to dim again as the lift groaned upward, its platform filling the doorway almost completely when it became flush with the ground. *Well done, Reggie*, thought Trick—he had, as promised, gotten the missile elevator back in "Def-Con" readiness. The platform budged not at all when the men dropped the Grand Arms upon it, nor when they all got on and rode down with it. As they sank into the lighted chamber below, Trick saw that the burdensome Grand Arms were indeed much like a carpet, but its edges were not square. In fact, the ends of the roll were quite irregular, and of many colors. He could tell nothing of it until he and the others muscled it off the lift and onto the chancel, where it was unrolled and recognized by all.

"Behold, gentle Knights," said Sir Kevin reverently, "One of the many treasures for the glory of King Arthur in his Abbey."

"Grand" was an understatement of the magnificence of the Grand Arms of the Knights of the Once and Forever King. The full heraldic "achievement," including a shield and crest and all the proper elements of a coat-of-arms, had been worked in meticulous detail in thick, plush yarns, latch-hooked by hand in a deep pile and sculpted into an almost three-dimensional appearance. It was at least twelve feet long and ten feet wide. The smaller versions Trick had seen on the door and in the chapel at Joyous Gard were poor "country craft" copies of this. The golden dragon, with its head turned backward, looked almost ready to spring from the red shield. Above the dragon, the top half of the shield was blue, with three golden crowns spaced across it. Atop the shield, a closed helmet positioned full-face supported another, more ornate crown, and from flames around the crown rose a golden phoenix. Around the helmet and shield twined a scrollwork of gold with an underside of silver, dotted with small black markings like arrowheads. To the left of the shield stood a baldpated gold lion with its tail between its legs and shackles around its neck and hind legs. On the right stood an eagle, similarly shorn and shackled. Both lion and eagle stood upon a likeness of the earth, with the western hemisphere visible, and beneath this, the motto, which Trick had heard spoken but never seen written, was lettered upon a broad ribbon.

All the Knights murmured respectfully as they admired the Grand Arms, and Trick was just as awed by its beauty as the rest. He was startled when Sir Kevin asked suddenly, "Jack, why don't you blazon the Grand Arms for us and prove that you learned something while you were at Joyous Gard."

Trick remembered the lessons in heraldry he'd studied diligently with his fellow apprentices at Joyous Gard, and recalled the blazon, or description in the language of heraldry, of the arms of the Knights, which he'd memorized, not fully understanding it. But as he carefully spoke the words, pointing to each element as he did so, the blazon came alive in his mind with new clarity: "Gules, a dragon rampant regardant Or, and in a chief Azure, three ancient coronets Or. For his crest, upon the royal helm, the Crown proper, issuant therefrom a phoenix Or rousant enflamed proper; and for his mantle, Or doubled Ermine. The supporters being upon the dexter a Lion coward Or, shorn of its mane, collared and shackled, and upon the sinister an Eagle unquilled and jessed, both rampant upon the Earth proper. And his motto shall be *Arthurus, Rex Quondam, Rexque Futurus.*" Trick was sure that it all symbolized something, but he would not become privy to that knowledge until he was Knighted.

"Well done, Jack!" praised Sir Kevin, and the other Knights offered a spattering of applause. "We'll need to work on your Latin pronunciation a bit, but the rest was all there and in the right order. If I had my sword, I'd Knight you, because you deserve it and you're long overdue for it—but if you can stand to wait a few more days, you can be Knighted by the King himself at the Convergence!"

Trick nodded. "I can wait, Sir Kevin. Thank you."

Sir Kevin clapped his hands together once and exclaimed to the gathered company, "Well, the Grand Arms won't wait until then, so let's get moving." The workers each took an edge and moved the huge wall-hanging closer to its home. The artist or artists who had created it had provided a number of hanging loops on the back. After some careful measuring and leveling, crew leader Reggie drove a series of heavy nails into the freshly painted concrete—which was now a smooth, warm buff rather than the severe institutional green—and the Grand Arms was raised upward and affixed to them.

Once the Grand Arms was hung, the men who had placed it there stood back in awe, for the sight of the magnificent tapestry, now properly displayed, was almost overwhelming. It covered the wall from the ceiling down to the top level of the chancel stage, and occupied almost a quarter of its expansive lateral space.

Then the reverent silence was broken by the voice of Sir Travis

Gawaine, announcing, "Saddle up, gents, it's paintball party time on the prairie!"

Trick felt the cautious, questioning eyes upon him before he actually saw them, and prepared to be left out again. He glanced at Reggie, who said merrily, as if he had read Trick's mind, "Yeah, you too, Jack boy. You're only this far from being a Knight—" He held thumb and forefinger about a quarter of an inch apart—"so you might as well start training like one." Some of the other Knights chimed in their agreement, and with a comradely slap on the back from Reggie, he followed the rest of the crowd to the surface.

Trick was not unfamiliar with the sport of paintball, although he'd never played. It was seldom played in his hometown area, since the desert mountains of the gateway to the Big Bend afforded little in the way of substantial vegetation for cover. His brother-in-law, who lived in San Antonio, was an avid outdoorsman who enjoyed all forms of hunting. If Trick had not known him well for nearly twenty-five years, he would have worried that his sister Sharon's otherwise respectable husband Mark was a homicidal maniac when he had boasted that his best "kills" were on paintball battlefields in the Hill Country of south central Texas. Trick was himself an adequate marksman, but carried a shotgun only for protection from snakes, cougars, and other dangerous creatures that preyed on cattle and the men who tended them. Having been a combat soldier in Vietnam, where he was required to be both prey and predator, this opportunity to "hunt" other humans did not excite him, and in fact gave him a queasy feeling; however, it was part of his acceptance into the greater mysteries of the Knights, and he would do whatever was required to learn those secrets.

A waxing gibbous moon had just risen over the hills behind the compound, casting a cool glow on the warm ground. In the moonlight, Trick saw some others, women as well as men, gathered near the missile launch area compound gate, where the flatbed truck was parked. The construction workers joined the group by the gate, and Sir Travis clambered up onto the truck bed, where he tossed open the lids of two large wooden crates that were jammed behind the cab. From the first box he pulled a handful of plastic masks with clear visors, which looked like welding masks, and tossed one to each of the twenty people assembled around the truck.

"We have a few newbies tonight, so everybody listen up," he announced. "The first and most important rule is to wear your mask at all times. Nobody needs to lose an eye when we're just playing for fun. The second rule is when you're hit, you're out, so raise your hands over your head to signal you've been 'killed.' And even if you're 'dead,' remember rule number one—don't take off your mask until you're completely clear of the field."

Sir Travis began handing out weapons to each participant. Trick examined his paintball pistol quizzically—it looked kind of like a long semi-automatic handgun with an accessory shoulder stock, but the "stock" was a cylindrical canister. Perched on top of it was a rather unwieldy bladder-shaped plastic container with a snap-to-seal lid.

"Okay, everybody, count off by twos," said Sir Travis. "Ones, you get yellow, twos, you get green." Trick was a "two," and was glad when Reggie also sounded off "two." He watched Reggie load the container on top of his pistol with dark, marble-size pellets from a large cardboard box, and he did likewise. The pellets felt smooth and slightly pliable as he poured a handful of them into the opening in his pistol's paintball "magazine."

"How do we tell each other apart?" asked one of the other Knights, who was filling her pistol with yellow pellets.

"Hm, good question." Sir Travis thought a moment, and then said, "Hey, I know—the green team is all guys. We'll be 'shirts and skins.' Shirts off, green team—and that'll give you extra motivation not to get hit!"

Trick unbuttoned his threadbare shirt apprehensively, and laid it on the truck bed with the shirts doffed by the others. He was the oldest person present, and he was painfully aware of it when he noticed the firm upper bodies of the younger Knights on his team

in the moonlight. However, he was in a little better shape than
Reggie, who had some "love handles" that drooped over the waistband of his jeans; he also had two large, old scars surrounded by
suture marks, which made odd shiny patterns in the short black
hair that covered his chest—his souvenirs of Vietnam.

"Your mission is to capture and hold New Glastonbury Tor,"
announced Sir Travis, and he pointed eastward to the craggy hill
that rose up behind the missile launch area, slightly taller and more
sharply peaked than the others around it. "Remember that the Tor
is as holy a place as the Abbey, and defend it as you would your
own home. Now, masks on, everybody, and test-fire your weapon
before you deploy."

Trick put on his protective mask and did as the others, firing at
the ground some distance away. The pistol recoiled only slightly as
a blast of compressed air from the canister hurled the paintball
with the sound of a tennis racquet hitting a ball—*thwock!*—and
splattered it harmlessly on the rocky ground. One player's pistol
malfunctioned, but a change of air canister made it right. Then Sir
Travis barked, "You have five minutes to take cover. When you
hear my signal, you may begin. Go!"

"Come on, Jack, you're with me," called Reggie, and dashed
toward the south side of the Tor with some of the other "skins."
Both he and Trick were slightly breathless when they huddled down
behind a clump of mesquite within a few yards of the base of the
Tor. When a whistle shrieked in the distance, Trick almost jumped
out of his skin. "Let's go!" Reggie whispered, and they launched
out of their hiding place and onto the "battlefield" at the base of
the Tor. Almost immediately, he heard the *thwock-thwock-thwock* of
paintball pistol fire around him. His long-dormant memories of
combat training bubbled to the surface, and he remembered to
stay low, to move in short, quick and erratic patterns, and to watch
every leaf and pebble. And with the memories of training came the
memories of his last battle in Vietnam . . . he could almost smell
the jungle around him, and feel the mud pulling at his feet. The

lightweight weapon in his hands suddenly gained the weight of an automatic rifle, and the sensation of hostility surrounding him almost overpowered him.

Though his finger trembled on the trigger, when a shadow moved into his sight, he squeezed off two quick shots—*thwock-thwock-pthack!* "Ouch!" yelped a "shirt," caught in the process of moving from his cover by Trick's second shot. He stood up and raised his arms over his head, revealing the dark wet splotch of green paint on his back.

"Good shootin', Trick!" praised Reggie as the "casualty" marched forlornly back to the base with his weapon raised high to signal his "demise." "We got the edge on these kids with the training we got from Uncle Sam!"

Trick was amazed at the satisfaction he felt—his queasiness had passed, and he was now charged up with the thrill of the hunt. He and Reggie forged up the gentle slope of the hillside, ducking paintballs that whizzed past their ears like giant mosquitoes. Reggie eliminated another "shirt" from the game while Trick covered him.

Mere yards from the crest of the Tor, the action was intense; the air was thick with paint. Trick and Reggie made a dash for the summit, firing in opposite directions as they ran. Then Trick heard a *thwock* at close range, and though only a fraction of a second passed, it seemed like half an hour until the projectile found its mark. It pounded onto the flesh of his chest, making a deep dent in his left pectoral before exploding into a yellow mist that splattered up onto his visor. It burned like a scorpion sting, and he stumbled. Reggie fired off three more rounds before he too received a yellow badge of paint across his darker chest, and fell beside Trick in the dirt near the top of the Tor.

"You okay?" panted Reggie. "Man, we were so close."

"Yeah," Trick answered, although he was scraped and sore, with a splotch of yellow paint covering up what would soon be a purple bruise. "Let's go be dead someplace else."

They struggled to their feet, and just as they turned to walk back down the hill, Trick caught another paintball on his bare back. "Damn!" he cried, and spun around to face his assailant. "Watch where you're shootin', man, I'm already dead."

The "shirt" who had shot him stood up and said, "Sorry! You didn't have your hands up, so I thought you were still a target. Are you okay?" He lifted his visor briefly to get a better look at his "victim."

"Yeah, I'm all right. I think." Trick briefly glimpsed the young Knight's face before he put his visor back down and resumed the game. He wasn't one of the work crew, he was one of the others who had joined the paintball party. He looked to be about eighteen, was tall and had dark eyes, but that was all Trick could tell about him. Yet there was something oddly familiar about him. As he and Reggie started back down the hill—weapons raised to signal they were out of the game—Trick asked, "Who was that kid who shot me the second time?"

"I didn't get a good look at him," answered Reggie, "but it sounded like Sir Brian Bedivere."

"Sir . . . Brian?"

"Yeah—a real smart kid, good with computers. He's Round Table, and from what I hear, pretty tight with Lord Arthur."

Brian! At last! Trick remembered seeing the young man in photographs at the home he had forsaken for New Cadbury. The most recent one had portrayed a pleasant-looking teenager with neatly combed chin-length brunette hair stroked behind his ears, bright brown eyes and an even white smile. He bore a slight resemblance to Tay through his mother. Trick turned and tried to get another look at him, but in the glow of the moonlight, all the combatants looked very much alike.

Finally, after almost two weeks, the mission he thought would take only ten minutes had been accomplished. Brian was alive, well enough to play an energetic game of paintball, and living with the Knights of the Once and Future King at their lair in Palo Pinto County. Trick had only to report this news somehow to Tay and get back to his life. But there were still many questions that needed answering about these Knights who hunted one another for sport, and this trek down the hill, covered in yellow paint, gave Trick an opportunity to ask some.

"Reg, what was the point of this exercise?"

"Paintball? Fun, mostly, but partly practice for the real thing," answered Reggie.

"*What* real thing?"

"We're Knights, Trick. One of these days, and it might be soon, we're going to have to defend our way of life and protect our King. Just like when we were in the Army. Only now, we're in Arthur's army. When the time comes, we have to be used to warfare."

"What do you mean, warfare? Who the hell are we gonna fight?"

"The King will name our enemy at the Convergence when he reveals the meaning of the prophecy. I shouldn't be telling you this, since you're not officially a Knight. But you ought to know what you're getting into."

Trick's stomach made a leap for his throat, silencing his voice in amazement. Did Reggie actually mean the Knights could be involved in bloodshed? What did they seek to gain by it? Part of him wanted to throw his weapon on the ground right then and run deep into the hills in the night, escaping before he heard one more word about prophecy or enemies. The rest of him wanted desperately to know what other surprises lay awaiting, and how Tay's nephew—not to mention himself—would survive them.

CHAPTER ELEVEN

Trick's commission to prepare the Convergence feast was both an honor and an obstacle. On Tuesday, at Sir Kevin's request, he made out his shopping list, which included twenty untrimmed beef briskets and the ingredients for his special seasoning, along with enough potatoes, pinto beans, and peaches to feed two hundred or more hungry Knights.

"Let me go with you to pick out the briskets," Trick said as he handed Sir Kevin his list.

"Better stay here, Jack," advised Sir Kevin as he scanned the list, written on a sheet from a yellow legal pad in Trick's distinctive, narrow hand.

"Well, there's kind of a trick to picking good ones," Trick protested.

"What is it?"

"You get the ones that are vacuum-packed, not shrink-wrapped on styrofoam. Pick 'em up and try to fold 'em in two—if it's too stiff, there's too much fat. If it's too floppy, there's air in the package and it's no good."

"You give up your secrets too easily, Jack," said the young Knight, with a grin. "I think I can get everything you need at the wholesale club. Maybe you'd better stay here and brush up on the Code of Chivalry, especially the third tenet about loyalty to the pledged word. That includes your vow of apprenticeship, in which you promised to keep secret all that you learn and to obey your liege lord."

Before Trick could protest, Sir Kevin walked away. Trick could see that he would not have won the argument anyway, and his feeling of imprisonment took another growth spurt. If it had not been for Reggie, he would have taken the opportunity of Sir Kevin's turned back to scale the chain-link fence and escape. Reggie's presence gave him a thread of familiarity and safety to cling to while he waited for whatever the Knights had in store for him.

Reggie had accepted with enthusiasm the challenge of "scrounging" a barbecue cooker. Trick had described the equipment he needed, and by the time Sir Kevin returned Tuesday afternoon with the provisions, Reggie appeared at the back door of the B.O.Q. kitchen with an unwieldy-looking apparatus crafted from castoff steel parts: an old barrel with a deep dent on one side, rusty hunks of old decking, and a bedframe complete with casters. The barrel was sawn in half lengthwise with hinges welded onto the back so that it opened like a cylindrical treasure chest, with a handle of rebar. A lopsided firebox made of metal decking, about half the size of the barrel, was welded to one end, covering a series of one-inch holes in the barrel; it, too, had a hinged door and rebar handle on its front side. The whole thing sat atop a trolley made of a bedframe, whose casters made the heavy, unattractive device somewhat portable.

"Perfect!" Trick declared. "Reggie, you've outdone yourself!"

Reggie displayed his gappy grin and remarked, "Well, the rest is up to you. Personally, I think you're too fair-complected to cook good barbecue, but your people have made some significant strides in the last several years."

"I never said I could jump, Sir Floyd, but I can cook."

"I look forward to the proof of that bold statement. Later, Trick."

After Reggie left, Trick kindled a fire in the box with dry mesquite twigs he'd collected, then brought from the B.O.Q. kitchen the cooking racks from the oven, which he placed side by side across the bottom of the barrel to hold the meat away from searing heat. Then he loaded in half a dozen briskets, each averaging about ten pounds and rubbed with a mixture of salt and spices. On the back of the rack he placed a small metal bowl filled with water, which would humidify the cooker just enough to keep the meat from drying out during the long cooking cycle. Finally, he shut the cooker lid and wiped his hands. Within an hour, a small pillar of aromatic smoke rose from the open bunghole of the barrel, signifying the beginning of the twelve-hour process that would yield fork-tender, savory beef.

The cooker's fire required constant stoking, but Trick managed to attend to it as well as to his regular kitchen duties. When the Knights gathered for the evening meal, there was much interest in the fragrance that drifted through the B.O.Q. mess hall on the summer breeze. It even drew some of the mysterious Round Table Knights out of hiding: Sir Kevin was there, of course, and Sir Travis Gawaine dropped in, along with the blond woman Trick had once seen in his company; her name, he learned, was Dame Rebecca Gareth. Reggie managed to drift by hopefully every half hour or so, and much to Trick's secret delight, Dame Valerie stopped by on her way to work in Dallas.

Trick took care of the after-dinner kitchen clean-up, then returned to his cooker to replenish the fire. It was almost dark and the stars were beginning to blink in the clear gray-blue sky when a pair of headlights appeared over the crest of the hill. It was a small sport utility vehicle like a Blazer, and it seemed familiar. There were three people in it, but Trick couldn't make them out as male or female before it wheeled into the shadows of the carport.

He returned his attention to his task, but in a moment, he heard footsteps approaching and voices, one male and one female, conversing in low tones. He looked up and saw that the voices belonged to Sir Joshua and Dame Tonya from Joyous Gard. Trick rose to greet them, smiling and wiping his hands on his kitchen apron. Then the third member of the party came into view: a small, stocky figure dressed in a magenta tie-dyed T-shirt ensemble, carrying a small suitcase and handbag.

Trick's stomach sagged to his knees when Diane cried out "Jack!" and ran between the two Knights. She dropped her luggage in the dirt on the way and spread her arms as wide as her smile. "Whoa, honey, I'm too dirty to hug," he cautioned before she reached him, hoping it would stop her.

"I don't care if you've rolled in doggie doo," Diane declared, and wrapped her arms around his neck tightly.

Trick reluctantly returned the embrace and then gracefully wiggled out of it before she suffocated him. "Well, this is a nice surprise," he said, as sincerely as he could. "I didn't think you'd be here until the Convergence."

"I didn't either. Oh, Jack, this is so exciting. I'm going to be Knighted by King Arthur himself at the Convergence, but the best part is—I get to be your assistant!"

Trick's stomach sank to about ankle height, and he asked, "How'd that happen?"

Sir Joshua and Dame Tonya had finally caught up with Diane, and Sir Joshua answered. "New Cadbury steals another good cook from Joyous Gard," he said. "Sir Kevin called earlier today and told Sir Jeffrey that you were already working on the Convergence feast and was worried that you were trying to do too much. Jeff bragged on Diane here a little too profusely, and so Kevin drafted her."

Diane giggled. "Just like you."

Quickly changing the subject, Trick said, "Can I get anybody something to eat or drink? I've already put supper away, but I can fix some sandwiches."

"No, thanks, we ate at Joyous Gard," said Dame Tonya. "Come on, Diane, I'll show you where you'll be sleeping, and you can put your things away. Jack, do you need any help tonight?"

"I think it's under control right now," he answered, and smiled warmly at Diane to brighten the look of disappointment that darkened her face. "I start cookin' breakfast about seven, and I'll need to get the beans on—see you then."

"Okay," agreed Diane, and with a loving glance backward, followed Dame Tonya into the B.O.Q. Sir Joshua turned and retreated to the private-quarters barracks. When all were out of sight, Trick groaned aloud and sank down onto the ground, covering his head with his arms; from this position, he found it impossible to kick himself.

Shortly after midnight, Reggie stopped by on his way out to the work site and declared, "Trick, if I don't get a taste of that barbecue pretty soon, I'm gonna go mad and bite."

"Whoa, we sure don't want that," replied Trick mischievously. He opened the cooker, speared the nearest brisket with a large fork and dragged it onto a carving board, then shut the cooker. In the dim light of a kerosene lantern, Trick approved of the even blackening of the brisket, which sizzled and steamed on the carving board as he sliced off a hamburger-sized piece from its thin end with a long curved knife. He quickly replaced the remainder in the cooker before preparing the piece he'd cut off. First, he scraped off all the fat and trimmed the overcooked edges. Then, as he held the piece of meat with the fork, he gracefully shaved off half a dozen thin slices. The meat was done on the outside but slightly rare on the inside, with a red edge beneath the crusty surface that proved that the seasoning and smoke had penetrated just right. Trick took the first bite, and a satisfied grin creased his face: It had the perfect combination of mildness and piquance and was as tender as butter. He served Reggie a slice and said, "Be honest now. Don't try to spare my feelings."

Reggie devoured his sample eagerly and licked the amber grease from his fingers. "Any man who can cook like that," he declared, his eyes shut in ecstasy, "is a brother of mine. I take back that racially insensitive remark I made earlier."

They each had another slice and shared a drink from Trick's can of tepid Dr Pepper. They were silent a moment in the quiet camaraderie of the starlight, then Trick dared to raise a few sensitive issues of his own. "Reggie, will you trade me a secret for the barbecue?"

"I dunno, Trick. What do you want to know?"

"I'm just confused about this whole business, Reg. I've been here the better part of a week and I'm tired of being clueless. I can't go to meetings, I can't leave the premises, and no one will talk to me but you. What's gonna happen Friday night after we chow down all this food?"

"Lord Arthur will reveal the meaning of the prophecy, among other things."

" 'The lion and eagle shall fall and the dragon shall rise'? You mean you don't already know?"

Reggie shrugged. "Well, in a general sense, but not the specifics. That's Round Table stuff, and I'm a long way from Round Table. But we'll all find out Friday from Lord Arthur."

"There really *is* a King Arthur? Have you seen him?"

"Oh, sure, lots of times! He stays pretty close to the Innermost Circle, though he does get out a couple of times a week with some of the Round Table Knights."

"Do you know where the Innermost Circle is? Have you been there?"

"Uh-huh . . . but I can't tell you that, Trick—sorry."

"Okay. One more question, and I'll shut up and cook. What happens after the Convergence?"

Reggie sighed, and knitted his dark brows for a second. He took another bite of barbecue and chewed it a long time. Finally, he said, "One of two things. One, the prophecy comes true, and our purpose comes to fruition. Two, the prophecy comes true . . . and we're all screwed."

Trick swallowed hard, dumping a lump of fear on top of the meat in his stomach. "What if it doesn't come true?"

The gappy grin showed briefly in the starlight. "O ye of little faith," said Reggie. "Thanks for the barbecue," he added, and gave Trick a friendly smack on the arm before disappearing into the darkness on the way to New Glastonbury Abbey.

Trick found it quite easy to remain awake with the cooker. A nagging, unspecific fear eroded his flagging confidence and stretched his nerves like a faucet dripping in the night. As the night wore on, his eyelids stung with smoke and sleeplessness, but he could not shut them for wondering what might lie ahead. *A man with half a brain would already have bailed,* Trick chided himself again and again. *Lord, I hope you're still in the business of looking out for idiots.*

In the long hours before sunrise, as he sat propped up against the building, Trick found himself nodding off, then jerking awake. After the third occurrence, he roused himself, grumbling, and stoked the fire. Overnight barbecue watch was never intended to be a solitary vigil; it usually involved a number of ersatz cooks, picnic coolers full of beer, and merrymaking beneath the stars. As he stuffed more mesquite twigs into the firebox, he recalled fondly the last time he had supervised a barbecue party—the previous Labor Day weekend, when his brother and sisters and their families had gathered at the ranch near Alpine for the annual McGuire family reunion. It had been an especially happy time, because Tay had been with him; and more so, because his parents, with whom he lived, gave tacit approval to his committed but unmarried relationship with Tay by not putting up a fuss about their sharing his room. Usually when Tay visited the ranch, she slept in the guest room out of courtesy to Hugh and Maureen's old-fashioned values. But with a houseful of company, there was no room for sleeping single, so they bunked together and no one said an unkind word about it. She was now part of the family.

The thought of happy times that might never come again burned his heart like the rebar handle on the firebox burned his fingers as he pushed the door shut. He used a singed, greasy potholder to secure it, then used it to fan away from his tired eyes the smoke from the refreshed fire. From the dark distance, Trick thought he saw a shadow slowly approaching, but it faded into the darkness like a puff of smoke from the cooker. He ignored it, blaming his fatigued imagination, and massaged his itchy eyes with the heels of his hands. When he looked up, he was not alone.

Standing a few feet away, barely within the feeble glow of the camp lantern, a short, stocky old man with a grizzled beard and a Merryborough costume regarded him curiously. Trick was momentarily startled, but smiled and said, "Well, hello there. Haven't seen you around in awhile."

The old man smiled in return, but said nothing.

"Want a bite of the brisket? I was just going to try it myself."

The old man moved a step closer, but shook his head.

"You don't know what you're missing," Trick teased, and opened the lid of the cooker. Swiftly, he carved a bit more from the brisket he and Reggie had sampled earlier, then closed the lid before trimming it out. He took a bite; it was almost perfect, and he hummed a satisfied little sound. "You're sure?" he asked the old man once again. As he raised the second bite toward his mouth, his eyes unfocused, and he suddenly felt as if he had been shoved backwards into a small, dark room with a tiny window in it. Then, just as suddenly, his focus and viewframe raced back into proportion, and he tasted the spicy coating of the meat just as he swallowed it. He did not remember chewing it.

"It is toothsome indeed, sir," said the old man, "and I beg your pardon for the liberty."

Trick choked a bit and coughed, not so much from the strange incident but from the surprise of hearing the old man speak—the first time since they had encountered one another in Merryborough.

The old man stepped backward, with a concerned expression on his weatherbeaten face.

"Excuse me," coughed Trick. "I'm okay. Got a little of it in the wrong pipe."

Without preface, the old man said, "I know why you are here."

Trick stifled a cough and stared at the old man who seemed to be blending into the darkness—or was the lantern merely low on fuel and dimming out?

"I, too, follow a quest for another's soul. Perhaps we may assist one another."

Trick took a step toward the old man, who put up a hand to stop him. "I will return," said the voice, which seemed to fade like the figure into the night and the swirling smoke. "Anon, be ye ware. He is a liar."

And he was gone.

Trick rubbed his eyes some more and shook his head hard, as if to clear away the smoke. "Wait a minute!" he called softly into the night, jogging a few steps in the direction into which the old man had vanished. "Who are you? What are you saying?" But the darkness yielded no answer. As he sank down onto the ground next to the building, Trick groaned and lamented his lack of sleep, which was making him hallucinate again. But now, not only was he seeing things, he was hearing and feeling things. Some part of it had to be real . . . didn't it?

A FEW MINUTES BEFORE SEVEN, AS HE WAS MEASURING COFFEE INTO A newly-acquired electric coffeemaker in the B.O.Q. kitchen, Diane appeared in her lavender outfit, reporting for duty. "Good morning, Jack," she said cheerfully. "I'm ready to work. What's first?"

"Oh, we kinda play breakfast by ear, since so many here work all night and sleep all day," he answered. "I guess you could go ahead and start setting out the plates and stuff—they're in the cupboard over here. We'll need about half a dozen kid-sized cereal bowls, too."

Diane quickly assimilated herself into the kitchen, chattering merrily as she worked. "I'm glad there are children here. I love little ones. I hope I can have a few of my own before that old biological clock of mine runs down."

Trick did not feel much like chattering, and only replied, "You got lots of time, honey."

"I like to hope we both do," she said, and touched him lightly on the arm.

Tired as he was, Trick estimated he could be over the chain-link within fifteen seconds. Fortunately, a woman, a man, and two children appeared in the mess hall door and saved Trick from having to respond more politely to Diane's early-morning adoration. He gently wriggled out of her grasp and said, "Honey, why don't you go introduce yourself and see what these folks want, and I'll get the grill fired up."

A better-than-average crowd showed up for breakfast that morning, and kept Trick and Diane busy for well over an hour. Afterward, they had a bit of breakfast themselves, then washed the dishes and cleaned the kitchen. By mid-morning, Trick was exhausted, and said, "Diane, we gotta get the beans on to soak pretty quick, but if I don't get some shut-eye, I'm gonna be useless. Can I leave you to do that for awhile?"

"Sure, Jack, just show me where everything is and I'll take care of it," she said eagerly.

"I knew I could count on you, honey."

"And you always can. Sweet dreams, sweetheart."

Trick left Diane picking through pounds of pinto beans and climbed wearily up the stairs to the room he shared with Reggie—who had not come to breakfast this morning but was not in his bunk—and several other single men. He climbed into his bunk and shut his eyes, which were itchy from fatigue and mesquite smoke, but sleep did not come right away. He had never felt so stressed in his life—his mind was playing tricks on him again; and if that weren't enough, a woman he did not love was in love with him. The woman he loved was estranged from him. The woman he lusted for was totally uninterested in him. And, depending on variables too cosmic for comprehension by the un-Knighted, the only thing certain about the future was that the lion and eagle were going to fall and the dragon would rise. As sleep finally overcame him in the warm morning light, he imagined that with his luck, the lion and eagle would fall right on top of him, and he'd enter the Pearly Gates covered in fur and feathers. It was an amusing thought until he began to see images of Vietnam in black and white . . . this time with an old man in rustic clothes who warned of danger, but not in time to save him.

CHAPTER TWELVE

AS THE SUN BEGAN TO SINK IN THE WEST ON THE EVENING OF THE Convergence, Trick paced the B.O.Q. mess hall kitchen, making certain everything was ready to go. The brisket was trimmed and sliced, ready to be served with his secret recipe sauce; the beans were cooked tender-firm, in a well-seasoned liquid (but without the beer for flavoring which produced Trick's favorite, *borracho* beans); the creamy potato salad, loaded with hard-boiled eggs and pickles, was blended and safely stored in the refrigerator until just before serving time; loaves of thick-sliced bread were buttered and wrapped in aluminum foil and staying warm on the stovetop; and a mammoth peach cobbler continued to bubble and brown in the oven, mingling its sweet and spicy fragrance with the other delicious aromas that permeated the otherwise dismal old building. Everything was set: Plastic dishes and flatware and paper napkins were stacked at the beginning of the serving line, and at the end, plastic cups were ready to be filled with ice from the half-dozen large plastic ice chests lined up neatly beneath the serving tables and with tea or water from insulated picnic coolers.

Is anyone gonna come help me eat all this food? Trick thought apprehensively, for at the moment, he was by himself in the mess hall. It was getting on toward nine; wasn't anybody going to show up until the Convergence itself, which was planned for midnight?

He had worked himself ragged since rising from his nap shortly after noon, and desperately needed to get a shower and put on clean clothes, but he could not leave his week's work unattended. But at last, Diane scurried into the kitchen, flushed and breathless, freshly showered and coiffed. She had taken special care to look nice on this Convergence evening, whether for the Convergence itself or for Trick's approval or both—she had coaxed her short frosted hair into curls, put on a few touches of makeup, and forsaken her perennial T-shirt ensemble for a denim skirt and dress shoes with low heels. However, the blue cotton blouse she wore was obviously one of her own creations, conservatively hand-decorated with colorful fabric appliqués outlined in raised metallic gold paint. Around her left arm she wore her embroidered red armband.

"Very pretty," remarked Trick as she breezed past him to wriggle into her apron, and her smile brightened the dimness of the mess hall at dusk.

"Thank you, kind sir," she replied demurely, with a little nod. Then she grabbed a cuptowel, rolled it into a rat-tail and flicked it at him mischievously. "Now scoot! I'm here, and I'll watch things while you go clean up."

"Thank you, darlin'," he said warmly, grateful for her assistance, if not her company. He hurried up the stairs to his dormitory room, where his roommates were in various stages of attire. To his dismay, he discovered that they had used all the hot water, so his shower was a brief and brisk one, but he did wash his hair. When he emerged, he quickly buttoned into his hand-me-down best—faded but intact jeans and a worn white dress shirt with a tiny cigarette burn on the pocket. He gave his boots a quick lick with a dry towel, then checked his reflection in the cracked mirror that hung on one end of the lockers in the room. He scarcely recognized himself: His hair and sparse beard were still slick and wet, and appeared darker than they really were. His own blue eyes looked back at him from a face that looked somehow ancient, wise. It was not a bad look, but it bothered him, because he knew this was not the face he had brought with him to New Cadbury. Briefly he considered shaving the beard, but there wasn't time. Remembering Diane wearing her armband, he stuffed his own carefully into his back pocket.

Reggie suddenly appeared in the stairway door and called out, "Hurry up, guys, they're starting to arrive, and we've gotta park 'em." He was smartly styled in deeply pleated gray dress slacks with shiny black shoes and a dark purple band-collar silk dress shirt. He slapped high-fives with the other dressed-up Knights as they bustled out of the room. Trick self-consciously dusted his shirt front as he took in Reggie's finery and once again lamented his lost snakeskin boots. He followed the others downstairs and returned to the kitchen. The others hurried outside to create order among the swarm of amber parking lights that were appearing in the twilight like dozens of oversize fireflies, visible to Trick through the cloudy kitchen windows. People began to file into the basement mess hall in groups of three or more, laughing and excited, and before very long, the crowd Trick had despaired of seeing was taking on multitudinous proportions.

Sir Kevin rushed into the kitchen and without greeting or preface, announced, "Jack, I need you to go ahead and fix up nine dinners 'to go' for Lord Arthur and the Round Table. Can you do that right now, please?"

"Yes, sir, Sir Kevin," answered Trick, and went into action. Diane overheard the orders and also snapped to, dealing out plastic plates on the serving counter for Trick to fill with generous portions of meat and sauce. She came in behind him and ladled up beans and scooped potato salad onto each plate. While Trick covered each plate with another, inverted plate and wrapped each meal individually in foil, she served up nine helpings of cobbler into plastic bowls and covered them. Sir Kevin stood by watchfully, his appetite adding to the urgency of the production.

When the mountain of foil-wrapped containers was ready to go, loaded into half a dozen plastic grocery sacks, Trick calmly asked,

"Do you need me to help you carry all this, Sir Kevin?" More than anything he hoped for a look at the "Innermost Circle."

"No, thank you, Jack," answered the seneschal of New Cadbury. "Sir Brian is on his way here to help me."

Trick's heart skipped a beat at that moment, and again a moment later, when the slender young man in loose-fitting white pants and shirt appeared in the kitchen doorway. For the first time, Trick got a good, close-up look at the boy who was the reason for everything he had experienced for the past two weeks, first at Joyous Gard, then at New Cadbury. "Sir" Brian wore his light brown hair in the same way as in the photograph Trick had seen—chin-length, parted in the middle, and swept back behind his ears. A few blemishes dotted the forehead and chin of a face that was just beginning to take on the angular definitions of maturity. Both ears were pierced; the left sported a twinkling white jewel, the other a small hoop with a miniature dagger dangling from it. The penetrating brown eyes in this friendly young face with a wry, asymmetrical grin gave Trick a little shiver—not so much because they bore a family resemblance to Tay's eyes, but because they seemed to be windows on something dark and secret. His armband featured the dragon emblem, and, like Sir Kevin's, three embroidered chevrons.

"Jack, have you met Sir Brian Bedivere?" asked Sir Kevin as the young Knight began to gather up the shopping bags.

"Yes, sir, briefly, but not formally," answered Trick, and seeing Brian's quizzical reaction, added, "The night we played paintball, Sir Brian—we were on opposite sides, and you nailed me a good one."

"Oh, I remember you now," said Brian cheerfully. "You and Sir Floyd had nearly made it to the top of the Tor, but I smoked your butts."

"You could say that," Trick said politely, omitting the mention of the minor detail about already having been "killed" when Brian had splattered him.

Sir Kevin and Brian moved out of the kitchen as quickly as

they could without unbalancing the shopping bags they carried. The elder Knight said to Trick, over his shoulder, "You can begin serving whenever you like. Let's get everyone fed and ready to go to New Glastonbury Abbey by eleven o'clock." He disappeared without waiting for a response.

The crowd began to queue up at his makeshift serving tables in a more or less orderly fashion. Among the dozens of strange faces were familiar ones he had not seen in several days: Dames Anne and Jennifer of Joyous Gard, along with Sirs Barry, Dylan, and Cody— but not Russell. Before Trick could do more than wonder about the conspicuous absence of the third un-Knighted member of the Joyous Gard household, Sir Jeffrey Lancelot's authoritative voice cut through the dull roar of happy greetings and excited speculations to silence the entire room.

"Knights, before we partake of the meal that is ready to be set before us, let us thank our Creator and our King in an attitude of supplication." The sound of right fists striking the left sides of chests echoed dully in the room like the footsteps of a distant army coming to attention. Trick and Diane mimicked this symbolic gesture and stood in meditative silence for a moment with the rest. Then Sir Jeffrey concluded aloud, "By the grace of God and His chosen servant Arthur, the Once and Forever King of this and all worlds, we accept this feast and ask that it strengthen our bodies for his service. Amen."

"Amen"s were murmured, and then the noise level immediately rose to the previous level and beyond as the crowd surged toward the serving tables. Trick and Diane swung into action, filling plastic plates with meat, beans, and salad as they were presented by each "customer." In between plates, Diane scooped ice into plastic cups so each person could pour his or her own drink from the picnic coolers.

Trick tried to count how many men, women, and older children held out empty plates to him to be filled, but he lost count after seventy-eight. Since the normally cavernous mess hall was packed tight with people, most crowded around the banquet tables, some standing and leaning against the wall as they ate, he estimated the number closer to two hundred; Sir Kevin's guess had been a good one. As an accessory to their "Sunday best," each person wore the familiar red armband, most with one chevron, some with two. Those who had earned three were not dining with the lesser mortals.

Once everyone had been served, and second helpings taken by some, Trick and Diane served themselves. Just as they were about to sit down on a couple of emptied ice chests, one last hungry patron hurried up to the serving line.

"Hi, guys, sorry I'm late," said Reggie sheepishly. "Finally got all the cars squared away. Hard to park 'em in the dark. I guess you figured I'd get here eventually, didn't you, er—Jack?"

"I know I can always count on you, Sir Floyd," said Trick with a grin, as he filled a plate with an extra-generous serving of everything for his friend. He pointed to the ice chests behind the tables and asked, "Join us? It may be the only seat left in the house."

"Thanks, but I've got a few last-minute chores to do down in the Abbey. I'll see you there in a little while. Besides," he added, "you two probably want a few minutes of peace and quiet after all the work you put in and before all the shoutin' starts. Save me some leftovers!"

"Will do," agreed Trick, and Reggie saluted him with his plastic tumbler of iced tea as he made a hasty exit.

Trick finally sat down to his own plate, famished. Diane was nearly finished with hers, and bubbling over with excitement. "Just think, Jack, in just about an hour, you and I will finally be Knighted! I can hardly wait!"

"Oh, yeah, I plumb forgot," he answered, his mouth full of a very satisfying combination of flavors.

She made a little sound of exasperation and rolled her blue eyes skyward. "Isn't that just like a man, to forget something that important! And look at you, you're not even wearing your armband that I made especially for you."

"It's in my pocket," he mumbled around a forkful of potato salad, and pointed with his chin in the general direction of his left hip. Diane reached over and plucked the band of red cloth from his pocket, fussed over its wrinkles, then wrapped it around his left arm. She secured the Velcro fastener and stroked the armband smooth around his sleeve; she clung briefly to his arm with both hands, gently clasping his bicep as if to steady herself. She was blushing when she released him, and said merrily, "Well, I guess these leftovers won't put themselves away." She bounced up and began scooping potato salad into a storage container, humming.

Trick's appetite ebbed as a lump of shame grew in his throat. In the early days of this masquerade, "Jack" had done nothing to discourage the feelings which Diane evidently had for him, and now it looked like she was altogether in love with him. Now it was clear that Diane was of no real value as a contact within the Knights, but he had allowed her to get too close to him. There was no reason for the character of "Jack" to resist her, and now Trick was stuck. He swallowed the guilt with the last bite of his barbecue, sighed, then said lightly, "No, I reckon they won't. Let's hurry so we can get on out to New Glastonbury Abbey and get good seats."

With both of them working, they got the leftovers safely stored, the serving trays and utensils rinsed and the trash bags tied with time to spare before the scheduled start of the ceremony, which would take place in the refurbished underground missile bunker. By this time, the mess hall was deserted. "Are you up for a late evening stroll, young lady?" Trick asked as he and Diane hung up their cuptowels. He even offered his arm gallantly, though it pained him to see how glad this small gesture made her.

"I wouldn't miss it for the whole world," answered Diane, and she looped her arm through his and squeezed it close to her soft body. Together they climbed the few steps from the mess hall to the surface and set off at a quick but leisurely pace to try to catch up with the few other stragglers whose silhouettes were visible against the bright, starry sky, across the unkempt terrain between the base and the bunkers.

The night was warm, slightly humid, and silent. There had been a moon earlier, but it had set, leaving nothing in the sky to pollute the starlight. The stars were bright and crisp, hardly twinkling, and so many were visible in the clear country darkness that it was difficult to pick out constellations among them—just like they were over the rugged Davis Mountains of Trick's West Texas home. Trick remembered his boyhood there, when he and his brother and his dad, and sometimes even his mom and sisters, would pitch a tent in a corner of the ranch, maybe a mile from their house. He and his dad always forsook the tent and lay on their backs in their sleeping bags, gazing for hours up at the dazzling display of stars that marched slowly across the night. Trick wondered: Had Tay's brother-in-law, Bob Brannan, ever done that with Brian? He thought not so, or perhaps there would have been better communication between them, and then Trick would not have ended up on this foolhardy covert mission he had devised.

Off to the side, Trick saw a sudden movement out of the corner of his eye, and turned his head to see his mysterious old friend walking along with them, a few yards away. The old man beckoned to him, but did not break stride. Trick's throat clenched with a strange dread, but he managed to say to Diane, "You go on ahead, honey, and I'll catch up in just a second." He gently wrestled his arm away from her and gave her a reassuring little pat on the elbow to keep her moving.

Trick veered off toward the old man, who had stopped behind a twisted mesquite tree, and came within touching distance of him. "Yes, sir, what can I do for you?" Trick asked softly, just in case he really was talking to a ghost.

The old man said, just as softly, "I beg you: Drink not from his cup. It is poison to the soul."

"What do you mean?"

"Hear him, but do not listen, for he lies wondrously, and even those who are strong of wit may be taken a fool. When you have heard all, and know the danger full well, I will come once more to you. Then if you will, may you wield my sword."

Boldly, Trick stated, "Wait just a minute there, old-timer. I'm not wielding a sword for anybody I don't know who they are."

The old man smiled through his white beard. "I am called Owain. That is all I may tell you now, but I will tell all when you are certain of your quest, which is our quest together. See there," he said, and pointed a thick finger in the direction of the bunker. Trick turned his head to see nothing more than the night, the wild shrubbery, and the gathering of the faithful. When he looked back, there was no trace of the old man.

Trick made a little sound of exasperation, and clenched his fists at the night in frustration. He then turned and stalked onward toward the underground assembly hall, trying to sort out whether or not he'd just had a conversation with a ghost named Owain who wanted him to be his swordsman, or if his tired, muddled brain was only conjuring hallucinations again.

He caught up with Diane just as she was about to pass through the last chain-link gate that protected the missile bunkers. She had an annoyed expression on her face and huffed, "Couldn't you have waited until you got here? Surely there are restrooms. What *is* it with guys?"

For a moment, Trick was puzzled, but a grin that was partly relief crept onto his face when it registered that Diane had not seen him talking to his phantom friend and only believed he had gone on an urgent mission of nature. "Sorry, honey, but when you gotta go, you gotta go," he said, and lightly touched the top of his zipper, as if to confirm its closure.

In the bright starlight, silhouettes of the ventilation hoods and doorway bunkers were outlined distinctly, and yellowish light emanated from the stairwell leading down into the central bunker that would serve as the Abbey. As their feet crunched in the gravel and dirt on the concrete surface of the missile launching area, Trick saw that the missile bay doors were open, and the elevator was raised so that its platform was flush with the surface. Light beamed through the narrow cracks all around it, giving it an eerie outline like a doorway into another dimension—just like in the opening titles of the old *Twilight Zone* television show, where just such an image had invited viewers in for a half hour of chills and suspense. Trick was already in enough suspense to last him a lifetime, and the chills that began racing one another up and down his spine were as real as this Midsummer's Eve in the hills west of Fort Worth.

A solitary sentinel stood at the top of the stairs, and called out when he saw Trick and Diane, "Hurry, we're about to start!" Nonetheless, he took time to confirm that they were wearing their regulation armbands before allowing them to descend into the glowing stairwell, toward the light and the buzz of excitement that filled the great room beyond.

"Oh, Jack," breathed Diane, "this is magnificent!"

Indeed it was: A great transformation had taken place since Trick's last visit. The light neutral color of paint which now coated every surface served to make the enormous room look even larger. The completed platform stood at the east end of the room, and was now decorated by a pleated black fabric skirt that masked its wooden supports. Upon the platform, in front of the Grand Arms but not obscuring them, had been placed one large, high-backed armchair built of dark mahogany and upholstered in a rich, wine-colored velvet. On either side of the elegant chair was a low, backless bench, long enough to seat four or five people side by side. On the floor in front of the platform was a small table covered with a white cloth, and upon it was a large open Bible, a smaller, red-covered book that Trick recognized as the so-called Malory Revelation, and a large golden goblet and small silver pitcher, which looked quite old. Beside the platform was an old upright piano that had been painted Wedgwood blue beneath an unskillfully applied antique finish.

The elevator, in its raised position, formed a dividing line in the center of the room. On the platform side, neat rows of folding chairs were set up, and in the first rows of these sat Knights whose armbands bore two chevrons. Behind them sat Knights with only one chevron. On the other side of the elevator were more rows of folding chairs, in which sat the remainder of Knights with one chevron on their armbands. Ushers—one of whom was Reggie— moved about, keeping order among the excited, restless crowd. The guard at the Abbey stair indicated to Trick and Diane that they should take seats on the very last row, next to a young man and a young woman whom Trick had not seen before. The newcomers acknowledged them with nervous smiles, and Trick noticed that their armbands lacked chevrons, also.

The restless crowd grew noiser and more impatient as the stated time of the Convergence passed. Time wore on until almost one o'clock. Finally, a rustling, like leaves blown in a stiff autumn breeze, fluttered through the Abbey as photocopied song sheets were passed along by hundreds of hands. A Knight with two chevrons on his armband stepped up onto the platform and raised his arms, and the noise attenuated to a dull roar.

"Knights, the hour is at hand," he announced. "Let us wel- come the time of Convergence with a glad voice of singing." A young female Knight struck a chord on the blue piano, which was slightly out of tune. Following the words typed on the sheet, Trick and the multitude sang to the familiar tune, "Old One-Hundredth," the new doxology of the Knights of the Once and Forever King:

> *Praise God, from whom all blessings flow;*
> *Soon all who dwell on earth shall know*
> *The day of Arthur now hath dawned,*
> *The King of Earth and Avalon.*

As the "Amen" faded, the sound of a trumpet echoing in the distance caused a hush to fall over the assembly. It echoed a second time, a little nearer—a short, jubilant fanfare of announcement and welcome. Every person in the cavernous room forbore breathing for a moment, and the sound of marching feet could be heard from the surface, crunching in the loose gravel, all perfectly in step. The footsteps halted abruptly, and then the trumpet called again; this time, it was directly above the Abbey, and all eyes turned upward toward the raised elevator in the center of the room.

The click of a switch set machinery into motion, and the reverent silence was drowned by the roar of the old missile elevator as it sank slowly down to its home position. As it descended, Trick saw the backs of nine figures, six male and three female, dressed all in white, with shield designs worked in exquisite detail, front and back, upon white felt tabards, and swords in scabbards belted at their sides.

But the tall central figure was robed in a flowing mantle of glowing red velvet, edged with white fur, and the left arm, visible only as a gleaming *coudière* of golden metal, held in its crook a golden helmet. Trick caught his breath at this magnificent figure, resplendent from head to toe in armor and royal mantling.

"Great gosh-a-mighty," he whispered incredulously. "There really *is* a king!"

CHAPTER THIRTEEN

FOR A FROZEN INSTANT, THE ONLY MOTION IN THE ENTIRE ROOM was the twinkle of a silvery digital-audio disc compact as it was loaded into a player; then the room was filled with a heroic fanfare that Trick recognized vaguely as perhaps the theme from some Spielberg movie or other. Its cascading notes were almost overwhelming as it reverberated in the concrete cathedral like trumpets of a legion of angels.

The congregation sat spellbound as the Knights dismounted the elevator platform and marched up a central aisle to take their places on the chancel beneath the Grand Arms. Not a soul in the room breathed as the music seemed to swirl around the one who stood in the center, like the Christ candle in an Advent wreath, turned and faced his subjects.

The King was in his mid- to late-fifties, with wavy shoulder-length walnut-brown hair liberally salted with silver. Fine lines of age traced spidery patterns around large, wide, blue eyes as disturbingly pale as a sled dog's. They were set close to a large but aristocratically curved nose above thin lips sternly set in a downward-curving bow. A dictionary definition of the word "king" could not have been better illustrated. In his robe and armor he was so stunning to behold that it seemed he radiated light rather than reflected it, and when he raised a gleaming golden gauntlet in greeting and benediction, a single voice shouted over the music, "Long live the Lord King Arthur!" Suddenly the spell was broken, and the cry echoed from voice to voice as the room filled to bursting with cheers and applause.

When the cheering crested, the two Knights nearest the King bowed to their lord, and the one at stage right carefully removed the King's heavy cape while the one at stage left accepted the gleaming plumed helmet. Together they enfolded the helmet inside the cape and situated them reverently behind the King's tall chair; then they returned to their places.

Even Trick gaped in amazement at the King and his splendid retinue, dazzled by their collective beauty. Once his eyes adjusted to their physical and spiritual radiance, Trick recognized most of them by name. At the King's left hand were Sir Jeffrey Lancelot, Dame Rebecca Gareth, Sir Travis Gawaine, and Sir Kevin Kay, who had taken his cape. At his right were a man and a woman Trick did not know, along with Dame Valerie Percival and Sir Brian Bedivere, who had taken the King's helmet.

Sir Travis Gawaine stepped forward to center stage. "Let us now repeat our pledge of allegiance to our Liege and Master's Arms," he said, and his voice at normal speaking volume was clearly audible in the concrete room, even as far back as where Trick was sitting.

Following the instructions of his apprenticeship, Trick followed suit with all the rest of the Knights and apprentices and turned his eyes upward to the Grand Arms, crossed his arms and upraised fist in the salute which he had first seen awkwardly demonstrated by Brian's father, and repeated the pledge that repetition had committed to memory: "I swear allegiance to the Arms of my Liege Lord Arthur, and to the Kingdom for which it stands, universal, eternal, upon Earth as it is in Avalon."

As the echo of the congregational pledge faded, King Arthur seated himself upon his throne, and the Round Table Knights sat as one upon the benches upon either side, careful of the swords at their sides. Only Sir Kevin remained standing, and he moved to center stage as the other Knight returned to his place. "You may be seated," he said, and paused while the two hundred or so in the large room settled themselves onto the squeaking metal folding chairs.

"On behalf of our Lord King Arthur," he continued, "I bid you all welcome to the First Midsummer Court at New Glastonbury Abbey. I am Sir Kevin Kay, Seneschal of New Cadbury. Permit me to introduce the other members of the Round Table: To my left are Sir Jeffrey Lancelot, Dame Rebecca Gareth, and Sir Travis Gawaine; to my right, Sir Brian Bedivere, Dame Valerie Percival, Dame Sarah Dinadan, and Sir Robert Tristram.

"This will be an unforgettable evening, for we shall witness the coronation of our King and share his joyous news of the coming Kingdom. But before we proceed, we have one important matter to attend to. Let us be about the glad business of welcoming into true fellowship and the path to eternal life those whose works have shown their merit for Knighthood. Will the following novices please come forward and stand before the platform: Brandon, Diane, Jack, and Megan."

Inexplicably elated with the same kind of excitement as he had felt prior to his long-ago wedding—glad anticipation mixed with stark terror—Trick made his way through the congregation with the others to stand before the platform. Three other Round Table Knights came forward and stood by Sir Kevin, one in front of each apprentice; Trick stood eye to belt buckle with Sir Kevin, Diane in front of Sir Jeffrey, their former liege from Joyous Gard. The four Knights drew their swords and held them high above the heads of the trembling apprentices as Sir Kevin said, "Will you now swear to obey the Lord King Arthur, the Returned King; to forsake the evil world that you once knew; and to live by the Code of Chivalry in this world and in the next, so help you God? If so, answer 'I will.'"

"I will," chorused Trick and his fellow inductees, and through the moist fabric of his shirt he felt the coolness of the flat side of Sir Kevin's sword touching him first upon the left shoulder, then upon the right. In spite of himself, he could not help but feel very proud—especially when the King himself nodded and raised a hand in benediction.

"Then take the name Pendragon as your own, for you are now a child of the Once and Forever King of Earth and Avalon, with the right to bear arms, resist evil, and mete justice within and without the holy empire now and in the fulfillment to come. Knights, I now present your new brothers and sisters, Sir Brandon, Dame Diane, Sir Jack, and Dame Megan. Be welcome and of service to this court, with all the rights and privileges appertaining to your rank."

Applause accompanied the return of the four newest Knights to their seats in the back of the room. As they took their seats, an usher pressed an embroidered chevron for their armbands into each of their right hands. Diane smiled as her fingers closed around hers, and with her other hand wiped tears away from her eyes. She turned to Trick and whispered lovingly, "I'll sew yours on for you tomorrow, Jack . . . I mean, *Sir* Jack."

"Honey, that's too fancy a name for this old cowboy," whispered Trick in return. "You better just call me plain Jack."

She shook her head. "It makes you even more special . . . especially to me." She wriggled closer to him and laid her hand lightly on his wrist. A sudden fanfare from the sound system saved him from having to reciprocate, as everyone in the room sat up a little straighter, expectantly.

"Brothers and sisters, all, attend," announced Sir Kevin. "We may now proceed with the ceremonies of Convergence. Please rise." When the entire congregation was respectfully on its feet, he announced, "His Highness, Arthur Pendragon, by the grace of God the Once and Forever King of Earth and Avalon!" The recorded fanfare reprised, and no one noticed as Sir Kevin turned and took his seat beside the King's throne—all eyes were riveted upon the

King, who rose slowly, as if the armor he wore were a burden upon him. But when he stood tall before his throne, with the light glittering upon him, he was majestic, breathtaking, terrifying.

Then the severe countenance brightened, adding the brilliance of a smile full of even white teeth to his supernatural radiance. "My children," said the King, in the mellifluous voice Trick had heard many times on tape at Joyous Gard. It needed no artificial amplification, and as this simple acknowledgment rang in every corner of the missile bunker, not even the sound of breathing could be discerned; Trick held his breath with the rest of the captivated congregation.

"My children," said the King, "I am so very glad you are here this night of nights. Tonight we shall witness the beginning of something altogether wonderful, something not yet seen in this world . . . something that will not be forgotten in a thousand lifetimes of men.

"Tonight I have gathered you unto myself in order to send you forth, for I may now set my seal upon the words of the prophecy that you have written upon your hearts. For tomorrow, as I have promised, the Lion and the Eagle shall fall, the Dragon shall arise, and our new kingdom of chivalry will come on earth!"

The King pivoted on his heel and raised his armored arms toward the Grand Arms on the wall behind him, as if reaching upward into an embrace. Like a television weatherman describing atmospheric variances on a map, he pointed out the charges on the Grand Arms with sweeping gestures of his arms. "Behold! The prophecies shewn upon our glorious escutcheon shall soon come to pass. See upon the shield the combination of our ancient arms and the arms of our new kingdom. See how the great Lion of England and the proud Eagle of America shall be shamed and shackled when the Dragon, wielding Excalibur, returns to claim once again his rightful throne. See the phoenix rising triumphantly from the flames—that is the emblem of our resurrection. For *I* am the Dragon . . . and I am reborn. For *I* am the King . . . and I have come to claim my crown!"

Another recorded fanfare sounded, and Sir Robert Tristram stood. The artisan responsible for the beautifully wrought swords of steel sold at Merryborough now held in his hands a satin-wrapped bundle, and he approached the King and knelt before him reverently. He allowed the covering to fall away, revealing a glittering golden crown. It was a tall circlet with four cross-shaped points on it, each set with shimmering jewels of white, red, and purple. The King reached out toward it with both hands and clasped it lovingly. He raised it high above his head as if in an offering to a greater lord. Then he lowered it slowly and placed it upon his own brow. Trick could almost hear the sound of sparkling as the King stood there, majestic, awesome, powerful, caught up in the glory of the moment. His arms slowly spread wide, reaching upward, his fingertips quivering like the wings of an aged eagle soaring skyward. Then, in a voice that almost rocked the earth and echoed throughout the underground chamber, he cried, "By God and by Excalibur, tonight I claim once again my crown, and I shall be King for all eternity!"

A mighty cheer rose from the crowd, and the King rode the adulation like a wave, his arms still outstretched as if to balance upon it. As the cheering crested and fell, his eyes closed, but his luminous smile did not diminish. His arms dropped slowly, and he crossed slowly to the edge of the platform, at center stage. He raised clenched fists and began speaking in a low, deliberate, measured voice.

"My children, my subjects, my soldiers, I may now speak freely. Our Kingdom is at hand. Many plans have been set in motion long ere this night, by me and by my Knights of the Round Table, in whom I trust utterly, and now these plans have come seamlessly together into an opportunity for our first strike against the godlessness and evil that have ruled the world since my first life among men. The battle for Avalon begins at the morrow's dawn, when the banner of the Independent and Sovereign Nation of Camelot is hoist above our lands. Henceforth we are no part of America, a colony traitorous to the ancient crown. Henceforth we are no part of what is now called Great Britain, our ancient homeland, which has been weakened by a succession of bastardy that has become a fattened burden upon the land. Henceforth we claim our birthright as the noble and blessed Celtic race, the rightful rulers of all the world!

"Aye, many events have come together to create this moment, some not of our own making but that of the hand of God Himself. For even now as we stand at alert, the Lion and the Eagle are moving into a place where they may be felled with one stroke of the Dragon's claw. Then all shall look to Camelot as the throne of the world where I, Arthur Pendragon, shall rule with wisdom, benevolence, and a firm hand of discipline. And as my Knights, you are empowered to enforce my obedience, even unto the death, for you need no longer heed any law but that of your King. You need no longer obey any command but that of your King. And you need no longer fear death, for your King has gone beyond that long night into this dawning of a bright new day. I swear by Excalibur that any who shall lose his life for my sake shall be reborn as I was reborn, and shall live forever!

"And now I call upon my Knights to hear and to choose: If you would follow, if you would serve, if you would live and die and live again in a world of Chivalry, if you will stand behind me and beside me in the days and decades to come; if you will obey without question the commands of your King, then at this time, say so, and prepare to receive his blessing. If you will not, then say so, and be cast out in dishonor, and prepare to meet judgment in the coming Kingdom. What say you?"

At first, hesitantly, by only a few: "We are with you, Lord Arthur!" And then, more, and still more, and the momentum of gathering voices built into a pandemonium that shivered the concrete walls of the missile bunker. In the midst of the thunderous approval and acceptance, the King stood with his arms raised, his eyes closed, and his crowned head thrown back, smiling, swaying slightly to the music of his adulation.

And then, without preface, he snapped once again to rigid attention. With a flourish, his right hand seized at the hilt of his sword, and it rang out of its scabbard with a clear, percussive, musical note that attenuated the cheering. He raised it high above his head and raised his left hand in a fist beside it. "Swear now the blood oath with your King and his captains!" he shouted, and the multitude stilled. Dame Rebecca and Dame Valerie rose and moved downstage to the small table, where Dame Rebecca carefully lifted the golden goblet and Dame Valerie the silver pitcher. Together they returned to the King's side.

Dame Valerie gently tugged off the King's left gauntlet, and Dame Rebecca held the chalice before him. With one deliberate motion, and without looking upward, the King crossed his hands at the wrists above his head and slowly drew the entire length of the blade across his left wrist. The blood did not appear for a moment; but when the sword tip had passed, it came in bright red rivulets, coursing down his arm to stain the exposed white sleeve of his shirt. He lowered his hand over the golden chalice, and several large drops of blood fell heavily into the ornamented vessel as he flexed his fingers convulsively over it. Dame Valerie then poured a dark, purplish liquid from the pitcher into the chalice. The King stood for a moment, shivering, eyes wide and unblinking, with his sword still tightly clutched in his other hand. But he shook himself to attention, sheathed the sword, and took the chalice from Dame Rebecca. He held it before himself at arm's length in a gesture of offering and said with surprising calmness, "This is my blood, which once was spilt in defense of Camelot on the field of Camlann, and now flows anew for the resurrection of that glorious kingdom upon this new and sacred land. Whosoever would drink of it shall be filled with the power of that resurrection and shall thereby swear to follow Arthur, the Once and Forever King, beyond death to eternal life." He slowly raised the chalice to his lips and drank.

The King then turned slowly around and served each of the Round Table Knights in turn, beginning with Dames Rebecca and Valerie, and concluding with Sir Kevin. When each member of the Round Table had drunk, he returned the chalice to Dame Rebecca, and sank down cautiously upon his throne. Dame Sarah Dinadan bound a white cloth around his wounded wrist and stood protectively beside him as the other two female Knights moved out into the congregation.

Sir Kevin came forward and said softly (with the help of amplification), "As the Grail is passed, let us each be in a spirit of silent meditation after the example of our King." The pianist began to play softly the now-familiar hymns of the Knights of the Once and Forever King as Dames Rebecca and Valerie efficiently served each person in the room a sip from the Grail. Some of the smaller children, who were being kept awake past their bedtimes, protested tearfully when their mothers or guardians dipped a finger into the grail and touched a drop of the ceremonial liquid to their pouting lips, but every man, woman, and child received a taste of the symbolic blood of King Arthur.

By the time the chalice made it to the back of the Abbey, Trick had resolved not to drink, for the words of the mysterious Owain rang over and over again in his mind: *Drink not from his cup.* He thought it possible that Owain spoke metaphorically—that he meant simply, "Don't believe what he says"—but it was also possible that he specifically warned against drinking from the ceremonial goblet. He knew that the actual blood in it had been diluted to nothing, for the cup had been refilled several times from Dame Valerie's silver pitcher, but the idea of drinking any amount of blood—and from a container shared by nearly two hundred others of undetermined oral hygiene—made him slightly nauseous.

Diane seemed enraptured, and gladly took a small sip from the chalice with her eyes closed reverently. Trick looked on sadly, wishing he could have discouraged her from drinking, just as he planned to do. Then it was his turn. He felt the cool, moist edge of the cup as Dame Rebecca held it to his lips. He clamped his upper lip down, so that no liquid would enter his mouth, but it would seem that he was taking a drink. Just as the warm fluid brushed his mustache, Dame Valerie smiled and and gave him a surreptitious, mischievous little wink that gave Trick such a start that he involuntarily released his liplock on the cup and got a healthy mouthful of some ordinary cheap, sweet wine. The wine went down in one easy gulp, and it was done.

Trick felt his stomach sink, as if the wine landing in it were a lead weight. It had a slight metallic tang to it, which he was sure was due to some acidic reaction to the metal of the cup in which it was served. Since no one at the front of the congregation seemed to be on the verge of convulsions—most were holding hands with his or her neighbor, and humming along to the piano underscore while swaying in time to the music—it seemed unlikely that there would be a replay of Jonestown at New Cadbury. Still, he had the discouraging feeling that he had somehow disappointed his ghostly friend.

At last, all had tasted the "blood" of King Arthur, and Dames Valerie and Rebecca returned to the stage, where all the while, the Round Table Knights had stood at attention while the King sat in silent contemplation upon his throne. When the pianist struck the final chord of the communion music, there was a moment of silence as the King slowly rose and stood tall above his subjects.

"It is done," he said, the kindly father smiling over a large, devoted family. "Ah, my dear children, how glad I am to know that you are with me. And I am with you always, even unto the end of the earth. Very soon you will all briefly experience the freedom of resurrection, as a taste of the immortality which is at hand. And at morrow's dawn, my children and my soldiers, once the standard of Camelot is raised above the land, my trusted captains shall claim the gift and go forth to bring to pass the prophecy. They shall become as I am: immortal, free, able to assume flesh at will. They shall become the Dragon's Claw, and the Lion and Eagle shall fall beneath them. Stand forth, my captains, my firstborn, and let us honor you!"

The Round Table Knights, who had stood at parade-rest during the passing of the goblet, came to attention at the King's utterance of "stand forth." As one, and as if exhaustively practiced, they drew the swords hanging in scabbards at their sides, clasped them by the blades just below the hilts as if holding a cross, and performed a ritual salute: They knelt and held aloft their swords in both hands, and offered the hilts to their Lord King Arthur. The King clapped his hands together, and the congregation followed, filling the auditorium with their applause. Then they all took their seats and a curious silence descended upon the crowd.

Near the back of the room, Trick began to feel dizzy, and sank down onto his folding chair as so many had already done. Next to him, Diane sat with eyes closed and head swaying from side to side, a smile on her drowsy face. Now Trick was certain that Owain had meant it literally—"Don't drink from the cup!"—because whatever drug had been spiked into the wine was taking effect. It seemed as if his consciousness was pulling out of his body, causing an elastic feeling of tension around his eyes and mouth. And then, inexplicably, he felt as if he stood beside himself, still linked yet separate from his flesh.

Suddenly Owain was there. "I warned you not to drink," he said, not with anger, but with pity. "I shall try to turn the poison, if you will permit."

Trick felt his alert consciousness nodding affirmatively, though he could not tell whether his corporeal head was doing so. The old man reached out his short arms to Trick as if to embrace him, then disappeared. For a moment, Trick's discorporate consciousness poured into a small, dark room, from which he could see as if through the viewfinder of a camcorder with its lens zoomed out for a wide-angle shot, with only a letterboxed range of view. But it was apparent that someone else was controlling the "camera," because he could not feel his body rising from the chair, nor shuffling toward the stairs, nor climbing upward into the starry darkness. A few yards away from the lighted stairwell, Trick saw the fingers of his left hand reaching for his mouth, but he did not feel the two first fingers thrust past his uvula, nor the spasms of vomiting that it caused as his stomach bucked and heaved like a rodeo bull, spewing his barbecue dinner and the cheap red wine onto the dusty gravel at his feet.

From his comfortable little compartment of consciousness, Trick watched what was happening with morbid fascination, feeling nothing at all except curiosity. Then, just as suddenly as his mind and his body had seemed to separate, they slammed back together with a jolt, and Trick tasted the sour, bitter vomit on his lips. His stomach was still heaving slightly, and his breath came in gasps, but the dizzy, discorporate feeling had passed and his head was amazingly clear once again.

Owain had reappeared, and his weathered face reflected concern. "Forgive me, sir. It was a ghastly business but it was necessary. Are you able to hear me and heed me?" Trick nodded, feeling it physically this time. Owain continued, "Then give me your ear quickly, while they"—he pointed to the stairs to indicate the people gathered below—"are yet besotted with his wine. Do you not yet fathom his evil design?"

Trick shook his head, wiping his mouth on his sleeve, leaving a purplish-brown stain like old blood and causing another wave of nausea to grip him; somehow, he managed to control his now-empty stomach, but could not control an awkward case of hiccups.

"Hear me! For a moment, you may have felt as if you arose and stood apart from your body. This is one of his many deceptions, which he claims is a taste of immortality. They will all awaken in a short time with the memory of this wondrous thing, and they will believe that they must only do as he says and they will be free, immortal, like him. But it is only drunkenness which enchants them; and even the poor fool who has allowed this creature to come into the world through him is intoxicated with the rest. This is no king, and no brave warrior. This is only a deceiver, a murderer, a thief who lusts for what he never had nor will ever have. He is called Mog Hwl, and I first heard his evil name in the year of Our Lord that your calendar would reckon as 1432. It was nigh upon the winter solstice in that year that I too was transformed."

"Transformed?"

"Changed from a living man into a Traveler, a being such as he. But there is no time now to explain how I came to be, nor the nature of my existence. You must know only that he is training those children"—and once more, Owain pointed to the open stairwell—"to be Travelers and intends to send them forth at morrow's dawn to do his wicked work. He has not told them that their bodies must die for this to come to pass; he has promised only that they shall 'sleep' while they 'fly.' And once they do 'fly,' as he would have it, he intends to have them bring to pass his absurd prophecy that 'the Lion and the Eagle shall fall.' Do you not yet grasp the meaning of these words?"

"Something about the Lion is England, and the Eagle is America," Trick ventured, the symbols beginning to take on a new, horrific shape in his mind.

"You guess correctly, but you do not know all, for here you are not allowed to know what occurs in the world. On the morrow, your American president and His Highness the Prince of Wales shall meet in the nearby city of Dallas to exchange cordial greetings between nations. They are closely guarded by their own trusted knights and retainers and feel as safe as they might in their watchful care. But when his eight favored children are transformed, they will heed their evil master's bidding and speed invisibly to the meeting. There, they will overwhelm the bodies of those who are trusted to the safety of their noble masters, then use those bodies to turn upon them, and strike them down. And then this demon who would be King will declare himself lord of all nations under the Crown."

"My God," whispered Trick, and his hiccups abruptly ceased.

His stomach began to plummet, not with nausea but with terror. Who was this fiend in the false armor of King Arthur, that he dared mark for assassination the President of the United States and the Prince of Wales? And to steal the souls of eight "children"— including that of Brian Brannan!—to carry out his demented scheme?

As if reading his thoughts, Owain said, "I know of your quest. You have come here of your own free will to try to save the soul and body of the child Brian, who is under the spell of Mog Hwl. You are a man of honor, a true knight and worthy, but you alone are no match for the wicked one who holds the child's life as a woman would grasp a pretty trinket. The path of your quest lies alongside mine, which is to free Mog Hwl from the gift and the curse of immortality that he has abused and perverted. I alone am no match for him, for he has sheltered himself in a strong and willing vessel and has gathered around himself faithful believers in his wicked cause. Yet together, we may be able to defeat him. And so I would ask you now, Patrick Allen McGuire, son of John Hugh, son of John Patrick: Will you take my sword and be my knight and champion in my quest, and thereby fulfill your own?"

The sound of his own name and the names of his father and grandfather spoken by the all-too-real apparition startled and frightened Trick more than anything he had heard so far. Yet Trick took one bold step in Owain's direction and demanded, "I told you I wouldn't take any sword that I don't know whose sword it is. So who—and what—are you?"

The image of the old man did not dim; instead, it became even more solid and the kindly visage hardened. "My name is Owain of Caergwyndwr, and in my time and in my land I was a king. No, not the king of legend, though the tale of Arthur of Britain was known even in my time. But now it is *your* time. Will you or will you not take my sword, Patrick McGuire? I implore you, for I am no longer a king to command you, and no longer a man to challenge you. But without your hand upon my sword, what Mog

Hwl has promised will surely come to pass, and you will lose forever the boy Brian as surely as the nations of your birth and of your ancient blood will be thrown into utter, bloody chaos."

Owain reached with his left hand to his right hip and drew forth from a leather scabbard a long sword that reflected the bright starlight along its smooth, polished blade. He said no more, but turned over the sword in a graceful gesture and offered the hilt to Trick.

Only half believing in the spectral king before him, but desperate beyond denying the half that did not believe, Trick reached out his hand toward the hilt. His cupped palm touched solid metal, hard and heavy, wrapped in leather soft upon his hand. Amazed by the sword's substance, he caught his breath, and his fingers curled slowly around the thick shaft.

His fist suddenly clamped shut on nothing but the night air, and Owain was gone.

Trick uttered a groan of exasperation and raised his hands in frustration. "*Now* what am I supposed to do?" he demanded of the darkness.

Swiftly now, while they linger in drunkenness, let us end this wickedness!

Owain's voice registered as clearly in Trick's consciousness as in his ears, though he was nowhere in sight. An unseen force that seemed to reside within his body compelled him to turn toward the stairwell, but he did not resist it. Together as one, Trick McGuire and Owain of Caergwyndwr descended into the supernatural silence of the Abbey.

CHAPTER FOURTEEN

T HERE YOU ARE," WHISPERED DIANE AS TRICK SANK BACK DOWN ON
the squeaky folding chair beside her. "I didn't see you go out."

"I got sick," replied Trick simply.

"Oh, dear, I hope it wasn't the potato salad." She reached up a
hand to pat his cheek comfortingly. "Wasn't it wonderful? I've
never felt so free and so . . . . so beautiful! Oh, I can hardly wait for
morning!"

"Honey, I gotta tell you something," he began, but the pianist
stroked a gentle chord from the instrument to signal for attention.
The King was standing once more at center stage, smiling out at his
subjects as they recovered from their brief experience of "immortality."

"My children, hear me," declared the King, and those in the
congregation who were murmuring and fidgeting as their drug-
induced moment of transcendence wore off came to rapt attention.
"You have had a taste of the freedom and power that awaits you in
the coming kingdom. On the morrow, when our standard is hoist
above our sovereign nation, I shall call upon you, my children and
my warriors, to stand with me to defend our brave new world of
Chivalry. You need not be afraid, for now you may be certain of
what lies beyond death's threshold. And we must be prepared, for
these worthy Knights who stand beside me, who through service

and accomplishment have earned my favor and who have pledged
their utmost loyalty to me, I shall send forth as my vanguard to
smite the Lion and the Eagle and make clear the way for the Dragon!"
The King outstretched his arms toward the Round Table Knights
at either side of him, as if he intended to gather them all into an
embrace. The expressions on their faces ranged from dour to radi-
ant, but all of them, including Brian, stood unwavering.

"They will become as I am, and they shall become as living
claws in the talons of the Dragon. Hence they will go forth to the
place where the Lion and the Eagle shall meet, and shall strike the
first blow for Chivalry!"

A voice suddenly rang out of the crowd: "Have you yet told
them they must first perish by your hand?"

The hush that settled over the crowd was preceded by a mass
gasp that seemed to draw all the air from the room. Trick had
heard the voice—it was his own!—but it seemed to be coming
from somewhere else. He had not thought the words, nor felt his
mouth and throat working to utter them. But they surely had
come from his lips, for all eyes turned suddenly upon him like
hundreds of tiny beacons, incredulous.

"Who speaks this blasphemy?" demanded the King, striding
toward the edge of the stage, as if the few extra paces forward could
help him see better.

Trick did not feel himself standing, nor Diane's hands clutching his arm, trying to keep him in his seat. But he saw, as if from a
window in a dark room, his point of perspective rising, and he
heard his voice declare, "If you would tell this much, you must tell
all. Tell how it is done, and spare no detail. These children you say
you cherish will see the dawn, but not the evening twilight, for you
will poison their young bodies as surely as you have poisoned their
hearts with your wicked promises."

The King hesitated a fraction of a second; then, he roared in
fury, his face suddenly livid. "Knights! Remove that unbeliever
from my sight! I will deal with him outside this holy place ere

daybreak."

Sir Travis, Sir Kevin, and Brian leaped from the chancel and raced toward the back of the Abbey where Trick stood with arms crossed defiantly across his chest. "What the hell's gotten into you, Jack?" whispered Sir Kevin as he and Sir Travis grabbed his arms and hustled him toward the stairs, with every stunned face staring at him. Trick caught a glimpse of Diane, her blue eyes wide and wet, both sets of fingertips pressed to her mouth; but he could not speak to her, for once more, Owain's words thundered out of his mouth.

"Drink no more from his evil cup, my friends," he cried as he struggled in the firm grasp of Sir Travis and Sir Kevin as they dragged him up the concrete steps. "You may yet be saved if you will hasten from this place at once! He is no King, and his words are as false as he. All that the dawn will bring will be terror and tragedy if you do not—"

"Shut up," snarled Brian, once they were out of view, and cracked his fist across Trick's mouth. Trick did not feel any pain from the contact, nor the snap of his head in recoil; nor did he taste the blood in his mouth. But his view dimmed slightly, as if a thin curtain had been drawn across the window of his vision.

Above in the bright starlight, Sir Travis and Sir Kevin dragged Trick farther across the blighted concrete expanse, toward the last of the three sets of steel doors flush with the ground and its corresponding "storm-cellar" pedestrian entrance. Brian jiggled the rusty padlock, and it opened easily. Raising the metal door itself was almost beyond his strength, but he hauled it upward and let it fall back with a dull clanging crash.

"You can cool your heels down here until Lord Arthur decides what to do with you," said Sir Kevin, as he and Sir Travis shoved Trick toward the pitch-black doorway. "Frankly, Jack, I'm really disappointed in you. I thought you were just about the best apprentice Knight we ever had. I guess I figured wrong."

"My loyalty is to a higher power than your false King," stated

Trick's voice without his conscious effort.

"There *is* no higher power than the Lord King Arthur!" cried Brian, and drew back his fist once again. Trick saw the knuckles coming, but nothing his conscious thoughts would do could move his face out of their viciously accurate path. He did not feel the blow, nor the tiny slivers of bone grinding together into his sinuses, nor the blood flowing in slick red rivulets down his chin, mingling with hot, stinging tears. But the veil across his vision thickened, and he heard Sir Kevin's voice say, "Take it easy, Brian. He'll come to realize that soon enough."

"He'll be sorry he was ever born," added Sir Travis. "Come on, let's dump him and get back to the Abbey."

Through the dim haze of his vision, Trick saw the darkness rising up to envelop him and heard, as if from a great distance, the metal door banging shut. Suddenly his own sentience raced forward, and for an instant, he was overwhelmed with pain; but then all awareness was smothered under a silent, heavy blanket of unconsciousness.

Bits of memories wafted through his disassociation, like thin shreds of vivid dreams. First he saw Tay reaching out to him, but he remained just beyond her grasp. Then he saw himself on horseback, twirling a lariat to rope something that stayed frustratingly out of reach. Finally, a favorite dog from his childhood scampered across the front yard of his home, carrying in its mouth a snakeskin boot.

Then he saw things he knew he had never seen before, but they had a troubling familiarity about them. He saw upon a hilltop surrounded by leafy green trees a tall battlement built of stones the size of small automobiles, and above, a sky so clear and blue that it seemed to go on forever. A gate in the wall swung open, and he could see people moving purposefully around in the courtyard inside, carrying bundles, herding sheep, going about their daily business. They were all dressed in Merryborough-style costumes . . . or was it their usual mode of apparel? He rode through the gate astride a black horse, and all the people stopped their activities long enough to wave and bow and call out to him in a language he did not know but somehow understood: "Good morrow to thee, *Arglwydd Owain!*"

Ringing the inside the of the battlement were low stone houses with thatched roofs where the people hurried to and fro. In the center, surrounded by its own, lower stone wall, was a house that towered two stories above all the rest. It was built all of stone, with a deep undercroft below and many small windows above, and from the top of its turreted tower, a colorful pennon snapped smartly in the summer breeze. Into this house he went, through its ornately carved gate, followed by men carrying spears, swords, and bows. Just inside the doorway was a tiny shrine with a crude but detailed wooden carving of the Virgin Mary above a small pottery bowl. He reached into the bowl and made the sign of the cross with moistened fingertips before continuing into a dim room lighted only by the blazing hearth that spanned most of the opposite wall. He could almost smell the rich mutton stew bubbling in a cauldron on the fire and the golden trenchers of bread in the brick oven beside it. One of the servant women tended the fire, and she smiled and curtsied as he passed but continued her chores.

Beyond the galley lay the great hall, which he knew soon would be set for the meal that was being prepared for him and the household, and beyond the hall, a stairway to the second story. He climbed the stone steps two at a time until he reached the top and a room where half a dozen women sat spinning, sewing, weaving and embroidering. Quickly but quietly, all but one gathered their workbaskets and tiptoed into rooms beyond. The one remaining put her work down beside her and arose from the low bench. She was dressed in a plain rose-colored kirtle with only a simple cap to cover her straw-colored hair, but the way she stood and carried herself made it clear that this was the lady of the castle. She smiled and held out her arms to him.

"Briallen," he said, and reached out to her. Their fingertips hovered, inches apart.

But before they could touch, the memory of the lovely woman suddenly dissolved into a haze, and when it resolved, the scene was quite different.

It began as before, with a view of the castle from a distance. The sky was gray as the stones of the castle wall, which were broken open and strewn into the denuded brown trees that stalwartly ringed the snow-covered foot of the hill. There was no horse beneath him this time, and as he slowly approached the castle on foot, he could see the castle gate lay splintered, and beyond, the low stone houses were only lifeless, scorched walls with blackened roof timbers scattered like toothpicks. The muddy, ravaged courtyard was deserted, except for an old woman who wandered shivering from one empty doorway to another, weeping, with her apron pressed to her face. The carcass of a dun horse lay near the gate, still saddled, frozen solid.

The great house in the center stood soot-blackened but strong, though its tower had fallen and its stones lay scattered across the courtyard. But it was empty. What had not been destroyed had been looted. Even the little figure of the Blessed Virgin and the stoup of holy water had been stolen away, either by the soldiers or by the thieves who followed after them like hungry dogs.

He did not go into the ruined house. Empty though it stood, it still held the memories of a life that no longer would be. Instead, he turned around and strode back through the fallen gate. He walked alone into the wintry forest, beyond the small, unmarked mounds of stones that were poor and common monuments to the lives of his soldiers, his servants . . . his family and friends. He paused by one that he had himself raised, stone by stone, above the woman he had chosen late in life to be his queen, who had been with child when the brightly-caparisoned attackers from the east had descended upon his home and his lands like a swarm of locusts.

He had fought them well, but not well enough. They were fearless, as if death held no terror for them, as knights should be. But they also were merciless, slaying the innocent citizens of Caergwyndwr as effortlessly as the knighted soldiers of the castle. Unstoppable, they left standing nothing that could tumble, alive nothing that breathed. They rallied round their captain worshipfully, though he never showed his face nor uttered a sound, but somehow they knew his deadly bidding and carried it out unquestioningly. He knew them not, but they were not English, for the standard beneath which they rode bore not the emblem of "King Richard's cat." No, the symbol upon their battle flag was a wicked caricature of the Welsh dragon, which seemed to have come to life in that mysterious captain; had he been given the opportunity, he might even have breathed fire.

And so it seemed he had. Like everything else within the castle walls, the church inside the castle keep was in ashes, and the priest with it. Who would hear the confession of Owain of Caergwyndwr this day, and who would absolve him of the mortal sins he had committed and wished to commit further to avenge the evil that had been visited upon him? It mattered not to him that he would die in the attempt; he did not fear death, for he was a Christian, but he did not wish to free his soul unshriven.

Deep in the forest, down by the river, lived Grufydd the hermit. Some said he was a priest of an ancient pagan order; others simply called him a sorcerer. He was seldom seen except by scouts on patrol of the forest, but he had lived quietly in the forest for years beyond reckoning. If Grufydd were any kind of priest at all, Owain reckoned, he would hear his confession and bless him before he set out for vengeance and his own certain death.

Night was swiftly falling amid the snowflakes, but he struggled onward to the rocky outcroppings by the old river to the south. In ages long past, the sea had been over the land, and had cut out dozens of little caves in the rocks. Now the sea was miles away, but it had left a small river as a reminder of its former glory. Dim fireglow from one of the caves beckoned silently to a place where he might find a bit of light and warmth on this cold winter's eve.

"Grufydd!" he called out as he approached, and was surprised at how strangled and weak his voice sounded. "If you yet live and you hear me, speak!"

A shadow passed through the orange glow, and then the shape of a man, heavily cloaked, appeared in the pathway ahead of him. "I hear you, *Owain ap Caergwyndwr*," said a low, gentle voice, barely louder than the snowflakes drifting onto the ground. "Come, and warm yourself by my poor hearth. Are you injured?"

He had not thought of his own days-old wounds, for the pain in his heart overwhelmed any hurt he had taken at the hands of the attackers. But he had been sorely cut across his shield arm when his shield had been cloven by the enemy horseman's sword, and he had taken a jarring blow to the head that might have finished him, had he not been wearing his best and strongest helm. Then, when his horse had turned for the charge, it had lost its footing on a patch of ice, slipped and fell, flinging him into a cluster of the stones that had fallen from the castle wall. The good horse was able to struggle to its feet, only to have its headstall seized by a soldier and to be galloped off to wherever the attackers were hoarding the spoils of the battle. At least the horse would live to fight another day—though under the enemy's dragon-crested standard.

"I am well enough," he answered, and thinking of the horse, added, "I have been spared to fight another day, though I know not why."

"It will not be this day. Come, Lord Owain, have a bit of my soup and rest you in safety until the morrow. It is the least I can offer you, who have suffered me to live upon your lands these many years."

"They are my lands no longer," he replied sadly.

"Perhaps not for the moment," said the hermit, and gave an awkward little bow as he pointed toward the glowing cave with his rag-wrapped hand.

Owain preceded Grufydd into the cave, which he noted was shallow, but turned just so that it blocked the cold winds that hurried the snowflakes all around them. Grufydd indicated for him to sit on a crude wooden bench that stood near a ring of stones on the floor, in which a few small tongues of flame licked at glowing embers. Grufydd tossed a few more dry twigs into the fire and it blazed up lightly, adding enough more warmth to be able to unwrap their faces, and enough more light to be able to see them.

As he dusted the clinging snowflakes out of his beard, he took his first close look at the hermit Grufydd. He did not appear to be as old as the knights of Caergwyndwr had always said; his hair and beard were no grayer than his own, the skin behind them no more weathered and crinkled. Owain had counted fifty-nine summers in his life, but Grufydd the hermit had seemed an old man when he had been just a carefree boy, the prince of Caergwyndwr. Only the pale blue eyes beneath the grizzled brows betrayed him: They were as deep as water wells, as clear as the sky in summer, as ancient as Gwynedd itself. They were also intensely piercing, as if they could stare right through one to the very backmost recesses of the soul—which they seemed to be doing.

Owain blinked away and looked at the other spare furnishings of the cave called home by the hermit. A pile of rags nearby represented a bed. There was a table of sorts, a plank upon a pedestal of carefully-stacked stones. Upon it were bits of candles, scraps of parchment, and a small earthen bowl. In the flickering shadows of the firelight, he could see tucked onto every ledge of stone, whether carved gracefully by the primordial sea or clumsily by human hand, small jars and flasks and boxes of all shapes, colors and descriptions. The hermit had a reputation as an herbalist; perhaps, thought Owain, these are ingredients for his curatives.

Grufydd took the bowl from the table and brought it to the fireside. With a wooden ladle, he stirred the contents of a small, black pot which stood at the fire's edge, then dipped some of the brownish liquid into the bowl. Before he handed the bowl to

Owain, he reached a hand into a fold of his tattered robe and drew out a tiny silver box. He shook in a few grains of a rust-colored powder, then swirled the bowl lightly to mix it in. "This will warm you," he said, and gave him the bowl. Owain cautiously took a sip of the broth—*cwningen*, coney, he supposed—and was happily surprised by its flavor, which had a piquance he had never before tasted. What exotic seasoning had the hermit added to make the broth seem hotter than it was, but without burning his mouth? He drank it eagerly, and it warmed him within and without.

As if he could read his thoughts, the hermit said, "It is a spice from India, the land faraway to the east. They call it *kari*."

"It is tasty indeed, and I thank you. Tell me more about this faraway land."

"I have never been there, my lord, I have only heard tales told by the merchants who travel the waters to and from the shores of Brittany, and overland far beyond. They say that in India, the knights are as dark as Saracens and as fierce, and they ride great leathery creatures, as big as houses, that bellow like thunder."

"Then I should like to have had some of those knights and their giant steeds, and perhaps I should not have lost all that I have held dear all the days of my life to that band of armored raiders beneath the counterfeit dragon flag."

The hermit looked up suddenly, stricken. "Did you say that the knights who laid waste to Caergwyndwr rode under the emblem of a dragon?"

"Aye, upon a field *Gules*, a dragon *rampant regardant Or*. I shall never forget how it seemed to be like the torch that lighted the fires, flying above their evil captain."

"Mog Hwl," whispered Grufydd. "I feared as much."

"Who is Mog Hwl? Where are his lands?"

The hermit rose from where he had crouched by the fire, and took a step toward the mouth of the cave. Outside the snowflakes were falling thick and fast, and he stared at them for a moment in silence before answering. "Mog Hwl is a Traveler, my lord. He is a prince of the powers of the air."

"A *cythraul*, a demon, do you mean?"

"No, my lord, he once was a living man, as are you and I. But now he is a being of spirit, yet more than a mere ghost. For he can become as flesh, to be seen and to be heard, sometimes even to be touched. But his greater power lies in the ability to take upon himself living flesh and to make it do his bidding. The captain you saw at the fall of Caergwyndwr may have been only a farmer, a juggler, a priest—but under Mog Hwl's spell, he is a fell conquering knight who will not rest until he has made himself king of all the lands, and all the people who will not kneel to him are slain."

Owain crossed himself. The thin broth in his stomach seemed to be boiling, in fear as well as anger. "You have spoken of two unnatural creatures this night. I fear not the giant beast of faraway India, for I cannot not see it even in my mind, but I quake at the thought of a beast in the flesh of a knight, which I have seen with my eyes. I will not ask how you know of these fell things, Grufydd, for you are ancient and wise and must know of many things both good and evil. But I will ask if you know how this Mog Hwl can be stopped, once and for all, for I would have my revenge upon him though it kill me."

The old hermit turned and took a long step toward the fire, which cast a feral orange glow upon his gray beard and flickered in his deep blue eyes. "I am not ashamed of my knowledge nor whence it comes, Lord Owain. There are vast and wondrous sources of power in the earth below us, the skies above us, the waters all around us. I am called a pagan, a Druid, a sorcerer, and many other things I am not. I am but a listener and a watcher and a learner from those who have gone before me for generations uncounted. Thus I have learned of Travelers, and I know that their number is few, and among them only Mog Hwl is evil. And I know that the flesh which the Traveler wears like a gauntlet may be killed, for it is only a man, but the immortal creature itself may be destroyed only by another Traveler."

For a moment, only the crackle of the small fire broke the muffled winter silence, but it was all Owain needed to make up his mind. "Then I must become a Traveler also, and I will destroy the evil thing that is abroad in our land. Will you help me?"

"Lord Owain, that is madness. You know not what you ask!"

"I did ask 'Will you help me?' and I will ask once more before I command it, as the king that I was before Mog Hwl stripped me of crown, of queen, of castle and lands! Grufydd, wise one, hear me: I have naught to lose save my life, and if I lose that, I shall be only a lonely ghost damned to wander eternity, powerless. As a Traveler, I might be the instrument of some good in the land, beginning with the destruction of Mog Hwl. Will you help me?"

Grufydd turned to stare at the snowfall, and then returned his gaze, gentle once again, to Owain. "My lord, I will do as you command, but I must work in secret for a time. If you will sleep now, while I work, by morrow's dawn, I shall have what is necessary to lead you toward your desire."

Owain politely refused Grufydd's offer of the ragpile bed, and instead, gathered some of the straw that was strewn upon the cave floor and a few small stones warmed by the fire and made himself as comfortable as he could in a notch on the other side of the cavern. He did not sleep that long night. In the slow, silent hours that passed, he heard Grufydd muttering and shuffling about from time to time, and the occasional crackle as another dry twig caught fire when tossed into the crude hearth. But he listened only to his own thoughts, and, as he reviewed the course of his life, he determined that his years of privilege had amounted to little in the end. He had done nothing of lasting significance in the world: His kingdom, which would have been his legacy to history, was no more. The ruins of Caergwyndwr would become as the ancient standing stones that were found throughout the countryside: mysterious monuments to a civilization that had vanished away, lost and nameless. Given its way, the creature called Mog Hwl would claim as his own kingdom the entire land of Gwynedd, even if it were nothing but a bleak field of sad, broken stones.

When morning began to dawn, a tiny ray of golden sunlight broke through the hazy gray clouds and cast a warm, hopeful glow across the snowy landscape. Owain took it as a fortunate omen and rose stiffly from his cold, hard bed. He found Grufydd hunched over his table, staring at the candle flame in which he held the round bottom of a small glazed ceramic jar. With his other hand he held a cracked parchment covered unevenly with small faded letters in the kind of runic writing Owain had seen on some of the ancient standing stones near Caergwyndwr.

"It is almost finished," whispered Grufydd, as gray wisps of smoke swirled around the tiny vessel, leaving traces of soot on its smooth sides. Abruptly, its bit of cork popped out with a minuscule puff of steam, and Grufydd removed it from the flame, recapping it before setting it carefully onto a small wooden trivet made to hold it upright. He turned to Owain and said, "What I have compounded is the liquor which, taken gradually in small amounts, prepares one who would be made a Traveler for the transformation. It is done over the full cycle of the moon, while the man steeps himself in prayer to make peace with his god or gods, and briefly travels out of his own body and back in preparation for the time when he leaves it forever."

"By Saint Dyfed!" bellowed Owain. "I will not wait patiently for a month while Mog Hwl rides on, murdering and destroying! If I will do this thing, I will do it at once, and be done with it. Give it me now!"

The hermit only tucked his hands inside the folds of his robe and said quietly, "Would you make first your confession? That is why you did seek me out, is it not?"

Owain caught his breath; he had not spoken that desire aloud, but somehow Grufydd had known. The old man continued, "I am no priest, Owain, but if you wish to be shriven before you go to your death, I will hear you. And so will your God, whose forgiveness you may receive with or without a confessor."

Without hesitation, Owain sank to his knees and crossed himself, then folded his hands beneath his chin and recited his sins. As he did so, he felt each one tear free from his heart, leaving a warm lightness in its place. When he reached the end of the list he had made while he lay sleepless the night before, he felt almost unbearably light and unburdened

Grufydd's voice whispered in his reverie, "While you are still near to your God, make the following solemn vows, which a Traveler must keep for eternity: Swear that as a Traveler, you will never take the flesh of a living man against his will; that when you do take flesh you will do so only to accomplish good works, and you will restore the living man unharmed; and that you will never harm another Traveler, unless that Traveler has forsaken these vows."

Still caught up in the reverie of confession, he whispered, "I, Owain ap Caergwyndwr, son of Maredudd, son of Llwelyn, do so swear." He opened his eyes and saw the small ceramic vessel lying in the withered palm of Grufydd's hand.

"Take one small sip only," cautioned the hermit. "You will know when to drink the rest."

Owain put the tiny bottle to his lips and tasted only a single bitter drop. After only a few moments, he felt dizzy, and an odd kind of tension around his eyes and mouth, as if a large, unseen hand were tugging at his face. And then, in the blink of an eye, he saw himself as if he were another person, standing to one side, but attached to the body by what appeared to be shimmering strands of gossamer. He saw his body still kneeling, with the little bottle clutched in his fingertips inches from his lips, and his eyes open. He saw Grufydd standing before the kneeling figure, and the hermit addressed that body, rather than the consciousness that hovered beside it, seeing all, hearing all.

"It is not too late, Owain. Return the vial to me, and the drunkenness will pass and you will awaken, a living man as ever, free to find your revenge and perhaps someday peace upon this mortal sod. And when you die, as one day you must, your soul will go to its rest and you will be reunited with your queen. But drink the rest, and you are doomed to be Owain of Caergwyndwr for all time and eternity, even after you take your vengeance upon Mog Hwl. And should you fail to do so, and he destroys you instead, the price is an eternity of utter aloneness, apart not only from man, but from God. So choose wisely, my king."

Owain hesitated. Was the destruction of the evil Mog Hwl, who could not otherwise be stopped before conquering all the lands enslaving all the people, worth the price of his immortal soul? He was only one man, one who deserved to live and someday to go to his eternal reward.

But he was also a king, and a king was more than a man. A king must do whatever is necessary for the greater good of his land and his people. He could not bring back the dead, nor rebuild a castle from its ashes, but he had one remarkable opportunity to make a difference in history yet to be written.

At his own unspoken command, the flesh beside him raised the tiny flask and drained it. He did not taste the last bitter drops; he did not feel the liquor racing toward his heart, nor his heart's final beat. Yet he heard his body's last breath, and watched with dumbstruck fascination as it slumped slowly to the ground and lay still. The slender, spider-thread strands between his living consciousness and the body that had been his snapped like harpstrings cloven by a sword, and disappeared. How strange it was to go on seeing, hearing, thinking and remembering, as if this were all happening in a dream!

Grufydd knelt and closed the staring eyes of Owain's body. He looked up and around the cave, and said, "It is done. If you yet linger near, Lord Owain, hear me: Do not attempt to confront Mog Hwl until you are accustomed to what you have become. Learn what you can do, what you cannot do; grow ever stronger, and one day make an end not only of Mog Hwl but whatever other evil you may encounter in the world. And may God have mercy upon your troubled soul."

With these words of absolution, the Traveler that had been Owain departed the cave by the river, and felt no cold as he moved out over the drifting snows, past the sad ruins of Caergwyndwr, and deep into the forests of Gwynedd where he would conceal himself and teach himself the craft for which there was no master. How hasty he had been! What was a day, a month, a year, or even a century to him, now that he had forever?

But Mog Hwl was already abroad in the world, and Owain could not allow him to stay his murderous course. If he could not yet face him equally, he could make of himself an obstacle in his path, to confound him, thwart him and delay him, and thus hinder his evil works. And then one day, when he had acquired sufficient skill and strength as a Traveler, he could challenge and conquer Mog Hwl.

As the days and nights passed, some swiftly and some slowly, just as they had in his life, Owain added one more solemn vow to the covenant of the Traveler: to find a means to an honorable end of his own immortal existence and perhaps find salvation and peace, once his mission had been fulfilled. Then he could sleep . . .

Darkness drowned his eyes as a jab of pain between them forced them to pop open. The silence was filled with the throbbing rushing of blood in his ears, but suddenly a shrill screech, like the cry of a hawk, pierced the silent blackness. He felt a presence bearing down swiftly upon him, and he raised a hand to shield his face from the claws of the vulture or cougar or whatever it was that was about to tear into him. He was only a little relieved when a thin beam of light flashed across his face, firing tiny arrows of agony into his retinas, and outlined a human form bending over him.

"Jeepers, Trick, you look awful," whispered a voice that Trick McGuire, fully and painfully aware of his own body, recognized as Reggie's. "Do you think you can stand up? I'm getting out of here, and you're going with me. I've let this go too far, and I gotta call for some backup before all hell breaks loose at daylight."

CHAPTER FIFTEEN

W ITH REGGIE'S ASSISTANCE, TRICK struggled to his feet on the concrete steps where he'd been lying head downward. It took a minute for his equilibrium to right itself, and he leaned on his friend while the dizziness passed and his rubbery knees firmed up. His head throbbed so intensely that Trick was certain the entire county could hear the thumping between his ears like a water pump about to explode. Breathing through his nose was not an option, but the blood dribbling into his spiky mustache forced him either to sniff or to lick, and the resulting wet inhale caused him to choke and cough. Even so, he felt fully in charge of himself once again; Owain's presence (and memories) had disappeared, and he rejoiced in the freedom to feel his own pain.

"You gonna be okay?" asked Reggie, offering a rough paper towel to dab at his face.

Trick nodded slightly. "I think so," he said, tasting the blood in his mouth.

"Then let's move. We're going AWOL from King Arthur's army, old buddy."

Trick did not resist as Reggie looped his arm over his shoulders and helped him climb the concrete stairs toward the starry heavens. Reggie hesitated just as their heads broke the surface, and they peered cautiously toward the center missile bunker doors from which light and music still streamed upward into the night. In the ambient glow, they could make out the silhouette of a sentry by the stairwell, but he was turned away from them, looking downward into the Abbey below.

Reggie motioned to Trick to be silent and to keep low, and released him. Trick crouched down and watched Reggie creep like a silent shadow across the concrete expanse toward the Abbey entrance. With the speed and agility of a man half his age, he pounced upon the sentry from behind, and the two of them went sprawling across the gravel in a muffled scuffle. But only Reggie arose, and he beckoned to Trick to follow, and to hurry.

Trick scrambled after Reggie as best he could, even though his head pounded so viciously that it forced him to clutch it with both hands as he ran. It helped only slightly. He did not look at the body lying on the ground next to the Abbey doors and did not want to know if Reggie had killed him.

The gate into the missile launch site enclosure was chained and locked, but the chain was slack and they managed to squeeze themselves between the fence and the gate, and into the main area of the compound. Even though all the buildings were dark and, they were certain, deserted, they clung to the shadows, making their way from the B.O.Q., to the "officers' barracks," and finally to the garage before they made a run for the main gate of New Cadbury. Like the gate at the missile site, the main gate was chained and securely padlocked, but in this one there was not enough slack in the chain to let a cat pass through.

"Well, I hate to have to do this to you, Trick, but we've gotta go over it," whispered Reggie, staring at the top of the fence where a canopy of three taut strands of barbed wire leaned over them. "Thank goodness it's not razor wire. We may get scratched, but at least we won't leave big hunks of us in it. I'll go first, and see if I can loosen it up for you."

Reggie jumped up on the chain-link fence and pulled himself up carefully, hand over hand. In the starlight, it seemed to Trick that Reggie was climbing the darkness itself, suspended in mid-air. He paused at the top to squeeze himself carefully between the top of the fence and the first row of barbed wire. Trick heard him swear quietly, but was gratified to see him twist around upright on the opposite side of the wire. "Come on up," Reggie said. "I'll hold the sharp stuff off your back."

Cautiously, Trick fitted his hands into the metal links and hauled himself up the ten jingling feet of it, jamming the toes of his boots into the links. When he got to the top, Reggie pushed up the lowest strand of barbed wire with his foot to give Trick a bit of extra space to squeeze through. Even so, one sharp barb caught his shoulder as he went over, tearing his shirt and scratching him deeply.

They both continued over the fence; Reggie dropped from the top of it to the ground, but Trick climbed down slowly until he was within less than three feet of the ground, and then let go. The small impact rattled his already rattled skull, and he landed unsteadily but safely in the grass of the overgrown bar ditch below.

"Okay?" whispered Reggie, clutching Trick's arm to help him upright himself, and Trick nodded. "Yeah," he said.

"Let's hustle. I got a safe house about two miles down the road from the front gate, and we can get some troops in here before daylight."

"Reg, what the hell are you talking about?" asked Trick as they set off slowly but steadily down the caliche roadway, moving farther away from the main highway into the deeper darkness of the undeveloped ranchland.

"Guess I'd better 'fess up. I've been lyin' like a rug ever since I set foot on King Arthur's hallowed ground about three months ago. I'm not just friendly 'Sir Floyd' who fixes mechanical things and scrounges stuff and follows King Arthur's orders like all the rest of the good little sheep. I'm an agent of the Postal Inspection Service."

Trick stared in disbelief at Reggie, but in the dimness of starlight he could not make out his features. Reggie continued as they hiked briskly down the road. "About a year ago, I was shown some literature bulk-mailed with a non-profit organization permit from a Fort Worth substation. The assistant postmaster there was suspicious that this group called the Knights of the Once and Forever King might not be eligible to mail at those rates, and they called in a Postal Inspector—me—to look into it. I read the literature, and I agreed that they might have a pretty serious little mail fraud going down, so I went to the address on the flier, which turned out to be Joyous Gard. They were sure nice people there, so I didn't flash brass at them but let them tell me what they were about. It sounded like a big steamin' shovelful to me, but I acted interested and they kept piling it on. I started to get a little suspicious that mail fraud might not be all they were into, so I thought I might stay and look a little deeper. I went home and called my boss down at the main Post Office in Fort Worth. He was kind of interested, but he didn't really want to launch an official covert operation. So I decided I'd do it myself. My wife had been dead nearly two years—I told you that much truth—and my grown kids have their own lives, and wouldn't miss me for awhile, so I asked for a leave of absence, packed a few things and went back to Joyous Gard. I figured it'd take a few days to sniff out whatever they might be hiding.

"You know what goes on there. They find out what you're good at, and put you to work doin' it—I guess you got to be the chief cook and bottlewasher. I was the handyman—I fixed the leaky plumbing, and built Sir Jeffrey's little privacy partition, stuff like that. Meanwhile, I learned about bein' a Knight, and they awarded me a First Degree. I was actually kind of proud of myself . . . thought I had accomplished something. Pretty soon they decided that they needed someone at New Cadbury who could make the missile elevator work in time for the Convergence, and they transferred me out here. Then I started learning more about what they were really about: Our so-called King was determined to be king of the whole world, starting with this country and the one he came from, and his only problems were that pesky president and prince. They sort of let on that the Knights had a plan to take care of them, but you know they don't give out all their information at once.

"So I hung in there, hoping they would decide I deserved to be Second Degree, so I could find out more. That's when they started the 'training' to travel out of your body. They give you a little teeny bit of the same kind of stuff they put in the wine tonight, and you build up a tolerance for it as they give you more and more. After the first time, it scared me so bad I started faking it when they passed the cup around. I thought I should blow the whistle on them right there for possessing and manufacturing illegal drugs, but I still didn't know everything I needed to know. And it didn't all come together for me until tonight, at the Convergence, when I heard you say what you did about the Round Table Knights having to die to become like King Arthur. Then it dawned on me what they meant by the Lion and the Eagle . . . we don't get to listen to TV or the radio out here, but I remembered hearing somewhere about the President going out campaigning and stopping in Dallas the same day the Prince of Wales is supposed to be in town for some kind of charity appearance, and they were going to meet at the airport or something. Trick, I think what's gonna happen at dawn is they're somehow gonna try to kill them both."

Trick stared at Reggie in the dark, amazed at his old friend's sagacity. So Owain was right about Mog Hwl's plan—the Round Table Knights, once "transformed," would make swift work of the two world leaders. They would be surrounded by multiple levels of security—the Secret Service would be guarding the Prince as well as the President, and the Prince would have his own guards as well— but they would be no shield for the unseen Travelers who would simply channel into the agents nearest the rulers and turn their own weapons upon them.

Reggie went on, "Oh, I know it sounds crazy, because you must have believed in the world of Chivalry they promised you or you wouldn't have come here. I don't know what got into you to say what you said back there in the Abbey, but I'm guessing you figured it out, too. When we get to the safe house—it's really my old Airstream fishing trailer, about half a mile up the road, on the right—I can get hold of my supervisor. He might think I'm crazy, too, but he knows I'm telling the truth, and he won't hesitate to wake up a judge and get a warrant. By good daylight, this road'll be crawling with enforcement division agents, and then you'll really see what we mean by 'going postal'!"

Trick wavered on the brink of telling Reggie that he, too, was on a "covert operation," but at the moment he began to speak, he saw behind them two sets of automobile headlights cresting the hill that concealed the encampment at New Cadbury from view from the road.

"Oh, damn, they must have gone back to check on you," whispered Reggie. "Quick, down in the ditch!"

Trick and Reggie dove into the shallow bar ditch, where they flattened themselves in the overgrown grass, but kept their heads up to watch. The lights hesitated at the gate while someone got out to unlock and open it, then they both turned toward the main highway and vanished in the red glow of tail lights through a cloud of caliche. Reggie heaved a sigh and said, "They figured you'd make for the highway. And they probably figured you had some help getting out—and if they called the roll, they'll know it was me. We gotta hurry now, for sure. Think you can run?"

"Guess I'd better try," gulped Trick, unsure if he could even stand up.

Reggie raised up first, and while still kneeling in the grass pulled up the right leg of his dusty, grass-stained dress slacks. In the dark Trick could not see what he was doing, but in an instant the starlight sparkled on the short barrel of a small handgun that appeared in his right hand. Trick did not feel safer. But Reggie's gappy grin brightened his dark face, and he said, "You never know—might be snakes in the road up yonder." He offered Trick his left hand to help him up and kept hold of it to help him sprint unsteadily down the unpaved road.

A pair of headlights blinked on behind them, and an engine roared to life. Tires spun in the caliche, and a dark-colored car that had been crouching in the blackness hurtled after them. Trick's heart was already hammering so hard that he could barely hear the car overtaking them, but the lights bore down on them inexorably, and it was clear that the driver had no misgivings about running them down at top speed.

"Break!" yelled Reggie, and he let go of Trick's hand. Like the last kid in line in a game of "crack the whip," the momentum hurled Trick off the roadway to the left. Though he had the presence of mind to try to roll as he fell, the impact jarred his already pain-filled head and body, and his consciousness flickered like an unstable ballast on a fluorescent light. He came to rest against part of a square haybale that had been dumped in the ditch for erosion control, and the slight rotten odor that emanated from it made his empty stomach buck weakly. But the sound of the pursuing car grinding to a gravel-slinging halt only yards away, followed by the familiar voice of Sir Kevin yelling, "Hold it right there, traitor!" constricted his throat so tightly that nothing larger than an air molecule could have escaped from it. Two sets of footsteps crunched toward him, and Trick flattened himself in the dry grass, wishing the ground would open up and swallow him before Sir Kevin and his companion reached him. Terror such as he had felt only once before in his life clenched at his chest and threatened to squeeze his heart into a moist, quivering lump of flesh.

Suddenly a single gunshot rang out, followed in quick succession by a volley. Down in the ditch, Trick cowered, clamping his hands over his ears to try to silence the ringing reverberations in his skull; it was no more effective than covering his eyes would have been to shut off the last horrific scenes of his Vietnam nightmare, which played over and over as if on a short video loop in his alert, wakeful mind.

He waited for death, but it did not come. As he lay still, the roaring in his head gradually attenuated until all he could hear was the light swishing of the rain-thirsty grass stirred by the light breeze. Slowly he opened his eyes and forced himself to raise his head, half expecting to see some kind of magical Excalibur stuck in the ground in front of him, as he had done in the last recurrence of his nightmare. But the high-beams of a black Honda Civic shone down the road at nothing but swirling caliche dust.

In the ambient glow of the headlights, Trick saw a body sprawled face up at the edge of the roadway, a mere arm's length away. He mustered all of his meager strength and courage to raise himself to his hands and knees, and to drag himself to its side. A wave of revulsion rippled through his guts when he identified Sir Kevin, with a large automatic pistol lying a few inches from his right hand—but the familiar horn-rimmed glasses were shattered in their frames over a deep hole where his right eye had been, and blood dribbled from the side of his slack mouth, through his neat Vandyke beard, and into a larger pool forming beneath his head. Trick quickly averted his gaze, and struggled to his feet.

"Reggie!" he whispered hoarsely into the night. "Reg! Where are you?" he called out, taking a few cautious steps across the road. There was no answer, and no sign of him or anyone else. Trick knew Reggie must have run to the right to escape the oncoming car, and he shuffled across the road to peer into the opposite ditch. At first he could make out only a shadow on the embankment, but in three more steps he could see that the shadow had substance, and in two more that it was Reggie, face down in the grass. His gun was still grasped loosely in his outstretched right hand.

"Oh, my God," gasped Trick, as he knelt beside his friend. Even in the dim starlight, Trick could see that the back of Reggie's dark silk shirt was wet, and so was its front when he grasped Reggie's shoulders and turned him over on his back. Reggie's golden eyes were partway open, but they did not see him. Trick shook him hard, pleading, "Reggie, come on, bud, you can't do this to me now!" He shook him again, but it availed nothing except to further loosen the grip on the gun in his hand.

"Oh, God, no!" wailed Trick, and all the pain of his injuries and the fear for his own life were overwhelmed by the grief and guilt that crashed down upon him. He wept aloud as he gathered the limp body into his arms and hugged him until the remainder of life's warmth was gone and Trick shivered with the coldness of Reggie's cheek against his own.

A tiny squeaking sound, as if of rusty springs, suddenly reminded Trick that there had been one other person on the scene, and a cold fire of anger and hatred began to seep into the emptiness that Reggie's death had torn out of his heart. He laid Reggie's body down carefully, then, after quickly casting his eyes about for movement, scrambled across the road to the place where Sir Kevin lay. He scooped up Sir Kevin's gun in both hands and deliberately snapped the clip out and in vigorously so that anyone listening would know he was now armed. But there was no sign of another person anywhere. Either there was another corpse lying around somewhere, or the other person had hightailed it back to New Cadbury on foot.

In either case, before him sat Sir Kevin's Honda—his easy means of escape to civilization, where he could make one phone call that would bring to an end the false King Arthur's plan to murder the President and the Prince of Wales. In no way would it ever even the score for Reggie's senseless murder, but at least Trick could derive some small satisfaction from completing his own—and Reggie's—secret mission.

He yanked open the driver door, and the dome light blinking on startled him, but not nearly as much as the sight of somebody cringing and bleeding in the back seat. Reflexively, Trick snapped the gun into position, ready to shoot.

"P-Please, Jack, don't kill me," sobbed the young man, who raised a hand streaked with fresh, wet blood in a feeble gesture of defense,

Trick stared, still aiming, his finger quivering on the trigger. It was not the voice of the cocky young Sir Brian Bedivere begging for his life, merely that of the terrified Brian Brannan.

Anger mixed with relief mixed with triumph, and Trick could see his mission coming to a better end than he had hoped. He kept the gun aimed, but he clicked on the safety mechanism so he wouldn't accidentally kill the kid he had at one time determined to rescue.

"I-I didn't mean to kill him," stammered Brian. "Sir Floyd was a good Knight. But he started shooting at Sir Kevin and me, so I started shooting back, and—"

"What, did you think this was another freakin' game of paintball?" cried Trick, thrusting the gun closer to Brian's ashen face. "How does it feel to splatter real blood? How about I splatter *you* a good one right now?" He lunged into the back seat, and Brian jerked his head back, his wet eyes popping wide and white in the glare of the dome light.

"Nooo, Jack, please!" he wailed, and he burst into wracking sobs punctuated by whimpers of pain.

But Trick did not back off. He pressed the barrel of the gun against Brian's nose and snarled, "What are you afraid of, *Sir* Brian? I thought you were good and ready to give it up to be—let me see, what was it?—a 'living claw in the Dragon's talons'? Since your so-called King Arthur's gonna kill you in the morning anyway, I'll just give you a couple of hours' head start."

"*Nooo!*" screamed Brian. "King Arthur says we won't die! We'll be transformed into a higher state, where we'll live forever!"

Trick chuckled, shook his head, then withdrew; his anger was vented. "I know someone who'd tell you that kind of immortality ain't what it's cracked up to be. Let me see what you've got there." He tucked the gun into the back of his jeans waistband and pried Brian's hand away from his wounded arm long enough to see that a bullet from Reggie's gun had penetrated the top of the bicep and emerged on the underside of his arm. The bleeding had slowed, but not stopped. By the amount of blood already soaking into his white shirt and pants, and smeared on the upholstery, it was clear that he could not afford to lose much more.

"What are you talking about?" panted Brian, who jerked away from him, but did not have the strength to try to escape.

"Never mind. What did you do with your gun?"

"Why do you want to know?" asked the boy suspiciously.

"I don't like you much, kid, since you broke my nose and killed my friend, but I'm gonna buy you an alibi. You're gonna need one—if you survive."

Brian sighed and closed his eyes. "I dropped it behind the car just before I got in."

"Stay put," ordered Trick, and shut the car door. The night was black again, and Trick fumbled in the darkness on his hands and knees behind the car until his fingers brushed against cold steel lying on the warm gravel. He picked it up with the loose tail of his shirt and polished the barrel and the cylinder and the grip until it gleamed to killing perfection in the fading starlight. Only the sound of his own feet crunching on the caliche followed him to the place where Sir Kevin lay still, and he knelt beside the sprawled body. Sir Kevin's hand was very cold now, and stiff, and no longer felt like it belonged to a human being, but Trick fitted Brian's gun into it and squeezed the rigid fingers around it until they curled slightly around the grip. He doubted that these machinations would fool a trained forensics expert, but if anyone from New Cadbury came upon the bodies of Sir Kevin and Reggie, their immediate impression would be that they had shot each other. That would leave them to wonder what had happened to Brian and "Jack," but Trick hoped that by the time anyone got around to such wondering that they would be far down the road to Fort Worth.

Brian winced when the dome light popped on again, as Trick opened the door and slid into the driver's seat. "You okay?" he asked, grasping the keys that jingled in the ignition, and started the car.

"Sure," replied Brian. "Duh!" he added sarcastically before the effort of coherent speech became a bigger burden than his weakened body could bear. He whimpered and sank down in the floor of the back seat.

With his hands on the wheel of the Honda, Trick quickly reviewed his options, and found that he had but few. Driving toward the highway meant risking an encounter with the other cars that had gone in that direction; Sir Kevin's car would be recognized instantly. He could travel farther down the road and hope to find a back road that would join up with another route to the highway, but that would waste precious time neither he nor the injured teenager in the back seat could spare. It was nearly an hour's drive to Fort Worth, and already the stars were fading; by the time they arrived, King Arthur's plan already would be underway. His only real choice was to find Reggie's nearby "safe house" and hope he could contact Tay from there. He did not stop to look again at the body of his friend, but turned off the headlights, shifted into first gear and drove forward slowly into the darkness.

Reggie's estimate had been correct. About half a mile down the road on the right, Trick spotted what looked like a junkyard. Old tires were piled high against the sagging fence, and rusted-out vehicles, scrap metal, and various castoffs too large for a city landfill were strewn on either side of an unmarked, rutted dirt road. Trick concluded that this was where Reggie had "scrounged" the parts for his barbecue cooker, and the memory of it made him all the more determined to succeed. In the midst of the junk sat a small camping trailer that looked as if it had seen better days, but its silvery color and aerodynamic shape clearly marked it as the Airstream that had been Reggie's hope of refuge. Slowly and carefully, Trick negotiated the narrow road and drove up close to the far side of the trailer, concealing the car from clear view from the road.

He hopped out of the car and tried the trailer door, but it was locked. Just as he was about to smash open a window with a piece of metal pipe, he was surprised to see a familiar figure appear, and he stopped. Owain's image was more ghostly than usual, but Trick could plainly see that he was pointing to a rusty coffee can pushed upside down into the ground beneath the trailer's tow bar. Trick knelt and grasped the edges of the can and pulled it easily from the loose dirt around it to reveal a small key on a ring with a dirty white plastic tag that bore a worn imprint of the U.S. Postal Service logo. He thrust the key into the door lock, and the handle turned easily. When he looked around, Owain was gone.

"Thanks, Owain," he said aloud anyway as he pulled open the door and stepped up into the trailer. Of course it was dark, but there was enough ambient light from outside to reveal a small flashlight on the floor by the door. He picked it up and thumbed the switch. Nothing. But when he gave it a little shake, it flickered feebly to light. He cast it about the tiny room quickly, and saw that it contained a bunk bed, a small dinette, and a miniature kitchen and water-closet. All were in disrepair and disarray, just as if the trailer were truly a part of the abandoned refuse strewn all around, with one notable exception: On the dinette table, a cellular phone sat in a charger, with a bit of duct tape covering the green LED that showed it was charged. A wire ran from the charger to a transformer to an unobtrusive solar panel in the trailer's front window that supplied power to the unit. "You go, Reg," Trick whispered appreciatively as he reached for the phone.

CHAPTER SIXTEEN

FIRST HE DIALED TAY'S HOME NUMBER, AND WAS SURPRISED TO HEAR her voice-mail pick up; he didn't take time to puzzle out why she did not answer personally, but said quickly and clearly, "Honey, it's me. I know you're gonna be mad but I don't have time to explain and you wouldn't believe me if I did, this is so weird. Listen close, now: Get all the help you can and get to the place that looks like an old military base that's about two miles down the first road south, off the I-20 service road heading back east to Fort Worth from the Millsap exit. You gotta get there before daylight or it'll be too late. And be careful, these people are seriously armed. I have Brian here with me in this trailer up the road from there. He's been shot but I think he'll be okay if I can get him to lie still. Hurry, honey, this is a very bad situation." He pressed the *End* button, and waited for the signal strength indicators to light up again. Then he dialed Tay's official FBI voice-mail number, where he left a similar message after her curt recorded greeting. Finally he dialed her personal pager, and at the prompt, entered *911*911*911*. If that didn't draw her attention to her other lines of communication, nothing would.

He replaced the phone in its charger and hid it behind the chair of the dinette, then went back out to the car, where Brian still sat slumped on the floor of the back seat, pale but alert. "Come on inside and lie down," said Trick. "I'll try to get that bleeding stopped. Help's on the way." Brian resisted, but even in Trick's weakened condition he was strong enough to pull the lanky teenager out of the back seat, and walk him unsteadily to the trailer. "It's a mess, but I call it home," said Trick as he helped Brian step up into the dark trailer.

"Who *are* you?" asked Brian, sinking down onto the narrow mattress, but remaining upright.

"Right now, I'm all that's keeping you from bleeding to death. Later, I might be either your best friend or your worst nightmare, but I'll let you pick. For now, you can call me Jack." Trick poked around in the storage compartments in the trailer, but found no first aid supplies. He tore a strip from the hem of the tattered, dusty curtain that covered the window and bound it snugly around Brian's arm.

"You won't get away with this," said Brian softly. "Once the others are transformed, they'll find me, and they'll take me to King Arthur. Then I'll be transformed, too, and I'll make you sorry you were ever born."

"You already are. Now lie down and be quiet."

Brian glared at him with eyes that would have glowed like coals had his injury not sapped his strength, but he complied. Trick stood up and stepped carefully out of the trailer, gazing toward the east and the help that he prayed would come swiftly from that direction. Unfortunately, the hint of a pale pink glow was creeping up onto the edge of the sky that signaled the approaching dawn. It was still deeply dark in the west, though, and his internal clock told him that it was around four-thirty; if he were at home in Alpine, he'd be enjoying his last half hour of sleep before rising for a day's work on the ranch. Would those days ever come again, he wondered?

"Our work is not yet finished," said Owain's voice suddenly, and Trick whirled to the darker west, where he saw the old man plainly. He stood with his sword in his hand, its blade pointed downward.

"Where have you been?" Trick demanded brusquely.

"Doing for you as you are doing for the lad in there: keeping you alive that I might accomplish my own task," replied Owain with equal directness. Then he raised the sword slightly and said more kindly, "For a time I bore the awareness of your pain myself, that your mind might rest more comfortably. If you did dream, you did walk for a time in my flesh, as I have done in yours."

Trick remembered everything he had dreamed through Owain's eyes, and was amazed at the explanation. "I did," he said simply, and Owain nodded, understanding.

"I sincerely regret all the discomfort I have already caused you, Patrick, but now I must ask you to return with me to New Cadbury and complete our task. At this moment, Mog Hwl's captains are preparing themselves for what they believe is their duty. They still do not believe that their King intends to slay them, and they do not know what they must do when they are transformed. They know only that they shall do the bidding of their beloved master, and if they are transformed, they *must* do as he says. Hear me, Patrick, even now they may be redeemed, if they are only shown Mog Hwl for what he truly is."

"Owain, you know that I want this stopped as much as you do, but listen: I can't go back there now. They'll kill me the instant they see me. Then I guess you could get yourself another set o' bones to walk you around, but I wouldn't want you to have to break your vows as a Traveler."

Owain laughed for the first time since Trick had been aware of him. "Ah, Patrick, what a sensible man you are. I chose you rightly as my champion. I did vow as a Traveler never to harm the flesh I take upon me, and I will not forsake that vow. But it is a risk we must take, my good friend, for we have no choice but to return. The dawning will come ere any help may arrive from the east, even at the speeds of this age. Therefore I must once again be cast as a caltrop into Mog Hwl's path, to hinder him and delay him, and yours must be the arm that hurls me." He turned the hilt of the sword toward Trick.

"Let me see about Brian first," sighed Trick, and turned back toward the trailer.

Owain smiled, and nodded. "I shall await."

Trick climbed back into the trailer and picked up the flashlight. He shined its feeble beam into the bunk area where Brian lay, pale and sweating. His eyes were closed, but they flickered open when the flashlight beam crossed his face. "Who are you talking to?" whispered Brian suspiciously.

"Santa Claus," Trick replied. "And he is really pissed. I wouldn't ask for a bicycle this Christmas."

A slight smile turned up one side of Brian's mouth, and Trick couldn't help but grin back. Out of hopeful curiosity, he tugged open the door of the small refrigerator and was elated to discover that Reggie had stocked it with two full liter bottles of Ozarka drinking water. They were room temperature, of course, but when Trick screwed off the cap of one and took a long drink of it, nothing had ever tasted so refreshing. He offered the bottle to Brian, who raised himself up and accepted it. He drank thirstily, too quickly, and he coughed and spluttered.

"Whoa, take it easy, a little at a time," cautioned Trick. "Finish it off. There's plenty more."

Brian drank a little more, then handed the bottle back to Trick. "Thanks," he said weakly, and eased himself back down. Trick replaced the cap and returned it to the inoperative refrigerator.

"Listen, Brian, I gotta leave you alone for a little while, but I or somebody else will be here to get you and take you where you can get that arm taken care of. Will you promise me you'll stay right where you are until someone comes for you?"

"I won't go anywhere with anyone but Lord Arthur."

"Fine. I'll send him right over. You promise?"

"Are you with the FBI?"

Trick hoped the darkness of the trailer camouflaged the look of surprise that must have shown on his face. "No," he said honestly. "Why do you ask?"

"No reason. I just thought . . . well, I got an aunt who works for the FBI. Thought my parents might have sic'ed her on me."

"Well, if they didn't, they should have. But no, honest to God, I'm not with the FBI, or any other agency. I'm just the Lone Ranger, trying to do what's right."

"So who's Santa Claus out there?"

"Nobody. My guardian angel."

"Sounded to me like some old dude."

The look of surprise jumped back onto Trick's face. "Did you hear him?"

"Yeah, but not real well. I heard him laugh. He *did* sound kinda like Santa Claus."

Trick smiled. So Owain wasn't just a figment of his own imagination after all! "Well, he's more like the Grinch, only with a *real* bad attitude, and you sure don't want to mess with him. I'm leaving him here to make sure you stay put. Promise you won't leave the trailer; I'd hate to come back and find what's left after he gets through with you."

A sigh, and then, "Okay. I promise. But I'm not leaving here with anyone except Lord Arthur or one of my brother Knights."

"I'm headed that way. I'll give 'em your message." Trick stood slowly and made his way carefully toward the door. He stepped out into the warm darkness and saw that what had been a pale pink glow in the eastern sky was now blended with golden highlights. Dew was settling on the scrubby weeds growing among the junk scattered all around him. The sun would be peeking over the horizon in a matter of minutes. He glanced at the black Honda, parked safely behind the trailer, but he knew that driving it back to New Cadbury was an invitation to ambush. He would have to return on foot, and even if he had had his full strength, he could not cover the distance in less than twenty minutes. He checked to be sure Sir Kevin's gun was still tucked safely into his waistband and set off, forsaking the road for the open country that rolled up to the chain-link fence surrounding the back of New Cadbury's grounds.

"We must hurry," said Owain's voice beside him.

"I *am* hurrying," replied Trick, breathing hard after only a few steps, "but this is as fast as this old beat-up flesh goes."

"What is a Grinch?"

Trick laughed aloud and jogged on.

He watched the ground at his feet carefully, alert to the dangers of uneven terrain and lurking reptiles, but he also watched the way ahead. As the sky grew lighter, his own dim shadow stretched out before him; Trick imagined that it was Owain, leading the way. In half the time he had imagined it would take, Trick found himself at the back fence of the installation, where the hill they called New Glastonbury Tor was a stubbly giant crouching between him and the old missile base. He remembered the night of paintball play, where he and Reggie had almost won the Tor until they each had taken a hit. That time, though, they had both gotten up. The memory of Reggie's body, now lying in the ditch and no doubt attracting fire ants, gave Trick an extra measure of determination to scale the fence that stood guard over the back of the compound and complete both their missions.

The climb was no easier the second time, and, at the top, he had to squeeze underneath the barbed wire by himself. This accomplished, not without some minor bloodletting, he decided that it was still better to climb at least partway down, rather than leaping from the top as Reggie had done. Once his boots hit the dirt on the inside of the fence, he turned to see Owain waiting for him. "Lucky you," panted Trick, rubbing his shoulder where the barbs had scratched him. "All you had to do was strain yourself through the wire."

"Quite the contrary; I did climb the fence by your side. And no matter what falsehoods Mog Hwl tells his poor disciples, Travelers cannot fly; we are as earthbound as living men. Shall you take the sword again now?" He drew the sword from its scabbard and turned the hilt toward him.

"Is this ceremony really necessary?" Trick asked impatiently. "We are in a hurry, you know."

"It is absolutely necessary. Indeed, I could walk into the halls of your thoughts as easily as opening a door, and you would not be able to resist me. But I was a man of honor, and I now honor the code of the Travelers, and I will not do so without your approval. Your acceptance of my sword is your acceptance of our conjoined charge."

Trick reached out his hand and wrapped his fingers around the hilt; again he was surprised by its weight and its corporeality, and then, by its sudden disappearance. But this time, though he felt Owain's presence, he did not feel like he had been thrust into a room where he was viewing what was happening as if on a television screen. He felt as though they were side by side, looking out of the same panoramic window at what lay before them.

The dawning slowly revealed the sparse features of New Glastonbury Tor as Trick carefully climbed its gentle incline, stepping carefully and quietly until he came to its crest. There he crouched down and waited, watching and listening. From this vantage point, he could see the entire compound, from the flat expanse of the missile launch area to the cluster of run-down buildings nearer the county road. In the middle of the buildings, near the B.O.Q., he could see the top of a bare flagpole. As he watched, he saw a new flag rise slowly to its pinnacle, and he heard a great cheer go up. At once he recognized the standard of the resurrected King Arthur: in the hoist, the three simple gold crowns on a blue background that symbolized the arms of the king of legend . . . but in the fly, the flaming golden dragon, ever watchful of its back, upon a blood-red field, that represented Mog Hwl.

Trick's heart sank as the flag rose. Had the deed already been done? Was the raising of the standard of the Independent and Sovereign Nation of Camelot the climax of a ceremony where the King now stood over the dead or dying bodies of his six remaining faithful captains?

No, it is not yet done, else I would be aware of them, said Owain's voice in his head, as plainly as his own thoughts. *But we must make speed.*

"After five hundred years, you're suddenly in a hurry," whispered Trick, even though he knew it was unnecessary to give voice to his thoughts. "I'll get us there, but I'm not going to get us— me—killed, if I can help it."

No guards patrolled the back side of the compound; Trick rose from his hiding place and made a run for the nearest building, the print shack. The downhill grade from the Tor gave him some momentum and some extra speed that he might not otherwise have managed, and in a matter of seconds he drew up in the deep shadow behind the small, stucco-covered shed. He still could not see anyone, but he could hear King Arthur's powerful voice addressing his Knights. As he spoke, Trick inched closer and closer to the gathering, hiding himself in the shadows opposite the sunrise, until he could see the multitude gathered beneath the flagpole, gazing toward their King. He stood on some raised platform facing east, and the rising sun sparkled on his brilliant armor, rendering it in colors of flame.

"My children, I grieve most piteously for our beloved Sir Kevin," said the King sadly, "and in due time we will gather to pay our final respects. His body now lies in the Innermost Circle. For the moment, let us take some small comfort in the knowledge that his murderer was likewise smitten down, and his untransformed soul shrieks in the pits of hell. And though Sir Kevin had not been transformed, his immortal soul awaits a resurrection in the coming Kingdom, which we shall set in motion this glorious midsummer morning.

"We know not the fate of our brave Sir Brian. It is believed that he was taken hostage by the traitor, Jack." The King spat. "May his name be cursed, and never spoken again inside this nation. But Sir Brian is wise and valiant and will wait steadfastly until the Kingdom has come, when he will overcome his captor and speed safely home to us. And lo, the Kingdom is at hand. My captains, it is time."

The six remaining Round Table Knights, who had stood at attention behind the King, stepped forward when he beckoned with his gauntleted right hand. They formed a circle around him and knelt, with their heads bowed and eyes closed. As Dame Valerie joined in the ceremony, Trick watched her no longer with desire but with pity. She looked tired; he reasoned that she must have been up all night. Did she—or any of the others, for that matter—have any idea what their beloved King had in store for them?

"Let us all be in a spirit of prayer for our brother and sister Knights as they prepare for their transformation," said the King, and a hush fell upon the gathered multitude as every head bowed, every eye closed.

Trick's hand moved slowly to his waistband, where Sir Kevin's gun rode safely out of sight. He was a better marksman with a rifle than with a handgun, but he had a clear shot and needed only to step out from his protective shade, aim quickly, and fire once. Though his instincts told him to proceed, his conscience and his symbiotic mentor resisted.

We cannot kill the flesh that Mog Hwl uses, said Owain's voice in his mind. *He will simply overpower another.*

So what do we do, boss? asked Trick's conscious mind in return.

We must await our moment, answered Owain.

In the stillness, Trick could hear a faint humming sound in the distance; he thought it might just be the sound of commuter traffic building on I-20, carrying through the moist early morning atmosphere. It didn't seem to bother the prayerful crowd around the flagpole, so he clung to the dark side of the building, and waited for Owain to name the moment for action.

The King raised his head and clapped his gloved hands; the small armor plates on them jingled, which summoned the rest of the gathering to attention. "Let us begin. Bring forth the Grail!"

Up from the crowd stepped Dame Anne from Joyous Gard. In her hands she cradled the golden chalice that had passed from one Knight to another during the ceremony of Convergence the night before. She presented it to the King and bowed gracefully before returning to the front row of the expectant company. The King lifted up the chalice and said, "Taste once more the blood of the resurrection, my dearest ones, and prepare for thy transformation into immortality. Take one small sip only, children."

Trick quivered impotently, restrained by Owain's greater will, as the chalice passed from Sir Jeffrey to Dame Rebecca, to Dame Sarah, Sir Robert, Sir Travis, and finally Dame Valerie. A bit of the dark liquid escaped from the corner of Sir Robert's mouth and dribbled down his chin, and Trick had a vision of Reggie, lying in the ditch, blood upon his lips. He clamped his hand over his mouth to stifle the sound of a sob.

Why can't we do something? he asked, watching the same dreamy look steal over each of the faces of the six Round Table Knights as they continued to kneel, swaying slightly in the intoxication that heralded their imminent transformation.

Then Trick stared in amazement as shimmering, translucent clouds flowed from their eyes, noses and mouths; formless at first, they assumed a vague humanoid shape just above and behind each of them. The ectoplasmic entities seemed to be standing behind the kneeling Knights, wrapped in a caul of gossamer that bound them to the mortal bodies from which they were separating.

You are seeing them as I see them, Owain said, and Trick remembered the discorporeal feeling after his taste of the wine in the chalice—and from his dream in Owain's memories, how Owain had felt as he knelt on the brink of his own transformation.

Then the King raised the cup to his own lips and took a sip. His eyes closed and his head lolled slightly, as not one but two spectral figures issued from his body. One was cloaked in the same ephemeral threads as the others and seemed to be in a moment of respite from great distress. But the second took shape completely separate from him, and as it resolved, Trick's amazement changed to horror—the entity's face was human enough, but its eyes were dead things, like a snake's eyes . . . like a dragon's eyes. He had seen in photos the same kind of peculiar glint in the eyes of others who had aspired to godhood, such as David Koresh of the doomed Branch Davidians, and Marshall Applewhite, known as "Do" to those who had followed him through Heaven's Gate. Trick shivered all the way down into his cracked cowhide boots when the eyes of Mog Hwl seemed to turn in his direction.

But they continued to turn, and Mog Hwl suddenly drew himself and the other entity back into the body they shared. Although a hush hung over the congregation, the King's hand rose up in a gesture demanding absolute silence. His eyes—the unnaturally pale but less disturbing ones of his human host—flicked from north to south, scanning the horizon for the source of the humming sound that had slowly increased in intensity as the sun climbed above the eastern ridge.

Trick could now make out the unmistakable guttural drone of an approaching helicopter. He risked a glance from behind the building, and he could plainly see in the distance its slim silhouette against the glowing sky as it moved purposefully toward the old missile base.

Thank God! She got my message! he thought happily. But when he saw the King's hardening visage, he suddenly wished Tay had chosen a stealthier conveyance.

"We are betrayed!" cried the King, thrusting his finger toward the approaching craft, and a frightened murmur rippled through the crowd as all heads turned in its direction. He grabbed the arm of the Knight kneeling nearest him, Dame Valerie. With Owain's eyes, Trick saw her discorporate self snap back into her body as the King wrenched her to her feet. "Go, quickly, and open the armory," he commanded. "Outfit all with weaponry and prepare my Knights to repel these invaders."

"My Knights, the battle is upon us!" shouted the King to the multitude. "What has begun here must not be delayed, and therefore Dame Valerie will lead you to arms. But once my other captains have been sent forth to fulfill the prophecy, I shall return to lead you in defense of our nation and our home."

Disappointment clouded Dame Valerie's tanned face as she realized that her transformation had been interrupted, but she obeyed the King's order. She rubbed her face with her hands, took a ragged breath, then called out, "Take the children to the Abbey where they'll be safer, and let one or two of you stay with them. The rest of you, follow me!" On slightly unsteady legs, she descended to ground level and pushed through the crowd, and the nearly two hundred anxious Knights of all ages and sizes streamed after her toward the missile launch area.

The King then returned his attention to the five remaining Knights, whose penultimate dose of the lethal elixir appeared to be wearing off. The ghostly figures surrounding them were diminishing, and Sir Travis was blinking and rubbing his temples, and attempting to stand up.

"Patience, my children," said the King, but there was a hint of desperation in his voice. "Now is our moment. Drink but one more sip, and thou shalt stand with me in eternity." He raised the chalice toward Sir Travis, and the young Knight's hands reached eagerly for it.

Now! cried Owain's voice in his head, and Trick launched like a missile from the shadows toward the concrete slab which served as an outdoor dais. He hurled himself between the King and Sir Travis and struck the chalice out of their hands. The goblet spun over the heads of the kneeling Knights, spilling its contents in a spiraling arc onto the concrete, and it landed with a dull *clunk* on the ground below. Trick also went down rolling, but immediately came to his feet with the gun in his hand, pointed squarely at the King.

Sir Travis started to rise, but Trick thrust the weapon closer to the King's face and the young captain shrank away. "Tell him to back off," panted Trick.

"Traitorous bastard," growled the King. "Stand away, Sir Travis, but do not fear for me. Even if he kills my body, my resurrected soul shall take refuge in another. Perhaps it shall even be yours."

"I think not so, Mog Hwl," said Owain with Trick's voice, and the King's sallow face lost the rest of its meager color.

"Speak not that name, betrayer. Thou dost not know me."

Trick took a step closer, and allowed Owain to continue to speak. "Thou didst not know *me*, Mog Hwl, yet thou murdered my family, destroyed my home, and laid waste to my lands. And this thou must have done for pleasure, for it gained thee no throne. Wilt thou murder again today merely to revel in the discord?"

"Who art thou, to speak such blasphemies to my face?"

"One who has traveled long and far to meet thee here."

The King's pale eyes bored into Trick's, and once again, Trick could see the malevolent visage behind the flesh. He himself might have cowered, but Owain held his body rigid, steadfast, and returned stare for stare.

"Caergwyndwr," said the King, and Owain nodded Trick's head slowly.

"There it began, Mog Hwl, but here it shall end. Owain, by right of land and the grace of God, King of Caergwyndwr am I. Release the unwilling flesh thou hast taken and meet me upon a field of honor."

A smile twisted the lips and crinkled the eyes of the King, and he laughed wickedly. "I will meet thee in hell, thou interfering fool. You cannot harm me, and you cannot stop these good and willing Knights from completing their transformation and fulfilling my prophecy."

Trick could feel Owain's rage and frustration building, and marveled at how well he held his temper in check. But he was utterly horrified when Owain turned and fired one round squarely into Sir Travis's thigh. The brawny, ponytailed Knight screamed and collapsed, moaning and bleeding, onto the concrete.

"I have already dealt with Sir Brian and Sir Kevin," said Owain calmly, and carefully moved his aim toward Sir Jeffrey, who shuffled backward and fell off the concrete slab, sprawling awkwardly in the dirt. Dames Sarah and Rebecca knelt to comfort Sir Travis and each other, and Sir Robert simply ran away, vanishing behind the nearby B.O.Q. Owain returned his aim to the King and said, "Verily, I cannot harm thee in thy flesh, Mog Hwl, but I will harm thy cause in any way I can."

The King stared malevolently at him, but the small smile that flickered on Trick's face was more his own than Owain's. He was proud of Owain's determination and his restraint, and felt confident that if only they could hold Mog Hwl at bay for just a little longer, help would arrive and the whole episode would be brought to a swift and satisfactory close. Already the helicopter, a small craft with some kind of official markings upon it that Trick could not quite make out, was making a slow, wide circle around the perimeter of the old missile base. No doubt its occupants already had spotted him and this small group in the center of the facility; he hoped that Tay was aboard, so she could see that he was all right, at least for the moment.

"Good and true Knights, hear me for only a moment," Owain began.

"Listen not to this traitor!" stormed the King, but Owain went on.

"You have been sorely deceived, for this is not King Arthur, nor even a king at all. His name is Mog Hwl, who is a Traveler, or, if you will, a wandering spirit. But this person you see before you is only a man whose name we do not know, willingly or unwillingly possessed by Mog Hwl for his own wicked purposes. You must now be told that the world of Chivalry he has promised for you is only a means to his own ends, for if his so-called prophecy had come to pass, it would have meant the deaths of the President of the United States and His Royal Highness the Prince of Wales. And you would have been the instruments of their death, upon your transformation into Travelers such as Mog Hwl and myself.

Indeed, I, too, am a Traveler, speaking through this good and willing man you call Jack. It is not my desire to harm anyone, but I will indeed do what must be done to assure that you are not made into creatures like Mog Hwl. It encourages me to see that you do still fear dying; know now that your next sip from the cup would have meant instant death for your young bodies and unending torment for your souls."

The four cowering Knights seemed to absorb Owain's words and glanced back and forth between him and the King, as if weighing what he had just said with all that they had come to believe. Trick sensed that their faith had been deeply shaken, and in this moment of indecision, they might come to the truth.

Then something else caught Sir Jeffrey's attention, and he looked upward in the direction of the buildings behind them. Trick noticed the movement, and followed Sir Jeffrey's gaze to the roof of the B.O.Q., where Sir Robert had just appeared, dragging a wooden crate shaped like a small coffin by its rope handle. *Is he gonna shoot us with paintballs?* Trick thought in confusion as he watched him toss open the crate. But the weapon he extracted looked like an oversized camcorder with a long cylinder that stretched out behind it, and when he flicked open the caps at either end, Trick recognized it as a Vietnam-era rocket launcher.

"Oh, my God," whispered Trick, and he could also feel Owain's sudden dread. Frozen by their shared fear, he could only stand and watch as Sir Robert raised the weapon to his shoulder and sighted directly at him through an optical viewfinder. For a moment, Trick could almost see straight down the barrel of the launcher to the tip of the tiny missile, and only Owain's more courageous presence in his mind kept the perennially-cued Vietnam nightmare loop from playing again in his memory and eradicating all other coherent thought.

The helicopter made a slow turn around the missile launch site and headed back for another pass around the base. Sir Robert slowly turned his aim from the human targets he had only teased to his true mark as it approached at a low altitude.

Tay's on that chopper!

"Nooo!" Trick screamed, and pushed away from the King and Knights, charging helplessly toward the B.O.Q.

Too late; with a percussive *whump!* the rocket was away, in a cloud of propellant gas. Instantly, the early morning sky was brightened by a brief but brilliant fireball that erupted over New Glastonbury Tor, then was darkened by clouds of black smoke that billowed from the remains of the helicopter as it slammed into the hillside.

CHAPTER SEVENTEEN

NEW GLASTONBURY TOR BLAZED LIKE A TORCH, TRANSPOSING THE tranquil colors of morning sunlight with the feral colors of dusk. The flaming wreckage kindled the dry grass and thirsty shrubbery, and white smoke poured into the sky alongside the black as the secondary fire steadily gnawed its way up and down the hillside.

For a moment, all was silent except the insistent crackling of the fire crawling down the hill toward the back fence of the compound. Then one of the female Knights crouching beside Sir Travis choked on a sob, and for a millisecond, Trick saw Tay as he had last seen her: bundled in terrycloth, smiling from her front porch as he drove away, unaware of the path to hell that Trick was paving for her with his good intentions.

With a roar of fury, Trick raised the gun and squeezed off three shots at the roof of the B.O.Q. He saw Sir Robert go down, but did not know if he had been hit or was only diving for cover. He did not stop to check, but wheeled about and charged the concrete platform where the King and Knights had been standing. Sir Travis was now upright, with the aid of Sir Jeffrey and Dames Rebecca and Sarah, and the four of them scrambled awkwardly in the direction of the underground facility. Trick ignored them, and pursued the King, who had already bolted in the opposite direction.

Never before in his life had Trick been so enraged and at the same time so empowered. Reggie's death had torn out his heart, but now it lay in a charred lump on the hillside along with the woman he had loved as he had loved no other. In its place pounded an icy ball of steel that pumped anger into every cell of his body. Now Owain was merely a passenger in his mind, but his presence, and the memory of his own murdered beloved, gave Trick an extra measure of courage and passion.

The King had disappeared from sight, but Trick's earlier surveillance had given him a clue where to look. He raced directly to the print shack, and found its solid wooden door shut and locked. A quick glance through the cracked, cloudy window showed him he was on the right track: The door inside, to the "closet," was slightly ajar, and it was slowly swinging to. Still fueled by his wrath, he kicked at the door with his boot heel again and again until the weathered wood splintered out of its frame. He jammed his arm through the breach and turned the knob on the inside, and dashed past the duplicator and scattered paper and supplies to catch the inside door before its latch could click shut.

Beyond the door lay a small concrete landing, and below it, steps descending into darkness. With no hesitation, Trick galloped down twenty steps until he stumbled forward on level ground. As the gravity slowly closed the door above, blackness engulfed him, and his forward steps reverberated dully, as if in a padded cavern. He stopped and listened, holding his breath, and he could just make out tiny echoes of careful footfalls in the black distance. He kept his right hand thrust forward clutching his weapon, but trailed his left hand along the moist concrete beside him. His fingers passed over wide cracks where plant roots had penetrated the tunnel wall, and he moved steadily, swiftly, through the narrow passageway. The air was heavy, musty-smelling, and stale, but he paid it little attention as he pressed on through the gloom, alert to the possibility that the King or one of his minions could be crouching in ambush anywhere ahead.

At last, after what Trick estimated was a quarter of a mile, his footsteps echoed less hollowly, and he felt more confined, as if the tunnel had narrowed to a point. The nose of his gun bumped into a dead end, startling him, but he gathered his wits and began feeling along the featureless wall for a door. In only a moment, he found one; it had only a simple metal handle, but when he pulled on it, he found that it was as heavy and solid as a bank vault door. He had to pocket his gun and use both hands to haul it open , and before he stepped through it, he drew the weapon once more.

His feet now stood on carpet; its smell was a curious mixture of new fibers and the ancient mildew of the tunnel he had just traversed. He hesitated just inside the door, knowing that the King had to be somewhere nearby. Keeping his back close to the wall, he moved slowly to the left, and after only three tentative steps bumped into something soft. He reached out to it gingerly, and discovered an upholstered side chair; further tactile exploration conveyed that it was a wingback chair, covered in some kind of acrylic jacquard fabric. A fringed throw pillow lay in the seat.

Carefully he moved around it, still searching with his left hand, and his fingers curled around a cool, polished metal cylinder about an inch in diameter. He could hardly believe his luck as his hand slid up the pole to discover a small dangling chain: a floor lamp!

He switched it on. Forty watts of light stabbed his unacclimatized eyes, and he winced, but when they adjusted, he took in the sight of a small, formal living room. The walls were textured plaster, not cement, and they were painted in a warm neutral color that complemented the mingled neutrals of the thick Berber carpet on the floor. Another wingback chair sat in one corner of the room at an angle to the first, the lamp between them. Across the room was a long sofa of the same forest green fabric as the chairs, and in front of it was a low coffee table with a glass top. On either side of the sofa were occasional tables with brass lamps that matched the floor lamp. Above it, upon the wall, was a smaller replica of the Grand Arms, also made of hooked yarns.

In the wall opposite the door Trick had entered was another door. This one was made up of decorative wood panels and was polished to a high sheen. Its handle was a graceful dragon carved of wood. On a small display stand by the door sat the King's golden helmet. It had been placed there carefully, probably in the interim between the ceremony of Convergence and the aborted sunrise transformation service. Trick was certain that he had at last gained access to the Innermost Circle. He wrapped his hand around the dragon-shaped handle and wrenched open the door.

It was dark beyond, but Trick's fingers fumbled upon the wall beside the door for a light switch. He found a surface-mounted box with two switches, and flicked them both up. Fluorescent lights wobbled on, illuminating a long, rectangular conference table with ten fabric-covered, junior executive-style desk chairs neatly tucked up to it. Trick smirked at the incongruity: The so-called Round Table actually had corners. Across the room was another door, and yet another one to the left. He went to the one on the left first and pushed it open. It led into a small bedroom, which was simply furnished with a full bed, an antique wardrobe, and a wingback chair similar to the ones in the living room area. Another door inside the room was standing open, and Trick could see that it was a small private bath. The bed was made, but the spread appeared to have been lain on recently; one pillow was uncovered and still bore the depression made by someone's head. *I guess our King grabbed him a little shut-eye before coming upstairs to kill his kids*, Trick thought grimly.

Trick moved on to the next door, and beyond it he found a kitchen containing apartment-size appliances, but enough pots and pans and dishes stacked on open shelves to cook for a large family. More open shelves served as the well-stocked pantry for the Innermost Circle; there was as much food stored here as there was for all the rest of the residents of New Cadbury. In one corner of the kitchen, a large trash bin lined with a plastic bag contained the remains of the previous night's feast that Brian and Kevin had brought from the main dining hall ... which now seemed like days rather than hours ago. Trick recalled bitterly his role in its preparation—how he had enjoyed the task, before he had known whose table he was spreading! The trash bin stood beside yet another door, and he strode through it as he had done all the rest.

It was a utility room, with still another door opposite, and a narrow stairway leading upward right beside it. The room contained an old washer and dryer and the ordinary accoutrements of housekeeping. It also contained the body of Sir Kevin. Startled, Trick gasped and nearly stumbled on it. The body lay face up on the floor, pushed up against the wall beside the stairway, and partially covered by a worn, flower-printed bedsheet. The waxy, sunken face was still caked with dirt and blood. Next to his head sat a large, family-size box of laundry detergent: *Cheer*, it read. Trick had gotten the impression that the martyred Sir Kevin was lying in state before an altar surrounded by candles, not lying in the dark like a pile of dirty laundry. Nonetheless, it was a better place than Reggie had earned. The memory of Reggie pumped another spurt of anger and adrenaline into Trick's veins, and he passed the stairs and pushed through the next door on his quest for the King.

He stepped out into a long, narrow corridor that turned sharply to the right, where light and sound were vaguely discernible from its end. With his back to the wall, Trick edged slowly toward the light, and as he drew closer to what became visible as an open portal, he could hear voices speaking in agitated but controlled tones. He risked a peek through the opening. Beyond was another missile bunker, just like the cavernous concrete box in the ground that had been converted into New Glastonbury Abbey, but this one was unimproved—the institutional green paint still coated the tall walls, with all the stenciled warnings in black and red just as they had been for forty years or more. The elevator platform appeared to be rusted into its lowered position. Most, if not all, of the adult Knights who had followed Dame Valerie from the aborted sunrise transformation ceremony, including the members of the Round

Table, were each clutching a rifle or a handgun or both, and their attention was riveted on the far corner of the room. There stood the King, in his wrinkled and disarrayed royal finery, upon a make-shift platform of drywall panels stacked two feet high.

The King's voice rang out over all the others, and he declared, "It is not too late to complete the transformation, dear children, and bring our wondrous prophecy to pass. We have already struck one blow for the dragon; the battle is upon us, and we cannot turn away now."

"I don't *want* to go to battle!" wailed a young female voice, followed by a chorus of affirmative murmurs.

"We must! How else will our Independent and Sovereign Nation of Camelot be forged unless we are challenged? America and the Crown must acknowledge our independence, else we are no nation at all, and our dream of a world of Chivalry must remain that—only a dream."

"But why kill the President and the Prince of Wales?" asked the voice of Sir Jeffrey. "How will that bring about a world of Chivalry? Lord Arthur—Mog Hwl—whatever your name is—all that will accomplish is getting us all killed! Don't you know that who-ever sent that helo is going to send all kinds of reinforcements? We're probably surrounded right now!"

Dame Rebecca chimed in, "And you never told us that our transformation would kill us. We believed we would be able to travel farther out of our bodies but then return to them. What else have you lied to us about?"

"I will not listen to this blasphemy!" stormed the King. "You have been deceived by a clever traitor. Why will you abandon all you have experienced, all that you have learned, all that you have hoped for, all you have come to believe?"

After a pause, Dame Rebecca spoke up again. "We can't forget all we've learned, and we still hope for a world where Chivalry will be the law of all lands. But I just don't think we believe in *you* anymore."

Suddenly sweet and solicitous, the King spread his arms and smiled. "Dear children, why would you abandon me now, when our freedom and liberty are but one glorious battle away? Why, where would all of you Texans be if there had been no battle of the Alamo? Today is our battle, and New Glastonbury Abbey is our Alamo. Will you not rise with me to defend it?"

Now is your moment, lad, said Owain's voice in his mind, *and in but a moment, it will be mine.* Owain's will directed their shared body to pocket the gun, and together they walked slowly and deliberately into the missile bunker.

"Your knowledge of Texas history's lacking, Mog Hwl," said Trick, with his eyes staring directly at the King and ignoring the Knights, who had fallen absolutely silent, and who cleared out of his way as he marched a straight line up to the platform. "But ironically enough, it's the first honest thing I've heard you say."

Trick stepped up on the opposite side of the small platform and looked out over the hundred and fifty or more armed Knights who were staring incredulously at him. "So this will be our Alamo, will it? Does anyone here remember what happened at the Alamo?"

There was some uncertain murmuring, and Trick continued, "That's what I thought—nobody *really* remembers the Alamo! Well, let me tell you: Every brave man inside its walls, including the legendary Davy Crockett, ended up being slaughtered! Afterward, all the bodies were dragged into one giant heap and burned, like a bunch of animal carcasses. See, I went to public school before they invented political correctness, and back then they taught history like it really was—and some of it was pretty gruesome. Your King wants to make heroes out of you. Is that the kind of heroes you all want to be—dead ones?"

The murmuring in the room began again, but the King shouted, "Silence! I will not be humiliated by this traitor in my own home. Knights, I command you: Destroy this betrayer!"

"Call not upon the children to do the father's work," said Owain, who suddenly seized control of Trick's voice. "Destroy me thyself,

Mog Hwl, if thou darest."

Trick's left hand reached to his right side, but he did not grasp the gun, which was tucked into the waistband of his jeans. Instead, he felt his hand close around the soft leather that cushioned the steel of Owain's sword. He could even hear the ringing of the blade as it slid out of its scabbard, but he was not completely amazed until he actually saw the steel glittering in the harsh glare of the incandescent lights caged in the ceiling above. The simultaneous sudden intake of breath by all the Knights in the room seemed to suck all the oxygen from the air.

"Thou wouldst not meet me upon a field of honor, Mog Hwl," said Owain, as he traced a circle in the air with the point of the blade. "Now, I will meet thee in thy dwelling, as thou didst come to mine, in *combat à la outrance*, to the death. If there is aught of a king's mettle in thee, thou godless fiend, draw now thy sword!"

The King's face grew livid, and he quivered all over, as if he were about to spontaneously combust. Then, with a terrifying roar, another blade appeared out of the thinned air, and the King lunged forward.

The two swords collided with a loud, ringing crash that reverberated throughout the room, and the force of it threw Trick backward, hard, upon the concrete floor below the stack of drywall. Stunned, disoriented, he struggled to raise himself before the King's sword could smite him again. But he saw as he regained his footing that the King had also been hurled backward by the blow, and lay stunned on the floor a few yards away from him. The Knights nearest to the platform recoiled from it, and Trick looked upward to see the battle still raging—but now, it was Owain and Mog Hwl, visible to all, face to face and hand to hand.

The battle was terrible to behold, but everyone in the missile bunker stood transfixed by it. Steel rang upon steel, and sparks showered from the two blades as they collided over and over with a deadly intensity. The substance of the two Travelers vacillated from solid to ethereal, and the accompanying sounds of the struggle varied in volume according to their visibility. The small stack of drywall slid and scattered as their feet, when corporeal, stamped upon it and they stumbled, but the two combatants fought on. Their conflict moved out into the crowd, and the Knights cleared the way for them, for the swords, when solid, gouged into the strewn drywall panels and flung white gypsum dust into the air. Even when barely visible, the swinging swords could leave a stinging welt upon skin, as one of the Knights discovered as he reached out his hand to try to touch one of the ethereal beings. He backed off with a yelp, and the Knights around him recoiled even farther from the ghostly contest.

In the midst of it all, Trick heard Owain's voice in his mind, shouting, *Get them out, Patrick! Get them all out, now! Hurry!*

Still unsteady on his feet, Trick scrambled over to Dame Valerie and caught her by the arms. She stared at him in a mixture of terror and admiration as he gasped, "We've all gotta get out of here, now!"

"Jack, I—" she began, reaching her hands toward him in a gesture of supplication.

"No time for discussion! Get some of them out by the main stairs, and some out by the stairs in the utility room, but don't try to go out through the tunnel. Don't let anyone take weapons out of here—if they do, they're a target waiting to happen if there are any officers topside. Get Rebecca and Jeffrey to help you. Sarah, you help Travis." Trick turned to the Knight whose face was contorted by pain as he struggled to stand. "Sorry, man, it wasn't my idea," said Trick, as he helped Dame Sarah haul him to his feet.

"I know," said Sir Travis through gritted teeth. "But I'm still going to kick your ass."

In the brief echoing calm between periods of the combatants' corporeality, Dame Valerie shouted from the bottom of the main stairs, "Quickly now, but orderly, everybody evacuate. South side, follow Sir Jeffrey! North side, come with Dame Rebecca and me. Leave all weapons behind! I repeat, take no firearms with you!

We'll all gather together when we get outside, and wait for new orders. Move!"

Trick had to admire the element of the Knights' training that compelled them to obey orders. They lay their firearms down on the floor where they stood before they moved, and then there was a surge toward the exits. Even in these desperate moments as the Knights crowded into the stairways to the surface, most of the male Knights allowed the female Knights to go ahead of them. *Chivalry is still alive*, Trick thought with a wry smile.

The battle between Owain and Mog Hwl did not diminish as the minutes ticked past—it grew in intensity. Unencumbered by physical bodies, the two immortal creatures fought on and on, tirelessly. As they did, their visible aspect grew less and less material and more spectral, and an oppressive, electrical energy filled the room, as though a thunderstorm were building within its concrete walls. Flashes of electrical current crackled intermittently on the steel beams supporting the launch door and upon the wire cages that protected the light bulbs. The hair on Trick's arms and the back of his neck raised up like porcupine quills as he helped herd the Knights nearest him toward the main stairwell.

When the last of them had their feet on the steps, Trick took one more quick look around and found one stray: the King. The man who had been the host body for Mog Hwl still lay face down on the floor next to a broken piece of sheetrock, his red robe dusted with chalky gypsum, his arms covering his head. Avoiding the burgeoning maelstrom of energy that swirled about the room, Trick made a dash for him, almost swimming through the suffocating atmosphere.

"Leave me!" cried the voice of the King when Trick put his hands on the man's shoulders, but it no longer carried the authority that Mog Hwl's words had given it—now it was only the voice of an anguished old man. "What have I done? Oh, God, what have I allowed to happen?" he sobbed. "Go away, leave me! I want to die."

"Maybe later," said Trick, and he wrestled the man to his feet. His pale eyes were reddened with tears, his formerly aristocratic countenance screwed into a mask of agony.

"You don't understand! I allowed that beastly—thing!—to enter my body, and it has made me a murderer. Oh, God, how many more would I have slain?"

Trick pushed the image of the burning wreckage on the hillside out of his mind for a moment and insisted, "Well, it's gone now. Come on, pal, let's make ourselves scarce, too." He looped the King's arm over his shoulders and with his right arm around his waist, led him firmly toward the main stairs.

"What's your name?" Trick asked as they fought through air as heavy and noxious as transparent smoke, which undulated with the erratic rhythm of the incorporeal combatants.

"Arthur," said the man, and a sound that was at once a bitter chuckle and a sob tore from his throat. "That, of all I was forced to say, was true. My name is Arthur Edward Cossett, and I am a fool."

"Well, then, you're in good company—lots of 'em here, including me. Come on, up we go." Trick allowed Cossett to go ahead of him up the narrow stairs and gave him a little push to start him climbing. He looked over his shoulder to see that the entire chamber was filled with a pulsing, swirling glow like a tiny captive sun about to go nova.

Trick emerged from the first of the three missile bunkers into a bright morning, cloudless except for the white smoke that billowed straight upward from the smoldering Tor and the area just inside the compound fence. The fire had already blackened the Tor, and now blazed on an adjacent hillside. All the Knights were nearby, milling around nervously on the surface, watching the grass fire creeping toward the decrepit buildings of the main base.

The ground beneath Trick's feet trembled slightly, as if a heavy truck or a train were passing close by. "Move back!" shouted Trick, and waved his arms at the Knights to get their attention. "Get clear of here!" The crowd shuffled uncertainly, but all the Knights moved *en masse* past the second missile bunker—the Abbey—toward the third.

The Abbey's pedestrian door clanged open, and one of the young female Knights emerged, holding a bawling toddler on her hip. "What's happening?" she cried, and the baby wailed louder.

"Everybody out of the Abbey, now!" yelled Sir Jeffrey over the crackling of the fire and the slight rumbling that now accompanied the vibrating of the ground around the first missile bunker. The young Knight dashed back down the stairs, then reappeared holding a larger child by the hand, as well as the baby. She was closely followed by another woman who carried an infant in one arm and guided two young school-age children with the other. Some older grade-schoolers emerged by themselves, bravely leading younger ones, and then another adult appeared, carrying a sleeping toddler, oblivious to all the excitement. She beckoned desperately to whomever was still below on the stairs.

Arthur Cossett moved slowly, as if in a trance, drained of all the energy and vigor that Mog Hwl had conveyed to him. Trick grabbed his arm to hasten him along, and said, "Hurry up, man, none of the rest of us wants to die of old age waiting for you."

"Betrayer!" cried a voice nearby. "Take your hands off my King!"

Trick spun around just in time to see Diane, still standing partway in the Abbey stairwell a few yards away, raising up a small revolver with both hands. Her round, delicate face was flushed and her jaw was set, and her blue eyes were like melting ice behind narrow slits.

"Honey—" he said, and she squeezed the trigger.

His consciousness registered four gunshots, but he felt only the first one as it burned into his chest, and then no pain at all. For a moment, he thought that perhaps Owain had returned and was bearing the awareness of pain for him, as he had done before. He could see the sky pulling away from him but did not feel it when his body slammed backward onto the uneven gravel and concrete surface of the missile launch area.

The world was spinning, and as it spun, it hummed, louder and louder. The ground beneath him quivered, and he dimly recalled the unusual but minor earthquake that had rumbled the mountains of his Big Bend area home in 1996. When he saw the huge steel missile bay doors swing upward like window shutters in a stiff Texas breeze, his deteriorating consciousness protested feebly that they were designed to swing down; then a brilliant white comet of energy blasted through them, straight through the brownish-white clouds of smoke into the blue sky beyond, and for a moment, the morning sky gleamed as bright as noon. The brightness dimmed rapidly as the comet disintegrated in the cooler stratosphere, and its minute fragments dispersed and disappeared like a spent Fourth of July rocket. For Trick, the light kept on dimming until all was blackness, but with it came a deep, satisfying sensation of closure, of contentment, of peace.

CHAPTER EIGHTEEN

"JIMINY CHRISTMAS, THE PLACE IS ALREADY ON FIRE!" OBSERVED ROOKIE FBI agent Lonnie Baxter as the unmarked car in which he rode raced down the gravel road toward the source of the smoke that was visible for miles along Interstate 20 west of Weatherford. "The least they could have done was wait till we got here to torch the place, so they'd have someone to blame."

At the wheel of the white Crown Victoria, Diego Benavides winced at the memory of the botched Branch Davidian operation. He had been on another assignment that day, but he would never forget the effect it had had on every man and woman in the entire agency. His friends in the Bureau of Alcohol, Tobacco and Firearms felt the blame even more acutely, and though years had passed since that fateful April morning, the images were still vivid in their minds. Mistakes were made, no doubt about it, but the media had made certain that the knowledge of all the procedures scrupulously followed, correct actions taken, and proper responses made in the suddenly incendiary situation were eclipsed by the more sensational news of what had gone so tragically awry.

And now, right before his very eyes, it appeared to be happening again. He ignored Baxter's thoughtless attempt at humor and said only, "I just wish we could have done something sooner."

"We did what we could," Baxter replied, and gripped the door handle and dashboard as Benavides braked to a sliding, gravel-scattering stop behind a Texas state trooper's pursuit vehicle parked on the side of the road opposite the fenced compound. A law enforcement anachronism on wheels, the late model Chevy Z28, painted black and white and arrayed with a light bar, siren, and multiple antennae, sat at an angle on the raked road embankment as if lurking in wait for speeding civilian sports cars. The trooper in his gray uniform and matching Stetson hat stood in its open door and gazed through binoculars at the blazing hillside beyond the chain-link fence.

"FBI," announced Benavides as he and Baxter leaped out of the car and flashed their badges for the wary officer.

The trooper stood at attention and said respectfully, "Sir, there's a chopper down on the hill over there, I'm sure of it. But it's not one of ours—could it be one of yours?"

Benavides shook his head. "I don't think so. Our backup's coming in transports, along with an ATF assault team. They're about five minutes behind us."

"No structures are involved yet. This is all grass fire, except for the wreckage you can see through the binocs, but it's getting mighty close to the old missile base buildings. I've called the county sheriff and the volunteer fire department. Sir, if you don't mind telling, what's going on here?"

"I'm not really sure myself. Let's just hope we can sort it out as quickly as possible." Benavides turned to his junior partner and said, "Bax, get on the comm and see if we're missing a helo, and if we're not, who is." The younger man nodded and ducked back into the car, which was fully outfitted with top-of-the-line mobile communications equipment. In only a moment, he was in direct telephone contact with a dispatcher, and on a notebook computer he had the vast resources of the Internet and the restricted FBI database at his fingertips. Benavides smiled a little, glad that the kids coming up through the ranks these days had cut their teeth on computers, so that older ones like himself could still get out and do the old-fashioned legwork once in awhile.

Benavides and the state trooper exchanged what little knowledge they each had about the scene and the situation, and in less than the estimated five minutes, the first army-green personnel transport truck rumbled over the crest of the hill. It bore the markings of the U.S. National Guard, but the dozen officers that piled out of the back of it all were wearing dark jackets and caps with the letters *FBI* clearly stenciled in high-visibility yellow. A second troop transport ground to a halt beside the first, but the ten officers that dismounted from it were dressed in riot gear and carried assault rifles in plain sight. The next vehicle on the scene was a long, hulking recreational vehicle specially equipped to serve as a mobile command center. It drove past the officers already on the scene, and parked almost directly across the road from the missile base gate. Another half dozen ATF officers emerged from the back door of the craft, including one in a coat and tie, who strode purposefully over to Benavides.

"Nice to see you again, Isbell," said Benavides, accepting his ATF counterpart's handshake.

"You, too, Benavides," answered Isbell. "What's the situation?" While Benavides brought Isbell up to date, all of the FBI agents gathered around Benavides, their commander on scene, and the Kevlar-clad ATF operatives waited for Isbell's orders.

Some minutes later, a fire engine pumper—old but painstakingly polished, bearing the markings of the Palo Pinto County Volunteer Fire Department—and a water truck lumbered over the ridge. The fire chief viewed the armed FBI and ATF officers with dismay, and called out from the cab of the pumper, "Is it okay if we go put out that fire, or do you guys have some tanks you want to roll in first?"

"No, sir, chief, but we are about to execute a legal search warrant," answered Benavides deferentially, but with an edge on his voice that conveyed his lack of amusement.

"Won't be much left to search if you don't let us in, and those old rickety buildings back there catch," answered the chief, unfazed by the display of Benavides' and Isbell's badges.

"Special Agent Benavides, I have an update," called Baxter from the car, speaking formally in the presence of fellow officers. Benavides gestured to the fire chief to wait and then hurried over to the car.

"What do you know, Bax?" he asked.

"Well, it's definitely not one of ours, nor the Highway Patrol's. But I just heard on the scanner what sounds like someone calling a craft that's not responding." Baxter tuned the radio scanner until a female voice, calm but strained, repeated, "Traffic One, do you read? Please respond, over."

"TV station, maybe?" speculated Baxter.

"Could be," answered Benavides. "Or radio. Tay said she knows a pilot who flies the traffic 'copter for that Dallas all-news station, who'd help us if we needed...geez, I hope that's not him up there."

"Where *is* Tay, anyway? You'd think the brains of this operation would be the first one on the scene."

"You'd think so, now that she's finally convinced our boss that something's actually going on out here. She said when I talked to her before daylight that she was going to get some help and would be out here as quick as she could." A sudden realization struck Benavides hard, just above his belt buckle. "Oh, my God, the chopper..."

Baxter's head jerked up and his eyes widened. He shook his head in disbelief and gazed up to the blackened hillside. "No, Jim, it can't be."

Benavides clenched his jaw and both fists and said, "I'm not waiting for Padgett. Our part of this op is commencing right now, and our first objective is to recover that—whoa, what's that noise?"

A deep bass rumble poured over the hill cloaking the missile base like a tidal wave, and the gravel road beneath their feet trembled. The aerials on the Crown Victoria, the Z28, and the command unit began to sway wildly, as if caught by a sudden sharp wind. At Isbell's barked command, the ATF assault team snapped to atten-

tion and began advancing toward the chain-link fence, weapons up
and ready. Then, with a final, wrenching pulse that shook one
agent off of the fence he was scaling, a huge white fireball shot
skyward with such velocity that its dim tracer could scarcely keep
up with it. For a moment, the ground below was bathed in the
stark white light of a prolonged lightning flash as the fireball rock-
eted into the atmosphere. High above the brown smoke, in the
deep blue of the new day's clear sky, it silently disintegrated into a
million twinkling fragments and vanished.

For a moment, not so much as the sound of breathing could be
heard on the gravel road. Every single FBI and ATF operative, as
well as the state and county officials, stood gazing up into the sky
with jaws dropped in astonishment.

"Jiminy *Christmas!*" gasped Lonnie Baxter at last. "What in the
cat hair was *that?*"

"That had to have been some kind of missile," declared Isbell.
"We don't need your search warrant now—we're going in. Have
your men back us up, Jim—no telling what we'll find in there."

Benavides found his voice, once he had gulped down a huge
lump of incredulity and restarted his brain. "Wait for me!" he cried
to Isbell, as well as to his own agents, but they were already racing
toward the fence. He stopped Baxter and whispered urgently, "Bax,
get back on the horn and get hold of NORAD and see if anything
registered on their scopes. Find out if anybody got a seismograph
reading on that tremor. Somewhere, somehow, get us some evidence, or else no one will believe what we just saw—whatever it
was, it was no missile."

"I'll do what I can," said Baxter, and dove back into the car.

The fire chief sat impatiently in the driver's seat of the vintage
fire engine, and called out, "Hey, J. Edgar! Can we go put out that
fire now?"

Benavides wheeled around, and for an instant, the fire in his
eyes burned hotter than the hillsides. But by the time he got to the
pumper, he had forced his countenance into one of cool authority.

"Chief," he said slowly and firmly, "we apparently have a very volatile situation inside the fence. There is a helicopter crashed on the hillside over there, which may be the cause of the fire. I doubt there will be survivors, but just the same, I would like for you to call for medical backup before you approach the fire. And I think it would be better if you went in from the other side, just in case things get more dangerous than they already seem to be. If it does turn hostile, you get your men out of there and let the grass burn. Do you understand me? Do you have any questions?"

"Yes, sir. No, sir," answered the chief, chastened. He restarted the engine of the old pumper and added as he drove away, "Sorry about the J. Edgar thing."

The fire trucks turned around awkwardly on the narrow gravel road, and hastened back to another gate in the fence where they could gain access to the blistered countryside. Benavides checked his weapon in its shoulder holster and hurried toward the gate, which the ATF agents had already broken down. They were scrambling over the crest of the hill with the FBI agents close behind.

Even though he knew full well the weight of his responsibility as leader of the FBI team, he could not help but glance toward the hillside, where fresh billows of light brown smoke cascaded into the air as the county firefighters began to pour water onto the fire. He hoped his imagination was only running away with him, but he had indeed heard Tay tell him that she was going to "get some help" and get out to the site "as soon as possible." If he knew Tay, she wouldn't hesitate to commandeer a helicopter. Earlier in their unofficial investigation, she had told him of Peter Maine, a pilot who flew helicopters for the pool of traffic reporters that worked for Dallas-Fort Worth area radio stations, who had agreed to help them if needed. He had only to put two and two together to deduce that this had come to pass . . . and now, tragically, to an end. Jim Benavides felt another lump rising in his throat, for he had become more than fond of Tay over the past weeks of their covert operation, and he was certain that in some measure, the feelings were becoming mutual.

He had to push it all out of his mind and concentrate on what lay ahead. As he crested the hill, only a few paces behind his men, the first row of dilapidated barracks came into clear view, and just behind them, the rest of the old military base. A colorful flag was flapping in the gentle breeze on a pole situated somewhere in the middle of the buildings, but as he watched, it was hauled down the pole and another one was run up—a plain white one, probably a towel or part of a bedsheet—indicating surrender.

Benavides and Isbell called out simultaneously, "Halt!" and the almost two dozen FBI and ATF agents stopped in their tracks. They glanced at the newly hoist flag, then backward at their leaders. Isbell said, "Let's keep moving in, but more slowly. And be alert—it may just be a trick."

The agents continued advancing; their leaders moved forward in the pack, but kept themselves cautiously behind the armored front line. They passed the first row of barracks and saw the cars parked inside—and just beyond them, probably sixty or seventy more, all lined up neatly, as if they had been parked by valets.

"Good God, how many are here?" Isbell wondered aloud. He glanced over at Benavides and said, "These people think they're *Knights?*"

Benavides shrugged and said, "I told you everything I know. The guy on the inside, Tay Silvestri's ex-boyfriend, will give us the details."

"I know Silvestri," said Isbell. "Why isn't she here? This is her collar, isn't it?"

Benavides shook his head and started to venture his theory about the helicopter when two people emerged from the cluster of buildings just ahead of them: a black-haired man of about thirty, and a younger blond woman. Both had their hands up, and worried expressions on their faces. The agents on the front line dropped into crouching fire positions, but Isbell snapped, "Hold your fire!"

The two froze in their tracks, and Benavides stepped forward, with his badge in one hand and his service revolver, pointed upward, in the other. "Special Agent Diego Benavides, Federal Bureau of Investigation. This is Officer Donald Isbell, Bureau of Alcohol, Tobacco and Firearms. If you have weapons concealed on your persons, slowly reveal them and place them on the ground in front of you."

"We're unarmed," said the young man, and the woman beside him nodded. He started to lower his hands, but the locked-and-loaded agents tightened their aim and his hands rose upward again.

"You want to tell us who you are and what's going on here?" asked Isbell.

"I'm Sir . . . I'm Jeffrey Matthews. This is Rebecca Gill. We've come to tell you that . . . that what we had here is over, and we all want to go home. We don't want any trouble. We all just want to get out of this place."

Benavides and Isbell looked at one another suspiciously: *This is too easy*, they each seemed to say. "Well, that might be doable," said Benavides, "but it's not that simple, Mr. Matthews. In the first place, there's a crashed helicopter on the hillside over there. What can you tell me about that?"

Jeffrey ducked his head and gulped, "It was a mistake."

"If it was deliberately downed, I'd say, uh-huh, a big one. But go on: What was that missile you launched a minute ago?"

Both Jeffrey and Rebecca shook their heads, and Jeffrey said, "We don't know what that was. All we know is we were deceived, and except for the helicopter, we didn't do anything. We just want out of here, no trouble."

"How many are here?"

"Including the two of us, there are one hundred and eighty-six men, women and children at New Cadbury. Sirs, there are six of us, including Dame Rebecca—I mean, Miss Gill—and myself, who will accept all responsibility for all that has happened here today."

"No, there is but one," said a voice behind them, and all eyes turned and stared as a third person appeared, hands in the air—

upon which were golden gauntlets that glittered in the morning sunlight. A man of about sixty, with a tangle of shoulder-length, graying brown hair, wearing a golden breastplate, and trailing the tatters of what had been a fine red velvet cape, approached from the buildings beyond. His shoulders were squared, and his head was held high, but his seamed face was pulled tightly forward, as if it were holding back a tempest of emotions.

"Lord Arthur!" gasped Rebecca in astonishment.

"No, no, no lord. Arthur am I, but no king, and lord of nothing but sorrows," he said with the same mellifluous voice with its lyrical Welsh cadences, although now cracked with fear and fatigue. "It is all my doing, and I shall tell you all, though you will think me quite mad. I think me quite mad, too," he added with a chuckle that ended in a sob. He turned to Jeffrey and Rebecca and said, "I thank you, dear young friends, but you need not share in this. Let it be all upon my head." He stepped past the two and slowly lowered his arms, hands down, in a gesture of supplication and surrender.

Dumbfounded once more, Benavides mustered his wits about him and placed his hand on the back of the pathetic old man's wrist. He pulled a set of cuffs from his belt and recited from memory the Miranda warnings as he locked them around the golden gauntlets: "You're under arrest for criminal trespass. You have the right to remain silent. You have the right to an attorney . . ."

Isbell reached into his coat pocket and pulled out a radio transceiver. He keyed the switch and said, "Ops, this is Isbell. Need secure transport for two hundred. Over."

"Say again, two *hundred*, over?" crackled the response from the mobile command center.

"That's affirm, Ops. Two hundred. Over."

"Roger. Out."

Benavides handed off custody of the suspect to one of his subordinates and said, "I guess this is a mere formality now," and reached into his inside coat pocket to draw out the legal document he carried. He showed it to Jeffrey and Rebecca, then pocketed it again. "So I guess you won't mind if we take a little look around. Why don't you come along and show me what you've done with the place?"

Accompanied by five of the FBI agents and all but two of the ATF operatives, Benavides and the two suspects entered the compound, where dozens of silent, apprehensive men, women and children stood in uneasy ranks as they marched from an area even farther beyond the old buildings. Some of the smaller children whimpered, but no one said a word. Pairs of agents ducked quickly inside each of the buildings as they passed, and emerged after a moment signaling "all clear" before moving on with the others.

The fence and buildings at the back of the compound showed some slight exterior smoke damage, but the grass fire had burned itself out before reaching them. One little building's door appeared to have been kicked in, revealing a small offset duplicator inside, but the agent who checked it indicated that it was otherwise empty.

Benavides and the others pressed on, until they came to the gate in the back of the chain-link perimeter that led out onto a wide, flat expanse of concrete with three distinct surface features, which he recognized as a missile launch site. The launch doors of the first bunker were splayed open and twisted backward onto the ground, as if they had been wrenched apart by giant, clumsy hands. A team of agents raced ahead to investigate that scene, while Benavides looked beyond it to the second bunker. There he saw five stragglers. The three standing included a brawny young man with long hair in a ponytail, his right thigh bloody but bandaged, who was leaning heavily on a young woman with brown hair cut in a short bob and tears streaking her face. An attractive woman with strawberry blond hair fraying out of a long braid down her back was hugging her arms tightly to her body, as if cold on this warm July morning, and was gazing down sadly at the last two.

A heavyset woman with short, frosted brown hair, dressed in a matching T-shirt and leggings outfit of tie-dyed blue, knelt on the ground sobbing, and clutching the lifeless body of a man with long reddish hair and a short, darker beard, who lay on his back on the dusty concrete, a pool of blood seeping out from beneath his shoulders.

"Jack, oh, Jack, I'm so sorry," she wailed over and over again. "I didn't know, I didn't mean it. Oh, God, Jack, no."

Benavides instantly recognized the downed man, in spite of the name the hysterical woman was moaning, and he tossed up his hands in frustration and rage. First Tay, and now Trick!

But before he could curse aloud the vagaries of fortune, a white minivan topped the hill and came tearing toward the launch site gate in a cloud of dust, knocking it fully open as it barreled through. It ground to a halt, but while it was still sliding, both front doors swung open. Out of the passenger side loomed up the daunting figure of O. D. Shackleford, FBI, retired. From the driver's door leaped Special Agent Tay Silvestri.

CHAPTER NINETEEN

Diego Benavides could not hide the smile of relief that brightened his face as he jogged toward the minivan to meet Tay. "Thank God you're here," he said, and he reached out to grasp her hand. But she already had spotted the weeping woman embracing the body on the ground, and the look of horror on her face told him that she could see nothing else. "Tay, wait, you shouldn't—" he began, but she pulled her hand away and sprinted across the concrete as nimbly as if she were wearing Reeboks instead of the dress pumps with heels that matched the suit with a conservatively short skirt and a jacket to cover her shoulder holster—which she had been wearing since the day before.

"Let her go," said Shackleford, putting a hand on Benavides's arm to stop him from following. "It may be the last time she'll ever see him. Give her that moment."

Tay slid in beside Trick like a base runner stealing second, almost knocking a pretty red-haired woman standing beside him off her feet. None too gently, she peeled the plump woman's arms off of him, ignoring her wails of protest, and saw his white shirt soaked with blood. In spite of the knot of fear clenching her stomach and the lump of anguish rising in her throat, Tay forced herself into emergency response mode. She ripped the shirt open and quickly spotted one small bullet entrance wound in the left chest and another beneath the ribs, both still bleeding. She pressed her ear to the middle of his chest, but heard nothing.

"Can we get a little CPR over here?" she shouted to the agents emerging from the underground building nearby. Her voice was clear and authoritative, but her courage was wavering, and she was on the verge of not caring if it showed. Her hopes rose a little when one of the ATF men who had just come up from the missile bunker tore off his riot mask and dashed over to them.

"Is he alive?" he asked, kneeling beside her and gently lifting Trick's eyelids.

"No, I killed him," wailed the woman kneeling on the ground. Her blue and white T-shirt was stained dark red across the front, and she hugged herself tightly as the weight of her grief pulled her off balance and she sat down heavily. "Oh, Jack, Jack, I loved you so much," she cried plaintively. "They told me you were a traitor. I didn't know you were the real king."

Tay glared in annoyance at the round-faced woman's babbling, but her obvious anguish accurately represented what Tay was suppressing. She blinked hard over her own tears and softened her gaze. The woman had loved Trick, just as Tay had, and—in spite of her frustrations with him and recent developments with Jim Benavides—still did. "Hush," said Tay firmly but gently, and the woman continued to sob, but more quietly. For the first time, Tay noticed a small handgun lying beside her, and quickly followed her instincts to retrieve it into evidence. Covering her hand like a mitten with one of the plastic evidence bags she carried in her coat pocket, she scooped it up and dropped it into a second bag. She tucked it safely into the pocket until she had the opportunity to hand it over to the lab.

Meanwhile, the ATF agent performed skillful CPR on Trick. Mindful of the gunshot wounds, he alternated chest compressions with mouth-to-mouth resuscitation, and after several long minutes of deliberate effort, he panted, "We got a little heartbeat happening now, ma'am."

Tay, the heavy woman, and the pretty woman all gasped in surprise and relief, as if the ATF man had spoken to them individually and the others were not there. He continued his efforts on Trick's behalf until two paramedics arrived, carrying a stretcher. They all watched as the two medical technicians checked vital signs and continued CPR until it was determined it was safe to move him. Trick was carefully lifted onto the stretcher, covered, and strapped down for safety in transit. When they lifted the stretcher, its wheel assembly unfolded and locked into place, and without a word, they hurried their emergency patient toward a waiting ambulance.

Tay allowed herself one sniffle and flicked away her tears with the back of her hand. She stood, arranged her skirt and her twisted, laddered hosiery. She offered a hand up to the woman quivering on the ground, and when she struggled to her feet, she put her arms around her and held her for a moment. *Thank you for loving Trick while I was...distracted,* Tay thought. *I know he loved you, too.*

She released the woman, and saw that some of the blood on her shirt had offset onto her jacket lapels. Tay dabbed at her own eyes as they teared up again, but she took a deep, ragged breath, pulled out her badge, turned to the redhead and said, "Special Agent Tay Silvestri, FBI. You're under arrest for criminal trespass." More gently, she said to the trembling woman whose tears had abated, "You're under arrest for criminal trespass and assault with a deadly weapon. You both have the right to remain silent..."

BY THE TIME DEPUTY DIRECTOR PADGETT ARRIVED ON THE SCENE, ALL the excitement was over, and the mop-up was proceeding apace. Buses from the Weatherford school district had been brought in to transport the nearly two hundred bewildered suspects back to Fort Worth, where holding cells were being cleared to keep them all until formal charges could be filed. In all, one hundred sixty-nine adults awaited charges of criminal trespass and possession of unlicensed firearms; arrangements were being made hastily with Child Protective Services for care of the children while their parents were in custody. Most of the firearms were found in the first missile bunker, which the apparent earthquake had partially caved in. ATF agents bravely entered the structure and recovered and bagged as many rifles and handguns as they could.

The volunteer firefighters had finally quenched the stubborn grass fire and reported uneasily that the downed helicopter had carried two passengers, but dental records would be required for their identification. The discovery of a body in the rubble of the first bunker, another on the roof of the two-story barracks building, and a third in the bar ditch almost a mile down the dirt road—all victims of gunshot wounds—brought the total fatalities to five. The spent rocket launcher on the roof with the dead man seemed to answer the question about the helicopter crash, but the three dead from gunfire were mysteries yet to be solved.

Tay saw Padgett driving up in a white Suburban, followed by two agents in another featureless car, and her jaw clenched with disdain. If she and Benavides had waited for him to accompany them to the scene, as he had insisted when she woke him up just after five o'clock this morning, the odd inhabitants of the missile base might have decided to dig in for a long standoff. God only knew when—and how—that would have ended. She knew he would immediately demand a Situation Report, and then, in spite of the apparent success of the operation he had grudgingly authorized, the ass-chewing would begin.

But Tay had something else to do. Almost forgotten in all the excitement was the reason why all this had come about in the first place—her missing nephew, Brian. She was surprised and somewhat disappointed with herself that she could not work up more concern for the kid's welfare at this point.

When her pager had gone off that morning at five, she had been dozing at her desk at the office, where she was catching up on the official paperwork she had neglected while conducting her un-official investigation. She retrieved Trick's desperate message from her voice-mail and immediately flew into action; first she called Jim Benavides, who took over the mechanics of the operation and implemented the plan they had devised for gaining a legal means of entry to the missile base should it become necessary. Then she called Padgett, and she was annoyed when his wife answered the phone, but she told him what was happening and begged for his official blessing; he had granted it, but only upon the condition that they wait until a "reasonable hour" to proceed. She crossed her fingers and agreed. Then she called Shackleford, because she knew she could count on his help—and he was glad to oblige, even at five in the morning, even though it was inconvenient.

Trick had told Tay in his message Brian had been shot, but probably would be all right until she got to the place where he had stashed him. Now she had but to go there and bring him out, and her original mission would be accomplished. This thought did not generate any enthusiasm for the task; it only made her angry.

She drove past Padgett on her way out, and pretended not to notice him waving and pointing and otherwise trying to get her to turn around. Following Trick's sketchy directions, she turned up the dirt road and drove slowly past the roadblock the highway patrolman had set up, and began looking for the old trailer he had described. She spotted it about half a mile beyond where yellow crime scene tape fluttered on wooden stakes, marking the spot where a body had been found.

Tay wheeled the minivan across the embankment that spanned the ditch, and killed the engine in the junkyard just beyond the fence. There among the old tires and junked cars sat a beat-up old Airstream camper. Parked behind it, completely out of sight from the road, was a newish black Honda Civic, which she recognized from the briefings Jim had given her on his surveillance.

Cautiously, she reached into her jacket, drew out her gun and chambered a round—with the car parked there, someone else had to be in the trailer with Brian. She approached carefully, her eyes shifting all about, and tried the door; it was unlocked. Now she wished she had brought a partner to open the door for her and cover her while she confronted whoever was behind it, or vice versa. It was foolish to attempt a forcible entry alone, but here she was, and her time and temper were short. She took a deep breath, yanked open the door with her left hand, and took aim with the gun in her right as she cried, "Nobody move! FBI!"

In the dim morning light inside the trailer, a human figure on the bed flinched and whimpered, and Tay kept her aim steady as she made certain it was the only occupant of the tiny trailer. "Brian?" she asked softly.

"Aunt Tay?" came a feeble whisper. Tay holstered her weapon and crossed the trailer in two steps, where she found her nephew trying to sit up on the bed but slumping weakly back down.

"Whoa, Brian, take it easy, it's okay," she said softly, and sat down beside him. She reached out and felt of his face, which was cool and clammy, and he groaned when she touched the bloody sleeve of his shirt. A strip of some threadbare, dusty cloth had been wrapped around his arm, just tightly enough to stanch the bleeding.

"Am I busted?" he asked as she undid the makeshift bandage to peek at the wound beneath.

"No, but consider yourself in my protective custody," she answered. The bullet wound had a clean entrance and exit through the bicep, and it appeared to have stabilized, but he was still shocky and pale.

"What happened out there? Was that an earthquake? Where's King Arthur?"

"Shh, be still. We have to get you to a doctor."

"I'm not leaving here with anybody but my lord King or one of my brother Knights. I told Jack so."

Tay recognized the alias Trick had apparently been using, and said, "Well, Jack's not here now, and there are no more Knights of the Once and Forever King. The man who calls himself King Arthur has been arrested, and he's going to jail with the rest of your friends. You come with me right now, and I won't let them take *you* there."

Tay could see Brian's whole world crumbling in his eyes, and turning to tears. He sobbed, and she gathered him into her arms and held him like she had done only hours after his birth seventeen years previously. For a moment, her anger was forgotten, and she held and rocked and patted him while he wept. There were a hundred questions she wanted to ask, but this was not the time.

"I only wanted to live forever," he sobbed. "The King promised me he would make me immortal, like himself."

She did not know how to respond, and so simply kept silent until his grief was spent.

Brian was too weak to walk, so Tay piggybacked him awkwardly out of the trailer and let him lie down on the floor in the back of the minivan. She started the engine and returned to the county road, then drove slowly up to the Highway Patrol roadblocks, where she was cleared to pass. The last of the buses was leaving for Fort Worth, and the ATF agents were packing up their riot gear. By now, all the medical personnel would have cleared out, so she determined to drive Brian to the hospital herself. She wanted to go wherever they had taken Trick, so she pulled out her car phone and dialed Jim Benavides' cellular number to ask him where that was.

As they passed the main gate of the old missile base, she saw one of the unmarked government cars pulling out. In its back seat sat a distinguished-looking older man, with long, graying brown hair whom she remembered Jim pointing out to her as the so-called King. His face was puckered into a grimace of deep emotional pain. Tay glanced into the back of her van to make sure Brian was still lying down so he couldn't see how terribly mortal the King truly was.

In spite of Agent Silvestri's insubordination, Gordon Padgett was very pleased with the way things had been handled as he walked up to the ATF's mobile command unit. There, Benavides and the ATF guy whose name Padgett couldn't remember were standing outside, drinking coffee from styrofoam cups. Benavides was talking on his cell phone, and the ATF officer was writing on a clipboard. They both looked tired and sad, even though it was only a quarter past eight and the radio weatherman had forecast a near-perfect summer day.

"Well, I guess we're not in for a standoff today," declared Padgett almost merrily.

Benavides thumbed the *end* switch on his phone and said to Padgett, "You sound disappointed."

Padgett chuckled. "No way. Not after I call the Director and tell him that we pulled off this operation without a hitch. Zero mistakes."

Who's this "we"? Benavides wanted to ask, but he held his tongue. He was not amused, and even Isbell had noted Padgett's patting himself on the back. Lonnie Baxter climbed out of the white Ford parked nearby and came over to the big RV, flipping through the pages of a yellow legal pad as he walked.

"Director Padgett," he acknowledged politely, but he offered his report to his immediate superior. "I got all the information you asked for, Jim. Good news for Tay: It definitely wasn't her friend Peter Maine flying the chopper. I picked up his two-way communications on the scanner—he's flying traffic for the KRLD morning drive-time show, as usual."

"I know she'll be relieved about that," answered Benavides. "Do you have any idea whose 'copter it was?"

"Yes, sir, I do. It was the Channel 17 news chopper, with their investigative reporter, what's-his-name, er—"

" 'Tabloid Talbot' McRae? The guy on TV in Dallas who always has those muckraking, sensational, manufactured stories?"

"The same. Apparently he got a tip that there was a separatist group operating out here, and he wanted to get a look at their 'compound.' He sure picked a bad time, huh? I bet I can get hold of the name of his source if I lean on his news director a little." He flipped a page of his tablet. "Okay. I got hold of the U.S. Geological Survey, and their seismograph registered a four-point tremor out here, a little one, according to the guy I talked to. They'll be sending out a team to assess geological damage, but I advised them to wait until we got through."

"Good idea," said Benavides. "What did you get from NORAD?"

"Not much. They said their satellites registered something, but they haven't figured out what it was yet, and they aren't going to say until they study the telemetry. The guy I talked to said it was probably a meteor—they notice lots of 'em on their satellites, but they burn up before we can see 'em from down here. When I told him that it was going the wrong way to be a meteor, he just laughed."

"Had to have been a missile," said Isbell. "If these people were able to get hold of a rocket launcher, they could get hold of a SAM. This was a Nike base, after all."

Padgett spoke up. "Whoa, what are you talking about? Meteors . . . missiles . . . *what?*"

"It's hard to explain, Gordon," said Benavides. "But here comes someone who might have an idea." All eyes followed his pointing finger across the road. Over the crest of the hill came O. D. Shackleford, headed in their direction. He had a worried look on his face that they could see even at that distance.

"What's *he* doing here?" demanded Padgett. "He's retired! He has no authority any more, and he sure as hell doesn't have any clearance."

"We didn't have any authority, either," replied Benavides, "but we needed some help, and when you wouldn't give us any, Tay called someone who would."

"I authorized this operation today, didn't I?"

"Yes, but if you'd done it when she first asked, maybe none of these five people would have died."

"Don't throw those victims at me, Benavides. I had no hard evidence upon which to base an investigation at that time. I still don't, except for what Tay told me her boyfriend said."

"I guess you don't have any instincts," he countered. "Haven't you ever just acted on a hunch that turned out to be right?"

"Intuition is in the women's department," retorted Padgett, "and if you ask me, there are too damn many of them in the Bureau these days."

Shackleford, who had just gotten within earshot, remarked, "Hey, Padgett, it's true what I hear—you really *are* a first-class yutz!"

Padgett's face went livid from the neck up, and his hand snapped upward to wag his finger in Shackleford's face, but he had to reach too high to make that point—especially after the big man drew himself up to full, intimidating height and rearranged his features into a menacing scowl. "What are you gonna do, Padgett, fire me? Have me charged with obstructing an investigation? You're the one who obstructed it in the first place, you witless wimp. Not every good collar has to originate from the Attorney General's office—sometimes your people dig them up on their own. Just on principle, I oughta pound your broad bureaucratic ass into a little greasy spot on the road, but your agents would be compelled to defend you, and I don't want to hurt two good men."

Padgett glared back, then whirled and snapped at one of the FBI agents who had come up to report, "What are you looking at? Come on, get it finished, and let's get out of here. Move, move, move!" He stalked off, barking orders at every agent still within earshot. Benavides and Baxter did not suppress their smiles.

"Damn, Shack," said Isbell, also grinning with admiration. "Now that you're retired from the FBI, you want to come work for us?"

Shackleford chuckled, and replied, "Thanks for the offer, Don, but now I'm working for the wife. She keeps me plenty busy. Listen, would you excuse us a minute? I need to talk to Jim and Bax privately."

Isbell gave Shackleford a comradely slap on the arm and went over to assist his men, who were loading up their equipment.

"What is it, Shack?" asked Benavides.

Shackleford sighed and looked down at the ground for a moment. "I wish Tay were here now, but I'll tell her later. I went down into the bunker and had a little look around while Isbell's guys were picking up weapons. It's a mess, as you might expect from that tremor, but it's a clean mess. There's no scorching, no scoring, no fusing or melting or pitting—no physical evidence at all that any kind of ignition or explosion occurred down there. Whatever went flying out of those missile bay doors wasn't anything manufactured by man."

"Say what?" asked Baxter incredulously.

"I knew it wasn't a missile," Benavides said. He knew that Tay and Shackleford had once worked together on an investigation that involved some kind of paranormal activity, but she had never told him anything about it.

"Then what was it?" demanded the rookie agent.

Shackleford shook his head. "I don't know. I can't even begin to guess. All any of us can do is pray that Trick McGuire lives to tell about it . . . otherwise, we'll *never* know."

They stood silently and uncomfortably for a minute, then Shackleford said, "You guys mind if I bum a ride with you back to Dallas?"

"Sure, Shack, no problem," said Benavides. "Let me make sure all my guys get back on the trucks, and then we can head out." He jogged over to the waiting transport trucks, leaving Baxter and Shackleford to walk to the car by themselves.

"You'll make a good agent, son," said Shackleford as he folded himself into the back seat of the Crown Victoria.

"Thanks, Mr. Shackleford," replied Lonnie from the front passenger seat. "That means a lot, coming from you." He paused.

"You know, I can't believe the media aren't all hovering out here like a bunch of buzzards. I haven't seen a single reporter trying to sneak through the roadblock."

"Oh, haven't you heard? The president and the Prince of Wales are both landing at Love Field today, and they're having a joint press conference there at noon. I'll bet you every reporter in Texas is already out there on that tarmac. What kind of news is bigger than a president and a prince in town on the same day?"

"Well, we had a civilian helicopter shot down, we arrested two hundred people for piling up enough guns to liberate Bosnia, we were at the epicenter of an earthquake, and we watched a . . . an anomaly . . . blast through foot-thick steel doors and rocket into the stratosphere like the Hale-Bopp comet. You're right—for news, nothing beats a couple of famous politicians, grinning into the camera and asking for money."

CHAPTER TWENTY

Trick McGuire saw many remarkable things before he opened his eyes.

The first thing he saw was a blindingly bright light all around him. *Am I dead?* he wondered. The light was what a lot of people described when they had had a near-death experience and lived to write a book about it. But the books also claimed he would see many of his departed loved ones, such as his grandparents, his funny Aunt Mary and stern Uncle Roy, his high school best friend Dale, who had died at eighteen in a rodeo accident . . . and Tay . . . especially Tay. It was peaceful and pleasant, but he seemed to be stuck in one place rather than moving toward the source of the light. Then the light began to fade and recede, and he found himself back in the dark again.

But he wasn't alone.

"You needn't be in such haste, my friend," said a familiar voice. "It will come sooner for you than it did for me, but it is still many years away."

"Owain?" asked Trick, and he was certain that he spoke aloud.

"It is I indeed, your old companion at arms." Owain's form stepped out of the darkness and stood in a dim beam of light that cast deep shadows upon his face and body, but Trick could see him plainly. He was no longer dressed in his rustic tunic and breeches like a Merryborough peasant, but in a handsome suit of ring-mail armor, with a dark green cape over his shoulders. His hair and beard were neatly groomed, and they showed less gray and more auburn, as if in death he had regained the appearance of younger, happier days. "We have done it, good Patrick. Mog Hwl is no more; the substance of his being is scattered upon the winds forever. I, too, have claimed at last that great gift, but unlike him will soon pass beyond into the wondrous Light. Before I leave for that happy land where I shall meet my Briallen at last, I have a gift for you. It is a token of my gratitude, my admiration, and affection, for you helped me to accomplish a quest I began more than five hundred years ago, and the world is now a better, safer, more honorable place."

Trick was curious, but apprehensive. "I really didn't do anything, Owain—you did all the important talking, which probably did more to stop what Mog Hwl was trying to do than anything else."

"Perhaps. But it was your brave heart and strong arm that made it possible. That is why I want you to have this." Owain reached to his side and drew his sword from its scabbard. He turned the hilt to Trick and held it out to him.

"No, I couldn't," said Trick, and he was certain he was shaking his head.

"The gift is not the sword itself, but what you will do with it. Take it, Patrick. Take it, and you will know what to do."

Trick hesitated, but then he slowly reached out and let the leather-wrapped hilt of Owain's sword sink slowly into his palm. He closed his fingers around it, and hefted its perfectly balanced weight as he raised up its gleaming steel blade. "Thank you," he said, and he was certain he gave a gallant little bow.

Owain retreated into the shadows, and he said as he disappeared, "Farewell, my friend. Live well."

Darkness overtook him once more, but only briefly. Then the curtain of his subconscious rose upon familiar images in black and white, with no soundtrack. There he lay, in his damp cot in the sweltering tent that was his in-country Vietnam home, until habit more than duty compelled him to roll out and head to the mess tent to begin breakfast for the combat troops. The dream played on, in minute detail and in real time—it seemed to go on for hours, just like the long-ago reality had done. There was chief cook Smitty, with his cigarette ashes flaking into the biscuit dough, then dying in a burst of machine gun fire; young Reggie, stumbling through a cloud of acrid smoke, bravely but vainly defending his camp in the wake of the Viet Cong assault; and poor Rodriguez, the first victim of the summary judgment upon the American captives, pitching face down into the mud.

Trick could hear his racing heart and his panting breath as the horrific scene wore on, moving beyond the point where he would wake up and be spared the knowledge of the dream's true end. He remembered a recent manifestation of the dream, when he had heard a voice thundering, *Behold Excalibur!* and a glittering sword had appeared within reach. But that did not occur this time; instead, the reality continued. Rodriguez fell, and Trick squeezed his eyes shut to await his turn. He flinched at the shot that killed Kaplan, the guy next to the guy next to him.

But it wasn't the Viet Cong who had shot Kaplan.

Trick opened his eyes. Out of the jungle roared the morning patrol, thirty grunts in all, with guns blazing. The four VC renegades died instantly, and their bullet-riddled corpses crumpled among the bodies of the Ops Support men they had executed for their own amusement.

Trick slowly melted into the mud, as if what little spine he had left had turned to butter. He was still too terrified to experience any sense of relief, even with the grim-faced ground-pounders hovering all around him. Although in the dream he did not hear it, he remembered all too well what had been said: A voice nearby whispered hoarsely, "Hey, Billy, I saw you shoot the Jew boy. Did you do it on purpose?"

"Naw, he was just between me and the gook," replied Billy casually. "But I would've aimed a little more careful if it'd been old Trick here. Good cooks are hard to come by."

Trick lay on the ground and his eyes popped open in disbelief at the soldier in the limp boonie hat who knelt down next to him, as unconcerned as if what he'd just done were no more serious than jaywalking. But when he saw that Trick was conscious, Billy's eyes narrowed to dark slits in the shadow of the brim of his hat. "You didn't hear anything, McGuire. Not a damn thing. You just forget all about it. Understand me?" he hissed. Then louder, more jovially, more to the other grunts on the scene than to Trick, "You're one lucky sumbitch, Trick! You're as good as homeward bound today. You'll probably get a Purple Heart just for pissing your pants!"

Laughter echoed all around as panic, humiliation, and rage whirled around in Trick's mind, and he could bear no more evil on one day. His consciousness simply slipped away into a cloud of vague images and indistinct memories of sounds. The next thing he would remember clearly was waking up two days later in a bed in the American hospital in Guam. He could not recall anything that had happened after the execution of the man before Kaplan. From that moment onward, whenever he relived the events in his nightmare, the flash and the sound of that gunshot would wake him in a veil of sweat.

But now, more than twenty-five years later, in the dream that had robbed him of a good night's sleep on too many occasions, something very different occurred. As he began to lose consciousness in the final moments of the now-concluded nightmare, he experienced the feeling of his awareness separating from his body, just as it had done when he drank the wine in King Arthur's chalice. For an instant, he felt as though his eyes and nose were being sucked off of his face by the tension as his sentience gathered outside his body, as if he were about to become a Traveler. With his elevated consciousness, he could see the fine, undulating gossamer

threads that bound him to his body—just as he could see those of
the Round Table Knights when he had been seeing them through
Owain's eyes. But the body to which he was bound was not the
one he currently occupied; instead, he was tethered to the body of
the twenty-year-old assistant camp cook, who lay cowering under
the burden of the knowledge of Kaplan's needless death by "friendly
fire" as well as from the horrifying ordeal he had survived.

Other tendrils of the living gossamer stretched from Trick's ethereal being, out beyond the pathetic soldier, to encircle the others in
that scene—the bodies of the victims, particularly Kaplan, who
had all sacrificed their lives as soldiers often must, but without any
hope of glory; the irresponsible, bigoted Billy, who might have
spared Kaplan's life had he not judged it to be of less worth than
the enemy's; the guy next to him, who had also survived, but whose
name Trick could not recall even now. Still other glowing threads
reached out of sight, but Trick knew one was wrapped around
Smitty, who had not been a friend or even a good boss, but who
had not needed to die that way; another one was connected to the
memory of Reggie, so foolhardy, then and now. Dozens of others
stretched out of view, but at the end of each one was a bitter memory
of Vietnam.

So many strands were spinning out from his discorporate self
that Trick felt like he was at the center of a giant spider web. When
they suddenly began to tighten, it was if garrottes of piano wire
were pulling taut around every part of his body. He panicked: If
only he could have a taste of Grufydd the hermit's elixir, he could
escape these awful, strangling memories!

Then he remembered the sword. It was already in his right
hand.

In slow motion, his left hand reached across to join its strength
with the right, and with all his might, he swung the upturned blade
like a Louisville Slugger at a fast ball. It seemed to take an hour for
the blade to pass all the way through a 180-degree arc, and as it
did, the filaments snapped like elastic; each one lashed at him with

a sharp, stinging recoil, but the pain quickly faded to numbness. As the last one was severed, the sword slipped from his grasp and sailed on, shimmering, into the darkness that descended like the final act curtain upon his dream, and disappeared.

In the last moments before the darkness overtook him, Trick was overwhelmed with gratitude for Owain's incredible gift: Never again would the stark, sickening scenes of Vietnam appear in his sleeping subconscious—he had confronted them at last, and he had conquered them. The sword Owain of Caergwyndwr had given him was a symbol of acceptance, of continuity, of the ability to face a challenge and to consummate it with courage and honor.

Trick had taken the sword prior to the duel with Mog Hwl, believing that he might be riding into his final battle, his *joust à la outrance*; now he realized that it had been only a fool's joust compared to the victory he had just won. The only thing that would have made his triumph complete would have been to have Tay beside him. But that would be another battle . . .

TRICK SAW MANY MORE REMARKABLE THINGS AFTER HE OPENED HIS EYES. The most remarkable sight of all was Tay Silvestri, who was beside him at every permitted moment while he lay in Intensive Care and nearly every time he awakened after he had been moved to a regular, private hospital room. When he was able to talk, he did not tell her he had believed her to be dead. He did not wish to create any new nightmares for himself or for her.

The second most remarkable sight—one that made him chuckle in spite of the pain it caused—was the snakeskin boot stuffed with a wildly colorful bouquet of flowers, which she placed on his bedside table when she arrived for her long evening visit on the fourth day of his hospitalization.

"You know me so well," he whispered, and his voice was still raspy from having had a breathing tube down his throat for the first two days of critical care. He was glad that Diane wasn't a good shot and only two of the four .22-caliber rounds she had fired at close range had struck him—otherwise, he would not be here to enjoy Tay's tastefully twisted sense of humor.

Tay greeted him by applying a kiss to his forehead; it was the only place on his face that wasn't bandaged or bruised. While he had been under anesthesia to close the bullet wound that had collapsed his lung, an assisting surgeon had repaired his broken nose—not for cosmetic purposes, which would have required the talents of a plastic surgeon, but to remove bone chips and restore free breathing.

She kicked off her loafers and sat beside him on the bed. "Not as well as I thought I did," she replied. "For instance, who were those two women who were obviously so crazy over you back at the missile base?"

"*Two* women?"

"The chunky one who confessed to shooting you, and the babe with the long red hair."

"Ah, Dame Valerie!" He grinned, pleased. He hadn't realized that he had made any impression upon the comely former rodeo queen. Maybe he was still pretty hot for an old guy after all.

"Well? I'm waiting!"

Trick's grin turned sheepish and he evaded the question by asking, "Did I get any shopping cart dents on my truck?"

"No, it didn't stay parked at the supermarket that long. It's been hogging my driveway since the night after you left. But now that you've given me a good reason, Mr. Studley, I'll take a tire tool to it when I get home." She gave him a gentle punch in the arm to end the discussion, and moved her hand down to clutch his.

"How's Brian?" asked Trick, giving her hand a firm squeeze.

"He's better. He'll probably leave the hospital tomorrow, but since he offered a confession, he's gotta go down to the Youth Justice Center and be booked on one count of manslaughter, along with the lesser charges. They won't keep him there, though; he gets a personal recognizance bond because I know the judge and she likes me." She grinned, but then her expression clouded again as she added, "His attorney will try to get the charge reduced to involuntary manslaughter, since he's agreed to testify against Arthur Cossett. He was pretty doggone irritated when he found out that the so-called King was a phony; he'd sold all the high-dollar computer stuff his dad got for him so he could buy his way into the Round Table."

"I kinda figured there was more to getting the big promotion than just learning all the lines." Trick sighed, and said, "It's possible he could get the lesser charge. I didn't actually see him shoot Reggie."

"Preliminary ballistics show that the bullet taken from the body of Reggie Floyd matched the gun found next to the body of Kevin Gaines. That's got the lab bumfuzzled, but they'll figure it out."

He only nodded. Unless he was under oath, he would never confess that he had placed Brian's gun in Kevin's hand after the fact. That was one more nightmare Tay didn't need to have, and if it gave him one, well, he could deal with it.

"Well, that's the subject of a future discussion," she said, more cheerily. "How soon do you think you'll feel like giving a deposition? I've heard nearly two hundred versions of the story so far, and I don't believe any of them. Especially the part about you being the real King."

"No? Well, maybe I was . . . for a little while." He saw her eyebrows raise, and said, "All that matters was that the Knights finally realized that Arthur *wasn't* the King he claimed to be, and they got smart before anything really bad could happen."

"Too bad they didn't get the news until after the chopper from Channel 17 got blown out of the sky. The Dallas media scene is treating the demise of 'Tabloid Talbot' and his pilot with the same reverence as that of Princess Diana, but amazingly, they're keeping their mouths shut about the incident itself until there's more information. I told you about Lonnie Baxter, the rookie who helped me; well, he cordially put the screws on the news director at Channel 17 and found out that Talbot had gotten his 'tip' from a disgruntled former resident of 4633 Redwing Drive in Fort Worth—also known as Joyous Gard."

"I bet it was Russell," Trick replied. "He was the only one of the people who lived there who didn't show up for the Convergence. I bet they kicked him out for being too dumb to learn the Code of Chivalry or something. He might have been the smartest one of us."

"Well, at least he wasn't there when some of our people paid Joyous Gard a visit. The place was deserted—everyone was out at the missile base, I guess—but they found a bunch more guns and even a few grenades in a locked cabinet in the garage. Your Knightly comrades definitely had the neighborhood's superior arsenal."

"Everybody needs a little home security these days."

"Yeah, right. I'll say one thing for them—they're all the most polite, most cooperative bunch of suspects I've ever dealt with. I guess they really took their lessons in Chivalry to heart. Many of them are saying that there was a plot to assassinate the president and the Prince of Wales while they were together in Dallas. Was Arthur planning to make himself King of the whole world?"

"It wasn't Arthur, himself, it was . . . well, it's a long story. You got time tonight, or are you on an early shift tomorrow?"

"I have lots of time before I have to go back to work," she answered lightly. "Thirty days, to be exact. The good and wise Mr. Padgett, of whom I believe you have heard, has given me a little vacation without pay to reconsider my renegade ways relative to his authority. Jim Benavides has been giving me daily updates."

"Honey, I'm sorry. I guess that's really my fault. If I hadn't butted in and—"

"—If you hadn't butted in, we might be mopping up a double assassination, and the whole world would be crowding into that proverbial handbasket. When the assassination plot started turning up in their depositions, we had to alert the State Department. So don't be surprised if someday soon you get one phone call from the Secret Service and another from MI-5, inviting you to tea and interrogation. No, I'm glad to have some time off. I'm working on my résumé and making some calls. And somebody has to look after you until you can go home—which, according to your doctor, might be early next week if things continue to go well. Your mom and dad are getting anxious to have you back on the ranch. I can't wait to hear their reaction when they see you're growing a beard. I hope you'll keep it. It does make you look sort of kingly."

"Mom will like it, too, I think, but Dad'll probably drag me out to the show barn, tie me down with a piggin string, and shear me like a goat." They both chuckled until it made him wince.

Trick was quiet a moment, and stroked his thumb across the back of Tay's warm hand. He shook his head lightly, and said, "Nobody will ever believe what really happened. They'll think I've just been watching too many episodes of 'The X-Files.' "

"Hey, they believed you before," she answered, alluding to testimony he had given on the extraordinary case where they had met, two years previously. "And I'll believe you. Whenever you're ready to talk about it, I'll be ready to listen. It better be good."

"Oh, it's a humdinger, and if you can imagine, it's even weirder than the last time. The problem is, there's no physical evidence to back up my story."

"I wouldn't be too sure. A certain Mr. Shackleford has been gathering a few very peculiar but very interesting bits of trace evidence. I have no idea about any of it, but I bet you'll be able to enlighten us."

Trick grinned. "Shack *is* pretty hard to discredit," he admitted. "I feel a little better now."

"Well, you look tired. Why don't I let you get some shut-eye? I'm dying to hear your story, but I can wait until you're ready to put it on the record. For now, I'll just sit over there for awhile and read the trashy novel I bought in the hospital gift shop."

"No, please, stay right here. I don't want you out of my sight, ever again." He clutched her hand tightly. "Here's one thing I want to go on the record right now: This old cowboy is out of the covert operations business, for good. I promise to keep what's left of my nose out of any and all of your investigative business, official or not."

"Well, cowboy, I'm going to hold you to that promise for as long as it applies, but if I can find some other way to make a living, it might be a moot point."

"You want a new job? I got one for you. Come out to West Texas with me . . . and you can be the queen of all you survey."

Tay had never been at a loss for a rejoinder, but it took her a moment to pick up her jaw. "Queen of *all* I survey? Cows and horses, too?"

"Snakes and scorpions, too, if you want 'em. And me."

She nodded slowly, with a thoughtful look on her face, and pretended to think out loud. "It would be a cut in pay, but there are probably some pretty good perqs for being queen. Yes, I'll accept the job. When shall I start?"

"Whenever you'd like. How about right now?"

Tay smiled. "I'd like that. Is there someplace near your mouth that doesn't hurt, where I can kiss you?"

"No, but kiss me anyway—I'll suffer."

Mindful of his IVs and bandages, Tay put her arms gingerly around Trick, but he pulled her to him as tightly as he ever had, and they kissed for a long time.

And as she lay beside him in the narrow hospital bed, her fingertips stroking the cleft in his chin now hidden by his coppery beard, he smiled considered that he had never felt more like a king— even when he had actually been one.

ABOUT THE AUTHOR

CRYSTAL WOOD's roots and heart are in Texas, the setting for *Fool's Joust* and her first novel, *Cut Him Out in Little Stars*. She studied journalism and theater arts at Hardin-Simmons University, then earned a master's degree in theater technology from Texas Tech University. She has worked professionally in theaters in New York and Texas, but is now a professional writer, editor, and consultant in Denton, Texas. She and her husband, George, enjoy life with their assortment of cats, attending science fiction conventions, and exploring Texas for its wealth of history and opportunity.